The Apology of the Augsburg Confession

Philip Melanchthon

Contents

THE APOLOGY OF THE AUGSBURG CONFESSION

BY

Philip Melanchthon

INTRODUCTION

Philip Melanchthon Presents His Greeting to the Reader. Wherefore we believe that troubles and dangers for the glory of Christ and the good of the Church should be endured, and we are confident that this our fidelity to duty is approved of God, and we hope that the judgment of posterity concerning us will be more just.

For it is undeniable that many topics of Christian doctrine whose existence in the Church is of the greatest moment have been brought to view by our theologians and explained; in reference to which we are not disposed here to recount under what sort of opinions, and how dangerous, they formerly lay covered in the writings of the monks, canonists, and sophistical theologians. [This may have to be done later.] We have the public testimonials of many good men, who give God thanks for this greatest blessing, namely, that concerning many necessary topics it has taught better things than are read everywhere in the books of our adversaries.

We shall commend our cause, therefore, to Christ, who some time will judge these controversies, and we beseech Him to look upon the afflicted and scattered churches, and to bring them back to godly and perpetual concord. [Therefore, if the known and clear truth is trodden under foot, we will resign this cause to God and Christ in heaven, who is the Father of orphans and the Judge of widows and of all the forsaken, who (as we certainly know) will judge and pass sentence upon this cause aright. Lord Jesus Christ, it is Thy holy Gospel, it is Thy cause; look Thou upon the many troubled hearts and consciences, and maintain and strengthen in Thy truth Thy churches and little flocks, who suffer anxiety and distress from the devil. Confound all hypocrisy and lies, and grant peace and unity, so that Thy glory may advance, and Thy kingdom, strong against all the gates of hell, may continually grow and increase.]

Part 1

Article I: *Of God.*

The First Article of our Confession our adversaries approve, in which we declare that we believe and teach that there is one divine essence, undivided, etc., and yet, that there are three distinct persons, of the same divine essence, and coeternal, Father, Son, and Holy Ghost. This article we have always taught and defended, and we believe that it has, in Holy Scripture, sure and firm testimonies that cannot be overthrown. And we constantly affirm that those thinking otherwise are outside of the Church of Christ, and are idolaters, and insult God.

Article II (I): *Of Original Sin.*

The Second Article, Of Original Sin, the adversaries approve, but in such a way that they, nevertheless, censure the definition of original sin, which we incidentally gave. Here, immediately at the very threshold, His Imperial Majesty will discover that the writers of the **Confutation** were deficient not only in judgment, but also in candor. For whereas we, with a simple mind, desired, in passing, to recount those things which original sin embraces, these men, by framing an invidious interpretation, artfully distort a proposition that has in it nothing which of itself is wrong. Thus they say: "To be without the fear of God, to be without faith, is actual guilt"; and therefore they deny that it is original guilt.

It is quite evident that such subtilties have originated in the schools, not in the council of the Emperor. But although this sophistry can be very easily refuted; yet, in order that all good men may understand that we teach in this matter nothing that is absurd, we ask first of all that the German Confession be examined. This will free us from the suspicion of novelty. For there it is written: ***Weiter wird gelehrt, dass nach dem Fall Adams alle Menschen, so natuerlich geboren werden, in Suenden empfangen und geboren werdenen, das ist, dass sie alle von Mutterleibe an voll boeser Lueste und Neigung sind, keine wahre Gottesfurcht, keinen wahren Glauben an Gott von Natur haben koennen.*** [It is further taught that since the Fall of Adam all men who are naturally born are conceived and born in sin, i.e., that they all, from their mother's womb, are full of evil desire and inclination, and can have by nature no true fear of God, no true faith in God.] This passage testifies that we deny to those propagated according to carnal nature not only the acts, but also the power or gifts of producing fear and trust in God. For we say that those thus born have concupiscence, and cannot produce true fear and trust in God. What is there here with which fault can be found? To good men, we think, indeed, that we have exculpated ourselves sufficiently. For in this sense the Latin description denies to nature [even to innocent infants] the power, i.e., it denies the gifts and energy by which to produce fear and trust in God, and, in adults [over and above this innate evil disposition of the heart, also] the acts, so that, when we mention concupiscence, we understand not only the acts or fruits, but the constant inclination of the nature [the evil inclination within, which does not cease as long as we are not born anew through the Spirit and faith].

But hereafter we will show more fully that our description agrees with the usual and ancient definition. For we must first show our design in preferring to employ these words in this place. In their schools the adversaries confess that "the material," as they call it, "of original sin is concupiscence." Wherefore, in framing the definition, this should not have been passed by, especially at this time, when some are philosophizing concerning it in a manner unbecoming teachers of religion [are speaking concerning this innate, wicked desire more after the manner of heathen from philosophy than according to God's Word, or Holy Scripture].

For some contend that original sin is not a depravity or corruption in the nature of man, but only servitude, or a condition of mortality [not an innate evil nature, but only a blemish or imposed load, or burden], which those propagated from

Adam bear because of the guilt of another [namely, Adam's sin], and without any depravity of their own. Besides, they add that no one is condemned to eternal death on account of original sin, just as those who are born of a bond-woman are slaves, and bear this condition without any natural blemish, but because of the calamity of their mother [while, of themselves, they are born without fault, like other men: thus original sin is not an innate evil but a defect and burden which we bear since Adam, but we are not on that account personally in sin and inherited disgrace]. To show that this impious opinion is displeasing to us, we made mention of "concupiscence," and, with the best intention, have termed and explained it as "diseases," that "the nature of men is born corrupt and full of faults" [not a part of man, but the entire person with its entire nature is born in sin as with a hereditary disease].

Nor, indeed, have we only made use of the term concupiscence, but we have also said that "the fear of God and faith are wanting." This we have added with the following design: The scholastic teachers also, not sufficiently understanding the definition of original sin, which they have received from the Fathers, extenuate the sin of origin. They contend concerning the fomes [or evil inclination] that it is a quality of [blemish in the] body, and, with their usual folly, ask whether this quality be derived from the contagion of the apple or from the breath of the serpent, and whether it be increased by remedies. With such questions they have suppressed the main point. Therefore, when they speak of the sin of origin, they do not mention the more serious faults of human nature, to wit, ignorance of God, contempt for God, being destitute of fear and confidence in God, hatred of God's judgment, flight from God [as from a tyrant] when He judges, anger toward God, despair of grace, putting one's trust in present things [money, property, friends], etc. These diseases, which are in the highest degree contrary to the Law of God, the scholastics do not notice; yea, to human nature they meanwhile ascribe unimpaired strength for loving God above all things, and for fulfilling God's commandments according to the substance of the acts; nor do they see that they are saying things that are contradictory to one another. For what else is the being able in one's own strength to love God above all things, and to fulfil His commandments, than to have original righteousness [to be a new creature in Paradise, entirely pure and holy]? But if human nature have such strength as to be able of itself to love God above all things, as the scholastics confidently affirm, what will original sin be? For what will there be need of the grace of Christ if we can be justified by our own righteousness [powers]? For what will there be need of the Holy Ghost if human strength can by itself love God above all things, and fulfil God's commandments? Who does not see what preposterous thoughts our adversaries entertain? The lighter diseases in the nature of man they acknowledge, the more severe they do not acknowledge; and yet of these, Scripture everywhere admonishes us, and the prophets constantly complain [as the 13th Psalm, and some other psalms say Ps. 14, 1-3; 5, 9; 140, 3; 36, 1], namely, of carnal security, of the contempt of God, of hatred toward God, and of similar faults born with us. [For Scripture clearly says that all these things are not blown at us, but born with us.] But after the scholastics mingled with Christian doctrine philosophy concerning the perfection of nature [light of reason], and ascribed to the free will and the acts springing therefrom more than was sufficient, and taught that men are justified before God by philosophic or civil righteousness (which we also confess to be subject to reason, and in a measure, within our power), they could not see the inner uncleanness of the nature of men. For this cannot be judged except from the Word of God, of which the scholastics, in their discussions, do not frequently treat.

These were the reasons why, in the description of original sin, we made mention of concupiscence also, and denied to man's natural strength the fear of God and trust in Him. For we wished to indicate that original sin contains also these diseases, namely, ignorance of God, contempt for God, the being destitute of the fear of God and trust in Him, inability to love God. These are the chief faults of human nature, conflicting especially with the first table of the Decalog.

Neither have we said anything new. The ancient definition understood aright expresses precisely the same thing when it says: "Original sin is the absence of original righteousness" [a lack of the first purity and righteousness in Paradise]. But what is righteousness? Here the scholastics wrangle about dialectic questions, they do not explain what original righteousness is. Now, in the Scriptures, righteousness comprises not only the second table of the Decalog [regarding good works in serving our fellow-man], but the first also, which teaches concerning the fear of God, concerning faith, concerning the love of God. Therefore original righteousness was to embrace not only an even temperament of the bodily qualities [perfect health and, in all respects, pure blood, unimpaired powers of the body, as they contend], but also these gifts, namely, a quite certain knowledge of God, fear of God, confidence in God, or certainly the rectitude and power to yield these affections [but the greatest feature in that noble first creature was a bright light in the heart to know God and His work, etc.]. And Scripture testifies to this, when it says, Gen. 1, 27, that man was fashioned in the image and likeness of God. What else is this than that there were embodied in man such wisdom and righteousness as apprehended God, and in which God was reflected, i.e., to man there were given the gifts of the knowledge of God, the fear of God, confidence in God, and the like? For thus Irenaeus and Ambrose interpret the likeness to God, the latter of whom not only says many things to this effect, but especially declares: That soul is not, therefore, in the image of God, in which God is not at all times. And Paul shows in the Epistles to the Ephesians, 5, 9, and Colossians, 3,10, that the image of God is the knowledge of God, righteousness, and truth. Nor does Longobard fear to say that original righteousness is the very likeness to God which God implanted in man. We recount the opinions of the ancients, which in no way interfere with Augustine's interpretation of the image.

Therefore the ancient definition, when it says that sin is the lack of righteousness, not only denies obedience with respect to man's lower powers [that man is not only corrupt in his body and its meanest and lowest faculties], but also denies the knowledge of God, confidence in God, the fear and love of God, or certainly the power to produce these affections [the light in the heart which creates a love and desire for these matters]. For even the theologians themselves teach in their schools that these are not produced without certain gifts and the aid of grace. In order that the matter may be understood, we term these very gifts the knowledge of God, and fear and confidence in God. From these facts it appears that the ancient definition says precisely the same thing that we say, denying fear and confidence toward God, to wit, not only the acts, but also the gifts and power to produce these acts [that we have no good heart toward God, which truly loves God, not only that we are unable to do or achieve any perfectly good work].

Of the same import is the definition which occurs in the writings of Augustine, who is accustomed to define original sin as concupiscence [wicked desire]. For he means that when righteousness had been lost, concupiscence came in its place. For inasmuch as diseased nature cannot fear and love God and believe God, it seeks and loves carnal things. God's judgment it either contemns when at ease, or hates, when thoroughly terrified. Thus Augustine includes both the defect and the vicious habit which has come in its place. Nor indeed is concupiscence only a corruption of the qualities of the body, but also, in the higher powers, a vicious turning to carnal things. Nor do those persons see what they say who ascribe to man at the same time concupiscence that is not entirely destroyed by the Holy Ghost, and love to God above all things.

We, therefore, have been right in expressing, in our description of original sin, both namely, these defects: the not being able to believe God, the not being able to fear and love God; and, likewise: the having concupiscence, which seeks carnal things contrary to God's Word, i.e., seeks not only the pleasure of the body, but also carnal wisdom and righteousness, and, contemning God, trusts in these as god things. Nor only the ancients [like Augustine and others], but also the more recent [teachers and scholastics], at least the wiser ones among them, teach that original sin is at the same time truly these namely, the defects which I have recounted and concupiscence. For Thomas says thus: Original sin comprehends the loss of original righteousness, and with this an inordinate disposition of the parts of the soul; whence it is not pure loss, but a corrupt habit [something positive]. And Bonaventura: When the question is asked, What is original sin? The correct answer is, that it is immoderate [unchecked] concupiscence. The correct answer is also, that it is want of the righteousness that is due. And in one of these replies the other is included. The same is the opinion of Hugo, when he says that original sin is ignorance in the mind and concupiscence in the flesh. For he thereby indicates that when we are born, we bring with us ignorance of God unbelief, distrust, contempt, and hatred of God. For when he mentions ignorance, he includes these. And these opinions [even of the most recent teachers] also agree with Scripture. For Paul sometimes expressly calls it a defect [a lack of divine light], as 1 Cor. 2, 14: The natural man receiveth not the things of the Spirit of God. In another place, Rom. 7, 5, he calls it concupiscence working in our members to bring forth fruit unto death. We could cite more passages relating to both parts, but in regard to a manifest fact there is no need of testimonies. And the intelligent reader will readily be able to decide that to be without the fear of God and without faith are more than actual guilt. For they are abiding defects in our unrenewed nature.

In reference to original sin we therefore hold nothing differing either from Scripture or from the Church catholic, but cleanse from corruptions and restore to light most important declarations of Scripture and of the Fathers, that had been covered over by the sophistical controversies of modern theologians. For it is manifest from the subject itself that modern theologians have not noticed what the Fathers meant when they spake of defect [lack of original righteousness]. But the knowledge of original sin is necessary. For the magnitude of the grace of Christ cannot be understood [no one can heartily long and have a desire for Christ for the inexpressibly great treasure of divine favor and grace which the Gospel offers], unless our diseases be recognized. [As Christ says Matt. 9, 12; Mark 2, 17: They that are whole need not a physician.] The entire righteousness of man is mere hypocrisy [and abomination] before God, unless we acknowledge that our heart is naturally destitute of love, fear, and confidence in God [that we are miserable sinners who are in disgrace with God]. For this reason the prophet Jeremiah, 31, 19, says: After that I was instructed, I smote upon my thigh. Likewise Ps. 116, 11: I said in my haste, All men are liars, i.e., not thinking aright concerning God.

Here our adversaries inveigh against Luther also because he wrote that, "Original sin remains after Baptism." They add that this article was justly condemned by Leo X. But His Imperial Majesty will find on this point a manifest slander. For our adversaries know in what sense Luther intended this remark that original sin remains after Baptism. He always wrote thus, namely, that Baptism removes the guilt of original sin, although the material, as they call it, of the sin, i.e., concupiscence, remains. He also added in reference to the material that the Holy Ghost, given through Baptism, begins to mortify the concupiscence, and creates new movements [a new light, a new sense and spirit] in man. In the same manner, Augustine also speaks who says: Sin is remitted in Baptism, not in such a manner that it no longer exists, but so that it is not imputed. Here he confesses openly that sin exists, i.e., that it remains although it is not imputed. And this judgment was so agreeable to those who succeeded him that it was recited also in the decrees. Also against Julian, Augustine says: The Law, which is in the members, has been annulled by spiritual regeneration, and remains in the mortal flesh. It has been annulled because the guilt has been remitted in the Sacrament, by which believers are born again; but it remains, because it produces desires against which believers contend. Our adversaries know that Luther believes and teaches thus, and while they cannot reject the matter, they nevertheless pervert his words, in order by this artifice to crush an innocent man.

But they contend that concupiscence is a penalty, and not a sin [a burden and imposed penalty, and is not such a sin as is subject to death and condemnation]. Luther maintains that it is a sin. It has been said above that Augustine defines original sin as concupiscence. If there be anything disadvantageous in this opinion, let them quarrel with Augustine. Besides Paul says, Rom. 7, 7. 23: I had not known lust (concupiscence), except the Law had said, Thou shalt not covet. Likewise: I see another law in my members, warring against the law of my mind, and bringing me into captivity to the law of sin which is in my members. These testimonies can be overthrown by no sophistry. [All devils, all men cannot overthrow them.] For they clearly call concupiscence sin, which, nevertheless, is not imputed to those who are in Christ although by nature it is a matter worthy of death where it is not forgiven. Thus, beyond all controversy, the Fathers believe. For Augustine, in a long discussion refutes the opinion of those who thought that concupiscence in man is not a fault but an adiaphoron, as color of the body or ill health is said to be an adiaphoron [as to have a black or a white body is neither good nor evil].

But if the adversaries will contend that the fomes [or evil inclination] is an adiaphoron, not only many passages of Scripture but simply the entire Church [and all the Fathers] will contradict them. For [even if not entire consent, but only the inclination and desire be there] who ever dared to say that these matters, even though perfect agreement could not be attained, were adiaphora, namely, to doubt concerning God's wrath,: concerning God's grace, concerning God's Word, to be angry at the judgments of God, to be provoked because God does not at once deliver one from afflictions, to murmur because the wicked enjoy a better fortune than the good, to be urged on by wrath, lust, the desire for glory, wealth, etc.? And yet godly men acknowledge these in themselves, as appears in the Psalms and the prophets. [For all tried, Christian hearts know, alas! that these evils are wrapped up in man's skin, namely to esteem money, goods, and all other matters more highly than God, and to spend our lives in security; again, that after the manner of our carnal security we always imagine that God's wrath against sin is not as serious and great as it verily is. Again, that we murmur against the doing and will of God, when He does not succor us speedily in our tribulations, and arranges our affairs to please us. Again, we experience every day that it hurts us to see wicked people in good fortune in this world, as David and all the saints have complained. Over and above this, all men feel that their hearts are easily inflamed, now with ambition, now with anger and wrath, now with lewdness.] But in the schools they transferred hither from philosophy notions entirely different, that, because of passions, we are neither good nor evil, we are neither deserving of praise nor blame. Likewise, that nothing is sin, unless it be voluntary [inner desires and thoughts are not sins, if I do not altogether consent thereto]. These notions were expressed among philosophers with respect to civil righteousness, and not with respect to God's judgment. [For there it is true, as the jurists say, L. cogitationis, thoughts are exempt from custom and punishment. But God searches the hearts; in God's court and judgment it is different.] With no greater prudence they add also other notions, such as, that [God's creature and] nature is not [cannot in itself be] evil. In its proper place we do not censure this; but it is not right to twist it into an extenuation of original sin. And, nevertheless, these notions are read in the works of scholastics, who inappropriately mingle philosophy or civil doctrine concerning ethics with the Gospel. Nor were these matters only disputed in the schools, but, as is usually the case, were carried from the schools to the people. And these persuasions [godless, erroneous, dangerous, harmful teachings] prevailed, and nourished confidence in human strength, and suppressed the knowledge of Christ's grace. Therefore, Luther wishing to declare the magnitude of original sin and of human infirmity [what a grievous mortal guilt original sin is in the sight of God], taught that these remnants of original sin [after Baptism] are not, by their own nature, adiaphora in man, but that, for their non-imputation, they need the grace of Christ and, likewise for their mortification, the Holy Ghost.

Although the scholastics extenuate both sin and punishment when they teach that man by his own strength, can fulfil the commandments of God; in Genesis the punishment, imposed on account of original sin, is described otherwise. For there human nature is subjected not only to death and other bodily evils, but also to the kingdom of the devil. For there, Gen. 3, 16, this fearful sentence is proclaimed: I will put enmity between thee and the woman, and between thy seed and her seed. The defects and the concupiscence are punishments and sins. Death and other bodily evils and the dominion of the devil, are properly punishments. For human nature has been delivered into slavery, and is held captive by the devil, who infatuates it with wicked opinions and errors, and impels it to sins of every kind. But just as the devil cannot be conquered except by the aid of Christ, so by our own strength we cannot free ourselves from this slavery. Even the history of the world shows how great is the power of the devil's kingdom. The world is full of blasphemies against God and of wicked opinions, and the devil keeps entangled in these bands those who are wise and righteous [many hypocrites who appear holy] in the sight of the world. In other persons grosser vices manifest themselves. But since Christ was given to us to remove both these sins and these punishments, and to destroy the kingdom of the devil, sin and death, it will not be possible to recognize the benefits of Christ unless we understand our evils. For this reason our preachers have diligently taught concerning these subjects, and have delivered nothing that is new but have set forth Holy Scripture and the judgments of the holy Fathers.

We think that this will satisfy His Imperial Majesty concerning the puerile and trivial sophistry with which the adversaries have perverted our article. For we know that we believe aright and in harmony with the Church catholic of Christ. But if the adversaries will renew this controversy, there will be no want among us of those who will reply and defend the truth. For in this case our adversaries, to a great extent, do not understand what they say. They often speak what is contradictory, and neither explain correctly and logically that which is essential to [i.e., that which is or is not properly of the essence of] original sin, nor what they call defects. But we have been unwilling at this place to examine their contests with any very great subtlety. We have thought it worth while only to recite, in customary and well-known words, the belief of the holy Fathers, which we also follow.

PART 2

Article III: *Of Christ.*

The Third Article the adversaries approve, in which we confess that there are in Christ two natures, namely, a human nature, assumed by the Word into the unity of His person; and that the same Christ suffered and died to reconcile the Father to us; and that He was raised again to reign, and to justify and sanctify believers, etc., according to the Apostles' Creed and the Nicene Creed.

Article IV (II): *Of Justification.*

In the Fourth, Fifth, Sixth, and, below, in the Twentieth Article, they condemn us, for teaching that men obtain remission of sins, not because of their own merits, but freely for Christ's sake, through faith in Christ. [They reject quite stubbornly both these statements.] For they condemn us both for denying that men obtain remission of sins because of their own merits, and for affirming that, through faith, men obtain remission of sins, and through faith in Christ are justified. But since in this controversy the chief topic of Christian doctrine is treated, which, understood aright, illumines and amplifies the honor of Christ [which is of especial service for the clear, correct understanding of the entire Holy Scriptures, and alone shows the way to the unspeakable treasure and right knowledge of Christ, and alone opens the door to the entire Bible], and brings necessary and most abundant consolation to devout consciences, we ask His Imperial Majesty to hear us with forbearance in regard to matters of such importance. For since the adversaries understand neither what the remission of sins, nor what faith, nor what grace, nor what righteousness is, they sadly corrupt this topic, and obscure the glory and benefits of Christ and rob devout consciences of the consolations offered in Christ. But that we may strengthen the position of our Confession, and also remove the charges which the adversaries advance against us, certain things are to be premised in the beginning, in order that the sources of both kinds of doctrine, i. e., both that of our adversaries and our own, may be known.

All Scripture ought to be distributed into these two principal topics, the Law and the promises. For in some places it presents the Law, and in others the promise concerning Christ, namely, either when [in the Old Testament] it promises that Christ will come, and offers, for His sake, the remission of sins justification, and life eternal, or when, in the Gospel [in the New Testament], Christ Himself, since He has appeared, promises the remission of sins, justification, and life eternal. Moreover, in this discussion, by Law we designate the Ten Commandments, wherever they are read in the Scriptures. Of the ceremonies and judicial laws of Moses we say nothing at present.

Of these two parts the adversaries select the Law, because human reason naturally understands, in some way, the Law (for it has the same judgment divinely written in the mind); [the natural law agrees with the law of Moses, or the Ten Commandments] and by the Law they seek the remission of sins and justification. Now, the Decalog requires not only outward civil works, which reason can in some way produce, but it also requires other things placed far above reason, namely, truly to fear God, truly to love God, truly to call upon God, truly to be convinced that God hears us, and to expect the aid of God in death and in all afflictions; finally, it requires obedience to God, in death and all afflictions, so that we may not flee from these, or refuse them when God imposes them.

Here the scholastics, having followed the philosophers, teach only a righteousness of reason, namely, civil works, and fabricate besides that without the Holy Ghost reason can love God above all things. For, as long as the human mind is at ease, and does not feel the wrath or judgment of God, it can imagine that it wishes to love God, that it wishes to do good for God's sake. [But it is sheer hypocrisy.] In this manner they teach that men merit the remission of sins by doing what is in them, i.e., if reason, grieving over sin, elicit an act of love to God, or for God's sake be active in that which is good. And because this opinion naturally flatters men, it has brought forth and multiplied in the Church many services, monastic vows, abuses of the mass; and, with this opinion the one has, in the course of time, devised this act of worship and observances, the other that. And in order that they might nourish and increase confidence in such works, they have affirmed that God necessarily gives grace to one thus working, by the necessity not of constraint, but of immutability [not that He is constrained, but that this is the order which God will not transgress or alter].

In this opinion there are many great and pernicious errors, which it would be tedious to enumerate. Let the discreet reader think only of this: If this be Christian righteousness, what difference is there between philosophy and the doctrine of Christ? If we merit the remission of sins by these elicit acts [that spring from our mind], of what benefit is Christ? If we can be justified by reason and the works of reason, wherefore is there need of Christ or regeneration [as Peter declares, 1 Pet. 1, 18 ff.]? And from these opinions the matter has now come to such a pass that many ridicule us because we teach that an other than the philosophic righteousness must be sought after. [Alas! it has come to this, that even great theologians at Louvain, Paris, etc., have known nothing of any other godliness or righteousness (although every letter and syllable in Paul teaches otherwise) than the godliness which philosophers teach. And although we ought to regard this as a strange teaching, and ought to ridicule it, they rather ridicule us, yea, make a jest of Paul himself.] We have heard that some, after setting aside the Gospel, have, instead of a sermon, explained the ethics of Aristotle. [I myself have heard a great preacher who did not mention Christ and the Gospel, and preached the ethics of Aristotle. Is this not a childish, foolish way to preach to Christians?] Nor did such men err if those things are true which the adversaries defend [if the doctrine of the adversaries be true, the Ethics is a precious book of sermons, and a fine new Bible]. For Aristotle wrote concerning civil morals so learnedly that nothing further concerning this need be demanded. We see books extant in which certain sayings of Christ are compared with the sayings of Socrates, Zeno, and others, as though Christ had come for the purpose of delivering certain laws through which we might merit the remission of sins, as though we did not receive this gratuitously, because of His merits. Therefore, if we here receive the doctrine of the adversaries, that by the works of reason we merit the remission of sins and justification, there will be no difference between philosophic, or certainly pharisaic, and Christian righteousness.

Although the adversaries, not to pass by Christ altogether, require a knowledge of the history concerning Christ, and ascribe to Him that it is His merit that a habit is given us, or, as they say, **prima gratia**, "first grace," which they understand as a habit, inclining us the more readily to love God; yet what they ascribe to this habit is of little importance [is a feeble, paltry, small, poor operation, that would be ascribed to Christ], because they imagine that the acts of the will are of the same kind before and after this habit. They imagine that the will can love God; but nevertheless this habit stimulates it to do the same the more cheerfully. And they bid us first merit this habit by preceding merits; then they bid us merit by the works of the Law an increase of this habit and life eternal. Thus they bury Christ, so that men may not avail themselves of Him as a Mediator, and believe that for His sake they freely receive remission of sins and reconciliation, but may dream that by their own fulfilment of the Law they merit the remission of sins, and that by their own fulfilment of the Law they are accounted righteous before God; while, nevertheless, the Law is never satisfied, since reason does nothing except certain civil works, and, in the mean time neither [in the heart] fears God, nor truly believes that God cares for it. And although they speak of this habit, yet, without the righteousness of faith, neither the love of God can exist in man, nor can it be understood what the love of God is.

Their feigning a distinction between **meritum congrui** and **meritum condigni** [due merit and true, complete merit] is only an artifice in order not to appear openly to Pelagianize, For, if God necessarily gives grace for the **meritum congrui** [due merit], it is no longer **meritum congrui**, but **meritum condigni** [a true duty and complete merit]. But they do not know what they are saying. After this habit of love [is there], they imagine that man can acquire **merit de condigno**. And yet they bid us doubt whether there be a habit present. How, therefore, do they know whether they acquire merit **de congruo** or **de condigno** [in full, or half]? But this whole matter was fabricated by idle men [But, good God! these are mere inane ideas and dreams of idle, wretched, inexperienced men who do not much reduce the Bible to practise], who did not know how the remission of sins occurs, and how, in the judgment of God and terrors of conscience, trust in works is driven out of us. Secure hypocrites always judge that they acquire ***merit de condigno***, whether the habit be present or be not present, because men naturally trust in their own righteousness, but terrified consciences waver and hesitate, and then seek and accumulate other works in order to find rest. Such consciences never think that they acquire merit ***de condigno***, and they rush into despair unless they hear, in addition to the doctrine of the Law, the Gospel concerning the gratuitous remission of sins and the righteousness of faith. [Thus some stories are told that when the Barefooted monks had in vain praised their order and good works to some good consciences in the hour of death, they at last had to be silent concerning their order and St. Franciscus, and to say: "Dear man, Christ has died for you." This revived and refreshed in trouble, and alone gave peace and comfort.]

Thus the adversaries teach nothing but the righteousness of reason, or certainly of the Law, upon which they look just as the Jews upon the veiled face of Moses, and, in secure hypocrites who think that they satisfy the Law, they excite presumption and empty confidence in works [they place men on a sand foundation, their own works] and contempt of the grace of Christ. On the contrary, they drive timid consciences to despair, which, laboring with doubt, never can experience what faith is, and how efficacious it is; thus, at last they utterly despair.

Now, we think concerning the righteousness of reason thus, namely, that God requires it, and that, because of God's commandment, the honorable works which the Decalog commands must necessarily be performed, according to the passage Gal. 3, 24: The Law was our schoolmaster; likewise 1 Tim. 1, 9: The Law is made for the ungodly. For God wishes those who are carnal [gross sinners] to be restrained by civil discipline, and to maintain this, He has given laws, letters, doctrine, magistrates, penalties. And this righteousness reason, by its own strength, can, to a certain extent, work, although it is often overcome by natural weakness, and by the devil impelling it to manifest crimes. Now, although we cheerfully assign this righteousness of reason the praises that are due it (for this corrupt nature has no greater good [in this life and in a worldly nature, nothing is ever better than uprightness and virtue], and Aristotle says aright: Neither the evening star nor the morning star is more beautiful than righteousness, and God also honors it with bodily rewards), yet it ought not to be praised with reproach to Christ.

For it is false [I thus conclude, and am certain that it is a fiction, and not true] that we merit the remission of sins by our works.

False also is this, that men are accounted righteous before God because of the righteousness of reason [works and external piety].

False also is this that reason, by its own strength, is able to love God above all things, and to fulfil God's Law, namely, truly to fear God to be truly confident that God hears prayer, to be willing to obey God in death and other dispensations of God, not to covet what belongs to others, etc.; although reason can work civil works.

False also and dishonoring Christ is this, that men do not sin who, without grace, do the commandments of God [who keep the commandments of God merely in an external manner, without the Spirit and grace in their hearts]. We have testimonies for this our belief, not only from the Scriptures, but also from the Fathers. For in opposition to the Pelagians, Augustine contends at great length that grace is not given because of our merits. And in **De Natura et Gratia** he says: If natural ability, through the free will, suffice both for learning to know how one ought to live and for living aright, then Christ has died in vain, then the offense of the Cross is made void. Why may I not also here cry out? Yea I will cry out, and, with Christian grief, will chide them: Christ has become of no effect unto you whosoever of you are justified by the Law; ye are fallen from grace. Gal. 5, 4; cf. 2, 21. For they, being ignorant of God's righteousness, and going about to establish their own righteousness, have not submitted themselves unto the righteousness of God. For Christ is the end of the Law for righteousness to every one that believeth. Rom. 10 3. 4. And John 8, 36: If the Son therefore shall make you free, ye shall be free indeed. Therefore by reason we cannot be freed from sins and merit the remission of sins. And in John 3, 5 it is written: Except a man be born of water and of the Spirit, he cannot enter into the kingdom of God. But if it is necessary to be born again of the Holy Ghost the righteousness of reason does not justify us before God, and does not fulfil the Law, Rom. 3, 23: All have come short of the glory of God, i.e., are destitute of the wisdom and righteousness of God, which acknowledges and glorifies God. Likewise Rom. 8, 7. 8: The carnal mind is enmity against God; for it is not subject to the Law of God, neither indeed can be. So then they that are in the flesh cannot please God. These testimonies are so manifest that, to use the words of Augustine which he employed in this case, they do not need an acute understanding, but only an attentive hearer. If the carnal mind is enmity against God, the flesh certainly does not love God; if it cannot be subject to the Law of God, it cannot love God. If the carnal mind is enmity against God, the flesh sins even when we do external civil works. If it cannot be subject to the Law of God, it certainly sins even when, according to human judgment, it possesses deeds that are excellent and worthy of praise. The adversaries consider only the precepts of the Second Table which contain civil righteousness that reason understands. Content with this, they think that they satisfy the Law of God. In the mean time they do not see the First Table which commands that we love God, that we declare as certain that God is angry with sin, that we truly fear God, that we declare as certain that God hears prayer. But the human heart without the Holy Ghost either in security despises God's judgment, or in punishment flees from, and hates, God when He judges. Therefore it does not obey the First Table. Since, therefore, contempt of God, and doubt concerning the Word of God and concerning the threats and promises, inhere in human nature, men truly sin, even when, without the Holy Ghost, they do virtuous works, because they do them with a wicked heart, according to Rom. 14, 23: Whatsoever is not of faith is sin. For such persons perform their works with contempt of God, just as Epicurus does not believe that God cares for him, or that he is regarded or heard by God. This contempt vitiates works seemingly virtuous, because God judges the heart.

Lastly, it was very foolish for the adversaries to write that men who are under eternal wrath merit the remission of sins by an act of love, which springs from their mind, since it is impossible to love God, unless the remission of sins be apprehended first by faith. For the heart, truly feeling that God is angry, cannot love God, unless He be shown to have been reconciled. As long as He terrifies us, and seems to cast us into eternal death, human nature is not able to take courage, so as to love a wrathful, judging, and punishing God [poor, weak nature must lose heart and courage, and must tremble before such great wrath, which so fearfully terrifies and punishes, and can never feel a spark of love before God Himself comforts]. It is easy for idle men to feign such dreams concerning love as, that a person guilty of mortal sin can love God above all things, because they do not feel what the wrath or judgment of God is. But in agony of conscience and in conflicts [with Satan] conscience experiences the emptiness of these philosophical speculations. Paul says, Rom. 4,15: The Law worketh wrath. He does not say that by the Law men merit the remission of sins. For the Law always accuses and terrifies consciences. Therefore it does not justify, because conscience terrified by the Law flees from the judgment of God. Therefore they err who trust that by the Law, by their own works, they merit the remission of sins. It is sufficient for us to have said these things concerning the righteousness of reason or of the Law, which the adversaries teach. For after a while, when we will declare our belief concerning the righteousness of faith, the subject itself will compel us to adduce more testimonies, which also will be of service in overthrowing the errors of the adversaries which we have thus far reviewed.

Because, therefore, men by their own strength cannot fulfil the Law of God, and all are under sin, and subject to eternal wrath and death, on this account we cannot be freed by the Law from sin and be justified but the promise of the remission of sins and of justification has been given us for Christ's sake, who was given for us in order that He might make satisfaction for the sins of the world, and has been appointed as the [only] Mediator and Propitiator. And this promise has not the condition of our merits [it does not read thus: Through Christ you have grace salvation, etc., if you merit it], but freely offers the remission of sins and justification, as Paul says, Rom. 11, 6: If it be of works, then is it no more grace. And in another place, Rom. 3, 21: The righteousness of God without the Law is manifested, i.e., the remission of sins is freely offered. Nor does reconciliation depend upon our merits. Because, if the remission of sins were to depend upon our merits, and reconciliation were from the Law, it would be useless. For, as we do not fulfil the Law, it would also follow that we would never obtain the promise of reconciliation. Thus Paul reasons, Rom. 4, 14: For if they which are of the Law be heirs, faith is made void, and the promise made of none effect. For if the promise would require the condition of our merits and the Law, which we never fulfil, it would follow that the promise would be useless.

But since justification is obtained through the free promise, it follows that we cannot justify ourselves. Otherwise, wherefore would there be need to promise? [And why should Paul so highly extol and praise grace?] For since the promise cannot be received except by faith, the Gospel, which is properly the promise of the remission of sins and of justification for Christ's sake, proclaims the righteousness of faith in Christ, which the Law does not teach. Nor is this the righteousness of the Law. For the Law requires of us our works and our perfection. But the Gospel freely offers, for Christ's sake, to us, who have been vanquished by sin and death, reconciliation, which is received, not by works, but by faith alone. This faith brings to God not confidence in one's own merits, but only confidence in the promise, or the mercy promised in Christ. This special faith, therefore, by which an individual believes that for Christ's sake his sins are remitted him, and that for Christ's sake God is reconciled and propitious, obtains remission of sins and justifies us. And because in repentance, i.e. in terrors, it comforts and encourages hearts it regenerates us, and brings the Holy Ghost that then we may be able to fulfil God's Law, namely, to love God, truly to fear God, truly to be confident that God hears prayer, and to obey God in all afflictions; it mortifies concupiscence, etc. Thus, because faith, which freely receives the remission of sins, sets Christ, the Mediator and Propitiator, against God's wrath, it does not present our merits or our love [which would be tossed aside like a little feather by a hurricane]. This faith is the true knowledge of Christ, and avails itself of the benefits of Christ, and regenerates hearts, and precedes the fulfilling of the Law. And of this faith not a syllable exists in the doctrine of our adversaries. Hence we find fault with the adversaries, equally because they teach only the righteousness of the Law and because they do not teach the righteousness of the Gospel, which proclaims the righteousness of faith in Christ.

Part 3

What Is Justifying Faith?

The adversaries feign that faith is only a knowledge of the history, and therefore teach that it can coexist with mortal sin. Hence they say nothing concerning faith, by which Paul so frequently says that men are justified, because those who are accounted righteous before God do not live in mortal sin. But that faith which justifies is not merely a knowledge of history, [not merely this, that I know the stories of Christ's birth, suffering, etc. (that even the devils know,)] but it is to assent to the promise of God, in which for Christ's sake, the remission of sins and justification are freely offered. [It is the certainty or the certain trust in the heart, when, with my whole heart, I regard the promises of God as certain and true, through which there are offered me, without my merit, the forgiveness of sins, grace, and all salvation, through Christ the Mediator.] And that no one may suppose that it is mere knowledge we will add further: it is to wish and to receive the offered promise of the remission of sins and of justification. [Faith is that my whole heart takes to itself this treasure. It is not my doing, not my presenting or giving, not my work or preparation, but that a heart comforts itself, and is perfectly confident with respect to this, namely, that God makes a present and gift to us, and not we to Him, that He sheds upon us every treasure of grace in Christ.]

And the difference between this faith and the righteousness of the Law can be easily discerned. Faith is the *latreia* [divine service], which receives the benefits offered by God; the righteousness of the Law is the *latreia* [divine service] which offers to God our merits. By faith God wishes to be worshiped in this way, that we receive from Him those things which He promises and offers.

Now, that faith signifies, not only a knowledge of the history, but such faith as assents to the promise, Paul plainly testifies when he says, Rom. 4, 16: Therefore it is of faith, to the end the promise might be sure. For he judges that the promise cannot be received unless by faith. Wherefore he puts them together as things that belong to one another, and connects promise and faith. [There Paul fastens and binds together these two, thus: Wherever there is a promise faith is required and conversely, wherever faith is required there must be a promise.] Although it will be easy to decide what faith is if we consider the Creed where this article certainly stands: The forgiveness of sins. Therefore it is not enough to believe that Christ was born, suffered, was raised again, unless we add also this article, which is the purpose of the history: The forgiveness of sins. To this article the rest must be referred, namely, that for Christ's sake, and not for the sake of our merits, forgiveness of sins is given us. For what need was there that Christ was given for our sins if for our sins our merits can make satisfaction?

As often, therefore, as we speak of justifying faith, we must keep in mind that these three objects concur: the promise, and that, too, gratuitous, and the merits of Christ, as the price and propitiation. The promise is received by faith; the "gratuitous" excludes our merits, and signifies that the benefit is offered only through mercy; the merits of Christ are the price, because there must be a certain propitiation for our sins. Scripture frequently implores mercy, and the holy Fathers often say that we are saved by mercy. As often, therefore, as mention is made of mercy, we must keep in mind that faith is there required, which receives the promise of mercy. And, again, as often as we speak of faith, we wish an object to be understood, namely, the promised mercy. For faith justifies and saves, not on the ground that it is a work in itself worthy, but only because it receives the promised mercy.

And throughout the prophets and the psalms this worship, this *latreia*, is highly praised, although the Law does not teach the gratuitous remission of sins. But the Fathers knew the promise concerning Christ that God for Christ's sake wished to remit sins. Therefore, since they understood that Christ would be the price for our sins, they knew that our works are not a price for so great a matter [could not pay so great a debt]. Accordingly, they received gratuitous mercy and remission of sins by faith, just as the saints in the New Testament. Here belong those frequent repetitions concerning mercy and faith, in the psalms and the prophets, as this, Ps. 130, 3 sq.: If Thou Lord, shouldest mark iniquities, O Lord, who shall stand? Here

David confesses his sins and does not recount his merits. He adds; But there is forgiveness with Thee. Here he comforts himself by his trust in God's mercy, and he cites the promise: My soul doth wait and in His Word do I hope, i.e., because Thou hast promised the remission of sins, I am sustained by this Thy promise. Therefore the fathers also were justified, not by the Law but by the promise and faith. And it is amazing that the adversaries extenuate faith to such a degree, although they see that it is everywhere praised as an eminent service, as in Ps. 50, 15: Call upon Me in the day of trouble: I will deliver thee. Thus God wishes Himself to be known, thus He wishes Himself to be worshiped, that from Him we receive benefits, and receive them, too, because of His mercy, and not because of our merits. This is the richest consolation in all afflictions [physical or spiritual, in life or in death as all godly persons know]. And such consolations the adversaries abolish when they extenuate and disparage faith, and teach only that by means of works and merits men treat with God [that we treat with God, the great Majesty, by means of our miserable, beggarly works and merits].

Part 4

That Faith in Christ Justifies.

I n the first place, lest any one may think that we speak concerning an idle knowledge of the history, we must declare how faith is obtained [how the heart begins to believe]. Afterward we will show both that it justifies, and how this ought to be understood, and we will explain the objections of the adversaries. Christ, in the last chapter of Luke 24, 47, commands that repentance and remission of sins should be preached in His name. For the Gospel convicts all men that they are under sin, that they all are subject to eternal wrath and death, and offers for Christ's sake remission of sin and justification, which is received by faith. The preaching of repentance, which accuses us, terrifies consciences with true and grave terrors. [For the preaching of repentance, or this declaration of the Gospel: Amend your lives! Repent! When it truly penetrates the heart, terrifies the conscience, and is no jest, but a great terror, in which the conscience feels its misery and sin and the wrath of God.] In these, hearts ought again to receive consolation. This happens if they believe the promise of Christ, that for His sake we have remission of sins. This faith, encouraging and consoling in these fears, receives remission of sins, justifies and quickens. For this consolation is a new and spiritual life [a new birth and a new life]. These things are plain and clear, and can be understood by the pious, and have testimonies of the Church [as is to be seen in the conversion of Paul and Augustine]. The adversaries nowhere can say how the Holy Ghost is given. They imagine that the Sacraments confer the Holy Ghost *ex opere operato*, without a good emotion in the recipient, as though, indeed, the gift of the Holy Ghost were an idle matter.

But since we speak of such faith as is not an idle thought, but of that which liberates from death and produces a new life in hearts [which is such a new light, life, and force in the heart as to renew our heart, mind, and spirit, makes new men of us and new creatures,] and is the work of the Holy Ghost; this does not coexist with mortal sin [for how can light and darkness coexist?], but as long as it is present, produces good fruits as we will say after a while. For concerning the conversion of the wicked, or concerning the mode of regeneration, what can be said that is more simple and more clear? Let them, from so great an array of writers, adduce a single commentary upon the Sententiae that speaks of the mode of regeneration. When they speak of the habit of love, they imagine that men merit it through works and they do not teach that it is received through the Word, precisely as also the Anabaptists teach at this time. But God cannot be treated with, God cannot be apprehended, except through the Word. Accordingly, justification occurs through the Word, just as Paul says, Rom. 1, 16: The Gospel is the power of God unto salvation to every one that believeth. Likewise 10, 17: Faith cometh by hearing. And proof can be derived even from this that faith justifies, because, if justification occurs only through the Word, and the Word is apprehended only by faith, it follows that faith justifies. But there are other and more important reasons. We have said these things thus far in order that we might show the mode of regeneration, and that the nature of faith [what is, or is not, faith], concerning which we speak, might be understood.

Now we will show that faith [and nothing else] justifies. Here, in the first place readers must be admonished of this, that just as it is necessary to maintain this sentence: Christ is Mediator, so is it necessary to defend that faith justifies, [without works]. For how will Christ be Mediator if in justification we do not use Him as Mediator; if we do not hold that for His sake we are accounted righteous? But to believe is to trust in the merits of Christ, that for His sake God certainly wishes to be reconciled with us. Likewise, just as we ought to maintain that, apart from the Law, the promise of Christ is necessary, so also is it needful to maintain that faith justifies. [For the Law does not preach the forgiveness of sin by grace.] For the Law cannot be performed unless the Holy Ghost be first received. It is, therefore, needful to maintain that the promise of Christ is necessary. But this cannot be received except by faith. Therefore, those who deny that faith justifies, teach nothing but the Law, both Christ and the Gospel being set aside.

But when it is said that faith justifies, some perhaps understand it of the beginning, namely, that faith is the beginning of justification or preparation for justification, so that not faith itself is that through which we are accepted by God, but the works which follow; and they dream, accordingly, that faith is highly praised, because it is the beginning. For great is the importance of the beginning, as they commonly say, ***Archae aemioy pantos***, The beginning is half of everything; just as if one would say that grammar makes the teachers of all arts, because it prepares for other arts, although in fact it is his own art that renders every one an artist. We do not believe thus concerning faith, but we maintain this, that properly and truly, by faith itself, we are for Christ's sake accounted righteous, or are acceptable to God. And because "to be justified" means that out of unjust men just men are made, or born again, it means also that they are pronounced or accounted just. For Scripture speaks in both ways. [The term "to be justified" is used in two ways: to denote, being converted or regenerated; again, being accounted righteous.] Accordingly we wish first to show this, that faith alone makes of an unjust, a just man, i.e., receives remission of sins.

The particle alone offends some, although even Paul says, Rom. 3, 28: We conclude that a man is justified by faith, without the deeds of the Law. Again, Eph. 2, 8: It is the gift of God; not of works, lest any man should boast. Again, Rom. 3, 24: Being justified freely. If the exclusive alone displeases, let them remove from Paul also the exclusives freely, not of works, it is the gift, etc. For these also are [very strong] exclusives. It is, however, the opinion of merit that we exclude. We do not exclude the Word or Sacraments, as the adversaries falsely charge us. For we have said above that faith is conceived from the Word, and we honor the ministry of the Word in the highest degree. Love also and works must follow faith. Wherefore, they are not excluded so as not to follow, but confidence in the merit of love or of works is excluded in justification. And this we will clearly show.

Part 5

That We Obtain Remission of Sins by Faith Alone in Christ.

We think that even the adversaries acknowledge that, in justification, the remission of sins is necessary first. For we all are under sin. Wherefore we reason thus:-To attain the remission of sins is to be justified, according to Ps. 32, 1: Blessed is he whose transgression is forgiven. By faith alone in Christ, not through love, not because of love or works, do we acquire the remission of sins, although love follows faith. Therefore by faith alone we are justified, understanding justification as the making of a righteous man out of an unrighteous, or that he be regenerated.

It will thus become easy to declare the minor premise [that we obtain forgiveness of sin by faith, not by love] if we know how the remission of sins occurs. The adversaries with great indifference dispute whether the remission of sins and the infusion of grace are the same change [whether they are one change or two]. Being idle men, they did not know what to answer [cannot speak at all on this subject]. In the remission of sins, the terrors of sin and of eternal death, in the heart, must be overcome, as Paul testifies, 1 Cor. 15, 56 sq.: The sting of death is sin, and the strength of sin is the Law. But thanks be to God, which giveth us the victory through our Lord Jesus Christ. That is, sin terrifies consciences, this occurs through the Law, which shows the wrath of God against sin; but we gain the victory through Christ. How? By faith, when we comfort ourselves by confidence in the mercy promised for Christ's sake. Thus, therefore we prove the minor proposition. The wrath of God cannot be appeased if we set against it our own works, because Christ has been set forth as a Propitiator, so that, for His sake, the Father may become reconciled to us. But Christ is not apprehended as a Mediator except by faith.

Therefore, by faith alone we obtain remission of sins when we comfort our hearts with confidence in the mercy promised for Christ's sake. Likewise Paul, Rom. 5, 2, says: By whom also we have access, and adds, by faith. Thus, therefore, we are reconciled to the Father, and receive remission of sins when we are comforted with confidence in the mercy promised for Christ's sake. The adversaries regard Christ as Mediator and Propitiator for this reason, namely, that He has merited the habit of love; they do not urge us to use Him now as Mediator, but, as though Christ were altogether buried, they imagine that we have access through our own works, and, through these, merit this habit and afterwards, by this love, come to God. Is not this to bury Christ altogether, and to take away the entire doctrine of faith? Paul, on the contrary, teaches that we have access, i.e., reconciliation, through Christ. And to show how this occurs, he adds that we have access by faith. By faith, therefore, for Christ's sake, we receive remission of sins. We cannot set our own love and our own works over against God's wrath.

Secondly. It is certain that sins are forgiven for the sake of Christ, as Propitiator, Rom. 3, 25: Whom God hath set forth to be a propitiation. Moreover, Paul adds: through faith. Therefore this Propitiator thus benefits us, when by faith we apprehend the mercy promised in Him, and set it against the wrath and judgment of God. And to the same effect it is written, Heb. 4, 14. 16: Seeing, then, that we have a great High Priest, etc., let us therefore come with confidence. For the Apostle bids us come to God, not with confidence in our own merits, but with confidence in Christ as a High Priest; therefore he requires faith.

Thirdly. Peter, in Acts 10, 43, says: To Him give all the prophets witness that through His name, whosoever believeth on Him, shall receive remission of sins. How could this be said more clearly? We receive remission of sins, he says, through His name i.e., for His sake; therefore, not for the sake of our merits, not for the sake of our contrition, attrition, love, worship, works. And he adds: When we believe in Him. Therefore he requires faith. For we cannot apprehend the name of Christ except by faith. Besides he cites the agreement of all the prophets. This is truly to cite the authority of the Church. [For when all the holy prophets bear witness, that is certainly a glorious, great excellent, powerful decretal and testimony.] But of this topic we will speak again after a while, when treating of "Repentance."

Fourthly. Remission of sins is something promised for Christ's sake. Therefore it cannot be received except by faith alone. For a promise cannot be received except by faith alone. Rom. 4, 16: Therefore it is of faith that it might be by grace, to the end that the promise might be sure; as though he were to say: "If the matter were to depend upon our merits, the promise would be uncertain and useless, because we never could determine when we would have sufficient merit." And this, experienced consciences can easily understand [and would not, for a thousand worlds, have our salvation depend upon ourselves]. Accordingly, Paul says, Gal. 3, 22: But the Scripture hath concluded all under sin, that the promise by faith of Jesus Christ might be given to them that believe. He takes merit away from us, because he says that all are guilty and concluded under sin; then he adds that the promise, namely, of the remission of sins and of justification, is given, and adds how the promise can be received, namely, by faith. And this reasoning, derived from the nature of a promise, is the chief reasoning [a veritable rock] in Paul, and is often repeated. Nor can anything be devised or imagined whereby this argument of Paul can be overthrown. Wherefore let not good minds suffer themselves to be forced from the conviction that we receive remission of sins for Christ's sake, only through faith. In this they have sure and firm consolation against the terrors of sin, and against eternal death and against all the gates of hell. [Everything else is a foundation of sand that sinks in trials.]

But since we receive remission of sins and the Holy Ghost by faith alone, faith alone justifies, because those reconciled are accounted righteous and children of God, not on account of their own purity, but through mercy for Christ's sake, provided only they by faith apprehend this mercy. Accordingly, Scripture testifies that by faith we are accounted righteous, Rom. 3, 26. We, therefore, will add testimonies which clearly declare that faith is that very righteousness by which we are accounted righteous before God, namely, not because it is a work that is in itself worthy, but because it receives the promise by which God has promised that for Christ's sake He wishes to be propitious to those believing in Him, or because He knows that Christ of God is made unto us wisdom, and righteousness, and sanctification, and redemption, 1 Cor. 1, 30.

In the Epistle to the Romans, Paul discusses this topic especially, and declares that, when we believe that God, for Christ's sake is reconciled to us, we are justified freely by faith. And this proposition, which contains the statement of the entire discussion [the principal matter of all Epistles, yea, of the entire Scriptures], he maintains in the third chapter: We conclude that a man is justified by faith, without the deeds of the Law, Rom. 3, 28. Here the adversaries interpret that this refers to Levitical ceremonies [not to other virtuous works]. But Paul speaks not only of the ceremonies, but of the whole Law. For he quotes afterward (7, 7) from the *Decalog*: Thou shalt not covet. And if moral works [that are not Jewish ceremonies] would merit the remission of sins and justification, there would also be no need of Christ and the promise, and all that Paul speaks of the promise would be overthrown. He would also have been wrong in writing to the Ephesians, 2, 8: By grace are ye saved through faith, and that not of yourselves; it is the gift of God, not of works. Paul likewise refers to Abraham and David, Rom. 4, 1. 6. But they had the command of God concerning circumcision. Therefore, if any works justified these works must also have justified at the time that they had a command. But Augustine teaches correctly that Paul speaks of the entire Law, as he discusses at length in his book, Of the Spirit and Letter, where he says finally: These matters, therefore, having been considered and treated, according to the ability that the Lord has thought worthy to give us, we infer that man is not justified by the precepts of a good life, but by faith in Jesus Christ.

And lest we may think that the sentence that faith justifies, fell from Paul inconsiderately, he fortifies and confirms this by a long discussion in the fourth chapter to the Romans, and afterwards repeats it in all his epistles. Thus he says, Rom. 4, 4. 5: To him that worketh is the reward not reckoned of grace, but of debt. But to him that worketh not, but believeth on Him that justifieth the ungodly, his faith is counted for righteousness. Here he clearly says that faith itself is imputed for righteousness. Faith, therefore, is that thing which God declares to be righteousness, and he adds that it is imputed freely, and says that it could not be imputed freely, if it were due on account of works. Wherefore he excludes also the merit of moral works [not only Jewish ceremonies, but all other good works]. For if justification before God were due to these, faith would not be imputed for righteousness without works. And afterwards, Rom. 4, 9: For we say that faith was reckoned to Abraham for righteousness. Chapter 5, 1 says: Being justified by faith, we have peace with God, i.e., we have consciences that are tranquil and joyful before God. Rom. 10, 10: With the heart man believeth unto righteousness. Here he declares that faith is the righteousness of the heart. Gal. 2, 15: We have believed in Christ Jesus that we might be justified by the faith of Christ, and not by the works of the Law. Eph. 2, 8. For by grace are ye saved through faith, and that not of yourselves; it is the gift of God; not of works, lest any man should boast.

John 1, 12: To them gave He power to become the sons of God, even to them that believe on His name; which were born, not of blood, nor of the will of the flesh nor of the will of man, but of God. John 3, 14. 15: As Moses lifted up the serpent in the wilderness, even so must the Son of Man be lifted up, that whosoever believeth in Him should not perish. Likewise, v. 17: For God sent not His Son into the world to condemn the world, but that the world through Him might be saved. He that believeth on Him is not condemned.

Acts 13, 38. 39: Be it known unto you therefore, men and brethren, that through this Man is preached unto you the forgiveness of sins; and by Him all that believe are justified from all things from which ye could not be justified by the Law of Moses. How could the office of Christ and justification be declared more clearly? The Law, he says, did not justify. Therefore Christ was given, that we may believe that for His sake we are justified. He plainly denies justification to the Law. Hence, for Christ's sake we are accounted righteous when we believe that God, for His sake, has been reconciled to us. Acts 4, 11. 12: This is the stone which was set at naught of you builders, which is become the head of the corner. Neither is there salvation in any other; for there is none other name under heaven given among men whereby we must be saved. But the name of Christ is apprehended only by faith. [I cannot believe in the name of Christ in any other way than when I hear His merit preached, and lay hold of that.] Therefore, by confidence in the name of Christ, and not by confidence in our works, we are saved. For "the name" here signifies the cause which is mentioned because of which salvation is attained. And to call upon the name of Christ is to trust in the name of Christ, as the cause or price because of which we are saved. Acts 15, 9: Purifying their hearts by faith. Wherefore that faith of which the Apostles speak is not idle knowledge, but a reality, receiving the Holy Ghost and justifying us [not a mere knowledge of history, but a strong powerful work of the Holy Ghost, which changes hearts].

Hab. 2, 4: The just shall live by his faith. Here he says, first that men are just by faith by which they believe that God is propitious and he adds that the same faith quickens, because this faith produces in the heart peace and joy and eternal life [which begins in the present life].

Is. 53, 11: By His knowledge shall He justify many. But what is the knowledge of Christ unless to know the benefits of Christ, the promises which by the Gospel He has scattered broadcast in the world? And to know these benefits is properly and truly to believe in Christ, to believe that that which God has promised for Christ's sake He will certainly fulfil.

But Scripture is full of such testimonies, since, in some places, it presents the Law, and in others the promises concerning Christ, and the remission of sins, and the free acceptance of the sinner for Christ's sake.

Here and there among the Fathers similar testimonies are extant. For Ambrose says in his letter to a certain Irenaeus: Moreover, the world was subject to him by the Law for the reason that, according to the command of the Law, all are indicted, and yet, by the works of the Law, no one is justified, i.e., because, by the Law, sin is perceived, but guilt is not discharged. The Law, which made all sinners, seemed to have done injury, but when the Lord Jesus Christ came, He forgave to all sin which no one could avoid, and, by the shedding of His own blood, blotted out the handwriting which was against us. This is what he says in Rom. 5, 20: "The Law entered that the offense might abound. But where sin abounded, grace did much more abound." Because after the whole world become subject, He took away the sin of the whole world, as he [John] testified, saying, John 1, 29: "Behold the Lamb of God, which taketh away the sin of the world." And on this account let no one boast of works, because no one is justified by his deeds. But he who is righteous has it given him because he was justified after the laver [of Baptism]. Faith, therefore, is that which frees through the blood of Christ, because he is blessed "whose transgression is forgiven, whose sin is covered," Ps. 32, 1. These are the words of Ambrose, which clearly favor our doctrine; he denies justification to works, and ascribes to faith that it sets us free through the blood of Christ. Let all the Sententiarists, who are adorned with magnificent titles, be collected into one heap. For some are called angelic; others, subtile; and others irrefragable [that is, doctors who cannot err]. When all these have been read and reread, they will not be of as much aid for understanding Paul as is this one passage of Ambrose.

To the same effect, Augustine writes many things against the Pelagians. In f the Spirit and Letter he says: The righteousness of the Law, namely, that he who has fulfilled it shall live in it, is set forth for this reason that when any one has recognized his infirmity he may attain and work the same and live in it, conciliating the Justifier not by his own strength nor by the letter of the Law itself (which cannot be done), but by faith. Except in a justified man, there is no right work wherein he who does it may live. But justification is obtained by faith. Here he clearly says that the Justifier is conciliated by faith, and that justification is obtained by faith. And a little after: By the Law we fear God; by faith we hope in God. But to those fearing punishment grace is hidden; and the soul laboring, etc., under this fear betakes itself by faith to God's mercy, in order that He may give what lie commands. Here he teaches that by the Law hearts are terrified, but by faith they receive consolation. He also teaches us to apprehend, by faith, mercy, before we attempt to fulfil the Law. We will shortly cite certain other passages.

Truly, it is amazing that the adversaries are in no way moved by so many passages of Scripture, which clearly ascribe justification to faith, and, indeed, deny it to works. Do they think that the same is repeated so often for no purpose? Do they think that these words fell inconsiderately from the Holy Ghost? But they have also devised sophistry whereby they elude them. They say that these passages of Scripture, (which speak of faith,) ought to be received as referring to a *fides formata*, i.e., they do not ascribe justification to faith except on account of love. Yea, they do not, in any way, ascribe justification to faith, but only to love, because they dream that faith can coexist with mortal sin. Whither does this tend, unless that they again abolish the promise and return to the Law? If faith receive the remission of sins on account of love, the remission of sins will always be uncertain, because we never love as much as we ought, yea, we do not love unless our hearts are firmly convinced that the remission of sins has been granted us. Thus the adversaries, while they require in the remission of sins and justification confidence in one's own love, altogether abolish the Gospel concerning the free remission of sins; although at the same time, they neither render this love nor understand it, unless they believe that the remission of sins is freely received.

We also say that love ought to follow faith as Paul also says, Gal. 5, 6: For in Jesus Christ neither circumcision availeth anything, nor uncircumcision, but faith which worketh by love. And yet we must not think on that account that by confidence in this love or on account of this love we receive the remission of sins and reconciliation just as we do not receive the remission of sins because of other works that follow. But the remission of sins is received by faith alone, and, indeed, by faith properly so called, because the promise cannot be received except by faith. But faith, properly so called, is that which assents to the promise [is when my heart, and the Holy Ghost in the heart, says: The promise of God is true and certain]. Of this faith Scripture speaks. And because it receives the remission of sins, and reconciles us to God, by this faith we are [like Abraham] accounted righteous for Christ's sake before we love and do the works of the Law, although love necessarily follows. Nor, indeed, is this faith an idle knowledge, neither can it coexist with mortal sin, but it is a work of the Holy Ghost, whereby we are freed from death, and terrified minds are encouraged and quickened. And because this faith alone receives the remission of sins, and renders us acceptable to God, and brings the Holy Ghost, it could be more correctly called *gratia gratum faciens*, grace rendering one pleasing to God, than an effect following, namely, love.

Thus far, in order that the subject might be made quite clear, we have shown with sufficient fulness, both from testimonies of Scripture, and arguments derived from Scripture, that by faith alone we obtain the remission of sins for Christ's sake, and that by faith alone we are justified, i.e., of unrighteous men made righteous, or regenerated. But how necessary the knowledge of this faith is, can be easily judged, because in this alone the office of Christ is recognized, by this alone we receive the benefits of Christ; this alone brings sure and firm consolation to pious minds. And in the Church [if there is to be a church, if there is to be a Christian Creed], it is necessary that there should be the [preaching and] doctrine [by which consciences are not made to rely on a dream or to build on a foundation of sand, but] from which the pious may receive the sure hope of salvation. For the adversaries give men bad advice [therefore the adversaries are truly unfaithful bishops, unfaithful preachers and doctors; they have hitherto given evil counsel to consciences, and still do so by introducing such doctrine] when they bid them doubt whether they obtain remission of sins. For how will such persons sustain themselves in death who have heard nothing of this faith, and think that they ought to doubt whether they obtain the remission of sins? Besides it is necessary that in the Church of Christ the Gospel be retained, i.e., the promise that for Christ's sake sins are freely remitted. Those who teach nothing of this faith, concerning which we speak, altogether abolish the Gospel. But the scholastics mention not even a word concerning this faith. Our adversaries follow them, and reject this faith. Nor do they see that, by rejecting this faith, they abolish the entire promise concerning the free remission of sins and the righteousness of Christ.

Part 6

Article III: *Of Love and the Fulfilling of the Law.*

Here the adversaries urge against us: If thou wilt enter into life, keep the commandments, Matt. 19, 17; likewise: The doers of the Law shall be justified, Rom. 2, 13, and many other like things concerning the Law and works. Before we reply to this, we must first declare what we believe concerning love and the fulfilling of the Law.

It is written in the prophet, Jer. 31, 33: I will put My Law in their inward parts, and write it in their hearts. And in Rom. 3, 31 Paul says: Do we, then, make void the Law through faith? God forbid! Yea, we establish the Law. And Christ says, Matt. 19, 17: If thou wilt enter into life, keep the commandments. Likewise, 1 Cor. 13, 3: If I have not charity, it profiteth me nothing. These and similar sentences testify that the Law ought to be begun in us, and be kept by us more and more [that we are to keep the Law when we have been justified by faith, and thus increase more and more in the Spirit]. Moreover, we speak not of ceremonies, but of that Law which gives commandment concerning the movements of the heart, namely, the ***Decalog***. Because, indeed, faith brings the Holy Ghost, and produces in hearts a new life, it is necessary that it should produce spiritual movements in hearts. And what these movements are, the prophet, Jer. 31, 33, shows, when he says: I will put My Law into their inward parts, and write it in their hearts. Therefore, when we have been justified by faith and regenerated, we begin to fear and love God, to pray to Him, to expect from Him aid, to give thanks and praise Him and to obey Him in afflictions. We begin also to love our neighbors, because our hearts have spiritual and holy movements [there is now, through the Spirit of Christ a new heart mind, and spirit within].

These things cannot occur until we have been justified by faith, and, regenerated, we receive the Holy Ghost: first, because the Law cannot be kept without [the knowledge of] Christ; and likewise the Law cannot be kept without the Holy Ghost. But the Holy Ghost is received by faith, according to the declaration of Paul, Gal. 3, 14: That we might receive the promise of the Spirit through faith. Then, too, how can the human heart love God while it knows that He is terribly angry, and is oppressing us with temporal and perpetual calamities? But the Law always accuses us, always shows that God is angry. [Therefore, what the scholastics say of the love of God is a dream.] God therefore is not loved until we apprehend mercy by faith. Not until then does He become a lovable object.

Although, therefore, civil works, i.e., the outward works of the Law, can be done, in a measure, without Christ and without the Holy Ghost [from our inborn light], nevertheless it appears from what we have said that those things which belong peculiarly to the divine Law, i.e., the affections of the heart towards God, which are commanded in the first table, cannot be rendered without the Holy Ghost. But our adversaries are fine theologians; they regard the second table and political works; for the first table [in which is contained the highest theology, on which all depends] they care nothing, as though it were of no matter; or certainly they require only outward observances. They in no way consider the Law that is eternal, and placed far above the sense and intellect of all creatures [which concerns the very Deity, and the honor of the eternal Majesty], Deut. 6, 5: Thou shalt love the Lord, thy God with all thine heart. [This they treat as such a paltry small matter as if it did not belong to theology.]

But Christ was given for this purpose, namely, that for His sake there might be bestowed on us the remission of sins, and the Holy Ghost to bring forth in us new and eternal life, and eternal righteousness [to manifest Christ in our hearts, as it is written John 16, 15: He shall take of the things of Mine, and show them unto you. Likewise, He works also other gifts, love, thanksgiving, charity, patience, etc.]. Wherefore the Law cannot be truly kept unless the Holy Ghost be received through faith. Accordingly, Paul says that the Law is established by faith, and not made void; because the Law can only then be thus kept when the Holy Ghost is given. And Paul teaches 2 Cor. 3, 15 sq., the veil that covered the face of Moses cannot be removed except by faith in Christ, by which the Holy Ghost is received. For he speaks thus: But even unto this day, when Moses is read, the veil is upon their heart. Nevertheless, when it shall turn to the Lord, the veil shall be taken away. Now the Lord is that Spirit, and where the Spirit of the Lord is, there is liberty. Paul understands by the veil the human opinion concerning the entire Law, the *Decalog* and the ceremonies, namely, that hypocrites think that external and civil works satisfy the Law of God and that sacrifices and observances justify before God *ex opere operato*. But then this veil is removed from us, i.e., we are freed from this error, when God shows to our hearts our uncleanness and the heinousness of sin. Then, for the first time, we see that we are far from fulfilling the Law. Then we learn to know how flesh, in security and indifference, does not fear God, and is not fully certain that we are regarded by God, but imagines that men are born and die by chance. Then we experience that we do not believe that God forgives and hears us. But when, on hearing the Gospel and the remission of sins, we are consoled by faith, we receive the Holy Ghost, so that now we are able to think aright concerning God, and to fear and believe God, etc. From these facts it is apparent that the Law cannot be kept without Christ and the Holy Ghost.

We, therefore, profess that it is necessary that the Law be begun in us, and that it be observed continually more and more. And at the same time we comprehend both spiritual movements and external good works [the good heart within and works without]. Therefore the adversaries falsely charge against us that our theologians do not teach good works, while they not only require these, but also show how they can be done [that the heart must enter into these works, lest they be mere lifeless, cold works of hypocrites]. The result convicts hypocrites, who by their own powers endeavor to fulfil the Law, that they cannot accomplish what they attempt. [For are they free from hatred, envy, strife, anger, wrath, avarice, adultery, etc.? Why, these vices were nowhere greater than in the cloisters and sacred institutes.] For human nature is far too weak to be able by its own powers to resist the devil, who holds as captives all who have not been freed through faith. There is need of the power of Christ against the devil, namely, that, inasmuch as we know that for Christ's sake we are heard, and have the promise, we may pray for the governance and defense of the Holy Ghost, that we may neither be deceived and err, nor be impelled to undertake anything contrary to God's will. [Otherwise we should, every hour, fall into error and abominable vices.] Just as Ps. 68, 18 teaches: Thou hast led captivity captive; Thou hast received gifts for man. For Christ has overcome the devil, and has given to us the promise and the Holy Ghost, in order that, by divine aid, we ourselves also may overcome. And 1 John 3, 8: For this purpose the Son of God was manifested, that He might destroy the works of the devil. Again, we teach not only how the Law can be observed, but also how God is pleased if anything be done, namely, not because we render satisfaction to the Law, but because we are in Christ, as we shall say after a little. It is, therefore, manifest that we require good works. Yea, we add also this, that it is impossible for love to God, even though it be small, to be sundered from faith, because through Christ we come to the Father, and, the remission of sins having been received, we now are truly certain that we have a God, i.e., that God cares for us; we call upon Him, we give Him thanks, we fear Him, we love Him as John teaches in his first Epistle, 4, 19: We love Him he says, because He first loved us, namely, because He gave His Son for us, and forgave us our sins. Thus he indicates that faith precedes and love follows. Likewise the faith of which we speak exists in repentance i.e., it is conceived in the terrors of conscience, which feels the wrath of God against our sins, and seeks the remission of sins, and to be freed from sin. And in such terrors and other afflictions this faith ought to grow and be strengthened. Wherefore it cannot exist in those who live according to the flesh, who are delighted by their own lusts and obey them. Accordingly, Paul says, Rom. 8, 1: There is, therefore, now no condemnation to them that are in Christ Jesus, who walk not after the flesh, but after the Spirit. So, too, vv. 12. 13: We are debtors, not to the flesh, to live after the flesh. For if ye live after the flesh, ye shall die; but if ye, through the Spirit, do mortify the deeds of the body, ye shall live. Wherefore, the faith which receives remission of sins in a heart terrified and fleeing from sin does not remain in those who obey their desires, neither does it coexist with mortal sin.

From these effects of faith the adversaries select one, namely, love, and teach that love justifies. Thus it is clearly apparent that they teach only the Law. They do not teach that remission of sins through faith is first received. They do not teach of Christ as Mediator, that for Christ's sake we have a gracious God; but because of our love. And yet, what the nature of this love is they do not say, neither can they say. They proclaim that they fulfil the Law, although this glory belongs properly to

Christ; and they set against the judgment of God confidence in their own works; for they say that they ***merit de condigno*** (according to righteousness) grace and eternal life. This confidence is absolutely impious and vain. For in this life we cannot satisfy the Law, because carnal nature does not cease to bring forth wicked dispositions [evil inclination and desire], even though the Spirit in us resists them.

But some one may ask: Since we also confess that love is a work of the Holy Ghost, and since it is righteousness, because it is the fulfilling of the Law, why do we not teach that it justifies? To this we must reply: In the first place, it is certain that we receive remission of sins, neither through our love nor for the sake of our love, but for Christ's sake, by faith alone. Faith alone, which looks upon the promise, and knows that for this reason it must be regarded as certain that God forgives, because Christ has not died in vain, etc., overcomes the terrors of sin and death. If any one doubts whether sins are remitted him, he dishonors Christ, since he judges that his sin is greater or more efficacious than the death and promise of Christ although Paul says, Rom. 5, 20: Where sin abounded, grace did much more abound, i.e., that mercy is more comprehensive [more powerful, richer, and stronger] than sin. If any one thinks that he obtains the remission of sins because he loves, he dishonors Christ, and will discover in God's judgment that this confidence in his own righteousness is wicked and vain. Therefore it is necessary that faith [alone] reconciles and justifies. And as we do not receive remission of sins through other virtues of the Law, or on account of these namely, on account of patience, chastity, obedience towards magistrates, etc., and nevertheless these virtues ought to follow, so, too, we do not receive remission of sins because of love to God although it is necessary that this should follow. Besides, the custom of speech is well known that by the same word we sometimes comprehend by synecdoche the cause and effects. Thus in Luke 7, 47 Christ says: Her sins, which are many, are forgiven for she loved much. For Christ interprets Himself [this very passage] when He adds: Thy faith hath saved thee. Christ, therefore, did not mean that the woman, by that work of love, had merited the remission of sins. For that is the reason He says: Thy faith hath sated thee. But faith is that which freely apprehends God's mercy on account of God's Word [which relies upon God's mercy and Word, and not upon one's own work]. If any one denies that this is faith [if any one imagines that he can rely at the same time upon God and his own works], he does not understand at all what faith is. [For the terrified conscience is not satisfied with its own works, but must cry after mercy, and is comforted and encouraged alone by God's Word.] And the narrative itself shows in this passage what that is which He calls love. The woman came with the opinion concerning Christ that with Him the remission of sins should be sought. This worship is the highest worship of Christ. Nothing greater could she ascribe to Christ. To seek from Him the remission of sins was truly to acknowledge the Messiah. Now, thus to think of Christ, thus to worship Him, thus to embrace Him, is truly to believe. Christ, moreover, employed the word "love" not towards the woman, but against the Pharisee, because He contrasted the entire worship of the Pharisee with the entire worship of the woman. He reproved the Pharisee because he did not acknowledge that He was the Messiah, although he rendered Him the outward offices due to a guest and a great and holy man. He points to the woman and praises her worship, ointment, tears, etc., all of which were signs of faith and a confession, namely, that with Christ she sought the remission of sins. It is indeed a great example which, not without reason, moved Christ to reprove the Pharisee, who was a wise and honorable man, but not a believer. He charges him with impiety, and admonishes him by the example of the woman, showing thereby that it is disgraceful to him, that, while an unlearned woman believes God, he, a doctor of the Law, does not believe, does not acknowledge the Messiah, and does not seek from Him remission of sins and salvation. Thus, therefore, He praises the entire worship [faith with its fruits, but towards the Pharisee He names only the fruits which prove to men that there is faith in the heart] as it often occurs in the Scriptures that by one word we embrace many things; as below we shall speak at greater length in regard to similar passages, such as Luke 11, 41: Give alms of such things as ye have; and, behold, all things are clean unto you. He requires not only alms, but also the righteousness of faith. Thus He here says: Her sins, which are many, are forgiven, for she loved much i.e., because she has truly worshiped Me with faith and the exercises and signs of faith. He comprehends the entire worship. Meanwhile He teaches this, that the remission of sins is properly received by faith, although love, confession, and other good fruits ought to follow. Wherefore He does not mean this, that these fruits are the price, or are the propitiation, because of which the remission of sins, which reconciles us to God, is given. We are disputing concerning a great subject, concerning the honor of Christ, and whence good minds may seek for sure and firm consolation whether confidence is to be placed in Christ or in our works. Now, if it is to be placed in our works, the honor of Mediator and Propitiator will be withdrawn from Christ. And yet we shall find, in God's judgment, that this confidence is vain, and that consciences rush thence into despair. But if the remission of sins and reconciliation do not occur freely for Christ's sake, but for the sake of our love, no one will have remission of sins, unless when he has fulfilled the entire Law, because the Law does not justify as long as it can accuse us. Therefore it is manifest that, since justification is reconciliation for Christ's sake we are justified by faith, because it is very certain that by faith alone the remission of sins is received.

Now, therefore, let us reply to the objection which we have above stated: [Why does love not justify anybody before God?] The adversaries are right in thinking that love is the fulfilling of the Law, and obedience to the Law is certainly righteousness. [Therefore it would be true that love justifies us if we would keep the Law. But who in truth can say or boast that he keeps the Law, and loves God as the Law has commanded? We have shown above that God has made the promise of grace, because we cannot observe the Law. Therefore Paul says everywhere that we cannot be justified before God by the Law.] But they make a mistake in this that they think that we are justified by the Law. [The adversaries have to fail at this point, and miss the main issue, for in this business they only behold the Law. For all men's reason and wisdom cannot but hold that we must become pious by the Law, and that a person externally observing the Law is holy and pious. But the Gospel faces us about, directs us away from the Law to the divine promises, and teaches that we are not justified, etc.] Since, however, we are not justified by the Law [because no person can keep it], but receive remission of sins and reconciliation by faith for Christ's sake, and not for the sake of love or the fulfilling of the Law, it follows necessarily that we are justified by faith in Christ. [For before we fulfil one tittle of the Law, there must be faith in Christ by which we are reconciled to God and first obtain the remission of sin. Good God, how dare people call themselves Christians or say that they once at least looked into or read the books of the Gospel when they still deny that we obtain remission of sins by faith in Christ? Why, to a Christian it is shocking merely to hear such a statement.]

Again, [in the second place,] this fulfilling of the Law or obedience towards the Law, is indeed righteousness, when it is complete; but in us it is small and impure. [For, although they have received the first-fruits of the Spirit, and the new, yea the eternal life has begun in them, there still remains a remnant of sin and evil lust, and the Law still finds much of which it must accuse us.] Accordingly, it is not pleasing for its own sake, and is not accepted for its own sake. But although from those things which have been said above it is evident that justification signifies not the beginning of the renewal, but the reconciliation by which also we afterwards are accepted, nevertheless it can now be seen much more clearly that the inchoate fulfilling of the Law does not justify, because it is accepted only on account of faith. [Trusting in our own fulfilment of the Law is sheer idolatry and blaspheming Christ, and in the end it collapses and causes our consciences to despair. Therefore, this foundation shall stand forever, namely, that for Christ's sake we are accepted with God, and justified by faith, not on account of our love and works. This we shall make so plain and certain that anybody may grasp it. As long as the heart is not at peace with God, it cannot be righteous, for it flees from the wrath of God, despairs, and would have God not to judge it. Therefore the heart cannot be righteous and accepted with God while it is not at peace with God. Now, faith alone makes the heart to be content, and obtains peace and life Rom. 5, 1, because it confidently and frankly relies on the promise of God for Christ's sake. But our works do not make the heart content, for we always find that they are not pure. Therefore it must follow that we are accepted with God, and justified by faith alone, when in our hearts we conclude that God desires to be gracious to us, not on account of our works and fulfilment of the Law, but from pure grace, for Christ's sake. What can our opponents bring forward against this argument? What can they invent and devise against the plain truth? For this is quite certain, and experience teaches forcibly enough, that when we truly feel the judgment and wrath of God, or become afflicted, our works and worship cannot set the heart at rest. Scripture indicates this often enough as in Ps. 143, 2: Enter not into judgment with Thy servant; for in Thy sight shall no man living be justified. Here he clearly shows that all the saints, all the pious children of God, who have the Holy Ghost, if God would not by grace forgive them their sin, still have remnants of sin in the flesh. For when David in another place, Ps. 7, 8, says: Judge me O Lord, according to my righteousness, he refers to his cause, and not to his righteousness, and asks God to protect his cause and word, for he says: Judge, O Lord, my cause. Again, in Ps. 130, 3 he clearly states that no person, not even the greatest saints, can bear God's judgment, if He were to observe our iniquity, as he says: If Thou, Lord, shouldest mark iniquity, O Lord, who shall stand! And thus says Job, 9, 28: I was afraid of all my works (Engl. vers., sorrows). Likewise chap. 9, 30: If I wash myself with snow-water, and make my hands never so clean, yet shalt Thou plunge me in the ditch. And Prov. 20, 9: Who can say, I have made my heart clean? And 1 John 1, 8: If we say that we have no sin, we deceive ourselves and the truth is not in us. And in the Lord's Prayer the saints ask for the forgiveness of sins. Therefore even the saints have guilt and sins. Again in Num. 14, 18: The innocent will not be innocent. And Zechariah, 2, 13, says: Be silent O all flesh, before the Lord. And Isaiah 40, 6 sqq.: All flesh is grass, i.e., flesh and righteousness of the flesh cannot endure the judgment of God. And Jonah says, 2, 9: They that observe lying vanities forsake their own mercy. Therefore, pure mercy preserves us, our own works, merits, endeavors, cannot preserve us. These and similar declarations in the Scriptures testify that our works are unclean, and that we need mercy. Wherefore works do not render consciences pacified but only mercy apprehended by faith does.] Nor must we trust that we are accounted righteous before God by our own perfection and fulfilling of the Law, but rather for Christ's sake.

First [in the third place], because Christ does not cease to be Mediator after we have been renewed. They err who imagine that He has merited only a first grace, and that afterwards we please God and merit eternal life by our fulfilling of the Law. Christ remains Mediator, and we ought always to be confident that for His sake we have a reconciled God even although we are unworthy. As Paul clearly teaches when he says [By whom also we have access to God, Rom. 5, 2. For our best works, even after the grace of the Gospel has been received, as I stated, are still weak and not at all pure. For sin and Adam's fall are not such a trifling thing as reason holds or imagines, it exceeds the reason and thought of all men to understand what a horrible wrath of God has been handed on to us by that disobedience. There occurred a shocking corruption of the entire human nature, which no work of man, but only God Himself, can restore], 1 Cor. 4, 4: I know nothing by myself, yet am I not hereby justified, but he knows that by faith he is accounted righteous for Christ's sake, according to the passage: Blessed are they whose iniquities are forgiven, Ps. 32, 1; Rom. 4, 7. [Therefore we need grace, and the gracious goodness of God, and the forgiveness of sin, although we have done many good works.] But this remission is always received by faith. Likewise, the imputation of the righteousness of the Gospel is from the promise; therefore it is always received by faith, and it always must be regarded certain that by faith we are for Christ's sake, accounted righteous. If the regenerate ought afterwards to think that they will be accepted on account of the fulfilling of the Law, when would conscience be certain that it pleased God, since we never satisfy the Law? Accordingly, we must always recur to the promise; by this our infirmity must be sustained, and we must regard it as certain that we are accounted righteous for the sake of Christ, who is ever at the right hand of God, who also maketh intercession for us, Rom. 8, 34. If any one think that he is righteous and accepted on account of his own fulfilment of the Law, and not on account of Christ's promise, he dishonors this High Priest. Neither can it be understood how one could imagine that man is righteous before God when Christ is excluded as Propitiator and Mediator.

Again [in the fourth place], what need is there of a long discussion? [If we were to think that, after we have come to the Gospel and are born again, we were to merit by our works that God be gracious to us, not by faith, conscience would never find rest, but would be driven to despair. For the Law unceasingly accuses us, since we never can satisfy the Law.] All Scripture, all the Church cries out that the Law cannot be satisfied. Therefore this inchoate fulfilment of the Law does not please on its own account, but on account of faith in Christ. Otherwise the Law always accuses us. For who loves or fears God sufficiently? Who with sufficient patience bears the afflictions imposed by God? Who does not frequently doubt whether human affairs are ruled by God's counsel or by chance? Who does not frequently doubt whether he be heard by God? Who is not frequently enraged because the wicked enjoy a better lot than the pious, because the pious are oppressed by the wicked? Who does satisfaction to his own calling? Who loves his neighbor as himself? Who is not tempted by lust? Accordingly Paul says, Rom. 7, 19: The good that I would I do not; but the evil which I would not that I do. Likewise v. 25: With the mind I myself serve the Law of God, but with the flesh, the law of sin. Here he openly declares that he serves the law of sin. And David says, Ps. 143, 2: Enter not into judgment with Thy servant; for in Thy sight shall no man living be justified. Here even a servant of God prays for the averting of judgment. Likewise Ps. 32, 2: Blessed is the man unto whom the Lord imputeth not iniquity. Therefore, in this our infirmity there is always present sin, which could be imputed, and of which he says a little while after, v. 6: For this shall every one that is godly pray unto Thee. Here he shows that even saints ought to seek remission of sins. More than blind are those who do not perceive that wicked desires in the flesh are sins, of which Paul, Gal. 5, 17, says: The flesh lusteth against the Spirit, and the Spirit against the flesh. The flesh distrusts God, trusts in present things, seeks human aid in calamities, even contrary to God's will, flees from afflictions, which it ought to bear because of God's commands, doubts concerning God's mercy, etc. The Holy Ghost in our hearts contends with such dispositions [with Adam's sin] in order to suppress and mortify them [this poison of the old Adam, this desperately wicked disposition], and to produce new spiritual movements. But concerning this topic we will collect more testimonies below, although they are everywhere obvious not only in the Scriptures, but also in the holy Fathers.

Well does Augustine say: All the commandments of God are fulfilled when whatever is not done, is forgiven. Therefore he requires faith even in good works [which the Holy Spirit produces in us], in order that we may believe that for Christ's sake we please God, and that even the works are not of themselves worthy and pleasing. And Jerome, against the Pelagians, says: Then, therefore, we are righteous when we confess that we are sinners, and that our righteousness consists not in our own merit, but in God's mercy. Therefore, in this inchoate fulfilment of the Law, faith ought to be present, which is certain that for Christ's sake we have a reconciled God. For mercy cannot be apprehended unless by faith, as has been repeatedly said above. [Therefore those who teach that we are not accepted by faith for Christ's sake but for the sake of our own works, lead consciences into despair.] Wherefore, when Paul says, Rom. 3, 31: We establish the Law through faith, by this we ought to understand, not only that those regenerated by faith receive the Holy Ghost, and have movements agreeing with God's Law, but it is by far of the greatest importance that we add also this, that we ought to perceive that we are far distant from the perfection of the Law. Wherefore we cannot conclude that we are accounted righteous before God because of our fulfilling of the Law, but in order that the conscience may become tranquil, justification must be sought elsewhere.

For we are not righteous before God as long as we flee from God's judgment, and are angry with God. Therefore we must conclude that, being reconciled by faith, we are accounted righteous for Christ's sake, not for the sake of the Law or our works, but that this inchoate fulfilling of the Law pleases on account of faith, and that, on account of faith, there is no imputation of the imperfection of the fulfilling of the Law, even though the sight of our impurity terrifies us. Now, if justification is to be sought elsewhere, our love and works do not therefore justify. Far above our purity, yea, far above the Law itself ought to be placed the death and satisfaction of Christ, presented to us that we might be sure that because of this satisfaction, and not because of our fulfilling of the Law, we have a gracious God.

Paul teaches this in Gal. 3, 13, when he says: Christ hath redeemed us from the curse of the Law, being made a curse for us, i.e. the Law condemns all men, but Christ, because without sin He has borne the punishment of sin, and been made a victim for us has removed that right of the Law to accuse and condemn those who believe in Him, because He Himself is the propitiation for them for whose sake we are now accounted righteous. But since they are accounted righteous, the Law cannot accuse or condemn them, even though they have not actually satisfied the Law. To the same purport he writes to the Colossians, 2, 10: Ye are complete in Him, as though he were to say: Although ye are still far from the perfection of the Law, yet the remnants of sin do not condemn you, because for Christ's sake we have a sure and firm reconciliation, if you believe, even though sin inhere in your flesh.

The promise ought always to be in sight that God, because of His promise, wishes for Christ's sake, and not because of the Law or our works, to be gracious and to justify. In this promise timid consciences ought to seek reconciliation and justification, by this promise they ought to sustain themselves, and be confident that for Christ's sake, because of His promise, they have a gracious God. Thus works can never render a conscience pacified, but only the promise can. If, therefore, justification and peace of conscience must be sought elsewhere than in love and works, love and works do not justify, although they are virtues and pertain to the righteousness of the Law, in so far as they are a fulfilling of the Law. So far also this obedience of the Law justifies by the righteousness of the Law. But this imperfect righteousness of the Law is not accepted by God, unless on account of faith. Accordingly it does not justify, i.e., it neither reconciles, nor regenerates, nor by itself renders us accepted before God.

From this it is evident that we are justified before God by faith alone [i.e., it obtains the remission of sins and grace for Christ's sake and regenerates us. Likewise, it is quite clear that by faith alone the Holy Ghost is received; again, that our works and this inchoate fulfilling of the Law do not by themselves please God. Now, even if I abound in good works like Paul or Peter, I must seek my righteousness elsewhere, namely, in the promise of the grace of Christ, again, if only faith calms the conscience, it must, indeed be certain that only faith justifies before God. For, if we wish to teach correctly, we must adhere to this, that we are accepted with God not on account of the Law, not on account of works, but for Christ's sake. For the honor, due Christ, must not be given to the Law or our-miserable works.] because by faith alone we receive remission of sins and reconciliation, because reconciliation or justification is a matter promised for Christ's sake, and not for the sake of the Law. Therefore it is received by faith alone, although, when the Holy Ghost is given, the fulfilling of the Law follows.

Part 7

Reply to the Arguments of the Adversaries.

Now, when the grounds of this case have been understood, namely, the distinction between the Law and the promises, or the Gospel, it will be easy to resolve the objections of the adversaries. For they cite passages concerning the Law and works, and omit passages concerning the promises. But a reply can once for all be made to all opinions concerning the Law, namely, that the Law cannot be observed without Christ, and that if civil works are wrought without Christ, they do not please God. [God is not pleased with the person.] Wherefore, when works are commended, it is necessary to add that faith is required, that they are commended on account of faith, that they are the fruits and testimonies of faith. [This our doctrine is, indeed, plain; it need not fear the light, and may be held against the Holy Scriptures. We have also clearly and correctly presented it here, if any will receive instruction and not knowingly deny the truth. For rightly to understand the benefit of Christ and the great treasure of the Gospel (which Paul extols so greatly), we must separate, on the one hand, the promise of God and the grace that is offered, and, on the other hand the Law, as far as the heavens are from the earth. In shaky matters many explanations are needed, but in a good matter one or two thoroughgoing explanations dissolve all objections which men think they can raise.] Ambiguous and dangerous cases produce many and various solutions. For the judgment of the ancient poet is true:

"An unjust cause, being In Itself sick, requires skilfully applied remedies."

But in just and sure cases one or two explanations derived from the sources correct all things that seem to offend. This occurs also in this case of ours. For the rule which I have just recited, explains all the passages that are cited concerning the Law and works [namely, that without Christ the Law cannot be truly observed, and although external works may be performed, still the person doing them does not please God outside of Christ]. For we acknowledge that Scripture teaches in some places the Law, and in other places the Gospel, or the gratuitous promise of the remission of sins for Christ's sake. But our adversaries absolutely abolish the free promise when they deny that faith justifies, and teach that for the sake of love and of our works we receive remission of sins and reconciliation. If the remission of sins depends upon the condition of our works, it is altogether uncertain. [For we can never be certain whether we do enough works, or whether our works are sufficiently holy and pure. Thus, too, the forgiveness of sins is made uncertain, and the promise of God perishes, as Paul says, Rom. 4, 14: The promise is made of none effect, and everything is rendered uncertain.] Therefore the promise will be abolished. Hence we refer godly minds to the consideration of the promises, and we teach concerning the free remission of sins and concerning reconciliation, which occurs through faith in Christ. Afterwards we add also the doctrine of the Law. [Not that by the Law we merit the remission of sins, or that for the sake of the Law we are accepted with God, but because God requires good works.] And it is necessary to divide these things aright, as Paul says, 2 Tim. 2, 15. We must see what Scripture ascribes to the Law, and what to the promises. For it praises works in such a way as not to remove the free promise [as to place the promise of God and the true treasure, Christ, a thousand leagues above it].

For good works are to be done on account of God's command, likewise for the exercise of faith [as Paul says, Eph. 2, 10: We are His workmanship, created in Christ Jesus unto good works], and on account of confession and giving of thanks. For these reasons good works ought necessarily to be done, which, although they are done in the flesh not as yet entirely renewed, that retards the movements of the Holy Ghost, and imparts some of its uncleanness, yet, on account of Christ, are holy, divine works, sacrifices, and acts pertaining to the government of Christ, who thus displays His kingdom before this world. For in these He sanctifies hearts and represses the devil, and, in order to retain the Gospel among men, openly opposes to the kingdom of the devil the confession of saints, and, in our weakness, declares His power. The dangers, labors, and sermons of the Apostle Paul, of Athanasius, Augustine, and the like, who taught the churches, are holy works, are true sacrifices acceptable to God, are contests of Christ through which He repressed the devil, and drove him from those who believed. David's labors, in waging wars and in his home government, are holy works, are true sacrifices, are contests of God, defending the people who had the Word of God against the devil, in order that the knowledge of God might not be entirely extinguished on earth. We think thus also concerning every good work in the humblest callings and in private affairs. Through these works Christ celebrates His victory over the devil, just as the distribution of alms by the Corinthians, 1 Cor. 16, 1, was a holy work and a sacrifice and contest of Christ against the devil, who labors that nothing may be done for the praise of God. To disparage such works, the confession of doctrine, affliction, works of love, mortifications of the flesh would be indeed to disparage the outward government of Christ's kingdom among men. Here also we add something concerning rewards and merits. We teach that rewards have been offered and promised to the works of believers. We teach that good works are meritorious, not for the remission of sins, for grace or justification (for these we obtain only by faith), but for other rewards, bodily and spiritual, in this life and after this life because Paul says, 1 Cor. 3, 8: Every man shall receive his own reward, according to his own labor. There will, therefore, be different rewards according to different labors. But the remission of sins is alike and equal to all, just as Christ is one, and is offered freely to all who believe that for Christ's sake their sins are remitted. Therefore the remission of sins and justification are received only by faith, and not on account of any works, as is evident in the terrors of conscience, because none of our works can be opposed to God's wrath, as Paul clearly says, Rom. 5, 1: Being justified by faith, toe have peace with God through our Lord Jesus Christ, by whom also we have access by faith, etc. But because faith makes sons of God, it also makes coheirs with Christ. Therefore, because by our works we do not merit justification, through which we are made sons of God, and coheirs with Christ, we do not by our works merit eternal life; for faith obtains this, because faith justifies us and has a reconciled God. But eternal life is due the justified, according to the passage Rom. 8, 30: Whom He justified, them He also glorified. Paul, Eph. 6, 2, commends to us the commandment concerning honoring parents, by mention of the reward which is added to that commandment where he does not mean that obedience to parents justifies us before God, but that, when it occurs in those who have been justified, it merits other great rewards. Yet

God exercises His saints variously, and often defers the rewards of the righteousness of works in order that they may learn not to trust in their own righteousness, and may learn to seek the will of God rather than the rewards, as appears in Job, in Christ, and other saints. And of this, many psalms teach us, which console us against the happiness of the wicked, as Ps. 37, 1: Neither be thou envious. And Christ says, Matt. 5, 10: Blessed are they which are persecuted for righteousness' sake; for theirs is the kingdom of heaven. By these praises of good works, believers are undoubtedly moved to do good works. Meanwhile, the doctrine of repentance is also proclaimed against the godless, whose works are wicked; and the wrath of God is displayed, which He has threatened all who do not repent. We therefore praise and require good works, and show many reasons why they ought to be done.

Thus of works Paul also teaches when he says, Rom. 4, 9 sq., that Abraham received circumcision, not in order that by this work he might be justified; for by faith he had already attained it that he was accounted righteous. But circumcision was added in order that he might have in his body a written sign, admonished by which he might exercise faith, and by which also he might confess his faith before others, and by his testimony might invite others to believe. By faith Abel offered unto God a more excellent sacrifice, Heb. 11, 4. Because, therefore, he was just by faith, the sacrifice which he made was pleasing to God, not that by this work he merited the remission of sins and grace, but that he exercised his faith and showed it to others, in order to invite them to believe.

Although in this way good works ought to follow faith, men who cannot believe and be sure that for Christ's sake they are freely forgiven, and that freely for Christ's sake they have a reconciled God, employ works far otherwise. When they see the works of saints, they judge in a human manner that saints have merited the remission of sins and grace through these works. Accordingly, they imitate them, and think that through similar works they merit the remission of sins and grace; they think that through these works they appease the wrath of God, and attain that for the sake of these works they are accounted righteous. This godless opinion concerning works we condemn. In the first place, because it obscures the glory of Christ when men offer to God these works as a price and propitiation. This honor, due to Christ alone, is ascribed to our works. Secondly, they nevertheless do not find, in these works, peace of conscience, but in true terrors, heaping up works upon works, they at length despair because they find no work sufficiently pure [sufficiently important and precious to propitiate God, to obtain with certainty eternal life, in a word, to tranquilize and pacify the conscience]. The Law always accuses, and produces wrath. Thirdly, such persons never attain the knowledge of God [nor of His will]; for, as in anger they flee from God, who judges and afflicts them, they never believe that they are heard. But faith manifests the presence of God, since it is certain that God freely forgives and hears us.

Moreover, this godless opinion concerning works always has existed in the world [sticks to the world quite tightly]. The heathen had sacrifices, derived from the fathers. They imitated their works. Their faith they did not retain, but thought that the works were a propitiation and price on account of which God would be reconciled to them. The people in the law [the Israelites] imitated sacrifices with the opinion that by means of these works they would appease God, so to say, *ex opere operato*. We see here how earnestly the prophets rebuke the people: Ps. 50, 8: I will not reprove thee for thy sacrifices, and Jer. 7, 22: I spake not unto your fathers concerning burnt offerings. Such passages condemn not works, which God certainly had commanded as outward exercises in this government, but they condemn the godless opinion according to which they thought that by these works they appeased the wrath of God, and thus cast away faith. And because no works pacify the conscience, new works, in addition to God's commands, were from time to time devised [the hypocrites nevertheless used to invent one work after another, one sacrifice after another, by a blind guess and in reckless wantonness, and all this without the word and command of God, with wicked conscience as we have seen in the Papacy]. The people of Israel had seen the prophets sacrificing on high places [and in groves]. Besides, the examples of the saints very greatly move the minds of those, hoping by similar works to obtain grace just as these saints obtained it. [But the saints believed.] Wherefore the people began, with remarkable zeal, to imitate this work, in order that by such a work [they might appease the wrath of God] they might merit remission of sins, grace, and righteousness. But the prophets had been sacrificing on high places, not that by these works they might merit the remission of sins and grace, but because on these places they taught, and, accordingly, presented there a testimony of their faith. The people had heard that Abraham had sacrificed his son. Wherefore they also, in order to appease God by a most cruel and difficult work, put to death their sons. But Abraham did not sacrifice his son with the opinion that this work was a price and propitiatory work for the sake of which he was accounted righteous. Thus in the Church the Lord's Supper was instituted that by remembrance of the promises of Christ, of which we are admonished in this sign, faith might be strengthened in us, and we might publicly confess our faith, and proclaim the benefits of Christ, as Paul says, 1 Cor. 11, 26: As often as ye eat this bread and drink this cup, ye do show the Lord's death, etc. But our adversaries contend that the mass is a work that justifies us ***ex opere operato***, and removes the guilt and liability to punishment in those for whom it is celebrated, for thus writes Gabriel.

Anthony, Bernard, Dominicus, Franciscus, and other holy Fathers selected a certain kind of life either for the sake of study [of more readily reading the Holy Scriptures] or other useful exercises. In the mean time they believed that by faith they were accounted righteous for Christ's sake, and that God was gracious to them, not on account of those exercises of their own. But the multitude since then has imitated not the faith of the Fathers, but their example without faith, in order that by such works they might merit the remission of sins, grace, and righteousness: they did not believe that they received these freely on account of Christ as Propitiator. [Thus the human mind always exalts works too highly, and puts them in the wrong place. And this error the Gospel reproves which teaches that men are accounted righteous not for the sake of the Law, but for the sake of Christ alone. Christ, however, is apprehended by faith alone; wherefore we are accounted righteous by faith alone for Christ's sake.] Thus the world judges of all works that they are a propitiation by which God is appeased; that they are a price because of which we are accounted righteous. It does not believe that Christ is Propitiator; it does not believe that by faith we freely attain that we are accounted righteous for Christ's sake. And, nevertheless, since works cannot pacify the conscience, others are continually chosen, new rites are performed, new vows made, and new orders of monks formed beyond the command of God, in order that some great work may be sought which may be set against the wrath and judgment of God. Contrary to Scripture, the adversaries uphold these godless opinions concerning works. But to ascribe to our works these things, namely, that they are a propitiation, that they merit the remission of sins and grace that for the sake of these and not by faith for the sake of Christ as Propitiator we are accounted righteous before God, what else is this than to deny Christ the honor of Mediator and Propitiator? Although, therefore, we believe and teach that good works must necessarily be done (for the inchoate fulfilling of the Law ought to follow faith), nevertheless we give to Christ His own honor. We believe and teach that by faith, for Christ's sake, we are accounted righteous before God, that we are not accounted righteous because of works without Christ as Mediator, that by works we do not merit the remission of sins, grace, and righteousness, that we cannot set our works against the wrath and justice of God, that works cannot overcome the terrors of sin, but that the terrors of sin are overcome by faith alone, that only Christ the Mediator is to be presented by faith against the wrath and judgment of God. If any one think differently, he does not give Christ due honor, who has been set forth that He might be a Propitiator, that through Him we might have access to the Father. We are speaking now of the righteousness through which we treat with God not with men, but by which we apprehend grace and peace of conscience. Conscience however, cannot be pacified before God, unless by faith alone, which is certain that God for Christ's sake is reconciled to us, according to Rom. 5, 1: Being justified by faith, we have peace because justification is only a matter freely promised for Christ's sake, and therefore is always received before God by faith alone.

Now, then, we will reply to those passages which the adversaries cite, in order to prove that we are justified by love and works. From 1 Cor. 13, 2 they cite: Though I have all faith, etc., and hove not charity, I am nothing. And here they triumph greatly. Paul testifies to the entire Church, they say, that faith alone does not justify. But a reply is easy after we have shown above what we hold concerning love and works. This passage of Paul requires love. We also require this. For we have said above that renewal and the inchoate fulfilling of the Law must exist in us, according to Jer. 31, 33: I will put My Law in their inward parts, and write it in their hearts. If any one should cast away love, even though he have great faith, yet he does not retain it, for he does not retain the Holy Ghost [he becomes cold and is now again fleshly, without Spirit and faith; for the Holy Ghost is not where Christian love and other fruits of the Spirit are not]. Nor indeed does Paul in this passage treat of the mode of justification, but he writes to those who, after they had been justified, should be urged to bring forth good fruits lest they might lose the Holy Ghost. The adversaries, furthermore, treat the matter preposterously: they cite this one passage, in which Paul teaches concerning fruits, they omit very many other passages, in which in a regular order he discusses the mode of justification. Besides, they always add a correction to the other passages, which treat of faith, namely, that they ought to be understood as applying to *fides formata*. Here they add no correction that there is also need of the faith that holds that we are accounted righteous for the sake of Christ as Propitiator. Thus the adversaries exclude Christ from justification, and teach only a righteousness of the Law. But let us return to Paul. No one can infer anything more from this text than that love is necessary. This we confess. So also not to commit theft is necessary. But the reasoning will not be correct if some one would desire to frame thence an argument such as this: "Not to commit theft is necessary. Therefore, not to commit theft justifies." Because justification is not the approval of a certain work, but of the entire person. Hence this passage from Paul does not harm us; only the adversaries must not in imagination add to it whatever they please. For he does not say that love justifies, but: ["And if I have not love"] "I am nothing," namely, that faith, however great it may have been, is extinguished. He does not say that love overcomes the terrors of sin and of death that we can set our love against the wrath and judgment of God, that our love satisfies God's Law, that without Christ as Propitiator we have access, by our love, to God, that by our love we receive the promised remission of sins. Paul says nothing of this. He does not, therefore, think that love justifies, because we are justified only when we apprehend Christ as Propitiator, and believe that for Christ's sake God is reconciled to us. Neither is justification even to be dreamed of with the omission of Christ as Propitiator. If there be no need of Christ, if by our love we can overcome death, if by our love, without Christ as Propitiator' we have access to God, then let our adversaries remove the promise concerning Christ, then let them abolish the Gospel [which teaches that we have access to God through Christ as Propitiator, and that we are accepted not for the sake of our fulfilling of the Law, but for Christ's sake]. The adversaries corrupt very many passages, because they bring to them their own opinions, and do not derive the meaning from the passages themselves. For what difficulty is there in this passage if we remove the interpretation which the adversaries, who do not understand what justification is or how it occurs [what faith is, what Christ is, or how a man is justified before God], out of their own mind attach to it? The Corinthians, being justified before, had received many excellent gifts. In the beginning they glowed with zeal, just as is generally the case. Then dissensions [factions and sects] began to arise among them as Paul indicates; they began to dislike good teachers. Accordingly, Paul reproves them, recalling them [to unity and] to offices of love. Although these are necessary, yet it would be foolish to imagine that works of the Second Table, through which we have to do with man and not properly with God, justify us. But in justification we have to treat with God; His wrath must be appeased, and conscience must be pacified with respect to God. None of these occur through the works of the Second Table [by love, but only by faith, which apprehends Christ and the promise of God. However, it is true that losing love involves losing the Spirit and faith. And thus Paul says: If I have not love, I am nothing. But he does not add the affirmative statement, that love justifies in the sight of God].

But they object that love is preferred to faith and hope. For Paul says, 1 Cor. 13, 13: The greatest of these is charity. Now, it is reasonable that the greatest and chief virtue should justify, although Paul, in this passage, properly speaks of love towards one's neighbor, and indicates that love is the greatest, because it has most fruits. Faith and hope have to do only with God; but love has infinite offices externally towards men. [Love goes forth upon earth among the people, and does much good, by consoling, teaching, instructing, helping, counseling privately and publicly.] Nevertheless, let us, indeed, grant to the adversaries that love towards God and our neighbor is the greatest virtue, because the chief commandment is this: Thou shalt love the Lord, thy God Matt. 22, 37. But how will they infer thence that love justifies? The greatest virtue, they say, justifies. By no means. [It would be true if we had a gracious God because of our virtue. Now, it was proven above that we are accepted and justified for Christ's sake, not because of our virtue, for our virtue is impure.] For just as even the greatest or first Law does not justify, so also the greatest virtue of the Law does not justify. [For, as the Law and virtue is higher, and our ability to do the same proportionately lower, we are not righteous because of love.] But that virtue justifies which apprehends Christ, which communicates to us Christ's merits, by which we receive grace and peace from God. But this virtue is faith. For as it has been often said, faith is not only knowledge, but much rather willing to receive or apprehend those things which are offered in the promise concerning Christ. Moreover this obedience towards God, namely, to wish to receive the offered promise, is no less a divine service, *latreia*, than is love. God wishes us to believe Him, and to receive from Him blessings, and this He declares to be true divine service.

But the adversaries ascribe justification to love because they everywhere teach and require the righteousness of the Law. For we cannot deny that love is the highest work of the Law. And human wisdom gazes at the Law, and seeks in it justification. Accordingly, also the scholastic doctors, great and talented men, proclaim this as the highest work of the Law, and ascribe to this work justification. But deceived by human wisdom, they did not look upon the uncovered, but upon the veiled face of Moses, just as the Pharisees, philosophers, Mahometans. But we preach the foolishness of the Gospel, in which another righteousness is revealed, namely, that for the sake of Christ, as Propitiator, we are accounted righteous, when we believe that for Christ's sake God has been reconciled to us. Neither are we ignorant how far distant this doctrine is from the judgment of reason and of the Law. Nor are we ignorant that the doctrine of the Law concerning love makes a much greater show; for it is wisdom. But we are not ashamed of the foolishness of the Gospel. For the sake of Christ's glory we defend this, and beseech Christ, by His Holy Ghost, to aid us that we may be able to make this clear and manifest.

The adversaries, in the Confutation, have also cited against us Col. 3, 14: Charity, which is the bond of perfectness. From this they infer that love justifies because it renders men perfect. Although a reply concerning perfection could here be made in many ways, yet we will simply recite the meaning of Paul. It is certain that Paul spoke of love towards one's neighbor. Neither must we indeed think that Paul would ascribe either justification or perfection to the works of the Second Table, rather than to those of the First. And if love render men perfect, there will then be no need of Christ as Propitiator, [However, Paul teaches in all places that we are accepted on account of Christ, and not on account of our love, or our works, or of the Law; for no saint (as was stated before) perfectly fulfils the Law. Therefore since he in all places writes and teaches that in this life there is no perfection in our works, it is not to be thought that he speaks here of personal perfection.] for faith apprehends Christ only as Propitiator. This, however, is far distant from the meaning of Paul, who never suffers Christ to be excluded as Propitiator. Therefore he speaks not of personal perfection, but of the integrity common to the Church [concerning the unity of the Church and the word which they interpret as perfection means nothing else than to be not rent]. For on this account he says that love is a bond or connection, to signify that he speaks of the binding and joining together, with each other, of the many members of the Church. For just as in all families and in all states concord should be nourished by mutual offices, and tranquillity cannot be retained unless men overlook and forgive certain mistakes among themselves; so Paul commands that there should be love in the Church in order that it may preserve concord, bear with the harsher manners of brethren as there is need, overlook certain less serious mistakes, lest the Church fly apart into various schisms, and enmities and factions and heresies arise from the schisms.

For concord must necessarily he rent asunder whenever either the bishops impose [without cause] upon the people heavier burdens, or have no respect to weakness in the people. And dissensions arise when the people judge too severely [quickly censure and criticize] concerning the conduct [walk and life] of teachers [bishops or preachers], or despise the teachers because of certain less serious faults; for then both another kind of doctrine and other teachers are sought after. On the other hand, perfection, i.e., the integrity of the Church, is preserved, when the strong bear with the weak, when the people take in good part some faults in the conduct of their teachers [have patience also with their preachers], when the bishops make some allowances for the weakness of the people [know how to exercise forbearance to the people, according to circumstances, with respect to all kinds of weaknesses and faults]. Of these precepts of equity the books of all the wise are full, namely, that in every day life we should make many allowances mutually for the sake of common tranquillity. And of this Paul frequently teaches both here and elsewhere. Wherefore the adversaries argue indiscreetly from the term "perfection" that love justifies, while Paul speaks of common integrity and tranquillity. And thus Ambrose interprets this passage: Just as a building is said to be perfect or entire when all its parts are fitly joined together with one another. Moreover, it is disgraceful for the adversaries to preach so much concerning love while they nowhere exhibit it. What are they now doing? They are rending asunder churches, they are writing laws in blood, and are proposing to the most clement prince, the Emperor, that these should be promulgated; they are slaughtering priests and other good men, if any one have [even] slightly intimated that he does not entirely approve some manifest abuse. [They wish all dead who say a single word against their godless doctrine.] These things are not consistent with those declamations of love, which if the adversaries would follow, the churches would be tranquil and the state have peace. For these tumults would be quieted if the adversaries would not insist with too much bitterness [from sheer vengeful spite and pharisaical envy, against the truth which they have perceived] upon certain traditions, useless for godliness, most of which not even those very persons observe who most earnestly defend them. But they easily forgive themselves, and yet do not likewise forgive others, according to the passage in the poet: I forgive myself, Maevius said. But this is very far distant from those encomiums of love which they here recite from Paul, nor do they understand the word any more than the walls which give it back. From Peter they cite also this sentence, 1 Pet. 4, 8: Charity shall cover the multitude of sins. It is evident that also Peter speaks of love towards one's neighbor, because he joins this passage to the precept by which he commands that they should love one another. Neither could it have come into the mind of any apostle that our love overcomes sin and death; that love is the propitiation on account of which to the exclusion of Christ as Mediator, God is reconciled; that love is righteousness without Christ as Mediator. For this love, if there would be any, would be a righteousness of the Law, and not of the Gospel, which promises to us reconciliation and righteousness if we believe that, for the sake of Christ as Propitiator, the Father has been reconciled, and that the merits of Christ are bestowed upon us. Peter, accordingly, urges us, a little before, to come to Christ that we may be built upon Christ. And he adds, 1 Pet. 2, 4-6: He that believeth on Him shall not be confounded. When God judges and convicts us, our love does not free us from confusion [from our works and lives, we truly suffer shame]. But faith in Christ liberates us in these fears, because we know that for Christ's sake we are forgiven.

Besides, this sentence concerning love is derived from Prov. 10,12, where the antithesis clearly shows how it ought to be understood: Hatred stirreth up strifes; but love covereth all sins. It teaches precisely the same thing as that passage of Paul taken from Colossians, that if any dissensions would occur, they should be moderated and settled by our equitable and lenient conduct. Dissensions, it says, increase by means of hatred, as we often see that from the most trifling offenses tragedies arise [from the smallest sparks a great conflagration arises]. Certain trifling offenses occurred between Caius Caesar and Pompey, in which, if the one had yielded a very little to the other, civil war would not have arisen. But while each indulged his own hatred, from a matter of no account the greatest commotions arose. And many heresies have arisen in the Church only from the hatred of the teachers. Therefore it does not refer to a person's own faults, but to the faults of others, when it says: Charity covereth sins, namely, those of others, and that, too, among men, i.e., even though these offenses occur, yet love overlooks them, forgives, yields, and does not carry all things to the extremity of justice. Peter, therefore, does not mean that love merits in God's sight the remission of sins, that it is a propitiation to the exclusion of Christ as Mediator, that it regenerates and justifies, but that it is not morose, harsh, intractable towards men, that it overlooks some mistakes of its friends, that it takes in good part even the harsher manners of others, just as the well-known maxim enjoins: Know, but do rot hate, the manners of a fiend. Nor was it without design that the apostle taught so frequently concerning this office what the philosophers call epieicheia, leniency. For this virtue is necessary for retaining public harmony [in the Church and the civil government], which cannot last unless pastors and Churches mutually overlook and pardon many things [if they want to be extremely particular about every defect, and do not allow many things to flow by without noticing them].

From James they cite 2, 24: Ye see, then how by works a man is justified, and not by faith alone. Nor is any other passage supposed to be more contrary to our belief. But the reply is easy and plain. If the adversaries do not attach their own opinions concerning the merits of works, the words of James have in them nothing that is of disadvantage. But wherever there is mention of works, the adversaries add falsely their own godless opinions, that by means of good works we merit the remission of sins; that good works are a propitiation and price on account of which God is reconciled to us; that good works overcome the terrors of sin and of death; that good works are accepted in God's sight on account of their goodness; and that they do not need mercy and Christ as Propitiator. None of all these things came into the mind of James, which the adversaries nevertheless, defend under the pretext of this passage of James.

In the first place, then, we must ponder this, namely, that the passage is more against the adversaries than against us. For the adversaries teach that man is justified by love and works. Of faith, by which we apprehend Christ as Propitiator, they say nothing. Yea they condemn this faith; nor do they condemn it only in sentences and writings, but also by the sword and capital punishments they endeavor to exterminate it in the Church. How much better does James teach, who does not omit faith, or present love in preference to faith, but retains faith, so that in justification Christ may not be excluded as Propitiator! Just as Paul also, when he treats of the sum of the Christian life, includes faith and love, 1 Tim. 1, 5: The end of the commandment is charity out of a pure heart, and of a good conscience, and of faith unfeigned.

Secondly, the subject itself declares that here such works are spoken of as follow faith, and show that faith is not dead, but living and efficacious in the heart. James, therefore, did not believe that by good works we merit the remission of sins and grace. For he speaks of the works of those who have been justified, who have already been reconciled and accepted, and have obtained remission of sins. Wherefore the adversaries err when they infer that James teaches that we merit remission of sins and grace by good works, and that by our works we have access to God, without Christ as Propitiator.

Part 8

Thirdly, James has spoken shortly before concerning regeneration, namely, that it occurs through the Gospel. For thus he says 1, 18: Of His own will begat He us with the Word of Truth, that we should be a kind of first-fruits of His creatures. When he says that we have been born again by the Gospel, he teaches that we have been born again and justified by faith. For the promise concerning Christ is apprehended only by faith, when we set it against the terrors of sin and of death. James does not, therefore, think that we are born again by our works.

From these things it is clear that James does not contradict us, who, when censuring idle and secure minds, that imagine that they have faith, although they do not have it, made a distinction between dead and living faith. He says that that is dead which does not bring forth good works [and fruits of the Spirit: obedience, patience, chastity, love]; he says that that is living which brings forth good works. Furthermore, we have frequently already shown what we term faith. For we do not speak of idle knowledge [that merely the history concerning Christ should be known], such as devils have, but of faith which resists the terrors of conscience, and cheers and consoles terrified hearts [the new light and power which the Holy Ghost works in the heart, through which we overcome the terrors of death, of sin, etc.]. Such faith is neither an easy matter, as the adversaries dream [as they say: Believe, believe, how easy it is to believe! etc.], nor a human power [thought which I can form for myself], but a divine power, by which we are quickened, and by which we overcome the devil and death. Just as Paul says to the Colossians, 2, 12, that faith is efficacious through the power of God, and overcomes death: Wherein also ye are risen with Him through the faith of the operation of God. Since this faith is a new life, it necessarily produces new movements and works. [Because it is a new light and life in the heart, whereby we obtain another mind and spirit, it is living, productive, and rich in good works.] Accordingly, James is right in denying that we are justified by such a faith as is without works. But when he says that we are justified by faith and works, he certainly does not say that we are born again by works. Neither does he say this, that partly Christ is our Propitiator, and partly our works are our propitiation. Nor does he describe the mode of justification, but only of what nature the just are, after they have been already justified and regenerated. [For he is speaking of works which should follow faith. There it is well said: He who has faith and good works is righteous; not, indeed, on account of the works, but for Christ's sake, through faith. And as a good tree should bring forth good fruit, and yet the fruit does not make the tree good, so good works must follow the new birth, although they do not make man accepted before God; but as the tree must first be good, so also must man be first accepted before God by faith for Christ's sake. The works are too insignificant to render God gracious to us for their sake, if He were not gracious to us for Christ's sake. Therefore James does not contradict St. Paul, and does not say that by our works we merit, etc.] And here to be justified does not mean that a righteous man is made from a wicked man, but to be pronounced righteous in a forensic sense, as also in the passage Rom. 2, 13: The doers of the Law shall be justified. As, therefore, these words: The doers of the Law shall be justified, contain nothing contrary to our doctrine, so, too, we believe concerning the words of James: By works a man is justified, and not by faith alone, because men having faith and good works are certainly pronounced righteous. For, as we have said, the good works of saints are righteous, and please on account of faith. For James commends only such works as faith produces, as he testifies when he says of Abraham, 2, 21: Faith wrought with his works. In this sense it is said: The doers of the Law are justified, i.e., they are pronounced righteous who from the heart believe God, and afterwards have good fruits which please Him on account of faith, and accordingly, are the fulfilment of the Law. These things, simply spoken, contain nothing erroneous, but they are distorted by the adversaries who attach to them godless opinions out of their mind. For it does not follow hence that works merit the remission of sins; that works regenerate hearts; that works are a propitiation, that works please without Christ as Propitiator; that works do not need Christ as Propitiator. James says nothing of these things, which, nevertheless, the adversaries shamelessly infer from the words of James.

Certain other passages concerning works are also cited against us. Luke 6, 37: Forgive, and ye shall be forgiven. Is. 58, 7 [9]: Is it not to deal thy bread to the hungry?...Then shalt thou call, and the Lord will answer. Dan. 4, 24 [27]: Break off thy sins, by showing mercy to the poor. Matt. 5, 3: Blessed are the poor in spirit; for theirs is the kingdom of heaven; and v. 7: Blessed are the merciful; for they shall obtain mercy. Even these passages would contain nothing contrary to us if the adversaries would not falsely attach something to them. For they contain two things: The one is a preaching either of the Law or of repentance, which not only convicts those doing wrong, but also enjoins them to do what is right; the other is a promise which is added. But it is not added that sins are remitted without faith, or that works themselves are a propitiation. Moreover, in the preaching of the Law these two things ought always to be understood, namely: First, that the Law cannot be observed unless we have been regenerated by faith in Christ, just as Christ says, John 15, 5: Without Me ye can do nothing. Secondly, and though some external works can certainly be done, this general judgment: Without faith it is impossible to please God, which interprets the whole Law, must be retained: and the Gospel must be retained, that through Christ we have access to the Father, Heb. 10, 19, Rom. 5, 2. For it is evident that we are not justified by the Law. Otherwise, why would there be need of Christ or the Gospel, if the preaching of the Law alone would be sufficient? Thus in the preaching of repentance, the preaching of the Law, or the Word convicting of sin, is not sufficient, because the Law works wrath, and only accuses, only terrifies consciences, because consciences never are at rest, unless they hear the voice of God in which the remission of sins is clearly promised. Accordingly, the Gospel must be added, that for Christ's sake sins are remitted, and that we obtain remission of sins by faith in Christ. If the adversaries exclude the Gospel of Christ from the preaching of repentance, they are judged aright to be blasphemers against Christ.

Therefore, when Isaiah, 1, 16. 18, preaches repentance: Cease to do evil; learn to do well; seek judgment, relieve the oppressed, judge the fatherless, plead for the widow. Come now and let us reason together, saith the Lord; though your sine be as scarlet, they shall be white as snow, the prophet thus both exhorts to repentance, and adds the promise. But it would be foolish to consider in such a sentence only the words: Relieve the oppressed; judge the fatherless. For he says in the beginning: Cease to do evil, where he censures impiety of heart and requires faith. Neither does the prophet say that through the works: Relieve the oppressed, judge the fatherless, they can merit the remission of sins *ex opere operato*, but he commands such works as are necessary in the new life. Yet, in the mean time, he means that remission of sins is received by faith, and accordingly the promise is added. Thus we must understand all similar passages. Christ preaches repentance when He says: Forgive, and He adds the promise: And ye shall be forgiven, Luke 6, 37. Nor, indeed, does He say this, namely, that, when we forgive, by this work of ours we merit the remission of sins *ex opere operato*, as they term it, but He requires a new life, which certainly is necessary. Yet, in the mean time He means that remission of sins is received by faith. Thus, when Isaiah says, 58, 7: Deal thy bread to the hungry, he requires a new life. Nor does the prophet speak of this work alone, but, as the text indicates, of the entire repentance; yet, in the mean time, he intends that remission of sins is received by faith. For the position is sure, and none of the gates of hell can overthrow it, that in the preaching of repentance the preaching of the Law is not sufficient, because the Law works wrath and always accuses. But the preaching of the Gospel should be added, namely, that in this way remission of sins is granted us, if we believe that sins are remitted us for Christ's sake. Otherwise, why would there be need of the Gospel, why would there be need of Christ? This belief ought always to be in view, in order that it may be opposed to those who, Christ being cast aside and the Gospel being blotted out, wickedly distort the Scriptures to the human opinions, that by our works we purchase remission of sins.

Thus also in the sermon of Daniel, 4, 24, faith is required. [The words of the prophet which were full of faith and spirit, we must not regard as heathenish as those of Aristotle or any other heathen. Aristotle also admonished Alexander that he should not use his power for his own wantonness, but for the improvement of countries and men. This was written correctly and well; concerning the office of king nothing better can be preached or written. But Daniel is speaking to his king, not only concerning his office as king, but concerning repentance, the forgiveness of sins, reconciliation to God, and concerning sublime, great, spiritual subjects, which far transcend human thoughts and works.] For Daniel did not mean that the king should only bestow alms [which even a hypocrite can do], but embraces repentance when he says: Break off [Redeem, Vulg.] thy iniquities by showing mercy to the poor, i.e. break off thy sins by a change of heart and works. But here also faith is required. And Daniel proclaims to him many things concerning the worship of the only God, the God of Israel, and converts the king not only to bestow alms, but much more to faith. For we have the excellent confession of the king concerning the God of Israel: There is no other God that can deliver after this sort Dan. 3, 29. Therefore, in the sermon of Daniel there are two parts. The one part is that which gives commandment concerning the new life and the works of the new life. The other part is, that Daniel promises to the king the remission of sins. [Now, where there is a promise, faith is required. For the promise cannot be received in any other way than by the heart's relying on such word of God, and not regarding its own worthiness or unworthiness. Accordingly, Daniel also demands faith: for thus the promise reads: There will be healing for thy offenses.] And this promise of the remission of sins is not a preaching of the Law, but a truly prophetical and evangelical voice, of which Daniel certainly meant that it should be received in faith. For Daniel knew that the remission of sins in Christ was promised not only to the Israelites, but also to all nations. Otherwise he could not have promised to the king the remission of sins. For it is not in the power of man especially amid the terrors of sin, to assert without a sure word of God concerning God's will, that He ceases to be angry. And the words of Daniel speak in his own language still more clearly of repentance and still more clearly bring out the promise. Redeem thy sins by righteousness and thy iniquities by favors toward the poor. These words teach concerning the whole of repentance. [It is as much as to say: Amend your life! And it is true, when we amend our lives, we become rid of sin.] For they direct him to become righteous, then to do good works, to defend the miserable against injustice, as was the duty of a king. But righteousness is faith in the heart. Moreover, sins are redeemed by repentance, i.e. the obligation or guilt is removed, because God forgives those who repent, as it is written in Ezek. 18, 21. 22. Nor are we to infer from this that He forgives on account of works that follow, on account of alms, but on account of His promise He forgives those who apprehend His promise. Neither do any apprehend His promise, except those who truly believe, and by faith overcome sin and death. These, being regenerated, ought to bring forth fruits worthy of repentance, just as John says, Matt. 3, 8. The promise, therefore, was added: So, there will be healing for thy offenses, Dan. 4, 24. [Daniel does not only demand works, but says: Redeem thy sins by righteousness. Now, everybody knows that in Scripture righteousness does not mean only external works, but embraces faith, as Paul says: ***Iustus ex fide vivet***? The just shall live by his faith, Heb. 10, 38. Hence, Daniel first demands faith when he mentions righteousness and says: Redeem thy sins by righteousness, that is, by faith toward God, by which thou art made righteous. In addition to this do good works, administer your office, do not be a tyrant, but see that your government be profitable to your country and people, preserve peace, and protect the poor against unjust force. These are princely alms.] Jerome here added a particle expressing doubt, that is beside the matter, and in his commentaries contends much more unwisely that the remission of sins is uncertain. But let us remember that the Gospel gives a sure promise of the remission of sins. And to deny that there must be a sure promise of the remission of sins would completely abolish the Gospel. Let us therefore dismiss Jerome concerning this passage. Although the promise is displayed even in the word redeem. For it signifies that the remission of sins is possible that sins can be redeemed, i.e., that their obligation or guilt can be removed, or the wrath of God appeased. But our adversaries, overlooking the promises, everywhere, consider only the precepts, and attach falsely the human opinion that remission occurs on account of works, although the text does not say this, but much rather requires faith. For wherever a promise is, there faith is required. For a promise cannot be received unless by faith. [The same answer must also be given in reference to the passage from the Gospel: Forgive, and you will be forgiven. For this is just such a doctrine of repentance. The first part in this passage demands amendment of life and good works, the other part adds the promise. Nor are we to infer from this that our forgiving merits for us ***ex opere operato*** remission of sin. For that is not what Christ says, but as in other sacraments Christ has attached the promise to an external sign, so He attaches the promise of the forgiveness of sin in this place to external good works. And as in the Lord's Supper we do not obtain forgiveness of sin without faith, ***ex opere operato***, so neither in this when we forgive. For, our forgiving is not a good work, except it is performed by a person whose sins have been previously forgiven by God in Christ. If, therefore, our forgiving is to please God, it must follow after the forgiveness which God extends to us. For, as a rule, Christ combines these two, the Law and the Gospel, both faith and good works, in order to indicate that, where good works do not follow, there is no faith either that we may have external marks, which remind us of the Gospel and the forgiveness of sin, for our comfort and that thus our faith may be exercised in many ways. In this manner we are to understand such passages, otherwise they would directly contradict the entire Gospel, and our beggarly works would be put in the place of Christ, who alone is to be the propitiation, which no man is by any means to despise. Again, if these passages were to be understood as relating to works, the remission of sins would be quite uncertain; for it would rest on a poor foundation, on our miserable works.]

But works become conspicuous among men. Human reason naturally admires these, and because it sees only works, and does not understand or consider faith, it dreams accordingly that these works merit remission of sins and justify. This opinion of the Law inheres by nature in men's minds; neither can it be expelled, unless when we are divinely taught. But the mind must be recalled from such carnal opinions to the Word of God. We see that the Gospel and the promise concerning Christ have been laid before us. When, therefore, the Law is preached, when works are enjoined, we should not spurn the promise concerning Christ. But the latter must first be apprehended, in order that we may be able to produce good works, and our works may please God, as Christ says, John 16; 5: With out Me ye can do nothing. Therefore, if Daniel would have used such words as these: "Redeem your sins by repentance," the adversaries would take no notice of this passage. Now, since he has actually expressed this thought in apparently other words, the adversaries distort his words to the injury of the doctrine of grace and faith, although Daniel meant most especially to include faith. Thus, therefore, we reply to the words of Daniel, that, inasmuch as he is preaching repentance, he is teaching not only of works, but also of faith, as the narrative itself in the context testifies. Secondly, because Daniel clearly presents the promise, he necessarily requires faith which believes that sins are freely remitted by God. Although, therefore, in repentance he mentions works, yet Daniel does not say that by these works we merit remission of sins. For Daniel speaks not only of the remission of the punishment; because remission of the punishment is sought for in vain unless the heart first receive the remission of guilt. Besides, if the adversaries understand Daniel as speaking only of the remission of punishment, this passage will prove nothing against us, because it will thus be necessary for even them to confess that the remission of sin and free justification precede. Afterwards even we concede that the punishments by which we are chastised, are mitigated by our prayers and good works, and finally by our entire repentance, according to 1 Cor. 11, 31: For if we would judge ourselves, we should not be judged. And Jer. 15, 19: If thou return, then will I bring thee again. And Zech. 1, 3: Turn ye unto Me, and I will turn unto you. And Ps. 50, 15: Call upon Me in the day of trouble.

Let us, therefore, in all our encomiums upon works and in the preaching of the Law retain this rule: that the Law is not observed without Christ. As He Himself has said: Without Me ye can do nothing. Likewise that: Without faith it is impossible to please God, Heb. 11, 6. For it is very certain that the doctrine of the Law is not intended to remove the Gospel, and to remove Christ as Propitiator. And let the Pharisees, our adversaries, be cursed, who so interpret the Law as to ascribe the glory of Christ to works namely, that they are a propitiation, that they merit the remission of sins. It follows, therefore, that works are always thus praised, namely, that they are pleasing on account of faith, as works do not please without Christ as Propitiator. By Him we have access to God, Rom. 5, 2, not by works, without Christ as Mediator. Therefore, when it is said, Matt. 19, 17: If thou wilt enter into life, keep the commandments, we must believe that without Christ the commandments are not kept, and without Him cannot please. Thus in the Decalog itself, in the First Commandment Ex. 20, 6: Showing mercy unto thousands of them that love Me and keep My commandments, the most liberal promise of the Law is added. But this Law is not observed without Christ. For it always accuses the conscience which does not satisfy the Law, and therefore in terror, flies from the judgment and punishment of the Law. Because the Law worketh wrath, Rom. 4, 15. Man observes the Law, however, when he hears that for Christ's sake God is reconciled to us, even though we cannot satisfy the Law. When, by this faith, Christ is apprehended as Mediator, the heart finds rest, and begins to love God and observe the Law, and knows that now, because of Christ as Mediator, it is pleasing to God, even though the inchoate fulfilling of the Law be far from perfection and be very impure. Thus we must judge also concerning the preaching of repentance. For although in the doctrine of repentance the scholastics have said nothing at all concerning faith, yet we think that none of our adversaries is so mad as to deny that absolution is a voice of the Gospel. And absolution ought to be received by faith, in order that it may cheer the terrified conscience.

Therefore the doctrine of repentance, because it not only commands new works, but also promises the remission of sins, necessarily requires faith. For the remission of sins is not received unless by faith. Therefore, in those passages that refer to repentance, we should always understand that not only works, but also faith is required, as in Matt. 6, 14. For if ye forgive men their trespasses, your heavenly Father will also forgive you. Here a work is required, and the promise of the remission of sins is added which does not occur on account of the work, but through faith, on account of Christ. Just as Scripture testifies in many passages: Acts 10, 43: To Him give all the prophets witness that through His name, whosoever believeth in Him, shall receive remission of sins; and 1 John 2, 12: Your sins are forgiven you for His name's sake; Eph. 1, 7: In whom we have redemption through His blood the forgiveness of sins. Although what need is there to recite testimonies? This is the very voice peculiar to the Gospel, namely, that for Christ's sake, and not for the sake of our works, we obtain by faith remission of sins. Our adversaries endeavor to suppress this voice of the Gospel by means of distorted passages which contain the doctrine of the Law, or of works. For it is true that in the doctrine of repentance works are required, because certainly a new life is required. But here the adversaries wrongly add that by such works we merit the remission of sins, or justification. And yet Christ often connects the promise of the remission of sins to good works not because He means that good works are a propitiation, for they follow reconciliation; but for two reasons. One is, because good fruits must necessarily follow. Therefore He reminds us that, if good fruits do not follow the repentance is hypocritical and feigned. The other reason is, because we have need of external signs of so great a promise, because a conscience full of fear has need of manifold consolation. As, therefore, Baptism and the Lord's Supper are signs that continually admonish, cheer, and encourage desponding minds to believe the more firmly that their sins are forgiven, so the same promise is written and portrayed in good works, in order that these works may admonish us to believe the more firmly. And those who produce no good works do not excite themselves to believe, but despise these promises. The godly on the other hand, embrace them, and rejoice that they have the signs and testimonies of so great a promise. Accordingly, they exercise themselves in these signs and testimonies. Just as, therefore, the Lord's Supper does not justify us *ex opere operato*, without faith, so alms do not justify us without faith, *ex opere operato*.

So also the address of Tobias, 4, 11, ought to be received: Alms free from every sin and from death. We will not say that this is hyperbole, although it ought thus to be received, so as not to detract from the praise of Christ, whose prerogative it is to free from sin and death. But we must come back to the rule that without Christ the doctrine of the Law is of no profit. Therefore those alms please God which follow reconciliation or justification, and not those which precede. Therefore they free from sin and death, not *ex opere operato*, but, as we have said above concerning repentance, that we ought to embrace faith and its fruits, so here we must say concerning alms that this entire newness of life saves [that they please God because they occur in believers]. Alms also are the exercises of faith, which receives the remission of sins and overcomes death, while it exercises itself more and more, and in these exercises receives strength. We grant also this, that alms merit many favors from God [but they cannot overcome death, hell, the devil, sins, and give the conscience peace (for this must occur alone through faith in Christ)], mitigate punishments, and that they merit our defense in the dangers of sins and of death, as we have said a little before concerning the entire repentance. [This is the simple meaning, which agrees also with other passages of Scripture. For wherever in the Scriptures good works are praised, we must always understand them according to the rule of Paul, that the Law and works must not be elevated above Christ, but that Christ and faith are as far above all works as the heavens are above the earth.] And the address of Tobias, regarded as a whole shows that faith is required before alms, 4, 5: Be mindful of the Lord, thy God, all thy days And afterwards, v. 19. Bless the Lord, thy God, always, and desire of Him that thy ways be directed. This, however, belongs properly to that faith of which we speak, which believes that God is reconciled to it because of His mercy, and which wishes to be justified, sanctified, and governed by God. But our adversaries, charming men, pick out mutilated sentences, in order to deceive those who are unskilled. Afterwards they attach something from their own opinions. Therefore, entire passages are to be required, because, according to the common precept, it is unbecoming, before the entire Law is thoroughly examined, to judge or reply when any single clause of it is presented. And passages, when produced in their entirety, very frequently bring the interpretation with them.

Luke 11, 41 is also cited in a mutilated form, namely: Give alms of such things as ye have; and, behold, all things are clean unto you. The adversaries are very stupid [are deaf, and have callous ears; therefore, we must so often etc.]. For time and again we have said that to the preaching of the Law there should be added the Gospel concerning Christ, because of whom good works are pleasing, but they everywhere teach [without shame] that, Christ being excluded, justification is merited by the works of the Law. When this passage is produced unmutilated, it will show that faith is required. Christ rebukes the Pharisees who think that they are cleansed before God i.e. , that they are justified by frequent ablutions [by all sorts of **baptismata carnis**, that is, by all sorts of baths, washings, and cleansings of the body, of vessels, of garments]. Just as some Pope or other says of the water sprinkled with salt that it sanctifies and cleanses the people; and the gloss says that it cleanses from venial sins. Such also were the opinions of the Pharisees which Christ reproved, and to this feigned cleansing He opposes a double cleanness, the one internal, the other external. He bids them be cleansed inwardly [(which occurs only through faith)], and adds concerning the outward cleanness: Give alms of such things as ye have; and, behold, all things are clean unto you. The adversaries do not apply aright the universal particle all things; for Christ adds this conclusion to both members: "All things will be clean unto you, if you will be clean within, and will outwardly give alms." For He indicates that outward cleanness is to be referred to works commanded by God, and not to human traditions, such as the ablutions were at that time, and the daily sprinkling of water, the vesture of monks, the distinctions of food, and similar acts of ostentation are now. But the adversaries distort the meaning by sophistically transferring the universal particle to only one part: "All things will be clean to those having given alms." [As if any one would infer: Andrew is present; therefore all the apostles are present. Wherefore in the antecedent both members ought to be joined: Believe and give alms. For to this the entire mission, the entire office of Christ points; to this end He is come that we should believe in Him. Now, if both parts are combined, believing and giving alms, it follows rightly that all things are clean: the heart by faith, the external conversation by good works. Thus we must combine the entire sermon, and not invert the parts, and interpret the text to mean that the heart is cleansed from sin by alms. Moreover, there are some who think that these words were spoken by Christ against the Pharisees ironically, as if He meant to say: Aye, my dear lords, rob and steal, and then go and give alms, and you will be promptly cleansed, so that Christ would in a somewhat sarcastic and mocking way puncture their pharisaical hypocrisy. For, although they abounded in unbelief, avarice, and every evil work, they still observed their purifications, gave alms, and believed that they were quite pure, lovely saints. This interpretation is not contrary to the text.] Yet Peter says, Acts 15, 9, that hearts are purified by faith. And when this entire passage is examined, it presents a meaning harmonizing with the rest of Scripture, that, if the hearts are cleansed and then outwardly alms are added, i.e., all the works of love, they are thus entirely clean i.e. not only within, but also without. And why is not the entire discourse added to it? There are many parts of the reproof, some of which give commandment concerning faith and others concerning works. Nor is it the part of a candid reader to pick out the commands concerning works, while the passages concerning faith are omitted.

Lastly, readers are to be admonished of this, namely, that the adversaries give the worst advice to godly consciences when they teach that by works the remission of sins is merited, because conscience, in acquiring remission through works, cannot be confident that the work will satisfy God. Accordingly, it is always tormented, and continually devises other works and other acts of worship until it altogether despairs. This course is described by Paul, Rom. 4, 6, where he proves that the promise of righteousness is not obtained because of our works, because we could never affirm that we had a reconciled God. For the Law always accuses. Thus the promise would be in vain and uncertain. He accordingly concludes that this promise of the remission of sins and of righteousness is received by faith, not on account of works. This is the true, simple, and genuine meaning of Paul, in which the greatest consolation is offered godly consciences, and the glory of Christ is shown forth, who certainly was given to us for this purpose, namely, that through Him we might have grace, righteousness, and peace.

Thus far we have reviewed the principal passages which the adversaries cite against us, in order to show that faith does not justify, and that we merit, by our works, remission of sins and grace. But we hope that we have shown clearly enough to godly consciences that these passages are not opposed to our doctrine; that the adversaries wickedly distort the Scriptures to their opinions; that the most of the passages which they cite have been garbled; that, while omitting the clearest passages concerning faith, they only select from the Scriptures passages concerning works, and even these they distort; that everywhere they add certain human opinions to that which the words of Scripture say; that they teach the Law in such a manner as to suppress the Gospel concerning Christ. For the entire doctrine of the adversaries is, in part, derived from human reason, and is, in part, a doctrine of the Law, not of the Gospel. For they teach two modes of justification, of which the one has been derived from reason and the other from the Law, not from the Gospel, or the promise concerning Christ.

The former mode of justification with them is, that they teach that by good works men merit grace both *de congruo and de condigno*. This mode is a doctrine of reason, because reason, not seeing the uncleanness of the heart, thinks that it pleases God if it perform good works, and for this reason other works and other acts of worship are constantly devised, by men in great peril, against the terrors of conscience. The heathen and the Israelites slew human victims, and undertook many other most painful works in order to appease God's wrath. Afterwards, orders of monks were devised, and these vied with each other in the severity of their observances against the terrors of conscience and God's wrath. And this mode of justification, because it is according to reason, and is altogether occupied with outward works, can be understood, and to a certain extent be rendered. And to this the canonists have distorted the misunderstood Church ordinances, which were enacted by the Fathers for a far different purpose, namely, not that by these works we should seek after righteousness, but that, for the sake of mutual tranquillity among men, there might be a certain order in the Church. In this manner they also distorted the Sacraments and most especially the Mass, through which they seek *ex opere operato* righteousness, grace, and salvation.

Part 9

Another mode of justification is handed down by the scholastic theologians when they teach that we are righteous through a habit infused by God, which is love, and that, aided by this habit, we observe the Law of God outwardly and inwardly and that this fulfilling of the Law is worthy of grace and of eternal life. This doctrine is plainly the doctrine of the Law. For that is true which the Law says: Thou shalt love the Lord, thy God, etc., Deut. 6, 5. Thou shalt love thy neighbor Lev. 19, 18. Love is, therefore, the fulfilling of the Law.

But it is easy for a Christian to judge concerning both modes, because both modes exclude Christ, and are therefore to be rejected. In the former, which teaches that our works are a propitiation for sin, the impiety is manifest. The latter mode contains much that is injurious. It does not teach that, when we are born again, we avail ourselves of Christ. It does not teach that justification is the remission of sins. It does not teach that we attain the remission of sins before we love but falsely represents that we rouse in ourselves the act of love, through which we merit remission of sins. Nor does it teach that by faith in Christ we overcome the terrors of sin and death. It falsely represents that, by their own fulfilling of the Law, without Christ as Propitiator, men come to God. Finally, it represents that this very fulfilling of the Law, without Christ as Propitiator, is righteousness worthy of grace and eternal life, while nevertheless scarcely a weak and feeble fulfilling of the Law occurs even in saints.

But if any one will only reflect upon it that the Gospel has not been given in vain to the world, and that Christ has not been promised, set forth, has not been born, has not suffered, has not risen again in vain, he will most readily understand that we are justified not from reason or from the Law. In regard to justification, we therefore are compelled to dissent from the adversaries. For the Gospel shows another mode; the Gospel compels us to avail ourselves of Christ in justification, it teaches that through Him we have access to God by faith; it teaches that we ought to set Him as Mediator and Propitiator against God's wrath; it teaches that by faith in Christ the remission of sins and reconciliation are received, and the terrors of sin and of death overcome. Thus Paul also says that righteousness is not of the Law, but of the promise, in which the Father has promised that He wishes to forgive, that for Christ's sake He wishes to be reconciled. This promise, however, is received by faith alone, as Paul testifies, Rom. 4,13. This faith alone receives remission of sins, justifies, and regenerates. Then love and other good fruits follow. Thus, therefore, we teach that man is justified, as we have above said, when conscience, terrified by the preaching of repentance, is cheered and believes that for Christ's sake it has a reconciled God. This faith is counted for righteousness before God, Rom. 4, 3. 5. And when in this manner the heart is cheered and quickened by faith, it receives the Holy Ghost, who renews us, so that we are able to observe the Law; so that we are able to love God and the Word of God, and to be submissive to God in afflictions, so that we are able to be chaste, to love our neighbor, etc. Even though these works are as yet far distant from the perfection of the Law, yet they please on account of faith, by which we are accounted righteous, because we believe that for Christ's sake we have a reconciled God. These things are plain and in harmony with the Gospel, and can be understood by persons of sound mind. And from this foundation it can easily be decided why we ascribe justification to faith, and not to love; although love follows faith, because love is the fulfilling of the Law. But Paul teaches that we are justified not from the Law, but from the promise which is received only by faith. For we neither come to God without Christ as Mediator, nor receive remission of sins for the sake of our love, but for the sake of Christ. Likewise we are not able to love God while He is angry, and the Law always accuses us, always manifests to us an angry God. Therefore, by faith we must first apprehend the promise that for Christ's sake the Father is reconciled and forgives. Afterwards we begin to observe the Law. Our eyes are to be cast far away from human reason, far away from Moses upon Christ, and we are to believe that Christ is given us, in order that for His sake we may be accounted righteous. In the flesh we never satisfy the Law. Thus, therefore, we are accounted righteous, not on account of the Law but on account of

Christ because His merits are granted us, if we believe on Him. If any one, therefore, has considered these foundations, that we are not justified by the Law because human nature cannot observe the Law of God and cannot love God, but that we are justified from the promise, in which, for Christ's sake, reconciliation, righteousness, and eternal life have been promised, he will easily understand that justification must necessarily be ascribed to faith, if he only will reflect upon the fact that it is not in vain that Christ has been promised and set forth, that He has been born and has suffered and been raised again; if he will reflect upon the fact that the promise of grace in Christ is not in vain, that it was made immediately from the beginning of the world apart from and beyond the Law; if he will reflect upon the fact that the promise should be received by faith, as John says, 1 Ep. 5, 10 sq.: He that believeth not God hath made Him a liar, because he believeth not the record that God gave of His Son. And this is the record that God hath given to us eternal life, and this life is in His Son. He that hath the Son hath life, and he that hath not the Son of God hath not life. And Christ says John 8, 36: If the Son, therefore, shall make you free, ye shall be free indeed. And Paul, Rom. 5, 2: By whom also we have access to God; and he adds: by faith. By faith in Christ, therefore, the promise of remission of sins and of righteousness is received. Neither are we justified before God by reason or by the Law.

These things are so plain and so manifest that we wonder that the madness of the adversaries is so great as to call them into doubt. The proof is manifest that, since we are justified before God not from the Law but from the promise, it is necessary to ascribe justification to faith. What can be opposed to this proof, unless some one wish to abolish the entire Gospel and the entire Christ? The glory of Christ becomes more brilliant when we teach that we avail ourselves of Him as Mediator and Propitiator. Godly consciences see that in this doctrine the most abundant consolation is offered to them, namely, that they ought to believe and most firmly assert that they have a reconciled Father for Christ's sake, and not for the sake of our righteousness, and that, nevertheless, Christ aids us, so that we are able to observe also the Law. Of such great blessings as these the adversaries deprive the Church when they condemn and endeavor to efface, the doctrine concerning the righteousness of faith. Therefore let all well-disposed minds beware of consenting to the godless counsels of the adversaries. In the doctrine of the adversaries concerning justification no mention is made of Christ, and how we ought to set Him against the wrath of God, as though, indeed, we were able to overcome the wrath of God by love, or to love an angry God. In regard to these things, consciences are left in uncertainty. For if they are to think that they have a reconciled God for the reason that they love, and that they observe the Law, they must needs always doubt whether they have a reconciled God, because they either do not feel this love, as the adversaries acknowledge, or they certainly feel that it is very small; and much more frequently do they feel that they are angry at the judgment of God, who oppresses human nature with many terrible evils, with troubles of this life, the terrors of eternal wrath, etc. When, therefore, will conscience be at rest, when will it be pacified? When, in this doubt and in these terrors, will it love God? What else is the doctrine of the Law than a doctrine of despair? And let any one of our adversaries come forward who can teach us concerning this love, how he himself loves God. They do not at all understand what they say they only echo, just like the walls of a house, the little word "love," without understanding it. So confused and obscure is their doctrine: it not only transfers the glory of Christ to human works, but also leads consciences either to presumption or to despair. But ours, we hope, is readily understood by pious minds, and brings godly and salutary consolation to terrified consciences. For as the adversaries quibble that also many wicked men and devils believe, we have frequently already said that we speak of faith in Christ, i.e., of faith in the remission of sins, of faith which truly and heartily assents to the promise of grace. This is not brought about without a great struggle in human hearts. And men of sound mind can easily judge that the faith which believes that we are cared for by God, and that we are forgiven and heard by Him, is a matter above nature. For of its own accord the human mind makes no such decision concerning God. Therefore this faith of which we speak is neither in the wicked nor in devils.

Furthermore, if any sophist cavils that righteousness is in the will, and therefore it cannot be ascribed to faith, which is in the intellect, the reply is easy, because in the schools even such persons acknowledge that the will commands the intellect to assent to the Word of God. We say also quite clearly: Just as the terrors of sin and death are not only thoughts of the intellect, but also horrible movements of the will fleeing God's judgment, so faith is not only knowledge in the intellect, but also confidence in the will, i.e., it is to wish and to receive that which is offered in the promise, namely, reconciliation and remission of sins. Scripture thus uses the term "faith," as the following sentence of Paul testifies, Rom. 5, 1: Being justified by faith, we have peace with God. Moreover, in this passage, to justify signifies, according to forensic usage, to acquit a guilty one and declare him righteous, but on account of the righteousness of another, namely, of Christ, which righteousness of another is communicated to us by faith. Therefore, since in this passage our righteousness is the imputation of the righteousness of another, we must here speak concerning righteousness otherwise than when in philosophy or in a civil court we seek after the righteousness of one's own work which certainly is in the will. Paul accordingly says, 1 Cor. 1, 30: Of Him are ye in Christ Jesus, who of God is made unto us Wisdom and Righteousness, and Sanctification, and Redemption. And 2 Cor. 5, 21: He hath mode Him to be sin for us who knew no sin, that we might be made the righteousness of God in Him. But because the righteousness of Christ is given us by faith, faith is for this reason righteousness in us imputatively, i.e., it is that by which we are made acceptable to God on account of the imputation and ordinance of God, as Paul says, Rom. 4, 3. 5: Faith is reckoned for righteousness. Although on account of certain captious persons we must say technically: Faith is truly righteousness, because it is obedience to the Gospel. For it is evident that obedience to the command of a superior is truly a species of distributive justice. And this obedience to the Gospel is reckoned for righteousness, so that, only on account of this, because by this we apprehend Christ as Propitiator, good works, or obedience to the Law, are pleasing. For we do not satisfy the Law, but for Christ's sake this is forgiven us, as Paul says, Rom. 8, 1: There is therefore now no condemnation to them which are in Christ Jesus. This faith gives God the honor, gives God that which is His own, in this, that, by receiving the promises, it obeys Him. Just as Paul also says, Rom. 4, 20: He staggered not at the promise of God through unbelief, but was strong in faith, giving glory to God. Thus the worship and divine service of the Gospel is to receive from God gifts, on the contrary, the worship of the Law is to offer and present our gifts to God. We can, however, offer nothing to God unless we have first been reconciled and born again. This passage too, brings the greatest consolation, as the chief worship of the Gospel is to wish to receive remission of sins, grace, and righteousness. Of this worship Christ says, John 6, 40: This is the will of Him that sent Me, that every one which seeth the Son, and believeth on Him, may have everlasting life. And the Father says, Matt. 17, 5: This is My beloved Son, in whom I am well pleased, hear ye Him. The adversaries speak of obedience to the Law; they do not speak of obedience to the Gospel, and yet we cannot obey the Law, unless, through the Gospel, we have been born again, since we cannot love God, unless the remission of sins has been received. For as long as we feel that He is angry with us, human nature flees from His wrath and judgment. If any one should make a cavil such as this: If that be faith which wishes those things that are offered in the promise, the habits of faith and hope seem to be confounded, because hope is that which expects promised things, to this we reply that these dispositions cannot in reality be severed, in the manner that they are divided by idle speculations in the schools. For also in the Epistle to the Hebrews faith is defined as the substance (*exspectatio*) of things hoped for, Heb. 11, 1. Yet if any one wish a distinction to be made, we say that the object of hope is properly a future event, but that faith is concerned with future and present things, and receives in the present the remission of sins offered in the promise.

From these statements we hope that it can be sufficiently understood both what faith is and that we are compelled to hold that by faith we are justified, reconciled, and regenerated, if, indeed, we wish to teach the righteousness of the Gospel, and not the righteousness of the Law. For those who teach that we are justified by love teach the righteousness of the Law, and do not teach us in justification to avail ourselves of Christ as Mediator. These things also are manifest namely, that not by love, but by faith, we overcome the terrors of sin and death, that we cannot oppose our love and fulfilling of the Law to the wrath of God, because Paul says, Rom. 5, 2: By Christ we have access to God by faith. We urge this sentence so frequently for the sake of perspicuity. For it shows most clearly the state of our whole case, and, when carefully considered, can teach abundantly concerning the whole matter, and can console well-disposed minds. Accordingly, it is of advantage to have it at hand and in sight, not only that we may be able to oppose it to the doctrine of our adversaries, who teach that we come to God not by faith, but by love and merits, without Christ as Mediator; and also, at the same time that, when in fear, we may cheer ourselves and exercise faith. This is also manifest, that without the aid of Christ we cannot observe the Law, as He Himself says John 15, 5: Without Me ye can do nothing. Accordingly, before we observe the Law, our hearts must be born again by faith. [From the explanations which we have made it can easily be inferred what answer must be given to similar quotations. For the rule so interprets all passages that treat of good works that outside of Christ they are to be worthless before God, and that the heart must first have Christ, and believe that it is accepted with God for Christ's sake, not because of its own works. The adversaries also bring forward some arguments of the schools, which are easily answered, if you know what faith is. Tried Christians speak of faith quite differently from the sophists, for we have shown before that to believe means to rely on the mercy of God, that He desires to be gracious for Christ's sake, without our merits. That is what it means to believe the article of the forgiveness of sin. To believe this does not mean to know the history only, which the devils also know. Therefore we can easily meet the argument of the schools when they say that the devils also believe, therefore faith does not justify. Aye, the devils know the history, but they do not believe the forgiveness of sin. Again, they say: To be righteous is to be obedient. Now, to perform works is certainly obedience; therefore works must justify. We should answer this as follows: To be righteous is a kind of obedience which God accepts as such. Now God is not willing to accept our obedience in works as righteousness; for it is not an obedience of the heart, because none truly keep the Law. For this reason He has ordained that there should be another kind of obedience which He will accept as righteousness, namely, that we are to acknowledge our disobedience, and trust that we are pleasing to God for Christ's sake, not on account of our obedience. Accordingly, to be righteous in this case means to be pleasing to God, not on account of our own obedience, but from mercy for Christ's sake. Again, to sin is to hate God; therefore, to love God must be righteousness. True, to love God is the righteousness of the Law. But nobody fulfils this Law. Therefore the Gospel teaches a new kind of righteousness, namely, that we are pleasing to God for Christ's sake, although we have not fulfilled the Law; and yet, we are to begin to do the Law. Again, what is the difference between faith and hope? Answer: Hope expects future blessings and deliverance from tribulation; faith receives the present reconciliation, and concludes in the heart that God has forgiven my sin, and that He is now gracious to me. And this is a noble service of God, which serves God by giving Him the honor, and by esteeming His mercy and promise so sure that without merit we can receive and expect from Him all manner of blessings. And in this service of God the heart should be exercised and increase, of which the foolish sophists know nothing.]

Hence it can also be understood why we find fault with the doctrine of the adversaries concerning ***meritum condigni***. The decision is very easy: because they do not make mention of faith, that we please God by faith for Christ's sake, but imagine that good works, wrought by the aid of the habit of love, constitute a righteousness worthy by itself to please God, and worthy of eternal life, and that they have no need of Christ as Mediator. [This can in no wise be tolerated.] What else is this than to transfer the glory of Christ to our works, namely that we please God because of our works, and not because of Christ? But this is also to rob Christ of the glory of being the Mediator who is Mediator perpetually, and not merely in the beginning of Justification. Paul also says, Gal. 2, 17, that If one justified in Christ have need afterwards to seek righteousness elsewhere, he affirms of Christ that He is a minister of sin, i.e., that He does not fully justify. [And this is what the holy, catholic, Christian Church teaches, preaches, and confesses, namely, that we are saved by mercy as we have shown above from Jerome.] And most absurd is that which the adversaries teach, namely, that good works merit ***grace de condigno***, as though indeed after the beginning of justification, if conscience is terrified, as is ordinarily the case, grace must be sought through a good work, and not by faith in Christ.

Secondly, the doctrine of the adversaries leaves consciences in doubt, so that they never can be pacified, because the Law always accuses us, even in good works. For always the flesh lusteth against the Spirit, Gal. 5, 17. How, therefore, will conscience here have peace without faith, if it believe that, not for Christ's sake, but for the sake of one's own work, it ought now to please God? What work will it find, upon what will it firmly rely as worthy of eternal life, if, indeed, hope ought to originate from merits? Against these doubts Paul says, Rom. 5, 1: Being justified by faith, we have peace with God; we ought to be firmly convinced that for Christ's sake righteousness and eternal life are granted us. And of Abraham he says Rom. 4, 18: Against hope he believed in hope.

Thirdly, how will conscience know when by the inclination of this habit of love, a work has been done of which it may affirm that it merits ***grace de condigno***? But it is only to elude the Scriptures that this very distinction has been devised, namely, that men merit at one time ***de congruo*** and at another time ***de condigno***, because, as we have above said, the intention of the one who works does not distinguish the kinds of merit; but hypocrites, in their security, think simply their works are worthy, and that for this reason they are accounted righteous. On the other hand, terrified consciences doubt concerning all works, and for this reason are continually seeking other works. For this is what it means to **merit de congruo**, namely to doubt and, without faith, to work, until despair takes place. In a word, all that the adversaries teach in regard to this matter is full of errors and dangers.

Fourthly, the entire [the holy, catholic, Christian] Church confesses that eternal life is attained through mercy. For thus Augustine speaks On Grace and Free Will, when indeed, he is speaking of the works of the saints wrought after justification: God leads us to eternal life not by our merits, but according to His mercy. And Confessions, Book IX: Woe to the life of man, however much it may be worthy of praise, if it be judged with mercy removed. And Cyprian in his treatise on the Lord's Prayer: Lest any one should flatter himself that he is innocent, and by exalting himself, should perish the more deeply, he is instructed and taught that he sins daily, in that he is bidden to entreat daily for his sins. But the subject is well known, and has very many and very clear testimonies in Scripture, and in the Church Fathers, who all with one mouth declare that, even though we have good works yet in these very works we need mercy. Faith looking upon this mercy cheers and consoles us. Wherefore the adversaries teach erroneously when they so extol merits as to add nothing concerning this faith that apprehends mercy. For just as we have above said that the promise and faith stand in a reciprocal relation, and that the promise is not apprehended unless by faith, so we here say that the promised mercy correlatively requires faith, and cannot be apprehended without faith. Therefore we justly find fault with the doctrine concerning **meritum condigni**, since it teaches nothing of justifying faith, and obscures the glory and office of Christ as Mediator. Nor should we be regarded as teaching anything new in this matter, since the Church Fathers have so clearly handed down the doctrine that even in good works we need mercy.

Scripture also often inculcates the same. In Ps. 143, 9: And enter not into judgment with Thy servant; for in Thy sight shall no man living be justified. This passage denies absolutely, even to all saints and servants of God, the glory of righteousness, if God does not forgive, but judges and convicts their hearts. For when David boasts in other places of his righteousness, he speaks concerning his own cause against the persecutors of God's Word, he does not speak of his personal purity; and he asks that the cause and glory of God be defended, as in Ps. 7, 8: Judge me, O Lord, according to Thy righteousness, and according to mine integrity that is in me. Likewise in Ps. 130, 3, he says that no one can endure God's judgment, if God were to mark our sins: If Thou, Lord, shouldest mark iniquities, O Lord, who shall stand? Job 9, 28: I am afraid of all my sorrows [Vulg., opera, works]; v. 30: If I wash myself with snow-water, and make my hands never so clean, yet Thou shalt plunge me in the ditch. Prov. 20, 9: Who can say, I have made my heart clean, I am pure from my sin? 1 John 1, 8: If we say that we have no sin, we deceive ourselves and the truth is not in us, etc. And in the Lord's Prayer the saints ask for the remission of sins. Therefore even the saints have sins. Num. 14, 18: The innocent shall not be innocent [cf. Ex. 34, 7]. Deut. 4, 24: The Lord, thy God, is a consuming fire. Zechariah also says, 2, 13: Be silent, O all flesh, before the Lord. Is. 40, 6: All flesh is as grass, and all the goodliness thereof is as the flower of the field; the grass withereth, the flower fadeth, because the Spirit of the Lord bloweth upon it, i. e., flesh and righteousness of the flesh cannot endure the judgment of God. Jonah also says, chap. 2, 8: They that observe lying vanities forsake their own mercy, i.e., all confidence is vain, except confidence in mercy; mercy delivers us; our own merits, our own efforts, do not. Accordingly, Daniel also prays, 9, 18 sq.: For we do not present our supplications before Thee for our righteousnesses but for Thy great mercies. O Lord, hear; O Lord, forgive; O Lord, hearken and do it; defer not for Thine own sake, O my God; for Thy city and Thy people are called by Thy name. Thus Daniel teaches us in praying to lay hold upon mercy, i.e., to trust in God's mercy, and not to trust in our own merits before God. We also wonder what our adversaries do in prayer, if, indeed, the profane men ever ask anything of God. If they declare that they are worthy because they have love and good works, and ask for grace as a debt, they pray precisely like the Pharisee in Luke 18, 11, who says: I am not as other men are. He who thus prays for grace and does not rely upon God's mercy, treats Christ with dishonor, who, since He is our High Priest, intercedes for us. Thus, therefore, prayer relies upon God's mercy, when we believe that we are heard for the sake of Christ the High Priest, as He Himself says, John 14, 13: Whatsoever ye shall ask the Father in My name, He will give it you. In My name, He says, because without this High Priest we cannot approach the Father.

[All prudent men will see what follows from the opinion of the adversaries. For if we shall believe that Christ has merited only the ***prima gratia***, as they call it, and that we afterwards merit eternal life by our works, hearts or consciences will be pacified neither at the hour of death, nor at any other time, nor can they ever build upon certain ground; they are never certain that God is gracious. Thus their doctrine unintermittingly leads to nothing but misery of soul and, finally, to despair. For God's Law is not a matter of pleasantry; it ceaselessly accuses consciences outside of Christ, as Paul says, Rom. 4, 15: The Law worketh wrath. Thus it will happen that if consciences feel the judgment of God, they have no certain comfort and will rush into despair.

Paul says: Whatsoever is not of faith is sin, Rom. 14, 23. But those persons can do nothing from faith who are first to attain to this that God is gracious to them only when they have at length fulfilled the Law. They will always quake with doubt whether they have done enough good works, whether the Law has been satisfied, yea, they will keenly feel and understand that they are still under obligation to the Law. Accordingly, they will never be sure that they have a gracious God, and that their prayer is heard. Therefore they can never truly love God, nor expect any blessing from Him, nor truly worship God. What else are such hearts and consciences than hell itself, since there is nothing in them but despair, fainting away grumbling, discontent, and hatred of God, and yet in this hatred they invoke and worship God, just as Saul worshiped Him

Here we appeal to all Christian minds and to all that are experienced in trials; they will be forced to confess and say that such great uncertainty, such disquietude, such torture and anxiety, such horrible fear and doubt follow from this teaching of the adversaries who imagine that we are accounted righteous before God by our own works or fulfilling of the Law which we perform, and point us to Queer Street by bidding us trust not in the rich, blessed promises of Grace, given us by Christ the Mediator, but in our own miserable works! Therefore, this conclusion stands like a rock, yea, like a wall, namely, that, although we have begun to do the Law, still we are accepted with God and at peace with Him, not on account of such works of ours, but for Christ's sake by faith; nor does God owe us everlasting life on account of these works. But just as forgiveness of sin and righteousness is imputed to us for Christ's sake, not on account of our works, or the Law, so everlasting life, together with righteousness, is offered us, not on account of our works, or of the Law, but for Christ's sake as Christ says, John 6, 40: This is the Father's will that sent He, that every one which seeth the Son, and believeth on Him may have everlasting life. Again, v. 47: He that believeth on the Son hath everlasting life. Now, the adversaries should be asked at this point what advice they give to poor consciences in the hour of death: whether they comfort consciences by telling them that they will have a blessed departure, that they will be saved, and have a propitiated God, because of their own merits or because of God's grace and mercy for Christ's sake. For St. Peter St. Paul, and saints like them cannot boast that God owes them eternal life for their martyrdom, nor have they relied on their works, but on the mercy promised in Christ.

Nor would it be possible that a saint, great and high though he be, could make a firm stand against the accusations of the divine Law, the great might of the devil, the terror of death, and, finally, against despair and the anguish of hell, if he would not grasp the divine promises, the Gospel, as a tree or branch in the great flood in the strong, violent stream, amidst the waves and billows of the anguish of death; if he does not cling by faith to the Word, which proclaims grace, and thus obtains eternal life without works, without the Law, from pure grace. For this doctrine alone preserves Christian consciences in afflictions and anguish of death. Of these things the adversaries know nothing, and talk of them like a blind man about color.

Here they will say: If we are to be saved by pure mercy, what difference is there between those who are saved, and those who are not saved? If merit is of no account, there is no difference between the evil and the good and it follows that both are saved alike. This argument has moved the scholastics to invent the *meritum condigni*; for there must be (they think) a difference between those who are saved and those who are damned.

We reply; in the first place, that everlasting life is accorded to those whom God esteems just, and when they have been esteemed just, they are become, by that act, the children of God and coheirs of Christ, as Paul says, Rom. 8, 30: Whom He justified, them He also glorified. Hence nobody is saved except only those who believe the Gospel. But as our reconciliation with God is uncertain if it is to rest on our works, and not on the gracious promise of God, which cannot fail, so, too, all that we expect by hope would be uncertain if it must be built on the foundation of our merits and works. For the Law of God ceaselessly accuses the conscience and men feel in their hearts nothing but this voice from the fiery, flaming cloud: I am the Lord, thy God; this thou shalt do; that thou art obliged to do; this I require of thee. Deut. 5, 6 ff. No conscience can for a moment be at rest when the Law and Moses assails the heart, before it apprehends Christ by faith. Nor can it truly hope for eternal life, unless it be pacified before. For a doubting conscience flees from God, despairs and cannot hope. However, hope of eternal life must be certain. Now, in order that it may not be fickle, but certain, we must believe that we have eternal life, not by our works or merits, but from pure grace, by faith in Christ.

In secular affairs and in secular courts we meet with both, mercy and justice. Justice is certain by the laws and the verdict rendered, mercy is uncertain. In this matter that relates to God the case is different; for grace and mercy have been promised us by a certain word, and the Gospel is the word which commands us to believe that God is gracious and wishes to save us for Christ's sake, as the text reads, John 3, 17: God sent not His Son into the world to condemn the world, but that the world through Him might be saved. He that believeth on Him is not condemned.

Now, whenever we speak of mercy, the meaning is to be this, that faith is required, and it is this faith that makes the difference between those who are saved, and those who are damned, between those who are worthy, and those who are unworthy. For everlasting life has been promised to none but those who have been reconciled by Christ. Faith, however, reconciles and justifies before God the moment we apprehend the promise by faith. And throughout our entire life we are to pray God and be diligent, to receive faith and to grow in faith. For, as stated before, faith is where repentance is, and it is not in those who walk after the flesh. This faith is to grow and increase throughout our life by all manner of afflictions. Those who obtain faith are regenerated, so that they lead a new life and do good works.

Now, just as we say that true repentance is to endure throughout our entire life, we say, too, that good works and the fruits of faith must be done throughout our life, although our works never become so precious as to be equal to the treasure of Christ, or to merit eternal life, as Christ says, Luke 17, 10: When ye shall have done all those things which are commanded you, say, We are unprofitable servants. And St. Bernard truly says: There is need that you must first believe that you cannot have forgiveness of sin except by the grace of God; next, that thereafter you cannot have and do any good work unless God grants it to you; lastly, that you cannot earn eternal life with your works, though it is not given you without merit. A little further on he says: Let no one deceive himself; for when you rightly consider the matter, you will undoubtedly find that you cannot meet with ten thousand him who approaches you with twenty thousand. These are strong sayings of St. Bernard; let them believe these if they will not believe us.

In order, then, that hearts may have a true certain comfort and hope, we point them, with Paul, to the divine promise of grace in Christ, and teach that we must believe that God gives us eternal life, not on account of our works, but for Christ's sake, as the Apostle John says in his Epistle, 1, 5, 12: He that hath the Son hath life, and he that hath not the Son of God hath not life.]

Part 10

Here belongs also the declaration of Christ, Luke 17, 10: So likewise ye, when ye shall have done all those things which are commanded you, say, We are unprofitable servants. These words clearly declare that God saves by mercy and on account of His promise, not that it is due on account of the value of our works. But at this point the adversaries play wonderfully with the words of Christ. In the first place, they make an antistrophe and turn it against us. Much more, they say, can it be said: "If we have believed all things, say, We are unprofitable servants." Then they add that works are of no profit to God, but are not without profit to us. See how the puerile study of sophistry delights the adversaries, and although these absurdities do not deserve a refutation, nevertheless we will reply to them in a few words. The antistrophe is defective. For, in the first place, the adversaries are deceived in regard to the term faith; because, if it would signify that knowledge of the history which is also in the wicked and in devils, the adversaries would be correct in arguing that faith is unprofitable when they say: "When we have believed all things, say, We are unprofitable servants." But we are speaking, not of the knowledge of the history, but of confidence in the promise and mercy of God. And this confidence in the promise confesses that we are unprofitable servants; yea, this confession that our works are unworthy is the very voice of faith, as appears in this example of Daniel, 9, 18, which we cited a little above: We do not present our supplications before Thee for our righteousnesses, etc. For faith saves because it apprehends mercy, or the promise of grace, even though our works are unworthy; and, thus understood, namely that our works are unworthy, the antistrophe does not injure us: "When ye shall have believed all things, say, We are unprofitable servants"; for that we are saved by mercy, we teach with the entire Church. But if they mean to argue from the similar: When you have done all things, do not trust in your works, so also, when you have believed all things, do not trust in the divine promise there is no connection. [The inference is wrong: "Works do not help; therefore, faith also does not help." We must give the uncultured men a homely illustration: It does not follow that because a half-farthing does not help, therefore a florin also does not help. Just as the florins is of much higher denomination and value than the half-farthing, so also should it be understood that faith is much higher and more efficacious than works. Not that faith helps because of its worth, but because it trusts in God's promises and mercy. Faith is strong, not because of its worthiness, but because of the divine promise.] For they are very dissimilar, as the causes and objects of confidence in the former proposition are far dissimilar to those of the latter. In the former, confidence is confidence in our own works. In the latter, confidence is confidence in the divine promise. Christ, however, condemns confidence in our works; He does not condemn confidence in His promise. He does not wish us to despair of God's grace and mercy. He accuses our works as unworthy, but does not accuse the promise which freely offers mercy. And here Ambrose says well: grace is to be acknowledged; but nature must not be disregarded. We must trust in the promise of grace and not in our own nature. But the adversaries act in accordance with their custom, and distort, against faith, the judgments which have been given on behalf of faith. [Hence, Christ in this place forbids men to trust in their own works; for they cannot help them. On the other hand, He does not forbid to trust in God's promise. Yea, He requires such trust in the promise of God for the very reason that we are unprofitable servants and works can be of no help. Therefore, the knaves have improperly applied to our trust in the divine promise the words of Christ which treat of trust in our own worthiness. This clearly reveals and defeats their sophistry. May the Lord Christ soon put to shame the sophists who thus mutilate His holy Word! Amen.] We leave, however, these thorny points to the schools. The sophistry is plainly puerile when they interpret "unprofitable servant " as meaning that the works are unprofitable to God, but are profitable to us. Yet Christ speaks concerning that profit which makes God a debtor of grace to us, although it is out of place to discuss here concerning that which is profitable or unprofitable. For "unprofitable servants" means "insufficient," because no one fears God as much, and loves God as much, and believes God as much as he ought. But let us dismiss these frigid cavils of the adversaries, concerning which, if at any time they are brought to the light, prudent men will easily decide what they should judge. They have found a flaw in words which are very plain and clear. But every one sees that in this passage confidence in our own works is condemned.

Let us, therefore, hold fast to this which the Church confesses, namely, that we are saved by mercy. And lest any one may here think: "If we are to be saved by mercy, hope will be uncertain, if in those who obtain salvation nothing precedes by which they may be distinguished from those who do not obtain it," we must give him a satisfactory answer. For the scholastics, moved by this reason, seem to have devised the ***meritum condigni***. For this consideration can greatly exercise the human mind. We will therefore reply briefly. For the very reason that hope may be sure, for the very reason that there may be an antecedent distinction between those who obtain salvation, and those who do not obtain it, it is necessary firmly to hold that we are saved by mercy. When this is expressed thus unqualifiedly, it seems absurd. For in civil courts and in human judgment, that which is of right or of debt is certain, and mercy is uncertain. But the matter is different with respect to God's judgment; for here mercy has a clear and certain promise and command from God. For the Gospel is properly that command which enjoins us to believe that God is propitious to us for Christ's sake. For God sent not His Son into the world to condemn the world, but that the world through Him might be saved, John 3, 17. 18. As often, therefore, as mercy is spoken of, faith in the promise must be added; and this faith produces sure hope, because it relies upon the Word and command of God. If hope would rely upon works, then, indeed, it would be uncertain, because works cannot pacify the conscience, as has been said above frequently. And this faith makes a distinction between those who obtain salvation, and those who do not obtain it. Faith makes the distinction between the worthy and the unworthy, because eternal life has been promised to the justified; and faith justifies.

But here again the adversaries will cry out that there is no need of good works if they do not merit eternal life. These calumnies we have refuted above. Of course, it is necessary to do good works. We say that eternal life has been promised to the justified. But those who walk according to the flesh retain neither faith nor righteousness. We are for this very end justified, that, being righteous we may begin to do good works and to obey God's Law. We are regenerated and receive the Holy Ghost for the very end that the new life may produce new works, new dispositions, the fear and love of God, hatred of concupiscence, etc. This faith of which we speak arises in repentance, and ought to be established and grow in the midst of good works, temptations, and dangers, so that we may continually be the more firmly persuaded that God for Christ's sake cares for us, forgives us, hears us. This is not learned with out many and great struggles. How often is conscience aroused, how often does it incite even to despair when it brings to view sins, either old or new, or the impurity of our nature! This handwriting is not blotted out without a great struggle, in which experience testifies what a difficult matter faith is. And while we are cheered in the midst of the terrors and receive consolation, other spiritual movements at the same time grow, the knowledge of God, fear of God, hope, love of God; and we are regenerated, as Paul says, Col. 3, 10 and 2 Cor. 3, 18, in the knowledge of God, and, beholding the glory of the Lord, are changed into the same image, i.e., we receive the true knowledge of God, so that we truly fear Him, truly trust that we are cared for and that we are heard by Him. This regeneration is, as it were, the beginning of eternal life, as Paul says, Rom. 8, 10: If Christ be in you, the body is dead because of sin; but the Spirit is life because of righteousness. And 2 Cor. 5, 2. 3: We are clothed upon, if so be that, being clothed, we shall not be found naked. From these statements the candid reader can judge that we certainly require good works, since we teach that this faith arises in repentance, and in repentance ought continually to increase; and in these matters we place Christian and spiritual perfection, if repentance and faith grow together in repentance. This can be better understood by the godly than those things which are taught by the adversaries concerning contemplation or perfection. Just as, however, justification pertains to faith, so also life eternal pertains to faith. And Peter says, 1 Pet. 1, 9: Receiving the end, or fruit, of your faith, the salvation of your souls. For the adversaries confess that the justified are children of God and coheirs of Christ. Afterwards works, because on account of faith they please God, merit other bodily and spiritual rewards. For there will be distinctions in the glory of the saints.

But here the adversaries reply that eternal life is called a reward, and that therefore it is merited ***de condigno*** by good works. We reply briefly and plainly: Paul, Rom. 6, 23, calls eternal life a gift, because by the righteousness presented for Christ's sake, we are made at the same time sons of God and coheirs of Christ, as John says, 3, 36: He that believeth on the Son hath everlasting life. And Augustine says, as also do very many others who follow him: God crowns His gifts in us. Elsewhere indeed, Luke 5, 23, it is written: Your reward is great in heaven. If these passages seem to the adversaries to conflict, they themselves may explain them. But they are not fair judges; for they omit the word gift. They omit also the sources of the entire matter [the chief part, how we are justified before God, also that Christ remains at all times the Mediator], and they select the word reward, and most harshly interpret this not only against Scripture, but also against the usage of the language. Hence they infer that inasmuch as it is called a reward, our works, therefore, are such that they ought to be a price for which eternal life is due. They are, therefore, worthy of grace and life eternal, and do not stand in need of mercy, or of Christ as Mediator, or of faith. This logic is altogether new; we hear the term reward, and therefore are to infer that there is no need of Christ as Mediator, or of faith having access to God for Christ's sake, and not for the sake of our works! Who does not see that these are anacoluthons? We do not contend concerning the term reward. We dispute concerning this matter, namely, whether good works are of themselves worthy of grace and of eternal life, or whether they please only on account of faith, which apprehends Christ as Mediator. Our adversaries not only ascribe this to works, namely, that they are worthy of grace and of eternal life, but they also state falsely that they have superfluous merits, which they can grant to others, and by which they can justify others, as when monks sell the merits of their orders to others. These monstrosities they heap up in the manner of Chrysippus, where this one word reward is heard, namely: "It is called a reward, and therefore we have works which are a price for which a reward is due; therefore works please by themselves, and not for the sake of Christ as Mediator. And since one has more merits than another, therefore some have superfluous merits. And those who merit them can bestow these merits upon others." Stop, reader; you have not the whole of this sorites. For certain sacraments of this donation must be added; the hood is placed upon the dead. [As the Barefooted monks and other orders have shamelessly done in placing the hoods of their orders upon dead bodies.] By such accumulations the blessings brought us in Christ, and the righteousness of faith have been obscured. [These are acute and strong arguments, all of which they can spin from the single word reward, whereby they obscure Christ and faith.]

We are not agitating an idle logomachy concerning the term reward [but this great, exalted, most important matter, namely, where Christian hearts are to find true and certain consolation; again, whether our works can give consciences rest and peace; again, whether we are to believe that our works are worthy of eternal life, or whether that is given us for Christ's sake. These are the real questions regarding these matters; if consciences are not rightly instructed concerning these, they can have no certain comfort. However, we have stated clearly enough that good works do not fulfil the Law, that we need the mercy of God, that by faith we are accepted with God, that good works, be they ever so precious, even if they were the works of St. Paul himself, cannot bring rest to the conscience. From all this it follows that we are to believe that we obtain eternal life through Christ by faith, not on account of our works, or of the Law. But what do we say of the reward which Scripture mentions?] If the adversaries will concede that we are accounted righteous by faith because of Christ, and that good works please God because of faith, we will not afterwards contend much concerning the term reward. We confess that eternal life is a reward, because it is something due on account of the promise, not on account of our merits. For the justification has been promised, which we have above shown to be properly a gift of God; and to this gift has been added the promise of eternal life, according to Rom. 8, 30: Whom He justified, them He also glorified. Here belongs what Paul says, 2 Tim. 4, 8: There is laid up for me a crown of righteousness which the Lord, the righteous Judge, shall give me. For the crown is due the justified because of the promise. And this promise saints should know, not that they may labor for their own profit, for they ought to labor for the glory of God; but in order that they may not despair in afflictions, they should know God's will, that He desires to aid, to deliver, to protect them. [Just as the inheritance and all possessions of a father are given to the son, as a rich compensation and reward for his obedience, and yet the son receives the inheritance, not on account of his merit, but because the father, for the reason that he is his father, wants him to have it. Therefore it is a sufficient reason why eternal life is called a reward, because thereby the tribulations which we suffer, and the works of love which we do, are compensated, although we have not deserved it. For there are two kinds of compensation: one, which we are obliged, the other, which we are not obliged, to render. I.e., when the emperor grants a servant a principality, he therewith compensates the servant's work; and yet the work is not worth the principality, but the servant acknowledges that he has received a gracious lien. Thus God does not owe us eternal life, still, when He grants it to believers for Christ's sake, that is a compensation for our sufferings and works.] Although the perfect hear the mention of penalties and rewards in one way, and the weak hear it in another way; for the weak labor for the sake of their own advantage. And yet the preaching of rewards and punishments is necessary. In the preaching of punishments the wrath of God is set forth, and therefore this pertains to the preaching of repentance. In the preaching of rewards, grace is set forth. And just as Scripture, in the mention of good works, often embraces faith,--for it wishes righteousness of the heart to be included with the fruits,--so sometimes it offers grace together with other rewards as in Is. 58, 8 f., and frequently in other places in the prophets. We also confess what we have often testified, that, although justification and eternal life pertain to faith, nevertheless good works merit other bodily and spiritual rewards [which are rendered both in this life and after this life; for God defers most rewards until He glorifies saints after this life, because He wishes them in this life to be exercised in mortifying the old man] and degrees of rewards, according to 1 Cor. 3, 8: Every man shall receive his own reward according to his own labor. [For the blessed will have reward, one higher than the other. This difference merit makes, according as it pleases God; and it is merit, because they do these good works whom God has adopted as children and heirs. For thus they have merit which is their own and peculiar as one child with respect to another.] For the righteousness of the Gospel, which has to do with the promise of grace, freely receives justification and quickening. But the fulfilling of the Law, which follows faith, has to do with the Law, in which a reward is offered and is due, not freely, but according to our works. But those who merit this are justified before they do the Law. Therefore as Paul says, Col. 1, 13; Rom. 8, 17, they have before been translated into the kingdom of God's Son, and been made joint-heirs with Christ. But as often as mention is made of merit, the adversaries immediately transfer the matter from other rewards to justification, although the Gospel freely offers justification on account of Christ's merits and not of our own; and the merits of Christ are communicated to us by faith. But works and afflictions merit, not justification, but other remunerations, as the reward is offered for the works in these passages: He which soweth sparingly shall reap also sparingly, and he which soweth bountifully shall reap also bountifully, 2 Cor. 9, 6. Here clearly the measure of the reward is connected with the measure of the work. Honor thy father and thy mother, that thy days may be long upon the land, Ex. 20, 12. Also here the Law offers a reward to a certain work. Although, therefore, the fulfilling of the Law merits a reward, for a reward properly pertains to the Law, yet we ought to be mindful of the Gospel, which freely offers justification for Christ's sake. We neither observe the Law nor can observe it, before we have been reconciled to God, justified, and regenerated. Neither would this fulfilling of the Law please God, unless we would be accepted on account of faith. And because men are accepted on account of faith, for this very reason the inchoate fulfilling of the Law pleases, and has a reward in this life and after this life. Concerning the term reward, very many other remarks might here be made derived from the nature of the Law, which as they are too extensive, must be explained in another connection.

But the adversaries urge that it is the prerogative of good works to merit eternal life, because Paul says, Rom. 2, 5: Who will render to every one according to his works. Likewise v. 10: Glory, honor, and peace to every man that worketh good. John 6, 29: They that have done good [shall come forth] unto the resurrection of life. Matt. 25 36: I was an hungred and ye gave Me meat etc. In these and all similar passages in which works are praised in the Scriptures, it is necessary to understand not only outward works, but also the faith of the heart, because Scripture does not speak of hypocrisy, but of the righteousness of the heart with its fruits. Moreover, as often as mention is made of the Law and of works, we must know that Christ as Mediator is not to be excluded. For He is the end of the Law, and He Himself says, John 16, 5: Without Me ye can do nothing. According to this rule we have said above that all passages concerning works can be judged. Wherefore, when eternal life is granted to works, it is granted to those who have been justified, because no men except justified men, who are led by the Spirit of Christ, can do good works; and without faith and Christ, as Mediator, good works do not please, according to Heb. 11, 6: Without faith it is impossible to please God. When Paul says: He will render to every one according to his works, not only the outward work ought to be understood, but all righteousness or unrighteousness. So: Glory to him that worketh good, i.e., to the righteous. Ye gave Me meat, is cited as the fruit and witness of the righteousness of the heart and of faith, and therefore eternal life is rendered to righteousness. [There it must certainly be acknowledged that Christ means not only the works, but that He desires to have the heart, which He wishes to esteem God aright, and to believe correctly concerning Him, namely, that it is through mercy that it is pleasing to God. Therefore Christ teaches that everlasting life will be given the righteous, as Christ says: The righteous shall go into everlasting life.] In this way Scripture, at the same time with the fruits, embraces the righteousness of the heart. And it often names the fruits, in order that it may be better understood by the inexperienced, and to signify that a new life and regeneration, and not hypocrisy, are required. But regeneration occurs, by faith, in repentance.

No sane man can judge otherwise, neither do we here affect any idle subtilty, so as to separate the fruits from the righteousness of the heart; if the adversaries would only have conceded that the fruits please because of faith, and of Christ as Mediator, and that by themselves they are not worthy of grace and of eternal life. For in the doctrine of the adversaries we condemn this, that in such passages of Scripture, understood either in a philosophical or a Jewish manner, they abolish the righteousness of faith, and exclude Christ as Mediator. From these passages they infer that works merit grace, sometimes de congruo, and at other times ***de condigno***, namely, when love is added; i.e., that they justify, and because they are righteousness they are worthy of eternal life. This error manifestly abolishes the righteousness of faith, which believes that we have access to God for Christ's sake, not for the sake of our works, and that through Christ, as Priest and Mediator, we are led to the Father, and have a reconciled Father, as has been sufficiently said above. And this doctrine concerning the righteousness of faith is not to be neglected in the Church of Christ, because without it the office of Christ cannot be considered, and the doctrine of justification that is left is only a doctrine of the Law. But we should retain the Gospel, and the doctrine concerning the promise, granted for Christ's sake.

[We are here not seeking an unnecessary subtilty, but there is a great reason why we must have a reliable account as regards these questions. For as soon as we concede to the adversaries that works merit eternal life, they spin from this concession the awkward teaching that we are able to keep the Law of God, that we are not in need of mercy, that we are righteous before God, that is, accepted with God by our works, not for the sake of Christ, that we can also do works of supererogations namely, more than the Law requires. Thus the entire teaching concerning faith is suppressed. However, if there is to be and abide a Christian Church, the pure teaching concerning Christ, concerning the righteousness of faith, must surely be preserved. Therefore we must fight against these great pharisaical errors, in order that we redeem the name of Christ and the honor of the Gospel and of Christ, and preserve for Christian hearts a true, permanent, certain consolation. For how is it possible that a heart or conscience can obtain rest, or hope for salvation, when in afflictions and in the anguish of death our works in the judgment and sight of God utterly become dust, unless it becomes certain by faith that men are saved by mercy, for Christ's sake, and not for the sake of their works, their fulfilling of the Law? And, indeed, St. Laurentius, when placed on the gridiron, and being tortured for Christ's sake did not think that by this work he was perfectly and absolutely fulfilling the Law, that he was without sin, that he did not need Christ as Mediator and the mercy of God. He rested his case, indeed, with the prophet, who says: Enter not into judgment with Thy servant; for in Thy sight shall no man living be justified, Ps. 143, 2. Nor did St. Bernard boast that his works were worthy of eternal life, when he says: ***Perdite vixi***, I have led a sinful life, etc. But he boldly comforts himself, clings to the promise of grace, and believes that he has remission of sins and life eternal for Christ's sake, just as Psalm 32, 1 teaches: Blessed is he whose transgression is forgiven, whose sin is covered. And Paul says, Rom. 4, 6: David also describeth the blessedness of the man to whom God imputeth righteousness without works. Paul, then, says that he is blessed to whom righteousness is imputed through faith in Christ, even though he have not performed any good works. That is the true, permanent consolation, by which hearts and consciences can be confirmed and encouraged, namely that for Christ's sake, through faith, the remission of sins, righteousness, and life eternal are given us. Now, if passages which treat of works are understood in such a manner as to comprise faith, they are not opposed to our doctrine. And, indeed, it is necessary always to add faith, so as not to exclude Christ as Mediator. But the fulfilment of the Law follows faith; for the Holy Ghost is present, who renews life. Let this suffice concerning this article.]

We are not, therefore, on this topic contending with the adversaries concerning a small matter. We are not seeking out idle subtilties when we find fault with them for teaching that we merit eternal life by works, while that faith is omitted which apprehends Christ as Mediator. For of this faith which believes that for Christ's sake the Father is propitious to us there is not a syllable in the scholastics. Everywhere they hold that we are accepted and righteous because of our works, wrought either from reason, or certainly wrought by the inclination of that love concerning which they speak. And yet they have certain sayings, maxims, as it were, of the old writers, which they distort in interpreting. In the schools the boast is made that good works please on account of grace, and that confidence must be put in God's grace. Here they interpret grace as a habit by which we love God, as though, indeed, the ancients meant to say that we ought to trust in our love, of which we certainly experience how small and how impure it is. Although it is strange how they bid us trust in love, since they teach us that we are not able to know whether it be present. Why do they not here set forth the grace, the mercy of God toward us? And as often as mention is made of this, they ought to add faith. For the promise of God's mercy, reconciliation, and love towards us is not apprehended unless by faith. With this view they would be right in saying that we ought to trust in grace, that good works please because of grace, when faith apprehends grace. In the schools the boast is also made that our good works avail by virtue of Christ's passion. Well said! But why add nothing concerning faith? For Christ is a propitiation, as Paul, Rom. 3, 25, says, through faith. When timid consciences are comforted by faith, and are convinced that our sins have been blotted out by the death of Christ, and that God has been reconciled to us on account of Christ's suffering, then, indeed, the suffering of Christ profits us. If the doctrine concerning faith be omitted, it is said in vain that works avail by virtue of Christ's passion.

And very many other passages they corrupt in the schools because they do not teach the righteousness of faith and because they understand by faith merely a knowledge of the history or of dogmas, and do not understand by it that virtue which apprehends the promise of grace and of righteousness, and which quickens hearts in the terrors of sin and of death. When Paul says, Rom. 10, 10: With the heart man believeth unto righteousness, and with the mouth confession is made unto salvation, we think that the adversaries acknowledge here that confession justifies or saves, not ***ex opere operato***, but only on account of the faith of the heart. And Paul thus says that confession saves, in order to show what sort of faith obtains eternal life; namely, that which is firm and active. That faith, however, which does not manifest itself in confession is not firm. Thus other good works please on account of faith, as also the prayers of the Church ask that all things may be accepted for Christ's sake. They likewise ask all things for Christ's sake. For it is manifest that at the close of prayers this clause is always added: Through Christ, our Lord. Accordingly, we conclude that we are justified before God, are reconciled to God and regenerated by faith, which in repentance apprehends the promise of grace, and truly quickens the terrified mind, and is convinced that for Christ's sake God is reconciled and propitious to us. And through this faith, says Peter, 1 Ep. 1, 5, we are kept unto salvation ready to be revealed. The knowledge of this faith is necessary to Christians, and brings the most abundant consolation in all afflictions, and displays to us the office of Christ because those who deny that men are justified by faith, and deny that Christ is Mediator and Propitiator, deny the promise of grace and the Gospel. They teach only the doctrine either of reason or of the Law concerning justification. We have shown the origin of this case, so far as can here be done, and have explained the objections of the adversaries. Good men, indeed, will easily judge these things, if they will think, as often as a passage concerning love or works is cited, that the Law cannot be observed without Christ, and that we cannot be justified from the Law, but from the Gospel, that is, from the promise of the grace promised in Christ. And we hope that this discussion, although brief, will be profitable to good men for strengthening faith, and teaching and comforting conscience. For we know that those things which we have said are in harmony with the prophetic and apostolic Scriptures, with the holy Fathers, Ambrose, Augustine and very many others, and with the whole Church of Christ, which certainly confesses that Christ is Propitiator and Justifier.

Nor are we immediately to judge that the Roman Church agrees with everything that the Pope, or cardinals, or bishops, or some of the theologians, or monks approve. For it is manifest that to most of the pontiffs their own authority is of greater concern than the Gospel of Christ. And it has been ascertained that most of them are openly Epicureans. It is evident that theologians have mingled with Christian doctrine more of philosophy than was sufficient. Nor ought their influence to appear so great that it will never be lawful to dissent from their disputations, because at the same time many manifest errors are found among them, such as, that we are able from purely natural powers to love God above all things. This dogma, although it is manifestly false, has produced many other errors. For the Scriptures the holy Fathers, and the judgments of all the godly everywhere make reply. Therefore, even though Popes, or some theologians, and monks in the Church have taught us to seek remission of sins, grace, and righteousness through our own works, and to invent new forms of worship, which have obscured the office of Christ, and have made out of Christ not a Propitiator and Justifier, but only a Legislator, nevertheless the knowledge of Christ has always remained with some godly persons. Scripture, moreover, has predicted that the righteousness of faith would be obscured in this way by human traditions and the doctrine of works. Just as Paul often complains (cf. Gal. 4, 9; 5, 7; Col. 2, 8, 16 sq.; 1 Tim. 4, 2 sq., etc.) that there were even at that time those who, instead of the righteousness of faith, taught that men were reconciled to God and justified by their own works and own acts of worship, and not by faith for Christ's sake; because men judge by nature that God ought to be appeased by works. Nor does reason see a righteousness other than the righteousness of the Law, understood in a civil sense. Accordingly, there have always existed in the world some who have taught this carnal righteousness alone to the exclusion of the righteousness of faith; and such teachers will also always exist. The same happened among the people of Israel. The greater part of the people thought that they merited remission of sins by their works they accumulated sacrifices and acts of worship. On the contrary, the prophets, in condemnation of this opinion, taught the righteousness of faith. And the occurrences among the people of Israel are illustrations of those things which were to occur in the Church. Therefore, let the multitude of the adversaries, who condemn our doctrine, not disturb godly minds. For their spirit can easily be judged, because in some articles they have condemned truth that is so clear and manifest that their godlessness appears openly. For the bull of Leo X condemned a very necessary article, which all Christians should hold and believe, namely, that we ought to trust that we have been absolved not because of our contrition, but because of Christ's word, Matt. 16, 19: Whatsoever thou shalt bind, etc. And now, in this assembly, the authors of the **Confutation** have in clear words condemned this, namely, that we have said that faith is a part of repentance, by which we obtain remission of sins, and overcome the terrors of sin, and conscience is rendered pacified. Who, however, does not see that this article that by faith we obtain the remission of sins, is most true, most certain, and especially necessary to all Christians? Who to all posterity, hearing that such a doctrine has been condemned, will judge that the authors of this condemnation had any knowledge of Christ?

And concerning their spirit, a conjecture can be made from the unheard-of cruelty, which it is evident that they have hitherto exercised towards most good men. And in this assembly we have heard that a reverend father, when opinions concerning our Confession were expressed, said in the senate of the Empire that no plan seemed to him better than to make a reply written in blood to the Confession which we had presented written in ink. What more cruel would Phalaris say? Therefore some princes also have judged this expression unworthy to be spoken in such a meeting. Wherefore, although the adversaries claim for themselves the name of the Church, nevertheless we know that the Church of Christ is with those who teach the Gospel of Christ, not with those who defend wicked opinions contrary to the Gospel, as the Lord says, John 10, 21: My sheep hear My voice. And Augustine says: The question is, Where is the Church! What, therefore, are we to do? Are we to seek it in our own words or in the words of its Head our Lord Jesus Christ? I think that we ought to seek it in the words of Him who is Truth, and who knows His own body best. Hence the judgments of our adversaries will not disturb us, since they defend human opinions contrary to the Gospel, contrary to the authority of the holy Fathers, who have written in the Church, and contrary to the testimonies of godly minds.

Part 11

Articles VII and VIII: *Of the Church.*

The Seventh Article of our Confession, in which we said that the Church is the congregation of saints, they have condemned and have added a long disquisition, that the wicked are not to be separated from the Church, since John has compared the Church to a threshing-floor on which wheat and chaff are heaped together, Matt. 3, 12, and Christ has compared it to a net in which there are both good and bad fishes, Matt. 13, 47. It is, verily, a true saying, namely, that there is no remedy against the attacks of the slanderer. Nothing can be spoken with such care that it can escape detraction. For this reason we have added the Eighth Article, lest any one might think that we separate the wicked and hypocrites from the outward fellowship of the Church, or that we deny efficacy to Sacraments administered by hypocrites or wicked men. Therefore there is no need here of a long defense against this slander. The Eighth Article is sufficient to exculpate us. For we grant that in this life hypocrites and wicked men have been mingled with the Church, and that they are members of the Church according to the outward fellowship of the signs of the Church, i.e., of Word, profession, and Sacraments, especially if they have not been excommunicated. Neither are the Sacraments without efficacy for the reason that they are administered by wicked men; yea, we can even be right in using the Sacraments administered by wicked men. For Paul also predicts, 2 Thess. 2, 4, that Antichrist will sit in the temple of God, i.e., he will rule and bear office in the Church. But the Church is not only the fellowship of outward objects and rites, as other governments, but it is originally a fellowship of faith and of the Holy Ghost in hearts. [The Christian Church consists not alone in fellowship of outward signs, but it consists especially in inward communion of eternal blessings in the heart, as of the Holy Ghost, of faith, of the fear and love of God]; which fellowship nevertheless has outward marks so that it can be recognized, namely, the pure doctrine of the Gospel, and the administration of the Sacraments in accordance with the Gospel of Christ. [Namely, where God's Word is pure, and the Sacraments are administered in conformity with the same, there certainly is the Church, and there are Christians.] And this Church alone is called the body of Christ, which Christ renews [Christ is its Head, and] sanctifies and governs by His Spirit, as Paul testifies, Eph. 1, 22 sq., when he says: And gave Him to be the Head over all things to the Church, which is His body, the fulness of Him that filleth all in all. Wherefore, those in whom Christ does not act [through His Spirit] are not the members of Christ. This, too, the adversaries acknowledge, namely, that the wicked are dead members of the Church. Therefore we wonder why they have found fault with our description [our conclusion concerning Church] which speaks of living members. Neither have we said anything new. Paul has defined the Church precisely in the same way, Eph. 6, 25 f., that it should be cleansed in order to be holy. And he adds the outward marks, the Word and Sacraments. For he says thus: Christ also loved the Church, and gave himself for it, that He might sanctify and cleanse it with the washing of water by the Word, that He might present it to Himself a glorious Church, not having spot, or wrinkle, or any such thing, but that it should be holy and without blemish. In the Confession we have presented this sentence almost in the very words. Thus also the Church is defined by the article in the Creed which teaches us to believe that there is a holy Catholic Church. The wicked indeed are not a holy Church. And that which follows, namely, the communion of saints, seems to be added in order to explain what the Church signifies, namely, the congregation of saints, who have with each other the fellowship of the same Gospel or doctrine [who confess one Gospel, have the same knowledge of Christ] and of the same Holy Ghost, who renews, sanctifies, and governs their hearts.

And this article has been presented for a necessary reason. [The article of the Church Catholic or Universal, which is gathered together from every nation under the sun, is very comforting and highly necessary.] We see the infinite dangers which threaten the destruction of the Church. In the Church itself, infinite is the multitude of the wicked who oppress it [despise, bitterly hate, and most violently persecute the Word, as, e.g., the Turks, Mohammedans, other tyrants, heretics, etc. For this reason the true teaching and the Church are often so utterly suppressed and disappear, as if there were no Church which has happened under the papacy, it often seems that the Church has completely perished]. Therefore, in order that we may not despair, but may know that the Church will nevertheless remain [until the end of the world], likewise that we may know that, however great the multitude of the wicked is, yet the Church [which is Christ's bride] exists, and that Christ affords those gifts which He has promised to the Church, to forgive sins, to hear prayer, to give the Holy Ghost, this article in the Creed presents us these consolations. And it says church Catholic, in order that we may not understand the Church to be an outward government of certain nations [that the Church is like any other external polity, bound to this or that land, kingdom, or nation, as the Pope of Rome will say], but rather men scattered throughout the whole world [here and there in the world, from the rising to the setting of the sun], who agree concerning the Gospel, and have the same Christ, the same Holy Ghost, and the same Sacraments, whether they have the same or different human traditions. And the gloss upon the Decrees says that the Church in its wide sense embraces good and evil; likewise, that the wicked are in the Church only in name, not in fact; but that the good are in the Church both in fact and in name. And to this effect there are many passages in the Fathers. For Jerome says: The sinner, therefore, who Has been soiled with any blotch cannot be called a member of the Church of Christ, neither can he be said to be subject to Christ.

Although, therefore, hypocrites and wicked men are members of this true Church according to outward rites [titles and offices], yet when the Church is defined, it is necessary to define that which is the living body of Christ, and which is in name and in fact the Church [which is called the body of Christ, and has fellowship not alone in outward signs, but has gifts in the heart, namely, the Holy Ghost and faith]. And for this there are many reasons. For it is necessary to understand what it is that principally makes us members, and that, living members, of the Church. If we will define the Church only as an outward polity of the good and wicked, men will not understand that the kingdom of Christ is righteousness of heart and the gift of the Holy Ghost [that the kingdom of Christ is spiritual, as nevertheless it is, that therein Christ inwardly rules, strengthens, and comforts hearts, and imparts the Holy Ghost and various spiritual gifts], but they will judge that it is only the outward observance of certain forms of worship and rites. Likewise, what difference will there be between the people of the Law and the Church if the Church is an outward polity? But Paul distinguishes the Church from the people of the Law thus, that the Church is a spiritual people, i.e., that it has been distinguished from the heathen not by civil rites [not in the polity and civil affairs], but that it is the true people of God, regenerated by the Holy Ghost. Among the people of the Law, apart from the promise of Christ, also the carnal seed [all those who by nature were born Jews and Abraham's seed] had promises concerning corporeal things, of government, etc. And because of these even the wicked among them were called the people of God, because God had separated this carnal seed from other nations by certain outward ordinances and promises; and yet, these wicked persons did not please God. But the Gospel [which is preached in the Church] brings not merely the shadow of eternal things, but the eternal things themselves, the Holy Ghost and righteousness, by which we are righteous before God. [But every true Christian is even here upon earth partaker of eternal blessings, even of eternal comfort, of eternal life, and of the Holy Ghost, and of righteousness which is from God, until he will be completely saved in the world to come.]

Therefore, only those are the people, according to the Gospel, who receive this promise of the Spirit. Besides, the Church is the kingdom of Christ, distinguished from the kingdom of the devil. It is certain, however, that the wicked are in the power of the devil, and members of the kingdom of the devil, as Paul teaches, Eph. 2, 2, when he says that the devil now worketh in the children of disobedience. And Christ says to the Pharisees, who certainly had outward fellowship with the Church, i.e., with the saints among the people of the Law (for they held office, sacrificed, and taught): Ye are of your father, the devil, John 8, 44. Therefore, the Church, which is truly the kingdom of Christ is properly the congregation of saints. For the wicked are ruled by the devil, and are captives of the devil; they are not ruled by the Spirit of Christ.

But what need is there of words in a manifest matter? [However, the adversaries contradict the plain truth.] If the Church, which is truly the kingdom of Christ, is distinguished from the kingdom of the devil, it follows necessarily that the wicked, since they are in the kingdom of the devil, are not the Church; although in this life, because the kingdom of Christ has not yet been revealed; they are mingled with the Church, and hold offices [as teachers, and other offices] in the Church. Neither are the wicked the kingdom of Christ, for the reason that the revelation has not yet been made. For that is always the kingdom which He quickens by His Spirit, whether it be revealed or be covered by the cross; just as He who has now been glorified is the same Christ who was before afflicted. And with this clearly agree the parables of Christ, who says, Matt. 13, 38, that the good seed are the children of the kingdom, but the tares are the children of the Wicked One. The field, He says, is the world, not the Church. Thus John [Matt. 3,12: He will throughly purge His floor, and gather His wheat into the garner; but He will burn up the chaff] speaks concerning the whole race of the Jews, and says that it will come to pass that the true Church will be separated from that people. Therefore, this passage is more against the adversaries than in favor of them, because it shows that the true and spiritual people is to be separated from the carnal people. Christ also speaks of the outward appearance of the Church when He says, Matt. 13, 47: The kingdom of heaven is like unto a net, likewise, to ten virgins; and He teaches that the Church has been covered by a multitude of evils, in order that this stumbling-block may not offend the pious; likewise, in order that we may know that the Word and Sacraments are efficacious even when administered by the wicked. And meanwhile He teaches that these godless men, although they have the fellowship of outward signs, are nevertheless not the true kingdom of Christ and members of Christ; for they are members of the kingdom of the devil. Neither, indeed, are we dreaming of a Platonic state, as some wickedly charge, but we say that this Church exists, namely, the truly believing and righteous men scattered throughout the whole world [We are speaking not of an imaginary Church, which is to be found nowhere; but we say and know certainly that this Church, wherein saints live, is and abides truly upon earth; namely, that some of God's children are here and there in all the world, in various kingdoms, islands, lands, and cities, from the rising of the sun to its setting, who have truly learned to know Christ and His Gospel.] And we add the marks: the pure doctrine of the Gospel [the ministry or the Gospel] and the Sacraments. And this Church is properly the pillar of the truth, 1 Tim. 3, 15. For it retains the pure Gospel, and, as Paul says, 1 Cor. 3, 11 [: "Other foundation can no man lay than that is laid, which is Jesus Christ"], the foundation, i.e., the true knowledge of Christ and faith. Although among these [in the body which is built upon the true foundation, i.e., upon Christ and faith] there are also many weak persons, who build upon the foundation stubble that will perish, i.e., certain unprofitable opinions [some human thoughts and opinions], which, nevertheless, because they do not overthrow the foundation are both forgiven them and also corrected. And the writings of the holy Fathers testify that sometimes even they built stubble upon the foundation, but that this did not overthrow their faith. But most of those errors which our adversaries defend, overthrow faith, as, their condemnation of the article concerning the remission of sins, in which we say that the remission of sins is received by faith. Likewise it is a manifest and pernicious error when the adversaries teach that men merit the remission of sins by love to God, prior to grace. [In the place of Christ they set up their works, orders, masses, just as the Jews, the heathen, and the Turks intend to be saved by their works.] For this also is to remove "the foundation," i.e., Christ. Likewise, what need will there be of faith if the Sacraments justify *ex opere operato*, without a good disposition on the part of the one using them? [without faith. Now, a person that does not regard faith as necessary has already lost Christ. Again, they set up the worship of saints, call upon them instead of Christ, the Mediator, etc.] But just as the Church has the promise that it will always have the Holy Ghost, so it has also the threatenings that there will be wicked teachers and wolves. But that is the Church in the proper sense which has the Holy Ghost. Although wolves and wicked teachers become rampant [rage and do injury] in the Church, yet they are not properly the kingdom of Christ. Just as Lyra also testifies, when he says: The Church does not consist of men with respect to power, or ecclesiastical or secular dignity, because many princes and archbishops and others of lower rank have been found to have apostatized from the faith. Therefore, the Church consists of those persons in whom there is a true knowledge and confession of faith and truth. What else have we said in our Confession than what Lyra here says [in terms so clear that he could not have spoken more clearly]?

But the adversaries perhaps require [a new Roman definition], that the Church be defined thus, namely, that it is the supreme outward monarchy of the whole world, in which the Roman pontiff necessarily has unquestioned power, which no one is permitted to dispute or censure [no matter whether he uses it rightly, or misuses it], to frame articles of faith; to abolish, according to his pleasure, the Scriptures [to pervert and interpret them contrary to all divine law, contrary to his own decretals, contrary to all imperial rights, as often, to as great an extent, and whenever it pleases him, to sell indulgences and dispensations for money]; to appoint rites of worship and sacrifices; likewise, to frame such laws as he may wish, and to dispense and exempt from whatever laws he may wish, divine, canonical, or civil; and that from him [as from the vicegerent of Christ] the Emperor and all kings receive, according to the command of Christ, the power and right to hold their kingdoms, from whom, since the Father has subjected all things to Him, it must be understood, this right was transferred to the Pope; therefore the Pope must necessarily be [a God on earth, the supreme Majesty,] lord of the whole world, of all the kingdoms of the world, of all things private and public, and must have absolute power in temporal and spiritual things, and both swords, the spiritual and temporal Besides this definition, not of the Church of Christ but of the papal kingdom, has as its authors not only the canonists, but also Daniel 11 36 ff. [Daniel, the prophet, represents Antichrist in this way.]

Now, if we would define the Church in this way [that it is such pomp, as is exhibited in the Pope's rule], we would perhaps have fairer judges. For there are many things extant written extravagantly and wickedly concerning the power of the Pope of Rome on account of which no one has ever been arraigned. We alone are blamed, because we proclaim the beneficence of Christ [and write and preach the clear word and teaching of the apostles], that by faith in Christ we obtain remission of sins, and not by [hypocrisy or innumerable] rites of worship devised by the Pope. Moreover, Christ, the prophets, and the apostles define the Church of Christ far otherwise than as the papal kingdom. Neither must we transfer to the Popes what belongs to the true Church, namely, that they are pillars of the truth, that they do not err. For how many of them care for the Gospel or judge that it [one little page, one letter of it] is worth being read? Many [in Italy and elsewhere] even publicly ridicule all religions, or, if they approve anything, they approve such things only as are in harmony with human reason, and regard the rest fabulous and like the tragedies of the poets. Wherefore we hold, according Scriptures, that the Church, properly so called, is the congregation of saints [of those here and there in the world], who truly believe the Gospel of Christ, and have the Holy Ghost.

And yet we confess that in this life many hypocrites and wicked men, mingled with these, have the fellowship of outward signs who are members of the Church according to this fellowship of outward signs, and accordingly bear offices in the Church [preach, administer the Sacraments, and bear the title and name of Christians]. Neither does the fact that the sacraments are administered by the unworthy detract from their efficacy, because, on account of the call of the Church, they represent the person of Christ, and do not represent their own persons, as Christ testifies, Luke 10, 16: He that heareth you heareth Me. [Thus even Judas was sent to preach.] When they offer the Word of God, when they offer the Sacraments, they offer them in the stead and place of Christ. Those words of Christ teach us not to be offended by the unworthiness of the ministers.

But concerning this matter we have spoken with sufficient clearness in the Confession that we condemn the Donatists and Wyclifites, who thought that men sinned when they received the sacraments from the unworthy in the Church. These things seem, for the present, to be sufficient for the defense of the description of the Church which we have presented. Neither do we see how, when the Church, properly so called, is named the body of Christ, it should be described otherwise than we have described it. For it is evident that the wicked belong to the kingdom and body of the devil, who impels and holds captive the wicked. These things are clearer than the light of noonday, however, if the adversaries still continue to pervert them, we will not hesitate to reply at greater length.

The adversaries condemn also the part of the Seventh Article in which we said that "to the unity of the Church it is sufficient to agree concerning the doctrine of the Gospel and the administration of the Sacraments; nor is it necessary that human traditions rites or ceremonies instituted by men should be alike everywhere." Here they distinguish between universal and particular rites, and approve our article if it be understood concerning particular rites, they do not receive it concerning universal rites. [That is a fine clumsy distinction!] We do not sufficiently understand what the adversaries mean. We are speaking of true, i.e., of spiritual unity [we say that those are one harmonious Church who believe in one Christ, who have one Gospel, one Spirit, one faith, the same Sacraments; and we are speaking, therefore, of spiritual unity], without which faith in the heart, or righteousness of heart before God cannot exist. For this we say that similarity of human rites, whether universal or particular, is not necessary, because the righteousness of faith is not a righteousness bound to certain traditions [outward ceremonies of human ordinances] as the righteousness of the Law was bound to the Mosaic ceremonies, because this righteousness of the heart is a matter that quickens the heart. To this quickening, human traditions, whether they be universal or particular, contribute nothing; neither are they effects of the Holy Ghost, as are chastity, patience, the fear of God, love to one's neighbor, and the works of love.

Neither were the reasons trifling why we presented this article. For it is evident that many [great errors and] foolish opinions concerning traditions had crept into the Church. Some thought that human traditions were necessary services for meriting justification [that without such human ordinances Christian holiness and faith are of no avail before God; also that no one can be a Christian unless he observe such traditions, although they are nothing but an outward regulation]. And afterwards they disputed how it came to pass that God was worshiped with such variety, as though, indeed, these observances were acts of worship, and not rather outward and political ordinances, pertaining in no respect to righteousness of heart or the worship of God, which vary, according to the circumstances, for certain probable reasons, sometimes in one way and at other times in another [as in worldly governments one state has customs different from another]. Likewise some Churches have excommunicated others because of such traditions, as the observance of Easter, pictures, and the like. Hence the ignorant have supposed that faith, or the righteousness of the heart before God, cannot exist [and that no one can be a Christian] without these observances. For many foolish writings of the Summists and of others concerning this matter are extant.

But just as the dissimilar length of day and night does not injure the unity of the Church, so we believe that the true unity of the Church is not injured by dissimilar rites instituted by men; although it is pleasing to us that, for the sake of tranquillity [unity and good order], universal rites be observed just as also in the churches we willingly observe the order of the Mass, the Lord's Day, and other more eminent festival days. And with a very grateful mind we embrace the profitable and ancient ordinances, especially since they contain a discipline by which it is profitable to educate and train the people and those who are ignorant [the young people]. But now we are not discussing the question whether it be of advantage to observe them on account of peace or bodily profit. Another matter is treated of. For the question at issue is, whether the observances of human traditions are acts of worship necessary for righteousness before God. This is the point to be judged in this controversy and when this is decided, it can afterwards be judged whether to the true unity of the Church it is necessary that human traditions should everywhere be alike. For if human traditions be not acts of worship necessary for righteousness before God, it follows that also they can be righteous and be the sons of God who have not the traditions which have been received elsewhere. F.i., if the style of German clothing is not worship of God, necessary for righteousness before God, it follows that men can be righteous and sons of God and the Church of Christ, even though they use a costume that is not German, but French.

Paul clearly teaches this to the Colossians, 2,16.17: Let no man, therefore, judge you in meat, or in drink, or in respect of an holy-day, or of the new moon, or of the Sabbath days, which are a shadow of things to come; but the body is of Christ. Likewise, v. 20 sqq.: If ye be dead with Christ from the rudiments of the world, why, as though living in the world, are ye subject to ordinances (touch not; taste not; handle not; which are to perish with the using), after the commandments and doctrines of men? Which things have, indeed, a show of wisdom in will-worship and humility. For the meaning is: Since righteousness of the heart is a spiritual matter, quickening hearts, and it is evident that human traditions do not quicken hearts and are not effects of the Holy Ghost, as are love to one's neighbor, chastity, etc., and are not instruments through which God moves hearts to believe, as are the divinely given Word and Sacraments, but are usages with regard to matters that pertain in no respect to the heart, which perish with the using, we must not believe that they are necessary for righteousness before God. [They are nothing eternal, hence, they do not procure eternal life, but are an external bodily discipline, which does not change the heart.] And to the same effect he says, Rom. 14, 17: The kingdom of God is not meat and drink, but righteousness and peace and joy in the Holy Ghost. But there is no need to cite many testimonies, since they are everywhere obvious in the Scriptures, and in our Confession we have brought together very many of them, in the latter articles. And the point to be decided in this controversy must be repeated after a while, namely, whether human traditions be acts of worship necessary for righteousness before God. There we will discuss this matter more fully.

The adversaries say that universal traditions are to be observed because they are supposed to have been handed down by the apostles. What religious men they are! They wish that the rites derived from the apostles be retained, they do not wish the doctrine of the apostles to be retained. They must judge concerning these rites just as the apostles themselves judge in their writings. For the apostles did not wish us to believe that through such rites we are justified, that such rites are necessary for righteousness before God. The apostles did not wish to impose such a burden upon consciences; they did not wish to place righteousness and sin in the observance of days, food, and the like. Yea, Paul calls such opinions doctrines of devils, 1 Tim. 4, 1. Therefore the will and advice of the apostles ought to be derived from their writings; it is not enough to mention their example. They observed certain days, not because this observance was necessary for justification, but in order that the people might know at what time they should assemble. They observed also certain other rites and orders of lessons whenever they assembled. The people [In the beginning of the Church the Jews who had become Christians] retained also from the customs of the Fathers [from their Jewish festivals and ceremonies], as is commonly the case, certain things which, being somewhat changed, the apostles adapted to the history of the Gospel as the Passover, Pentecost, so that not only by teaching, but also through these examples they might hand down to posterity the memory of the most important subjects. But if these things were handed down as necessary for justification, why afterwards did the bishops change many things in these very matters? For, if they were matters of divine right, it was not lawful to change them by human authority. Before the Synod of Nice some observed Easter at one time and others at another time. Neither did this want of uniformity injure faith. Afterward the plan was adopted by which our Passover [Easter] did not fall at the same time as that of the Jewish Passover. But the apostles had commanded the Churches to observe the Passover with the brethren who had been converted from Judaism. Therefore, after the Synod of Nice, certain nations tenaciously held to the custom of observing the Jewish time. But the apostles, by this decree, did not wish to impose necessity upon the Churches, the words of the decree testify. For it bids no one to be troubled, even though his brethren, in observing Easter, do not compute the time aright. The words of the decree are extant in Epiphanius: Do not calculate, but celebrate it whenever your brethren of the circumcision do; celebrate it at the same time with them, and even though they may have erred, let not this be a care to you.. Epiphanius writes that these are the words of the apostles presented in a decree concerning Easter, in which the discreet reader can easily judge that the apostles wished to free the people from the foolish opinion of a fixed time, when they prohibit them from being troubled, even though a mistake should be made in the computation. Some, moreover in the East, who were called, from the author of the dogma, Audians, contended, on account of this decree of the apostles, that the Passover should be observed with the Jews. Epiphanius, in refuting them, praises the decree and says that it contains nothing which deviates from the faith or rule of the Church, and blames the Audians because they do not understand aright the expression, and interprets it in the sense in which we interpret it because the apostles did not consider it of any importance at what time the Passover should be observed, but because prominent brethren had been converted from the Jews who observed their custom, and, for the sake of harmony, wished the rest to follow their example And the apostles wisely admonished the reader neither to remove the liberty of the Gospel, nor to impose necessity upon consciences, because they add that they should not be troubled even though there should be an error in making the computation.

Many things of this class can be gathered from the histories, in which it appears that a want of uniformity in human observances does not injure the unity of faith [separate no one from the universal Christian Church]. Although, what need is there of discussion? The adversaries do not at all understand what the righteousness of faith is, what the kingdom of Christ is, when they judge that uniformity of observances in food, days, clothing, and the like, which do not have the command of God, is necessary. But look at the religious men, our adversaries. For the unity of the Church they require uniform human observances, although they themselves have changed the ordinance of Christ in the use of the Supper, which certainly was a universal ordinance before. But if universal ordinances are so necessary, why do they themselves change the ordinance of Christ's Supper, which is not human, but divine? But concerning this entire controversy we shall have to speak at different times below.

The entire Eighth Article has been approved, in which we confess that hypocrites and wicked persons have been mingled with the Church, and that the Sacraments are efficacious even though dispensed by wicked ministers, because the ministers act in the place of Christ, and do not represent their own persons, according to Luke 10, 16: He that heareth you heareth Me. Impious teachers are to be deserted [are not to be received or heard], because these do not act any longer in the place of Christ, but are antichrists. And Christ says Matt. 7, 15: Beware of false prophets. And Paul, Gal. 1, 9: If any man preach any other gospel unto you, let him be accursed.

Moreover, Christ has warned us in His parables concerning the Church, that when offended by the private vices, whether of priests or people, we should not excite schisms, as the Donatists have wickedly done. As to those, however, who have excited schisms, because they denied that priests are permitted to hold possessions and property, we hold that they are altogether seditious. For to hold property is a civil ordinance. It is lawful, however, for Christians to use civil ordinances, just as they use the air, the light, food, drink. For as this order of the world and fixed movements of the heavenly bodies are truly God's ordinances and these are preserved by God, so lawful governments are truly God's ordinances, and are preserved and defended by God against the devil.

Part 12

Article IX: *Of Baptism.*

The Ninth Article has been approved, in which we confess that Baptism is necessary to salvation, and that children are to be baptized, and that the baptism of children is not in vain, but is necessary and effectual to salvation. And since the Gospel is taught among us purely and diligently, by God's favor we receive also from it this fruit, that in our Churches no Anabaptists have arisen [have not gained ground in our Churches], because the people have been fortified by God's Word against the wicked and seditious faction of these robbers. And as we condemn quite a number of other errors of the Anabaptists, we condemn this also, that they dispute that the baptism of little children is unprofitable. For it is very certain that the promise of salvation pertains also to little children [that the divine promises of grace and of the Holy Ghost belong not alone to the old, but also to children]. It does not, however, pertain to those who are outside of Christ's Church where there is neither Word nor Sacraments because the kingdom of Christ exists only with the Word and Sacraments. Therefore it is necessary to baptize little children, that the promise of salvation may be applied to them, according to Christ's command, Matt. 28, 19: Baptize all nations. Just as here salvation is offered to all, so Baptism is offered to all, to men, women, children, infants. It clearly follows, therefore, that infants are to be baptized, because with Baptism salvation [the universal grace and treasure of the Gospel] is offered. Secondly, it is manifest that God approves of the baptism of little children. Therefore the Anabaptists, who condemn the baptism of little children, believe wickedly. That God, however, approves of the baptism of little children is shown--by this, namely, that God gives the Holy

Ghost to those thus baptized [to many who have been baptized in childhood]. For if this baptism would be in vain, the Holy Ghost would be given to none, none would be saved, and finally there would be no Church. [For there have been many holy men in the Church who have not been baptized otherwise.] This reason, even taken alone, can sufficiently establish good and godly minds against the godless and fanatical opinions of the Anabaptists.

Part 13

Article X: *Of the Holy Supper.*

The Tenth Article has been approved, in which we confess that we believe, that in the Lord's Supper the body and blood of Christ are truly and substantially present, and are truly tendered, with those things which are seen, bread and wine to those who receive the Sacrament. This belief we constantly defend as the subject has been carefully examined and considered. For since Paul says, 1 Cor. 10, 16, that the bread is the communion of the Lord's body, etc., it would follow, if the Lord's body were not truly present, that the bread is not a communion of the body, but only of the spirit of Christ. And we have ascertained that not only the Roman Church affirms the bodily presence of Christ, but the Greek Church also both now believes, and formerly believed, the same. For the canon of the Mass among them testifies to this, in which the priest clearly prays that the bread may be changed and become the very body of Christ. And Vulgarius, who seems to us to be not a silly writer, says distinctly that bread is not a mere figure, but is truly changed into flesh. And there is a long exposition of Cyril on John 15, in which he teaches that Christ is corporeally offered us in the Supper. For he says thus: Nevertheless, we do not deny that we are joined spiritually to Christ by true faith and sincere love. But that we have no mode of connection with Him, according to the flesh, this indeed we entirely deny. And this, we say, is altogether foreign to the divine Scriptures. For who has doubted that Christ is in this manner a vine, and we the branches, deriving thence life for ourselves? Hear Paul saying 1 Cor. 10, 17; Rom. 12, 5; Gal. 3, 28: We are all one body in Christ; although we are many, we are, nevertheless, one in Him; for we are all partakers of that one bread. Does he perhaps think that the virtue of the mystical benediction is unknown to us? Since this is in us, does it not also, by the communication of Christ's flesh, cause Christ to dwell in us bodily? And a little after: Whence we must consider that Christ is in us not only according to the habit, which we call love, but also by natural participation, etc. We have cited these testimonies, not to undertake a discussion here concerning this subject, for His Imperial Majesty does not disapprove of this article, but in order that all who may read them may the more clearly perceive that we defend the doctrine received in the entire Church, that in the Lord's Supper the body and blood of Christ are truly and substantially present, and are truly tendered with those things which are seen, bread and wine. And we speak of the presence of the living Christ [living body]; for we know that death hath no more dominion over Him, Rom. 6, 9.

Part 14

Article XI: *Of Confession.*

The Eleventh Article, Of Retaining Absolutism in the Church, is approved. But they add a correction in reference to confession, namely, that the regulation headed, *Omnis Utriusque*, be observed, and that both annual confession be made, and, although all sins cannot be enumerated, nevertheless diligence be employed in order that they be recollected, and those which can be recalled be recounted. Concerning this entire article, we will speak at greater length after a while, when we will explain our entire opinion concerning repentance. It is well known that we have so elucidated and extolled [that we have preached, written, and taught in a manner so Christian, correct, and pure] the benefit of absolution and the power of the keys that many distressed consciences have derived consolation from our doctrine, after they heard that it is the command of God, nay, rather the very voice of the Gospel, that we should believe the absolution, and regard it as certain that the remission of sins is freely granted us for Christ's sake, and that we should believe that by this faith we are truly reconciled to God [as though we heard a voice from heaven]. This belief has encouraged many godly minds, and, in the beginning, brought Luther the highest commendation from all good men, since it shows consciences sure and firm consolation because previously the entire power of absolution [entire necessary doctrine of repentance] had been kept suppressed by doctrines concerning works, since the sophists and monks taught nothing of faith and free remission [but pointed men to their own works, from which nothing but despair enters alarmed consciences].

But with respect to the time, certainly most men in our churches use the Sacraments, absolution and the Lord's Supper, frequently in a year. And those who teach of the worth and fruits of the Sacraments speak in such a manner as to invite the people to use the Sacraments frequently. For concerning this subject there are many things extant written by our theologians in such a manner that the adversaries, if they are good men, will undoubtedly approve and praise them. Excommunication is also pronounced against the openly wicked [those who live in manifest vices, fornication, adultery, etc.] and the despisers of the Sacraments. These things are thus done both according to the Gospel and according to the old canons. But a fixed time is not prescribed, because all are not ready in like manner at the same time. Yea, if all are to come at the same time, they cannot be heard and instructed in order [so diligently]. And the old canons and Fathers do not appoint a fixed time. The canon speaks only thus: If any enter the Church and be found never to commune, let them be admonished that, if they do not commune, they come to repentance. If they commune [if they wish to be regarded as Christians], let them not be expelled; if they fail to do so, let them be excommunicated. Christ [Paul] says, I Cor. 11, 29, that those who eat unworthily eat judgment to themselves. The pastors, accordingly, do not compel those who are not qualified to use the Sacraments.

Concerning the enumeration of sins in confession, men are taught in such a way as not to ensnare their consciences. Although it is of advantage to accustom inexperienced men to enumerate some things [which worry them], in order that they may be the more readily taught, yet we are now discussing what is necessary according to divine Law. Therefore, the adversaries ought not to cite for us the regulation *Omnis Utriusque*, which is not unknown to us, but they ought to show from the divine Law that an enumeration of sins is necessary for obtaining their remission. The entire Church, throughout all Europe, knows what sort of snares this point of the regulation, which commands that all sins be confessed, has cast upon consciences. Neither has the text by itself as much disadvantage as was afterwards added by the Summists, who collect the circumstances of the sins. What labyrinths were there! How great a torture for the best minds! For the licentious and profane were in no way moved by these instruments of terror. Afterwards what tragedies [what jealousy and hatred] did the questions concerning one's own priest excite among the pastors and brethren [monks of various orders], who then were by no means brethren when they were warring concerning jurisdiction of confessions!

[for all brotherliness, all friendship, ceased, when the question was concerning authority and confessor's fees.] We, therefore, believe that, according to divine Law, the enumeration of sins is not necessary. This also is pleasing to Panormitanus and very many other learned jurisconsults. Nor do we wish to impose necessity upon the consciences of our people by the regulation **Omnis Utriusque**, of which we judge, just as of other human traditions, that they are not acts of worship necessary for justification. And this regulation commands an impossible matter, that we should confess all sins. It is evident, however, that most sins we neither remember nor understand [nor do we indeed even see the greatest sins], according to Ps. 19, 13: Who can understand his errors?

If the pastors are good men, they will know how far it is of advantage to examine [the young and otherwise] inexperienced persons but we do not wish to sanction the torture [the tyranny of consciences] of the Summists, which notwithstanding would have been less intolerable if they had added one word concerning faith, which comforts and encourages consciences. Now, concerning this faith which obtains the remission of sins, there is not a syllable in so great a mass of regulations, glosses, summaries, books of confession. Christ is nowhere read there. [Nobody will there read a word by which he could learn to know Christ, or what Christ is.] Only the lists of sins are read [to the end of gathering and accumulating sins, and this would be of some value if they understood those sins which God regards as such]. And the greater part is occupied with sins against human traditions, and this is most vain. This doctrine has forced to despair many godly minds, which were not able to find rest, because they believed that by divine Law an enumeration was necessary, and yet they experienced that it was impossible. But other faults of no less moment inhere in the doctrine of the adversaries concerning repentance, which we will now recount.

Part 15

Article XII (V): *Of Repentance.*

In the Twelfth Article they approve of the first part, in which we set forth that such as have fallen after baptism may obtain remission of sins at whatever time, and as often as they are converted. They condemn the second part, in which we say that the parts of repentance are contrition and faith [a penitent, contrite heart, and faith, namely that I receive the forgiveness of sins through Christ]. [Hear, now, what it is that the adversaries deny.] They [without shame] deny that faith is the second part of repentance. What are we to do here, O Charles, thou most invincible Emperor? The very voice of the Gospel is this, that by faith we obtain the remission of sins. [This word is not our word but the voice and word of Jesus Christ, our Savior.] This voice of the Gospel these writers of the *Confutation* condemn. We, therefore, can in no way assent to the *Confutation*. We cannot condemn the voice of the Gospel, so salutary and abounding in consolation. What else is the denial that by faith we obtain remission of sins than to treat the blood and death of Christ with scorn? We therefore beseech thee, O Charles most invincible Emperor, patiently and diligently to hear and examine this most important subject, which contains the chief topic of the Gospel, and the true knowledge of Christ, and the true worship of God [these great, most exalted and important matters which concern our own souls and consciences yea, also the entire faith of Christians, the entire Gospel, the knowledge of Christ, and what is highest and greatest, not only in this perishable, but also in the future life: the everlasting welfare or perdition of us all before God]. For all good men will ascertain that especially on this subject we have taught things that are true, godly, salutary, and necessary for the whole

Church of Christ [things of the greatest significance to all pious hearts in the entire Christian Church on which their whole salvation and welfare depends, and without instruction on which there can be or remain no ministry, no Christian Church]. They will ascertain from the writings of our theologians that very much light has been added to the Gospel, and many pernicious errors have been corrected, by which, through the opinions of the scholastics and canonists, the doctrine of repentance was previously covered.

Before we come to the defense of our position, we must say this first: All good men of all ranks, and also of the theological rank undoubtedly confess that before the writings of Luther appeared, the doctrine of repentance was very much confused. The books of the Sententiaries are extant, in which there are innumerable questions which no theologians were ever able to explain satisfactorily. The people were able neither to comprehend the sum of the matter, nor to see what things especially were required in repentance, where peace of conscience was to be sought for. Let any one of the adversaries come and tell us when remission of sins takes place. O good God, what darkness there is! They doubt whether it is in attrition or in contrition that remission of sins occurs. And if it occurs on account of contrition, what need is there of absolution, what does the power of the keys effect, if sins have been already remitted? Here, indeed, they also labor much more, and wickedly detract from the power of the keys. Some dream that by the power of the keys guilt is not remitted, but that eternal punishments are changed into temporal. Thus the most salutary power would be the ministry, not of life and the Spirit, but only of wrath and punishments. Others, namely, the more cautious imagine that by the power of the keys sins are remitted before the Church and not before God. This also is a pernicious error. For if the power of the keys does not console us before God, what, then, will pacify the conscience? Still more involved is what follows. They teach that by contrition we merit grace. In reference to which, if any one should ask why Saul and Judas and similar persons, who were dreadfully contrite, did not obtain grace, the answer was to be taken from faith and according to the Gospel, that Judas did not believe, that he did not support himself by the Gospel and promise of Christ. For faith shows the distinction between the contrition of Judas and of Peter. But the adversaries take their answer from the Law, that Judas did not love God, but feared the punishments. [Is not this teaching uncertain and improper things concerning repentance?] When, however, will a terrified conscience, especially in those serious, true, and great terrors which are described in the psalms and the prophets, and which those certainly taste who are truly converted, be able to decide whether it fears God for His own sake [out of love it fears God, as its God], or is fleeing from eternal punishments? [These people may not have experienced much of these anxieties, because they juggle words and make distinctions according to their dreams. But in the heart when the test is applied, the matter turns out quite differently, and the conscience cannot be set at rest with paltry syllables and words.] These great emotions can be distinguished in letters and terms; they are not thus separated in fact, as these sweet sophists dream. Here we appeal to the judgments of all good and wise men [who also desire to know the truth]. They undoubtedly will confess that these discussions in the writings of the adversaries are very confused and intricate. And nevertheless the most important subject is at stake, the chief topic of the Gospel, the remission of sins. This entire doctrine concerning these questions which we have reviewed, is, in the writings of the adversaries, full of errors and hypocrisy, and obscures the benefit of Christ, the power of the keys, and the righteousness of faith [to inexpressible injury of conscience].

These things occur in the first act. What when they come to confession? What a work there is in the endless enumeration of sins which is nevertheless, in great part, devoted to those against human traditions! And in order that good minds may by this means be the more tortured, they falsely assert that this enumeration is of divine right. And while they demand this enumeration under the pretext of divine right, in the mean time they speak coldly concerning absolution which is truly of divine right. They falsely assert that the Sacrament itself confers grace *ex opere operato* without a good disposition on the part of the one using it; no mention is made of faith apprehending the absolution and consoling the conscience. This is truly what is generally called *apienai pro tohn mustehriohn* departing before the mysteries. [Such people are called genuine Jews.]

The third act [of this play] remains, concerning satisfactions. But this contains the most confused discussions. They imagine that eternal punishments are commuted to the punishments of purgatory, and teach that a part of these is remitted by the power of the keys, and that a part is to be redeemed by means of satisfactions. They add further that satisfactions ought to be works of supererogation, and they make these consist of most foolish observances, such as pilgrimages, rosaries, or similar observances which do not have the command of God. Then, just as they redeem purgatory by means of satisfactions, so a scheme of redeeming satisfactions which was most abundant in revenue [which became quite a profitable, lucrative business and a grand fair] was devised. For they sell [without shame] indulgences which they interpret as remissions of satisfactions. And this revenue [this trafficking, this fair, conducted so shamelessly] is not only from the living, but is much more ample from the dead. Nor do they redeem the satisfactions of the dead only by indulgences, but also by the sacrifice of the Mass. In a word, the subject of satisfactions is infinite. Among these scandals (for we cannot enumerate all things) and doctrines of devils lies buried the doctrine of the righteousness of faith in Christ and the benefit of Christ. Wherefore, all good men understand that the doctrine of the sophists and canonists concerning repentance has been censured for a useful and godly purpose. For the following dogmas are clearly false, and foreign not only to Holy Scripture, but also to the Church Fathers:-I. That from the divine covenant we merit grace by good works wrought without grace.

II. That by attrition we merit grace.

III. That for the blotting out of sin the mere detestation of the crime is sufficient.

IV. That on account of contrition, and not by faith in Christ, we obtain remission of sins.

V. That the power of the keys avails for the remission of sins, not before God, but before the Church.

VI. That by the power of the keys sins are not remitted before God, but that the power of the keys has been instituted to commute eternal to temporal punishments, to impose upon consciences certain satisfactions, to institute new acts of worship, and to obligate consciences to such satisfactions and acts of worship.

VII. That according to divine right the enumeration of offenses in confession, concerning which the adversaries teach, is necessary.

VIII. That canonical satisfactions are necessary for redeeming the punishment of purgatory, or they profit as a compensation for the blotting out of guilt. For thus uninformed persons understand it. [For, although in the schools satisfactions are made to apply only to the punishment, everybody thinks that remission of guilt is thereby merited.]

IX. That the reception of the sacrament of repentance *ex opere operato*, without a good disposition on the part of the one using it, i.e., without faith in Christ, obtains grace.

X. That by the power of the keys our souls are freed from purgatory through indulgences

XI. That in the reservation of cases not only canonical punishment, but the guilt also, ought to be reserved in reference to one who is truly converted.

In order, therefore, to deliver pious consciences from these labyrinths of the sophists, we have ascribed to repentance [or conversion] these two parts, namely, contrition and faith. If any one desires to add a third namely, fruits worthy of repentance, i.e., a change of the entire life and character for the better [good works which shall and must follow conversion], we will not make any opposition. From contrition we separate those idle and infinite discussions, as to when we grieve from love of God, and when from fear of punishment. [For these are nothing but mere words and a useless babbling of persons who have never experienced the state of mind of a terrified conscience.] But we say that contrition is the true terror of conscience, which feels that God is angry with sin, and which grieves that it has sinned. And this contrition takes place in this manner when sins are censured by the Word of God, because the sum of the preaching of the Gospel is this, namely, to convict of sin, and to offer for Christ's sake the remission of sins and righteousness, and the Holy Ghost, and eternal life, and that as regenerate men we should do good works. Thus Christ comprises the sum of the Gospel when He says in the last chapter of Luke, v. 74: That repentance and remission of sins should be preached in My name among all nations. And of these terrors Scripture speaks, as Ps. 38, 4. 8: For mine iniquities are gone over mine head, as a heavy burden they are too heavy for me...I am feeble and sore broken; I have roared by reason of the disquietness of My heart. And Ps. 6, 2. 3: Have mercy upon me, O Lord; for I am weak; O Lord, heal me; for my bones are vexed. My soul is also sore vexed; but Thou, O Lord how long! And Is. 38, 10.13: I said in the cutting off of my days, I shall go to the gates of the grave: I am deprived of the residue of my years....I reckoned till morning that, as a lion, so will He break all my bones. [Again, v. 14: Mine eyes fail with looking upward; 0 Lord, I am oppressed.] In these terrors, conscience feels the wrath of God against sin, which is unknown to secure men walking according to the flesh [as the sophists and their like]. It sees the turpitude of sin, and seriously grieves that it has sinned; meanwhile it also flees from the dreadful wrath of God, because human nature, unless sustained by the Word of God, cannot endure it. Thus Paul says, Gal. 2, 19: I through the Law am dead to the Law, For the Law only accuses and terrifies consciences. In these terrors our adversaries say nothing of faith, they present only the Word, which convicts of sin. When this is taught alone, it is the doctrine of the Law, not of the Gospel. By these griefs and terrors, they say, men merit grace, provided they love God. But how will men love God in true terrors when they feel the terrible and inexpressible wrath of God What else than despair do those teach who in these terrors, display only the Law?

We therefore add as the second part of repentance, Of Faith in Christ, that in these terrors the Gospel concerning Christ ought to be set forth to consciences, in which Gospel the remission of sins is freely promised concerning Christ. Therefore, they ought to believe that for Christ's sake sins are freely remitted to them. This faith cheers, sustains, and quickens the contrite, according to Rom. 5, 1: Being justified by faith, we have peace with God. This faith obtains the remission of sins. This faith justifies before God, as the same passage testifies: Being justified by faith. This faith shows the distinction between the contrition of Judas and Peter, of Saul and of David. The contrition of Judas or Saul is of no avail, for the reason that to this there is not added this faith which apprehends the remission of sins, bestowed as a gift for Christ's sake. Accordingly, the contrition of David or Peter avails because to it there is added faith, which apprehends the remission of sins granted for Christ's sake. Neither is love present before reconciliation has been made by faith. For without Christ the Law [God's Law or the First Commandment] is not performed, according to [Eph. 2, 18; 3,12] Rom. 5, 2: By Christ we have access to God. And this faith grows gradually and throughout the entire life, struggles with sin [is tested by various temptations] in order to overcome sin and death. But love follows faith, as we have said above. And thus filial fear can be clearly defined as such anxiety as has been connected with faith, i.e., where faith consoles and sustains the anxious heart. It is servile fear when faith does not sustain the anxious heart [fear without faith, where there is nothing but wrath and doubt].

Moreover, the power of the keys administers and presents the Gospel through absolution, which [proclaims peace to me and] is the true voice of the Gospel. Thus we also comprise absolution when we speak of faith, because faith cometh by hearing, as Paul says Rom. 10, 17. For when the Gospel is heard and the absolution [i.e., the promise of divine grace] is heard, the conscience is encouraged and receives consolation. And because God truly quickens through the Word, the keys truly remit sins before God [here on earth sins are truly canceled in such a manner that they are canceled also before God in heaven] according to Luke 10,10: He that heareth you heareth Me Wherefore the voice of the one absolving must be believed not otherwise than we would believe a voice from heaven. And absolution [that blessed word of comfort] properly can be called a sacrament of repentance, as also the more learned scholastic theologians speak. Meanwhile this faith is nourished in a manifold way in temptations, through the declarations of the Gospel [the hearing of sermons, reading] and the use of the Sacraments. For these are [seals and] signs of [the covenant and grace in] the New Testament, i.e., signs of [propitiation and] the remission of sins. They offer, therefore, the remission of sins, as the words of the Lord's Supper clearly testify, Matt. 26, 26. 28: This is My body, which is given for you. This is the cup of the New Testament, etc. Thus faith is conceived and strengthened through absolution, through the hearing of the Gospel, through the use of the Sacraments, so that it may not succumb while it struggles with the terrors of sin and death. This method of repentance is plain and clear, and increases the worth of the power of the keys and of the Sacraments, and illumines the benefit of Christ, and teaches us to avail ourselves of Christ as Mediator and Propitiator.

But as the Confutation condemns us for having assigned these two parts to repentance, we must show that [not we, but] Scripture expresses these as the chief parts in repentance or conversion. For Christ says Matt. 11, 28: Come unto Me, all ye that labor and are heavy laden, and I will give you rest. Here there are two members. The labor and the burden signify the contrition, anxiety, and terrors of sin and of death. To come to Christ is to believe that sins are remitted for Christ's sake, when we believe, our hearts are quickened by the Holy Ghost through the Word of Christ. Here, therefore, there are these two chief parts, contrition and faith. And in Mark 1, 15 Christ says: Repent ye and believe the Gospel, where in the first member He convicts of sins, in the latter He consoles us, and shows the remission of sins. For to believe the Gospel is not that general faith which devils also have [is not only to believe the history of the Gospel], but in the proper sense it is to believe that the remission of sins has been granted for Christ's sake. For this is revealed in the Gospel. You see also here that the two parts are joined, contrition when sins are reproved and faith, when it is said: Believe the Gospel. If any one should say here that Christ includes also the fruits of repentance or the entire new life, we shall not dissent. For this suffices us, that contrition and faith are named as the chief parts.

Paul almost everywhere, when he describes conversion or renewal, designates these two parts, mortification and quickening, as in Col. 2, 11: In whom also ye are circumcised with the circumcision made without hands, namely, by putting off the body of the sins of the flesh. And afterward, v. 12: Wherein also ye are risen with Him through the faith of the operation of God. Here are two parts. [Of these two parts he speaks plainly Rom. 6, 2. 4. 11, that we are dead to sin, which takes place by contrition and its terrors, and that we should rise again with Christ, which takes place when by faith we again obtain consolation and life. And since faith is to bring consolation and peace into the conscience, according to Rom. 5, 1: Being justified by faith, we have peace, it follows that there is first terror and anxiety in the conscience. Thus contrition and faith go side by side.] One is putting off the body of sins; the other is the rising again through faith. Neither ought these words, mortification, quickening, putting off the body of sins, rising again, to be understood in a Platonic way, concerning a feigned change; but mortification signifies true terrors, such as those of the dying, which nature could not sustain unless it were supported by faith. So he names that as the putting off of the body of sins which we ordinarily call contrition, because in these griefs the natural concupiscence is purged away. And quickening ought not to be understood as a Platonic fancy, but as consolation which truly sustains life that is escaping in contrition. Here, therefore, are two parts: contrition and faith. For as conscience cannot be pacified except by faith, therefore faith alone quickens, according to the declaration, Hab. 2, 4; Rom. 1, 17: The just shall live by faith.

And then in Col. 2, 14 it is said that Christ blots out the handwriting which through the Law is against us. Here also there are two parts, the handwriting and the blotting out of the handwriting. The handwriting, however, is conscience, convicting and condemning us. The Law, moreover, is the word which reproves and condemns sins. Therefore, this voice which says, I have sinned against the Lord, as

David says, 2 Sam. 12, 13, is the handwriting. And wicked and secure men do not seriously give forth this voice. For they do not see, they do not read the sentence of the Law written in the heart. In true griefs and terrors this sentence is perceived. Therefore the handwriting which condemns us is contrition itself. To blot out the handwriting is to expunge this sentence by which we declare that we shall be condemned, and to engrave the sentence according to which we know that we have been freed from this condemnation. But faith is the new sentence, which reverses the former sentence, and gives peace and life to the heart.

However, what need is there to cite many testimonies since they are everywhere obvious in the Scriptures? Ps. 118, 18: The Lord hath chastened me sore, but He hath not given me over unto death. Ps. 119, 28: My soul melteth for heaviness; strengthen Thou me according unto Thy word. Here, in the first member, contrition is contained, and in the second the mode is clearly described how in contrition we are revived, namely, by the Word of God which offers grace. This sustains and quickens hearts. And 1 Sam. 2, 6 The Lord killeth and maketh alive; He bringeth down to the grave and bringeth up. By one of these, contrition is signified, by the other, faith is signified. And Is. 28, 21: The Lord shall be wroth that He may do His work, His strange work, and bring to pass His act, His strange act. He calls it the strange work of the Lord when He terrifies because to quicken and console is God's own work. [Other works, as, to terrify and to kill, are not God's own works, for God only quickens.] But He terrifies, he says, for this reason, namely, that there may be a place for consolation and quickening, because hearts that are secure and do not feel the wrath of God loathe consolation. In this manner Scripture is accustomed to join these two the terrors and the consolation, in order to teach that in repentance there are these chief members, contrition, and faith that consoles and justifies. Neither do we see how the nature of repentance can be presented more clearly and simply. [We know with certainty that God thus works in His Christians in the Church.]

For the two chief works of God in men are these, to terrify, and to justify and quicken those who have been terrified. Into these two works all Scripture has been distributed. The one part is the Law, which shows, reproves, and condemns sins. The other part is the Gospel, i.e., the promise of grace bestowed in Christ, and this promise is constantly repeated in the whole of Scripture, first having been delivered to Adam [I will put enmity, etc., Gen. 3, 15], afterwards to the patriarchs; then, still more clearly proclaimed by the prophets; lastly, preached and set forth among the Jews by Christ and disseminated over the entire world by the apostles. For all the saints were justified by faith in this promise, and not by their own attrition or contrition.

And the examples [how the saints became godly] show likewise these two parts. After his sin Adam is reproved and becomes terrified, this was contrition. Afterward God promises grace, and speaks of a future seed (the blessed seed, i.e., Christ), by which the kingdom of the devil, death, and sin will be destroyed, there He offers the remission of sins. These are the chief things. For although the punishment is afterwards added, yet this punishment does not merit the remission of sin. And concerning this kind of punishment we shall speak after a while.

So David is reproved by Nathan, and, terrified, he says, 2 Sam. 12, 13: I have sinned against the Lord. This is contrition. Afterward he hears the absolution: The Lord also hath put away thy sin; thou shalt not die. This voice encourages David, and by faith sustains, justifies, and quickens him. Here a punishment is also added, but this punishment does not merit the remission of sins. Nor are special punishments always added, but in repentance these two things ought always to exist, namely, contrition and faith, as Luke 7, 37. 38. The woman, who was a sinner, came to Christ weeping. By these tears the contrition is recognized. Afterward she hears the absolution: Thy sins are forgiven; thy faith hath saved thee; go in peace. This is the second part of repentance, namely, faith, which encourages and consoles her. From all these it is apparent to godly readers that we assign to repentance those parts which properly belong to it in conversion, or regeneration, and the remission of sin. Worthy fruits and punishments [likewise, patience that we be willing to bear the cross and punishments, which God lays upon the old Adam] follow regeneration and the remission of sin. For this reason we have mentioned these two parts, in order that the faith which we require in repentance [of which the sophists and canonists have all been silent] might be the better seen. And what that faith is which the Gospel proclaims can be better understood when it is set over against contrition and mortification.

But as the adversaries expressly condemn our statement that men obtain the remission of sins by faith, we shall add a few proofs from which it will be understood that the remission of sins is obtained not ***ex opere operato*** because of contrition, but by that special faith by which an individual believes that sins are remitted to him. For this is the chief article concerning which we are contending with our adversaries, and the knowledge of which we regard especially necessary to all Christians. As, however, it appears that we have spoken sufficiently above concerning the same subject, we shall here be briefer. For very closely related are the topics of the doctrine of repentance and the doctrine of justification.

When the adversaries speak of faith, and say that it precedes repentance, they understand by faith, not that which justifies, but that which, in a general way, believes that God exists, that punishments have been threatened to the wicked [that there is a hell], etc. In addition to this faith we require that each one believe that his sins are remitted to him. Concerning this special faith we are disputing, and we oppose it to the opinion which bids us trust not in the promise of Christ, but in the **opus operatum**, of contrition, confession, and satisfactions, etc. This faith follows terrors in such a manner as to overcome them, and render the conscience pacified. To this faith we ascribe justification and regeneration, inasmuch as it frees from terrors, and brings forth in the heart not only peace and joy, but also a new life. We maintain [with the help of God we shall defend to eternity and against all the gates of hell] that this faith is truly necessary for the remission of sins, and accordingly place it among the parts of repentance. Nor does the Church of Christ believe otherwise, although our adversaries [like mad dogs] contradict us.

Moreover, to begin with, we ask the adversaries whether to receive absolution is a part of repentance, or not. But if they separate it from confession as they are subtile in making the distinction, we do not see of what benefit confession is without absolution. If, however, they do not separate the receiving of absolution from confession, it is necessary for them to hold that faith is a part of repentance, because absolution is not received except by faith. That absolution, however is not received except by faith can be proved from Paul, who teaches Rom. 4, 16, that the promise cannot be received except by faith. But absolution is the promise of the remission of sins [nothing else than the Gospel, the divine promise of God's grace and favor]. Therefore, it necessarily requires faith. Neither do we see how he who does not assent to it may be said to receive absolution. And what else is the refusal to assent to absolution but charging God with falsehood, If the heart doubts, it regards those things which God promises as uncertain and of no account. Accordingly, in 1 John

5, 10 it is written: He that believeth not God hath made Him a liar, because he believeth not the record that God gave of His Son.

Secondly, we think that the adversaries acknowledge that the remission of sins is either a part, or the end, or, to speak in their manner, the ***terminus ad quem*** of repentance. [For what does repentance help if the forgiveness of sins be not obtained?] Therefore that by which the remission of sins is received is correctly added to the parts [must certainly be the most prominent part] of repentance. It is very certain, however, that even though all the gates of hell contradict us, yet the remission of sins cannot be received except by faith alone, which believes that sins are remitted for Christ's sake, according to Rom. 3, 25: Whom God hath set forth to be a propitiation through faith in His blood. Likewise Rom. 5, 2: By whom also we have access by faith unto grace, etc. For a terrified conscience cannot set against God's wrath our works or our love, but it is at length pacified when it apprehends Christ as Mediator, and believes the promises given for His sake. For those who dream that without faith in Christ hearts become pacified, do not understand what the remission of sins is, or how it came to us. Peter, 1 Ep. 2, 6, cites from Is. 49, 23, and 28, 16: He that believeth on Him shall not be confounded. It is necessary, therefore, that hypocrites be confounded, who are confident that they receive the remission of sins because of their own works, and not because of Christ. Peter also says in Acts 10, 43: To Him give all the prophets witness that through His name whosoever believeth in Him, shall receive remission of sins. What he says, through His name, could not be expressed more clearly and he adds: Whosoever believeth in Him. Thus, therefore, we receive the remission of sins only through the name of Christ, i.e., for Christ's sake, and not for the sake of any merits and works of our own. And this occurs when we believe that sins are remitted to us for Christ's sake.

Our adversaries cry out that they are the Church, that they are following the consensus of the Church [what the Church catholic universal, holds]. But Peter also here cites in our issue the consensus of the Church: To Him give all the prophets witness, that through His name, whosoever believeth in Him, shall receive remission of sins, etc. The consensus of the prophets is assuredly to be judged as the consensus of the Church universal. [I verily think that if all the holy prophets are unanimously agreed in a declaration (since God regards even a single prophet as an inestimable treasure), it would also be a decree, a declaration, and a unanimous strong conclusion of the universal, catholic, Christian, holy Church, and would be justly regarded as such.] We concede neither to the Pope nor to the Church the power to make decrees against this consensus of the prophets. But the bull of Leo openly condemns this article, Of the Remission of Sins and the adversaries condemn it in the Confutation. From which it is apparent what sort of a Church we must judge that of these men to be, who not only by their decrees censure the doctrine that we obtain the remission of sins by faith, not on account of our works, but on account of Christ, but who also give the command by force and the sword to abolish it, and by every kind of cruelty [like bloodhounds] to put to death good men who thus believe.

But they have authors of a great name Scotus, Gabriel, and the like, and passages of the Fathers which are cited in a mutilated form in the decrees. Certainly, if the testimonies are to be counted, they win. For there is a very great crowd of most trifling writers upon the Sententiae, who, as though they had conspired, defend these figments concerning the merit of attrition and of works, and other things which we have above recounted. [Aye, it is true, they are all called teachers and authors, but by their singing you can tell what sort of birds they are. These authors have taught nothing but philosophy, and have known nothing of Christ and the work of God, their books show this plainly.] But lest any one be moved by the multitude of citations, there is no great weight in the testimonies of the later writers, who did not originate their own writings, but only, by compiling from the writers before them, transferred these opinions from some books into others. They have exercised no judgment, but just like petty judges silently have approved the errors of their superiors, which they have not understood. Let us not, therefore, hesitate to oppose this utterance of Peter, which cites the consensus of the prophets, to ever so many legions of the Sententiaries. And to this utterance of Peter the testimony of the Holy Ghost is added. For the text speaks thus, Acts 10, 44: While Peter yet spake these words, the Holy Ghost fell on all them which heard the Word. Therefore, let pious consciences know that the command of God is this that they believe that they are freely forgiven for Christ's sake, and not for the sake of our works. And by this command of God let them sustain themselves against despair, and against the terrors of sin and of death. And let them know that this belief has existed among saints from the beginning of the world. [Of this the idle sophists know little; and the blessed proclamation, the Gospel, which proclaims the forgiveness of sins through the blessed Seed, that is, Christ, has from the beginning of the world been the greatest consolation and treasure to all pious kings all prophets, all believers. For they have believed in the same Christ in whom we believe; for from the beginning of the world no saint has been saved in any other way than through the faith of the same Gospel.] For Peter clearly cites the consensus of the prophets, and the writings of the apostles testify that they believe the same thing. Nor are testimonies of the Fathers wanting. For Bernard says the same thing in words that are in no way obscure: For it is necessary first of all to believe that you cannot have remission of sins except by the indulgence of God, but add yet that you believe also this, namely, that through Him sins are forgiven thee. This is the testimony which the Holy Ghost asserts in your heart, saying: "Thy sins are forgiven thee." For thus the apostle judges that man is justified freely through faith. These words of Bernard shed a wonderful light upon our cause, because he not only requires that we in a general way believe that sins are remitted through mercy but he bids us add special faith, by which we believe that sins are remitted even to us; and he teaches how we may be rendered certain concerning the remission of sins, namely when our hearts are encouraged by faith, and become tranquil through the Holy Ghost. What more do the adversaries require? [But how now, ye adversaries? Is St. Bernard also a heretic?] Do they still dare deny that by faith we obtain the remission of sins, or that faith is a part of repentance?

Thirdly, the adversaries say that sin is remitted; because an attrite or contrite person elicits an act of love to God [if we undertake from reason to love God], and by this act merits to receive the remission of sins. This is nothing but to teach the Law, the Gospel being blotted out, and the promise concerning Christ being abolished. For they require only the Law and our works, because the Law demands love. Besides they teach us to be confident that we obtain remission of sins because of contrition and love. What else is this than to put confidence in our works, not in the Word and promise of God concerning Christ? But if the Law be sufficient for obtaining the remission of sins, what need is there of the Gospel? What need is there of Christ if we obtain remission of sins because of our own work? We, on the other hand call consciences away from the Law to the Gospel, and from confidence in their own works to confidence in the promise and Christ, because the Gospel presents to us Christ, and promises freely the remission of sins for Christ's sake. In this promise it bids us trust, namely, that for Christ's sake we are reconciled to the Father, and not for the sake of our own contrition or love. For there is no other Mediator or Propitiator than Christ. Neither can we do the works of the Law unless we have first been reconciled through Christ. And if we would do anything, yet we must believe that not for the sake of these works, but for the sake of Christ, as Mediator and Propitiator, we obtain the remission of sins.

Yea, it is a reproach to Christ and a repeal of the Gospel to believe that we obtain the remission of sins on account of the Law, or otherwise than by faith in Christ. This method also we have discussed above in the chapter Of Justification, where we declared why we confess that men are justified by faith, not by love. Therefore the doctrine of the adversaries, when they teach that by their own contrition and love men obtain the remission of sins, and trust in this contrition and love, is merely the doctrine of the Law and of that, too, as not understood [which they do not understand with respect to the kind of love towards God which it demands], just as the Jews looked upon the veiled face of Moses. For let us imagine that love is present, let us imagine that works are present, yet neither love nor works can a propitiation for sin [or be of as much value as Christ]. And they cannot even be opposed to the wrath and judgment of God, according to Ps. 143, 2: Enter not into judgment with Thy servant; for in Thy sight shall no man living be justified. Neither ought the honor of Christ to be transferred to our works.

For these reasons Paul contends that we are not justified by the Law, and he opposes to the Law the promise of the remission of sins which is granted for Christ's sake and teaches that we freely receive the remission of sins for Christ's sake. Paul calls us away from the Law to this promise. Upon this promise he bids us look [and regard the Lord Christ our treasure], which certainly will be void if we are justified by the Law before we are justified through the promise, or if we obtain the remission of sins on account of our own righteousness. But it is evident that the promise was given us and Christ was tendered to us for the very reason that we cannot do the works of the Law. Therefore it is necessary that we are reconciled by the promise before we do the works of the Law. The promise, however, is received only by faith. Therefore it is necessary for contrite persons to apprehend by faith the promise of the remission of sins granted for Christ's sake, and to be confident that freely for Christ's sake they have a reconciled Father. This is the meaning of Paul, Rom. 4, 13, where he says: Therefore it is of faith that it might be by grace, to the end the promise might be sure. And Gal. 3, 22: The Scripture hath concluded all under sin, that the promise by faith of Jesus Christ might be given them that believe, i.e., all are under sin, neither can they be freed otherwise than by apprehending by faith the promise of the remission of sins. Therefore we must by faith accept the remission of sins before we do the works of the Law, although, as has been said above, love follows faith, because the regenerate receive the Holy Ghost, and accordingly begin [to become friendly to the Law and] to do the works of the Law.

We would cite more testimonies if they were not obvious to every godly reader in the Scriptures. And we do not wish to be too prolix, in order that this ease may be the more readily seen through. Neither, indeed, is there any doubt that the meaning of Paul is what we are defending, namely, that by faith we receive the remission of sins for Christ's sake, that by faith we ought to oppose to God's wrath Christ as Mediator, and not our works. Neither let godly minds be disturbed, even though the adversaries find fault with the judgments of Paul. Nothing is said so simply that it cannot be distorted by caviling. We know that what we have mentioned is the true and genuine meaning of Paul, we know that this our belief brings to godly consciences [in agony of death and temptation] sure comfort, without which no one can in God's judgment.

Therefore let these pharisaic opinions of the adversaries be rejected, namely, that we do not receive by faith the remission of sins, but that it ought to be merited by our love and works; that we ought to oppose our love and our works to the wrath of God. Not of the Gospel, but of the Law is this doctrine, which feigns that man is justified by the Law before he has been reconciled through Christ to God, since Christ says, John 15, 5: With out Me, ye can do nothing; likewise: I am the true Vine; ye are the branches. But the adversaries feign that we are branches, not of Christ, but of Moses. For they wish to be justified by the Law, and to offer their love and works to God before they are reconciled to God through Christ, before they are branches of Christ. Paul, on the other hand [who is certainly a much greater teacher than the adversaries], contends that the Law cannot be observed without Christ. Accordingly, in order that we [those who truly feel and have experienced sin and anguish of conscience must cling to the promise of grace, in order that they] may be reconciled to God for Christ's sake, the promise must be received before we do the works of the Law. We think that these things are sufficiently clear to godly consciences. And hence they will understand why we have declared above that men are justified by faith, not by love, because we must oppose to God's wrath not our love or works (or trust in our love and works), but Christ as Mediator [for all our ability, all our deeds and works, are far too weak to remove and appease God's wrath]. And we must apprehend the promise of the remission of sins before we do the works of the Law.

Lastly, when will conscience be pacified if we receive remission of sins on the ground that we love, or that we do the works of the Law? For the Law will always accuse us, because we never satisfy God's Law. Just as Paul says, Rom. 4, 15: The Law worketh wrath. Chrysostom asks concerning repentance, Whence are we made sure that our sins are remitted us? The adversaries also, in their "Sentences," ask concerning the same subject. [The question, verily, is worth asking blessed the man that returns the right answer.] This cannot be explained, consciences cannot be made tranquil, unless they know that it is God's command and the very Gospel that they should be firmly confident that for Christ's sake sins are remitted freely, and that they should not doubt that these are remitted to them. If any one doubts, he charges, as John says, 1 Ep. 5, 10, the divine promise with falsehood. We teach that this certainty of faith is required in the Gospel. The adversaries leave consciences uncertain and wavering. Consciences, however do nothing from faith when they perpetually doubt whether they have remission. [For it is not possible that there should be rest, or a quiet and peaceful conscience, if they doubt whether God be gracious. For if they doubt whether they have a gracious God, whether they are doing right, whether they have forgiveness of sins, how can, etc.] How can they in this doubt call upon God, how can they be confident that they are heard? Thus the entire life is without God [faith] and without the true worship of God. This is what Paul says, Rom. 14, 23: Whatsoever is not of faith is sin. And because they are constantly occupied with this doubt, they never experience what faith [God or Christ] is. Thus it comes to pass that they rush at last into despair [die in doubt, without God, without all knowledge of God]. Such is the doctrine of the adversaries, the doctrine of the Law, the annulling of the Gospel, the doctrine of despair. [Whereby Christ is suppressed, men are led into overwhelming sorrow and torture of conscience, and finally, when temptation comes, into despair. Let His Imperial Majesty graciously consider and well examine this matter, it does not concern gold or silver but souls and consciences.] Now we are glad to refer to all good men the judgment concerning this topic of repentance (for it has no obscurity), in order that they may decide whether we or the adversaries have taught those things which are more godly and healthful to consciences. Indeed, these dissensions in the Church do not delight us; wherefore, if we did not have great and necessary reasons for dissenting from the adversaries, we would with the greatest pleasure be silent. But now, since they condemn the manifest truth, it is not right for us to desert a cause which is not our own, but is that of Christ and the Church. [We cannot with fidelity to God and conscience deny this blessed doctrine and divine truth, from which we expect at last, when this poor temporal life ceases and all help of creatures fails, the only eternal, highest consolation: nor will we in anything recede from this cause, which is not only ours, but that of all Christendom, and concerns the highest treasure, Jesus Christ.]

We have declared for what reasons we assigned to repentance these two parts, contrition and faith. And we have done this the more readily because many expressions concerning repentance are published which are cited in a mutilated form from the Fathers [Augustine and the other ancient Fathers], and which the adversaries have distorted in order to put faith out of sight. Such are: Repentance is to lament past evils, and not to commit again deeds that ought to be lamented. Again: Repentance is a kind of vengeance of him who grieves, thus punishing in himself what he is sorry for having committed. In these passages no mention is made of faith. And not even in the schools, when they interpret, is anything added concerning faith. Therefore, in order that the doctrine of faith might be the more conspicuous, we have enumerated it among the parts of repentance. For the actual fact shows that those passages which require contrition or good works, and make no mention of justifying faith, are dangerous [as experience proves]. And prudence can justly be desired in those who have collected these centos of the "Sentences" and decrees. For since the Fathers speak in some places concerning one part, and in other places concerning another part of repentance, it would have been well to select and combine their judgments not only concerning one part, but concerning both, i.e., concerning contrition and faith.

For Tertullian speaks excellently concerning faith, dwelling upon the oath in the prophet, Ezek. 33, 11: As I live, saith the Lord God, I have no pleasure in the death of the wicked, but that the wicked turn from his way and live. For as God swears that He does not wish the death of a sinner, He shows that faith is required, in order that we may believe the one swearing, and be firmly confident that He forgives us. The authority of the divine promises ought by itself to be great in our estimation. But this promise has also been confirmed by an oath. Therefore, if any one be not confident that he is forgiven, he denies that God has sworn what is true, than which a more horrible blasphemy cannot be imagined. For Tertullian speaks thus: He invites by reward to salvation, even swearing. Saying, "I live," He desires that He be believed. Oh, blessed we, for whose sake God swears! Oh, most miserable if we believe not the Lord even when He swears! But here we must know that this faith ought to be confident that God freely forgives us for the sake of Christ, for the sake of His own promise, not for the sake of our works, contrition, confession, or satisfactions. For if faith relies upon these works, it immediately becomes uncertain, because the terrified conscience sees that these works are unworthy. Accordingly, Ambrose speaks admirably concerning repentance: Therefore it is proper for us to believe both that we are to repent, and that we are to be pardoned, but so as to expect pardon as from faith, which obtains it as from a handwriting. Again: It is faith which covers our sins. Therefore there are sentences extant in the Fathers, not only concerning contrition and works, but also concerning faith. But the adversaries, since they understand neither the nature of repentance nor the language of the Fathers, select passages concerning a part of repentance, namely, concerning works; they pass over the declarations made elsewhere concerning faith, since they do not understand them.

Part 16

Article VI: *Of Confession and Satisfaction.*

Good men can easily judge that it is of the greatest importance that the true doctrine concerning the abovementioned parts, namely, contrition and faith, be preserved. [For the great fraud of indulgences, etc., and the preposterous doctrines of the sophists have sufficiently taught us what great vexation and danger arise therefrom if a foul stroke is here made. How many a godly conscience under the Papacy sought with great labor the true way, and in the midst of such darkness did not find it!] Therefore, we have always been occupied more with the elucidation of these topics, and have disputed nothing as yet concerning confession and satisfaction. For we also retain confession, especially on account of the absolution, as being the word of God which, by divine authority, the power of the keys pronounces upon individuals. Therefore it would be wicked to remove private absolution from the Church. Neither do they understand what the remission of sins or the power of the keys is, if there are any who despise private absolution. But in reference to the enumeration of offenses in confession, we have said above that we hold that it is not necessary by divine right. For the objection, made by some, that a judge ought to investigate a ease before he pronounces upon it, pertains in no way to this subject; because the ministry of absolution is favor or grace, it is not a legal process, or law. [For God is the Judge, who has committed to the apostles, not the office of judges, but the administration of grace namely, to acquit those who desire, etc.] Therefore ministers in the Church have the command to remit sin, they have not the command to investigate secret sins. And indeed, they absolve from those that we do not remember; for which reason absolution, which is the voice of the Gospel remitting sins and consoling consciences, does not require judicial examination.

And it is ridiculous to transfer hither the saying of Solomon, Prov. 27, 23: Be thou diligent to know the state of thy flocks. For Solomon says nothing of confession, but gives to the father of a family a domestic precept, that he should use what is his own, and abstain from what is another's, and he commands him to take care of his own property diligently, yet in such a way that, with his mind occupied with the increase of his resources, he should not cast away the fear of God, or faith or care in God's Word. But our adversaries, by a wonderful metamorphosis, transform passages of Scripture to whatever meaning they please. [They produce from the Scriptures black and white, as they please, contrary to the natural meaning of the clear words.] Here to know signifies with them to hear confessions, the state, not the outward life, but the secrets of conscience; and the flocks signify men. [Sable, we think means a school within which there are such doctors and orators. But it has happened aright to those who thus despise the Holy Scriptures and all fine arts that they make gross mistakes in grammar.] The interpretation is assuredly neat, and is worthy of these despisers of the pursuits of eloquence. But if any one desires by a similitude to transfer a precept from a father of a family to a pastor of a Church, he ought certainly to interpret "state" [V. ***vultus***, countenance] as applying to the outward life. This similitude will be more consistent.

But let us omit such matters as these. At different times in the Psalms mention is made of confession, as, Ps. 32, 5: I said, I will confess my transgressions unto the Lord; and Thou forgavest the iniquity of my sin. Such confession of sin which is made to God is contrition itself. For when confession is made to God, it must be made with the heart not alone with the voice, as is made on the stage by actors. Therefore, such confession is contrition, in which, feeling God's wrath, we confess that God is justly angry, and that He cannot be appeased by our works, and nevertheless we seek for mercy because of God's promise. Such is the following confession, Ps. 51, 4: Against Thee only have I sinned, that Thou mightest be justified and be clear when Thou judgest, i.e., "I confess that I am a sinner, and have merited eternal wrath, nor can I set my righteousnesses, my merits, against Thy wrath; accordingly, I declare that Thou art just when Thou condemnest and punishest us, I declare that Thou art clear when hypocrites judge Thee to be unjust in punishing them or in condemning the well-deserving. Yea, our merits cannot be opposed to Thy judgment but we shall thus be justified, namely, if Thou justifiest us, if through Thy mercy Thou accountest us righteous." Perhaps some one may also cite Jas. 5, 16: Confess your faults one to another. But here the reference is not to confession that is to be made to the priests, but, in general, concerning the reconciliation of brethren to each other. For it commands that the confession be mutual.

Again, our adversaries will condemn many most generally received teachers if they will contend that in confession an enumeration of offenses is necessary according to divine Law. For although we approve of confession, and judge that some examination is of advantage in order that men may be the better instructed [young and inexperienced persons be questioned], yet the matter must be so controlled that snares are not cast upon consciences, which never will be tranquil if they think that they cannot obtain the remission of sins unless this precise enumeration be made. That which the adversaries have expressed in the ***Confutation*** is certainly most false, namely, that a full confession is necessary for salvation. For this is impossible. And what snares they here cast upon the conscience when they require a full confession! For when will conscience be sure that the confession is complete? In the Church-writers mention is made of confession, but they do not speak of this enumeration of secret offenses, but of the rite of public repentance. For as the fallen or notorious [those guilty of public crimes] were not received without fixed satisfactions [without a public ceremony or reproof], they made confession on this account to the presbyters, in order that satisfactions might be prescribed to them according to the measure of their offenses. This entire matter contained nothing similar to the enumeration concerning which we are disputing. This confession was made, not because the remission of sins before God could not occur without it, but because satisfactions could not be prescribed unless the kind of offense were first known. For different offenses had different canons.

And from this rite of public repentance there has been left the word "satisfaction." For the holy Fathers were unwilling to receive the fallen or the notorious, unless as far as it was possible, their repentance had been first examined into and exhibited publicly. And there seem to have been many causes for this. For to chastise those who had fallen served as an example, just as also the gloss upon the degrees admonishes, and it was improper immediately to admit notorious men to the communion [without their being tested]. These customs have long since grown obsolete. Neither is it necessary to restore them, because they are not necessary for the remission of sins before God. Neither did the Fathers hold this, namely, that men merit the remission of sins through such customs or such works, although these spectacles [such outward ceremonies] usually lead astray the ignorant to think that by these works they merit the remission of sins before God. But if any one thus holds, he holds to the faith of a Jew and heathen. For also the heathen had certain expiations for offenses through which they imagined to be reconciled to God. Now, however, although the custom has become obsolete, the name satisfaction still remains, and a trace of the custom also remains of prescribing in confession certain satisfactions, which they define as works that are not due. We call them canonical satisfactions. Of these we hold, just as of the enumeration, that canonical satisfactions [these public ceremonies] are not necessary by divine Law for the remission of sins, just as those ancient exhibitions of satisfactions in public repentance were not necessary by divine Law for the remission of sins. For the belief concerning faith must be retained, that by faith we obtain remission of sins for Christ's sake, and not for the sake of our works that precede or follow [when we are converted or born anew in Christ]. And for this reason we have discussed especially the question of satisfactions, that by submitting to them the righteousness of faith be not obscured, or men think that for the sake of these works they obtain remission of sins. And many sayings that are current in the schools aid the error, such as that which they give in the definition of satisfaction, namely, that it is wrought for the purpose of appeasing the divine displeasure.

But, nevertheless, the adversaries acknowledge that satisfactions are of no profit for the remission of guilt. Yet they imagine that satisfactions are of profit in redeeming from the punishments, whether of purgatory or other punishments. For thus they teach that in the remission of sins, God [without means, alone] remits the guilt, and yet, because it belongs to divine justice to punish sin, that He commutes eternal into temporal punishment. They add further that a part of this temporal punishment is remitted by the power of the keys, but that the rest is redeemed by means of satisfactions. Neither can it be understood of what punishments a part is remitted by the power of the keys, unless they say that a part of the punishments of purgatory is remitted, from which it would follow that satisfactions are only punishments redeeming from purgatory. And these satisfactions, they say, avail even though they are rendered by those who have relapsed into mortal sin, as though indeed the divine displeasure could be appeased by those who are in mortal sin. This entire matter is fictitious, and recently fabricated without the authority of Scripture and the old writers of the Church. And not even Longobardus speaks in this way of satisfactions. The scholastics saw that there were satisfactions in the Church; and they did not notice that these exhibitions had been instituted both for the purpose of example, and for testing those who desired to be received by the Church. In a word, they did not see that it was a discipline, and entirely a secular matter. Accordingly, they superstitiously imagined that these avail not for discipline before the Church, but for appeasing God. And just as in other places they frequently, with great inaptness, have confounded spiritual and civil matters [the kingdom of Christ, which is spiritual, and the kingdom of the world, and external discipline], the same happens also with regard to satisfactions. But the gloss on the canons at various places testifies that these observances were instituted for the sake of church discipline [should serve alone for an example before the Church].

Let us see, moreover, how in the Confutation which they had the presumption to obtrude upon His Imperial Majesty, they prove these figments of theirs. They cite many passages from the Scriptures, in order to impose upon the inexperienced, as though this subject which was unknown even in the time of Longobard, had authority from the Scriptures. They bring forward such passages as these: Bring forth, therefore, fruits meet for repentance, Matt. 3, 8, Mark 1, 15. Again: Yield your members servants to righteousness Rom. 6, 19. Again, Christ preaches repentance, Matt. 4, 17: Repent. Again, Christ Luke 24, 47, commands the apostles to preach repentance, and Peter preaches repentance Acts 2, 38. Afterward they cite certain passages of the Fathers and the canons, and conclude that satisfactions in the Church are not to be abolished contrary to the plain Gospel and the decrees of the Councils and Fathers [against the decision of the Holy Church]; nay, even that those who have been absolved by the priest ought to bring to perfection the repentance that has been enjoined, following the declaration of Paul, Titus 2, 14: Who gave Himself for us that He might redeem us from all iniquity, and purify unto Himself a peculiar people, zealous of good works.

May God put to confusion these godless sophists who so wickedly distort God's

Word to their own most vain dreams! What good man is there who is not moved by such indignity?" Christ says, Repent, the apostles preach repentance; therefore eternal punishments are compensated by the punishments of purgatory; therefore the keys have the power to remit part of the punishments of purgatory; therefore satisfactions redeem the punishments of purgatory"! Who has taught these asses such logic? Yet this is neither logic nor sophistry, but cunning trickery. Accordingly, they appeal to the expression repent in such a way that, when the inexperienced hear such a passage cited against us they may derive the opinion that we deny the entire repentance. By these arts they endeavor to alienate minds and to enkindle hatred, so that the inexperienced may cry out against us [Crucify! crucify!], that such pestilent heretics as disapprove of repentance should be removed from their midst. [Thus they are publicly convicted of being liars in this matter.]

But we hope that among good men these calumnies [and misrepresentations of Holy Scripture] may make little headway. And God will not long endure such impudence and wickedness. [They will certainly be consumed by the First and Second Commandments.] Neither has the Pope of Rome consulted well for his own dignity in employing such patrons, because he has entrusted a matter of the greatest importance to the judgment of these sophists. For since we include in the Confession almost the sum of the entire Christian doctrine, judges should have been appointed to make a declaration concerning matters so important and so many and various, whose learning and faith would have been more approved than that of these sophists who have written this Confutation. It was particularly becoming for you, O Campegius, in accordance with your wisdom, to have taken care that in regard to matters of such importance they should write nothing which either at this time or with posterity might seem to be able to diminish regard for the Roman See. If the Roman See judges it right that all nations should acknowledge her as mistress of the faith, she ought to take pains that learned and uncorrupt men make investigation concerning matters of religion. For what will the world judge if at any time the writing of the adversaries be brought to light? What will posterity judge concerning these reproachful judicial investigations? You see, O Campegius, that these are the last times, in which Christ predicted that there would be the greatest danger to religion. You, therefore, who ought, as it were, to sit on the watch-tower and control religious matters, should in these times employ unusual wisdom and diligence. There are many signs which, unless you heed them, threaten a change to the Roman state. And you make a mistake if you think that Churches should be retained only by force and arms. Men ask to be taught concerning religion. How many do you suppose there are, not only in Germany, but also in England, in Spain, in France, in Italy, and finally even in the city of Rome, who, since they see that controversies have arisen concerning of the greatest importance, are beginning here and there to doubt, and to be silently indignant that you refuse to investigate and judge aright subjects of such weight as these; that you do not deliver wavering consciences; that you only bid us be overthrown and annihilated by arms? There are many good men to whom this doubt is more bitter than death. You do not consider sufficiently how great a subject religion is, if you think that good men are in anguish for a slight cause whenever they begin to doubt concerning any dogma. And this doubt can have no other effect than to produce the greatest bitterness of hatred against those who, when they ought to heal consciences, plant themselves in the way of the explanation of the subject. We do not here say that you ought to fear God's judgment. For the hierarchs think that they can easily provide against this, for since they hold the keys, of course they can open heaven for themselves whenever they wish. We are speaking of the judgments of men and the silent desires of all nations, which, indeed, at this time require that these matters be investigated and decided in such a manner that good minds may be healed and freed from doubt. For, in accordance with your wisdom, you can easily decide what will take place if at any time this hatred against you should break forth. But by this favor you will be able to bind to yourself all nations, as all sane men regard it as the highest and most important matter, if you heal doubting consciences. We have said these things not because we doubt concerning our Confession. For we know that it is true, godly, and useful to godly consciences. But it is likely that there are many in many places who waver concerning matters of no light importance, and yet do not hear such teachers as are able to heal their consciences.

But let us return to the main point. The Scriptures cited by the adversaries speak in no way of canonical satisfactions, and of the opinions of the scholastics, since it is evident that the latter were only recently born. Therefore it is pure slander when they distort Scripture to their own opinions. We say that good fruits, good works in every kind of life, ought to follow repentance, i.e., conversion or regeneration [the renewal of the Holy Ghost in the heart]. Neither can there be true conversion or true contrition where mortifications of the flesh and good fruits do not follow [if we do not externally render good works and Christian patience]. True terrors, true griefs of mind, do not allow the body to indulge in sensual pleasures, and true faith is not ungrateful to God, neither does it despise God's commandments. In a word, there is no inner repentance unless it also produces outwardly mortifications of the flesh. We say also that this is the meaning of John when he says, Matt. 3, 8: Bring forth, therefore, fruits meet for repentance. Likewise of Paul when he says Rom. 6, 19: Yield your members servants to righteousness; just as he likewise says elsewhere, Rom. 12, 1: Present your bodies a living sacrifice, etc. And when Christ says Matt. 4, 17: Repent, He certainly speaks of the entire repentance, of the entire newness of life and its fruits, He does not speak of those hypocritical satisfactions which, the scholastics avail for compensating the punishment of purgatory or other punishments when they are made by those who are in mortal sin.

Many arguments, likewise, can be collected to show that these passages of Scripture pertain in no way to scholastic satisfactions. These men imagine that satisfactions are works that are not due [which we are not obliged to do]; but Scripture, in these passages, requires works that are due [which we are obliged to do]. For this word of Christ, Repent, is the word of a commandment. Likewise the adversaries write that if any one who goes to confession should refuse to undertake satisfactions, he does not sin, but will pay these penalties in purgatory. Now the following passages are, without controversy, precepts pertaining to this life: Repent; Bring forth fruits meet for repentance; Yield your members servants to righteousness. Therefore they cannot be distorted to the satisfactions which it is permitted to refuse. For to refuse God's commandments is not permitted. [For God's commands are not thus left to our discretion.] Thirdly, indulgences remit these satisfactions, as is taught by the Chapter, *De Poenitentiis et Remissione*, beginning *Quum ex eo*, etc. But indulgences do not free us from the commandments: Repent; Bring forth fruits meet for repentance. Therefore it is manifest that these passages of Scripture have been wickedly distorted to apply to canonical satisfactions. See further what follows. If the punishments of purgatory are satisfactions, or satispassions [sufferings sufficient], or if satisfactions are a redemption of the punishments of purgatory, do these passages also give commandment that souls be punished in purgatory?

[The above-cited passages of Christ and Paul must also show and prove that souls enter purgatory and there suffer pain.] Since this must follow from the opinions of the adversaries, these passages should be interpreted in a new way [these passages should put on new coats]: Bring forth fruits meet for repentance; Repent, i.e., suffer the punishments of purgatory after this life. But we do not care about refuting in more words these absurdities of the adversaries. For it is evident that Scripture speaks of works that are due, of the entire newness of life, and not of these observances of works that are not due, of which the adversaries speak. And yet, by these figments they defend orders [of monks], the sale of Masses and infinite observances, namely, as works which, if they do not make satisfaction for guilt, yet make satisfaction for punishment.

Since, therefore, the passages of Scripture cited do not say that eternal punishments are to be compensated by works that are not due, the adversaries are rash in affirming that these satisfactions are compensated by canonical satisfactions. Nor do the keys have the command to commute some punishments, and likewise to remit a part of the punishments. For where are such things [dreams and lies] read in the Scriptures? Christ speaks of the remission of sins when He says Matt. 18, 18: Whatsoever ye shall loose, etc. [i.e.], sin being forgiven, death eternal is taken away, and life eternal bestowed. Nor does Whatsoever ye shall bind speak of the imposing of punishments, but of retaining the sins of those who are not converted. Moreover, the declaration of Longobard concerning remitting a part of the punishments has been taken from the canonical punishments; a part of these the pastors remitted. Although, we hold that repentance ought to bring forth good fruits for the sake of God's glory and command, and good fruits, true fastings, true prayers, true alms, etc., have the commands of God, yet in the Holy Scriptures we nowhere find this, namely, that eternal punishments are not remitted except on account of the punishment of purgatory or canonical satisfactions, i.e., on account of certain works not due, or that the power of the keys has the command to commute their punishments or to remit a portion. These things the adversaries were to prove. [This they will not attempt.]

Besides, the death of Christ is a satisfaction not only for guilt, but also for eternal death, according to Hos. 13, 14: 0 death, I will be thy death. How monstrous, therefore, it is to say that the satisfaction of Christ redeemed from the guilt, and our punishments redeem from eternal death, as the expression, I will be thy death, ought then to be understood, not concerning Christ, but concerning our works, and, indeed, not concerning the works commanded by God, but concerning some frigid observances devised by men! And these are said to abolish death, even when they are wrought in mortal sin. It is incredible with what grief we recite these absurdities of the adversaries, which cannot but cause one who considers them to be enraged against such doctrines of demons, which the devil has spread in the Church in order to suppress the knowledge of the Law and Gospel, of repentance and quickening, and the benefits of Christ. For of the Law they speak thus: "God, condescending to our weakness, has given to man a measure of those things to which of necessity he is bound and this is the observance of precepts, so that from what is left, i.e., from works of supererogation, he can render satisfaction with reference to offenses that have been committed." Here men imagine that they can observe the Law of God in such a manner as to be able to do even more than the Law exacts. But Scripture everywhere exclaims that we are far distant from the perfection which the Law requires. Yet these men imagine that the Law of God has been comprised in outward and civil righteousness; they do not see that it requires true love to God "with the whole heart," etc., and condemns the entire concupiscence in the nature. Therefore no one does as much as the Law requires. Hence their imagination that we can do more is ridiculous. For although we can perform outward works not commanded by God's Law [which Paul calls beggarly ordinances], yet the confidence that satisfaction is rendered God's Law [yea, that more is done than God demands] is vain and wicked. And true prayers, true alms, true fastings, have God's command; and where they have God's command, they cannot without sin be omitted. But these works, in so far as they have not been commanded by God's Law, but have a fixed form derived from human rule are works of human traditions of which Christ says, Matt. 15, 9: In vain they do worship Me with the commandments of men, such as certain fasts appointed not for restraining the flesh, but that, by this work, honor may be given to God, as Scotus says, and eternal death be made up for; likewise, a fixed number of prayers, a fixed measure of alms when they are rendered in such a way that this measure is a worship ***ex opere operato*** giving honor to God, and making up for eternal death. For they ascribe satisfaction to these ***ex opere operato***, because they teach that they avail even in those who are in mortal sin. There are works which depart still farther from God's commands, as [rosaries and] pilgrimages; and of these there is a great variety: one makes a journey [to St. Jacob] clad in mail, and another with bare feet. Christ calls these "vain acts of worship," and hence they do not serve to appease God's displeasure, as the adversaries say. And yet they adorn these works with magnificent titles; they call them works of supererogation, to them the honor is ascribed of being a price paid instead of eternal death. Thus they are preferred to the works of God's commandments [the true works expressly mentioned in the Ten Commandments]. In this way the Law of God is obscured in two ways, one, because satisfaction is thought to be rendered God's Law by means of outward and civil works, the other, because human traditions are added whose works are preferred to the works of the divine Law.

Part 17

In the second place, repentance and grace are obscured. For eternal death is not atoned for by this compensation of works because it is idle, and does not in the present life taste of death. Something else must be opposed to death when it tries us. For just as the wrath of God is overcome by faith in Christ, so death is overcome by faith in Christ. Just as Paul says, 1 Cor. 16, 67: But thanks be to God which giveth us the victory through our Lord Jesus Christ. He does not say: "Who giveth us the victory if we oppose our satisfactions against death." The adversaries treat of idle speculations concerning the remission of guilt, and do not see how in the remission of guilt, the heart is freed by faith in Christ from God's anger and eternal death. Since, therefore, the death of Christ is a satisfaction for eternal death, and since the adversaries themselves confess that these works of satisfactions are works that are not due, but are works of human traditions, of which Christ says, Matt. 16, 9, that they are vain acts of worship, we can safely affirm that canonical satisfactions are not necessary by divine Law for the remission of guilt, or eternal punishment, or the punishment of purgatory.

But the adversaries object that vengeance or punishment is necessary for repentance, because Augustine says that repentance is vengeance punishing, etc.. We grant that vengeance or punishment is necessary in repentance, yet not as merit or price, as the adversaries imagine that satisfactions are. But vengeance is in repentance formally, i.e., because regeneration itself occurs by a perpetual mortification of the oldness of life. The saying of Scotus may indeed be very beautiful, that *poenitentia* is so called because it is, as it were, *poenae tenentia*, holding to punishment. But of what punishment, of what vengeance, does Augustine speak? Certainly of true punishment, of true vengeance, namely, of contrition, of true terrors. Nor do we here exclude the outward mortifications of the body, which follow true grief of mind. The adversaries make a great mistake if they imagine that canonical satisfactions [their juggler's tricks, rosaries, pilgrimages, and such like] are more truly punishments than are true terrors in the heart. It is most foolish to distort the name of punishment to these frigid satisfactions, and not to refer them to those horrible terrors of conscience of which David says, Ps. 18, 4; 2 Sam. 22, 5: The sorrows of death compassed me. Who would not rather, clad in mail and equipped, seek the church of James, the basilica of Peter, etc., than bear that ineffable violence of grief which exists even in persons of ordinary lives, if there be true repentance?

But they say that it belongs to God's justice to punish sin. He certainly punishes it in contrition, when in these terrors He shows His wrath. Just as David indicates when he prays, Ps. 6, 1: 0 Lord, rebuke me not in Thine anger. And Jeremiah, 10, 24: 0 Lord, correct me, but with judgment; not in Thine anger, lest Thou bring me to nothing. Here indeed the most bitter punishments are spoken of. And the adversaries acknowledge that contrition can be so great that satisfaction is not required. Contrition is therefore more truly a punishment than is satisfaction. Besides, saints are subject to death, and all general afflictions, as Peter says, 1 Ep. 4, 17: For the time is come that judgment must begin at the house of God; and if it first begin at us, what shall the end be of them that obey not the Gospel of God? And although these afflictions are for the most part the punishments of sin, yet in the godly they have a better end, namely, to exercise them, that they may learn amidst trials to seek God's aid, to acknowledge the distrust of their own hearts, etc., as Paul says of himself, 2 Cor. 1, 9: But we had the sentence of death in ourselves, that we should not trust in ourselves, but in God which raiseth the dead. And Isaiah says, 26, 16: They poured out prayer when Thy chastening was upon them i.e., afflictions are a discipline by which God exercises the saints. Likewise afflictions are inflicted because of present sin, since in the saints they mortify and extinguish concupiscence, so that they may be renewed by the Spirit, as Paul says, Rom. 8, 10: The body is dead because of sin, i. e., it is mortified [more and more every day] because of present sin which is still left in the flesh. And death itself serves this purpose, namely, to abolish this flesh of sin, that we may rise absolutely new. Neither is there now in the death of the believer, since by faith he has overcome the terrors of death, that sting and sense of wrath of which Paul speaks 1 Cor. 15, 56: The sting of death is sin; and the strength of sin is the Law. This strength of sin, this sense of wrath, is truly a punishment as long as it is present; without this sense of wrath, death is not properly a punishment. Moreover, canonical satisfactions do not belong to these punishments; as the adversaries say that by the power of the keys a part of the punishments is remitted. Likewise, according to these very men, the keys remit the satisfactions, and the punishments on account of which the satisfactions are made. But it is evident that the common afflictions are not removed by the power of the keys. And if they wish to be understood concerning punishments, why do they add that satisfaction is to be rendered in purgatory?

They oppose the example of Adam, and also of David, who was punished for his adultery. From these examples they derive the universal rule that peculiar temporal punishments in the remission of sins correspond to individual sins. It has been said before that saints suffer punishments, which are works of God; they suffer contrition or terrors, they also suffer other common afflictions. Thus, for example, some suffer punishments of their own that have been imposed by God. And these punishments pertain in no way to the keys because the keys neither can impose nor remit them, but God, without the ministry of the keys, imposes and remits them [as He will].

Neither does the universal rule follow: Upon David a peculiar punishment was imposed, therefore, in addition to common afflictions, there is another punishment of purgatory, in which each degree corresponds to each sin. Where does Scripture teach that we cannot be freed from eternal death except by the compensation of certain punishments in addition to common afflictions? But, on the other hand, it most frequently teaches that the remission of sins occurs freely for Christ's sake, that Christ is the Victor of sin and death. Therefore the merit of satisfaction is not to be patched upon this. And although afflictions still remain, yet Scripture interprets these as the mortifications of present sin [to kill and humble the old Adam], and not as the compensations of eternal death or as prices for eternal death.

Job is excused that he was not afflicted on account of past evil deeds, therefore afflictions are not always punishments or signs of wrath. Yea, terrified consciences are to be taught that other ends of afflictions are more important [that they should learn to regard troubles far differently, namely, as signs of grace], lest they think that they are rejected by God when in afflictions they see nothing but God's punishment and anger. The other more important ends are to be considered namely, that

God is doing His strange work so that He may be able to do His own work, etc., as Isaiah teaches in a long discourse, chap. 28. And when the disciples asked concerning the blind man who sinned, John 9, 2. 3, Christ replies that the cause of his blindness is not sin, but that the works of God should be made manifest in him. And in Jeremiah, 49, 12, it is said: They whose judgment was not to drink of the cup have assuredly drunken. Thus the prophets and John the Baptist and other saints were killed. Therefore afflictions are not always punishments for certain past deeds, but they are the works of God, intended for our profit, and that the power of God might be made more manifest in our weakness [how He can help in the midst of death].

Thus Paul says, 2 Cor. 12, 5. 9: The strength of God is made perfect in my weakness. Therefore, because of God's will, our bodies ought to be sacrifices, declare our obedience [and patience], and not to compensate for eternal death, for which God has another price namely, the death of His own Son. And in this sense Gregory interprets even the punishment of David when he says: If God on account of that sin had threatened that he would thus be humbled by his son, why, when the sin was forgiven, did He fulfil that which He had threatened against him? The reply is that this remission was made that man might not be hindered from receiving eternal life, but that the example of the threatening followed, in order that the piety of the man might be exercised and tested even in this humility. Thus also God inflicted upon man death of body on account of sin, and after the remission of sins He did not remove it, for the sake of exercising justice namely, in order that the righteousness of those who are sanctified might be exercised and tested.

Nor, indeed, are common calamities [as war, famine, and similar calamities], properly speaking, removed by these works of canonical satisfactions, i.e., by these works of human traditions, which, they say, ***avail ex opere operato***, in such a way that, even though they are wrought in mortal sin, yet they redeem from the punishments. [And the adversaries themselves confess that they impose satisfactions, not on account of such common calamities but on account of purgatory; hence, their satisfactions are pure imaginations and dreams.] And when the passage of Paul, 1 Cor. 11, 31, is cited against us: If we would judge ourselves, we should not be judged by the Lord [they conclude therefrom that, if we impose punishment upon ourselves, God will judge us the more graciously], the word to judge ought to be understood of the entire repentance and due fruits, not of works which are not due. Our adversaries pay the penalty for despising grammar when they understand to judge to be the same as to make a pilgrimage clad in mail to the church of St. James, or similar works. To judge signifies the entire repentance, it signifies to condemn sins. This condemnation truly occurs in contrition and the change of life. The entire repentance, contrition, faith, the good fruits, obtain the mitigation of public and private punishments and calamities, as Isaiah teaches chap. 1, 17, 19: Cease to do evil; learn to do well, etc. Though your sins be as scarlet, they shall be white as snow. If ye be willing and obedient, ye shall eat the good of the land. Neither should a most important and salutary meaning be transferred from the entire repentance, and from works due or commanded by God, to the satisfactions and works of human traditions. And this it is profitable to teach that common evils are mitigated by our repentance and by the true fruits of repentance, by good works wrought from faith, not, as these men imagine, wrought in mortal sin. And here belongs the example of the Ninevites, Jonah 3, 10, who by their repentance (we speak of the entire repentance) were reconciled to God, and obtained the favor that their city was not destroyed.

Moreover, the making mention, by the Fathers, of satisfaction, and the framing of canons by the councils, we have said above was a matter of church-discipline instituted on account of the example. Nor did they hold that this discipline is necessary for the remission either of the guilt or of the punishment. For if some of them made mention of purgatory, they interpret it not as compensation for eternal punishment [which only Christ makes], not as satisfaction, but as purification of imperfect souls. Just as Augustine says that venial [daily] offenses are consumed i.e., distrust towards God and other similar dispositions are mortified. Now and then the writers transfer the term satisfaction from the rite itself or spectacle, to signify true mortification. Thus Augustine says: True satisfaction is to cut off the causes of sin, i.e., to mortify the flesh, likewise to restrain the flesh, not in order that eternal punishments may be compensated for but so that the flesh may not allure to sin.

Thus concerning restitution, Gregory says that repentance is false if it does not satisfy those whose property we have taken. For he who still steals does not truly grieve that he has stolen or robbed. For he is a thief or robber, so long as he is the unjust possessor of the property of another. This civil satisfaction is necessary, because it is written Eph. 4, 28: Let him that stole, steal no more. Likewise

Chrysostom says: In the heart, contrition; in the mouth, confession; in the work, entire humility. This amounts to nothing against us. Good works ought to follow repentance, it ought to be repentance, not simulation, but a change of the entire life for the better.

Likewise, the Fathers wrote that it is sufficient if once in life this public or ceremonial penitence occur, about which the canons concerning satisfactions have been made. Therefore it can be understood that they held that these canons are not necessary for the remission of sins. For in addition to this ceremonial penitence, they frequently wish that penitence be rendered otherwise, where canons of satisfactions were not required.

The composers of the Confutation write that the abolition of satisfactions contrary to the plain Gospel is not to be endured. We, therefore, have thus far shown that these canonical satisfactions, i. e., works not due and that are to be performed in order to compensate for punishment, have not the command of the Gospel. The subject itself shows this. If works of satisfaction are works which are not due, why do they cite the plain Gospel? For if the Gospel would command that punishments be compensated for by such works, the works would already be due. But thus they speak in order to impose upon the inexperienced, and they cite testimonies which speak of works that are due, although they themselves in their own satisfactions prescribe works that are not due. Yea, in their schools they themselves concede that satisfactions can be refused without [mortal] sin. Therefore they here write falsely that we are compelled by the plain Gospel to undertake these canonical satisfactions.

But we have already frequently testified that repentance ought to produce good fruits: and what the good fruits are the [Ten] Commandments teach, namely, [truly and from the heart most highly to esteem, fear, and love God, joyfully to call upon Him in need], prayer, thanksgiving, the confession of the Gospel [hearing this Word], to teach the Gospel, to obey parents and magistrates, to be faithful to one's calling, not to kill, not to retain hatred, but to be forgiving [to be agreeable and kind to one's neighbor], to give to the needy, so far as we can according to our means, not to commit fornication or adultery, but to restrain and bridle and chastise the flesh, not for a compensation of eternal punishment, but so as not to obey the devil, or offend the Holy Ghost, likewise, to speak the truth. These fruits have God's injunction, and ought to be brought forth for the sake of God's glory and command; and they have their rewards also. But that eternal punishments are not remitted except on account of the compensation rendered by certain traditions or by purgatory, Scripture does not teach. Indulgences were formerly remission of these public observances, so that men should not be excessively burdened. But if, by human authority, satisfactions and punishments can be remitted, this compensation, therefore, is not necessary by divine Law, for a divine Law is not annulled by human authority. Furthermore, since the custom has now of itself become obsolete and the bishops have passed it by in silence, there is no necessity for these remissions. And yet the name indulgences remained. And just as satisfactions were understood not with reference to external discipline, but with reference to the compensation of punishment, so indulgences were incorrectly understood to free souls from purgatory. But the keys have not the power of binding and loosing except upon earth, according to Matt. 16, 19 : Whatsoever thou shalt bind on earth shall be bound in heaven, and whatsoever thou shalt loose on earth shall be loosed in heaven. Although as we have said above, the keys have not the power to impose penalties, or to institute rites of worship, but only the command to remit sins to those who are converted, and to convict and excommunicate those who are unwilling to be converted. For just as to loose signifies to remit sins, so to bind signifies not to remit sins. For Christ speaks of a spiritual kingdom. And the command of God is that the ministers of the Gospel should absolve those who are converted, according to 2 Cor. 10, 8: The authority which the Lord hath given us for edification. Therefore the reservation of eases is a secular affair. For it is a reservation of canonical punishment; it is not a reservation of guilt before God in those who are truly converted. Therefore the adversaries judge aright when they confess that in the article of death the reservation of eases ought not to hinder absolution.

We have set forth the sum of our doctrine concerning repentance, which we certainly know is godly and salutary to good minds [and highly necessary]. And if good men will compare our [yea, Christ's and His apostles'] doctrine with the very confused discussions of our adversaries, they will perceive that the adversaries have omitted the doctrine [without which no one can teach or learn anything that is substantial and Christian] concerning faith justifying and consoling godly hearts. They will also see that the adversaries invent many things concerning the merits of attrition, concerning the endless enumeration of offenses, concerning satisfactions, they say things [that touch neither earth nor heaven] agreeing neither with human nor divine law, and which not even the adversaries themselves can satisfactorily explain.

Part 18

Article XIII (VII): *Of the Number and Use of the Sacraments.*

In the Thirteenth Article the adversaries approve our statement that the Sacraments are not only marks of profession among men, as some imagine, but that they are rather signs and testimonies of God's will toward us, through which God moves hearts to believe [are not mere signs whereby men may recognize each other, as the watchword in war, livery, etc., but are efficacious signs and sure testimonies, etc.]. But here they bid us also count seven sacraments. We hold that it should be maintained that the matters and ceremonies instituted in the Scriptures, whatever the number, be not neglected. Neither do we believe it to be of any consequence, though, for the purpose of teaching, different people reckon differently, provided they still preserve aright the matters handed down in Scripture. Neither have the ancients reckoned in the same manner. [But concerning this number of seven sacraments, the fact is that the Fathers have not been uniform in their enumeration, thus also these seven ceremonies are not equally necessary.]

If we call Sacraments rites which have the command of God and to which the promise of grace has been added, it is easy to decide what are properly Sacraments. For rites instituted by men will not in this way be Sacraments properly so called. For it does not belong to human authority to promise grace. Therefore signs instituted without God's command are not sure signs of grace, even though they perhaps instruct the rude [children or the uncultivated], or admonish as to something [as a painted cross]. Therefore Baptism, the Lord's Supper, and Absolution, which is the Sacrament of Repentance, are truly Sacraments. For these rites have God's command and the promise of grace, which is peculiar to the New Testament. For when we are baptized, when we eat the Lord's body, when we are absolved, our hearts must be firmly assured that God truly forgives us for Christ's sake. And God, at the same time, by the Word and by the rite, moves hearts to believe and conceive faith, just as Paul says, Rom. 10, 17: Faith cometh by hearing. But just as the Word enters the ear in order to strike our heart, so the rite itself strikes the eye, in order to move the heart. The effect of the Word and of the rite is the same, as it has been well said by Augustine that a Sacrament is a visible word, because the rite is received by the eyes, and is, as it were, a picture of the Word, signifying the same thing as the Word. Therefore the effect of both is the same.

Confirmation and Extreme Unction are rites received from the Fathers which not even the Church requires as necessary to salvation, they do not have God's command. Therefore it is not useless to distinguish these rites from the former, which have God's express command and a clear promise of grace.

The adversaries understand priesthood not of the ministry of the Word, and administering the Sacraments to others, but they understand it as referring to sacrifice, as though in the New Testament there ought to be a priesthood like the Levitical, to sacrifice for the people, and merit the remission of sins for others. We teach that the sacrifice of Christ dying on the cross has been sufficient for the sins of the whole world, and that there is no need, besides, of other sacrifices, as though this were not sufficient for our sins. Men, accordingly, are justified not because of any other sacrifices, but because of this one sacrifice of Christ, if they believe that they have been redeemed by this sacrifice. They are accordingly called priests, not in order to make any sacrifices for the people as in the Law so that by these they may merit remission of sins for the people; but they are called to teach the Gospel and administer the Sacraments to the people. Nor do we have another priesthood like the Levitical, as the Epistle to the Hebrews sufficiently teaches. But if ordination be understood as applying to the ministry of the Word, we are not unwilling to call ordination a sacrament. For the ministry of the Word has God's command and glorious promises, Rom. 1, 16: The Gospel is the power of God unto salvation to every one that believeth. Likewise, Is. 55, 11: So shall My Word be that goeth forth out of My mouth; it shall not return unto Me void, but it shall accomplish that which I please. If ordination be understood in this way, neither will we refuse to call the imposition of hands a sacrament. For the Church has the command to appoint ministers, which should be most pleasing to us, because we know that God approves this ministry and is present in the ministry [that God will preach and work through men and those who have been chosen by men]. And it is of advantage, so far as can be done, to adorn the ministry of the Word with every kind of praise against fanatical men, who dream that the Holy Ghost is given not through the Word, but because of certain preparations of their own, if they sit unoccupied and silent in obscure places, waiting for illumination, as the Enthusiasts formerly taught, and the Anabaptists now teach.

Matrimony was not first instituted in the New Testament, but in the beginning, immediately on the creation of the human race. It has, moreover, God's command; it has also promises, not indeed properly pertaining to the New Testament, but pertaining rather to the bodily life. Wherefore, if any one should wish to call it a sacrament, he ought still to distinguish it from those preceding ones [the two former ones], which are properly signs of the New Testament, and testimonies of grace and the remission of sins. But if marriage will have the name of sacrament for the reason that it has God's command other states or offices also, which have God's command, may be called sacraments, as, for example, the magistracy.

Lastly, if among the Sacraments all things ought to be numbered which have God's command, and to which promises have been added, why do we not add prayer, which most truly can be called a sacrament? For it has both God's command and very many promises and if placed among the Sacraments, as though in a more eminent place, it would invite men to pray. Alms could also be reckoned here, and likewise afflictions, which are even themselves signs, to which God has added promises. But let us omit these things. For no prudent man will strive greatly concerning the number or the term, if only those objects still be retained which have God's command and promises.

It is still more needful to understand how the Sacraments are to be used. Here we condemn the whole crowd of scholastic doctors, who teach that the Sacraments confer grace *ex opere operato*, without a good disposition on the part of the one using them, provided he do not place a hindrance in the way. This is absolutely a Jewish opinion, to hold that we are justified by a ceremony, without a good disposition of the heart, i.e., without faith. And yet this impious and pernicious opinion is taught with great authority throughout the entire realm of the Pope. Paul contradicts this and denies, Rom. 4, 9, that Abraham was justified by circumcision, but asserts that circumcision was a sign presented for exercising faith. Thus we teach that in the use of the Sacraments faith ought to be added, which should believe these promises, and receive the promised things, there offered in the Sacrament. And the reason is plain and thoroughly grounded. [This is a certain and true use of the holy Sacrament, on which Christian hearts and consciences may risk to rely.] The promise is useless unless it is received by faith. But the Sacraments are the signs [and seals] of the promises. Therefore, in the use of the Sacraments faith ought to be added so that, if any one use the Lord's Supper, he use it thus. Because this is a Sacrament of the New Testament, as Christ clearly says, he ought for this very reason to be confident that what is promised in the New Testament namely, the free remission of sins, is offered him. And let him receive this by faith, let him comfort his alarmed conscience, and know that these testimonies are not fallacious, but as sure as though [and still surer than if] God by a new miracle would declare from heaven that it was His will to grant forgiveness. But of what advantage would these miracles and promises be to an unbeliever? And here we speak of special faith which believes the present promise, not only that which in general believes that God exists, but which believes that the remission of sins is offered. This use of the Sacrament consoles godly and alarmed minds.

Moreover, no one can express in words what abuses in the Church this fanatical opinion concerning the opus operate, without a good disposition on the part of the one using the Sacraments, has produced. Hence the infinite profanation of the Masses, but of this we shall speak below. Neither can a single letter be produced from the old writers which in this matter favors the scholastics. Yea Augustine says the contrary, that the faith of the Sacrament, and not the Sacrament justifies. And the declaration of Paul is well known, Rom. 10, 10: With the heart man believeth unto righteousness.

Part 19

Article XIV: *Of Ecclesiastical Order.*

The Fourteenth Article, in which we say that in the Church the administration of the Sacraments and Word ought to be allowed no one unless he be rightly called, they receive, but with the proviso that we employ canonical ordination. Concerning this subject we have frequently testified in this assembly that it is our greatest wish to maintain church-polity and the grades in the Church [old church-regulations and the government of bishops], even though they have been made by human authority [provided the bishops allow our doctrine and receive our priests]. For we know that church-discipline was instituted by the Fathers, in the manner laid down in the ancient canons with a good and useful intention. But the bishops either compel our priests to reject and condemn this kind of doctrine which we have confessed, or, by a new and unheard-of cruelty, they put to death the poor innocent men. These causes hinder our priests from acknowledging such bishops. Thus the cruelty of the bishops is the reason why the canonical government, which we greatly desired to maintain, is in some places dissolved. Let them see to it how they will give an account to God for dispersing the Church. In this matter our consciences are not in danger, because since we know that our Confession is true, godly, and catholic, we ought not to approve the cruelty of those who persecute this doctrine. And we know that the Church is among those who teach the Word of God aright, and administer the Sacraments aright and not with those who not only by their edicts endeavor to efface God's Word, but also put to death those who teach what is right and true towards whom, even though they do something contrary to the canons, yet the very canons are milder. Furthermore we wish here again to testify that we will gladly maintain ecclesiastical and canonical government, provided the bishops only cease to rage against our Churches. This our desire will clear us both before God and among all nations to all posterity from the imputation against us that the authority of the bishops is being undermined, when men read and hear that, although protesting against the unrighteous cruelty of the bishops, we could not obtain justice.

Part 20

Article XV (VIII): *Of Human Traditions in the Church.*

In the Fifteenth Article they receive the first part, in which we say that such ecclesiastical rites are to be observed as can be observed without sin, and are of profit in the Church for tranquility and good order. They altogether condemn the second part, in which we say that human traditions instituted to appease God, to merit grace, and make satisfactions for sins are contrary to the Gospel. Although in the Confession itself, when treating of the distinction of meats, we have spoken at sufficient length concerning traditions, yet certain things should be briefly recounted here.

Although we supposed that the adversaries would defend human traditions on other grounds, yet we did not think that this would come to pass, namely, that they would condemn this article: that we do not merit the remission of sins or grace by the observance of human traditions. Since, therefore, this article has been condemned, we have an easy and plain case. The adversaries are now openly Judaizing, are openly suppressing the Gospel by the doctrines of demons. For Scripture calls traditions doctrines of demons when it is taught that religious rites are serviceable to merit the remission of sins and grace. For they are then obscuring the Gospel, the benefit of Christ, and the righteousness of faith. [For they are just as directly contrary to Christ and to the Gospel as are fire and water to one another.] The Gospel teaches that by faith we receive freely, for Christ's sake, the remission of sins and are reconciled. The adversaries, on the other hand, appoint another mediator, namely these traditions. On account of these they wish to acquire remission of sins; on account of these they wish to appease God's wrath. But Christ clearly says,

Matt. 15, 9: In vain do they worship Me, teaching for doctrines the commandments of men.

We have above discussed at length that men are justified by faith when they believe that they have a reconciled God, not because of our works, but gratuitously, for Christ's sake. It is certain that this is the doctrine of the Gospel, because Paul clearly teaches Eph. 2, 8. 9: By grace are ye saved, through faith; and that not of yourselves: it is the gift of God; not of works. Now these men say that men merit the remission of sins by these human observances. What else is this than to appoint another justifier, a mediator other than Christ? Paul says to the Galatians, 5, 4: Christ has become of no effect unto you, whosoever of you are justified by the Law, i.e., if you hold that by the observance of the Law you merit to be accounted righteous before God, Christ will profit you nothing; for what need of Christ have those who hold that they are righteous by their own observance of the Law? God has set forth Christ with the promise that on account of this Mediator, and not on account of our righteousness, He wishes to be propitious to us. But these men hold that God is reconciled and propitious because of the traditions, and not because of Christ. Therefore they take away from Christ the honor of Mediator. Neither, so far as this matter is concerned is there any difference between our traditions and the ceremonies of Moses. Paul condemns the ceremonies of Moses, just as he condemns traditions, for the reason that they were regarded as works which merit righteousness before God. Thus the office of Christ and the righteousness of faith were obscured. Therefore, the Law being removed, and traditions being removed, he contends that the remission of sins has been promised not because of our works, but freely, because of Christ, if only by faith we receive it. For the promise is not received except by faith. Since, therefore, by faith we receive the remission of sins since by faith we have a propitious God for Christ's sake, it is an error and impiety to declare that because of these observances we merit the remission of sins. If any one should say here that we do not merit the remission of sins, but that those who have already been justified by these traditions merit grace, Paul again replies, Gal. 2, 17, that Christ would be the minister of sin if after justification we must hold that henceforth we are not accounted righteous for Christ's sake, but we ought first, by other observances, to merit that we be accounted righteous. Likewise Gal. 3, 15: Though it be but a man's covenant, no man addeth thereto. Therefore, neither to God's covenant, who promises that for Christ's sake He will be propitious to us ought we to add that we must first through these observances attain such merit as to be regarded as accepted and righteous.

However, what need is there of a long discussion? No tradition was instituted by the holy Fathers with the design that it should merit the remission of sins, or righteousness, but they have been instituted for the sake of good order in the Church and for the sake of tranquillity. And when any one wishes to institute certain works to merit the remission of sins, or righteousness, how will he know that these works please God since he has not the testimony of God's Word? How, without God's command and Word, will he render men certain of God's will? Does He not everywhere in the prophets prohibit men from instituting, without His commandment, peculiar rites of worship? In Ezek. 20, 18. 19 it is written: Walk ye not in the statutes of your fathers, neither observe their judgments, nor defile yourselves with their idols: I Am the Lord, your God. Walk in My statutes, and keep My judgements, and do them. If men are allowed to institute religious rites and through these rites merit grace, the religious rites of all the heathen will have to be approved, and the rites instituted by Jeroboam, 1 Kings 12, 26 f., and by others, outside of the Law, will have to be approved. For what difference does it make? If we have been allowed to institute religious rites that are profitable for meriting grace, or righteousness, why was the same not allowed the heathen and the Israelites? But the religious rites of the heathen and the Israelites were rejected for the very reason that they held that by these they merited remission of sins and righteousness, and yet did not know [the highest service of God] the righteousness of faith. Lastly, whence are we rendered certain that rites instituted by men without God's command justify, inasmuch as nothing can be affirmed of God's will without God's Word? What if God does not approve these services? How, therefore, do the adversaries affirm that they justify? Without God's Word and testimony this cannot be affirmed. And Paul says, Rom. 14, 23 Whatsoever is not of faith is sin. But as these services have no testimony of God's Word, conscience must doubt as to whether they please God.

And what need is there of words on a subject so manifest? If the adversaries defend these human services as meriting justification, grace, and the remission of sins, they simply establish the kingdom of Antichrist. For the kingdom of Antichrist is a new service of God, devised by human authority rejecting Christ, just as the kingdom of Mahomet has services and works through which it wishes to be justified before God; nor does it hold that men are gratuitously justified before God by faith for Christ's sake. Thus the Papacy also will be a part of the kingdom of Antichrist if it thus defends human services as justifying. For the honor is taken away from Christ when they teach that we are not justified gratuitously by faith, for Christ's sake, but by such services, especially when they teach that such services are not only useful for justification, but are also necessary, as they hold above in Art. VII, where they condemn us for saying that unto true unity of the Church it is not necessary that rites instituted by men should everywhere be alike. Daniel, 11, 38, indicates that new human services will be the very form and constitution of the kingdom of Antichrist. For he says thus: But in his estate shall he honor the god of forges; and a god whom his fathers knew not shall he honor with gold and silver and precious stones. Here he describes new services, because he says that such a god shall be worshiped as the fathers were ignorant of. For although the holy Fathers themselves had both rites and traditions, yet they did not hold that these matters are useful or necessary for justification they did not obscure the glory and office Christ, but taught that we are justified by faith for Christ's sake, and not for the sake of these human services. But they observed human rites for the sake of bodily advantage, that the people might know at what time they should assemble; that, for the sake of example, all things in the churches might be done in order and becomingly; lastly, that the common people might receive a sort of training. For the distinctions of times and the variety of rites are of service in admonishing the common people. The Fathers had these reasons for maintaining the rites, and for these reasons we also judge it to be right that traditions [good customs] be maintained. And we are greatly surprised that the adversaries [contrary to the entire Scriptures of the Apostles, contrary to the Old and New Testaments] contend for another design of traditions, namely, that they may merit the remission of sins, grace, or justification. What else is this than to honor God with gold and silver and precious stones [as Daniel says], i.e., to hold that God becomes reconciled by a variety in clothing, ornaments, and by similar rites [many kinds of church decorations, banners, tapers], as are infinite in human traditions?

Paul writes to the Colossians, 2, 23, that traditions have a show of wisdom.

And they indeed have. For this good order is very becoming in the Church, and for this reason is necessary. But human reason, because it does not understand the righteousness of faith, naturally imagines that such works justify men because they reconcile God, etc. Thus the common people among the Israelites thought, and by this opinion increased such ceremonies, just as among us they have grown in the monasteries [as in our time one altar after another and one church after another is founded]. Thus human reason judges also of bodily exercises, of fasts, although the end of these is to restrain the flesh, reason falsely adds that they are services which justify. As Thomas writes: Fasting avails for the extinguishing and the prevention of guilt. These are the words of Thomas. Thus the semblance of wisdom and righteousness in such works deceives men. And the examples of the saints are added [when they say: St. Francis wore a cap, etc.]; and when men desire to imitate these, they imitate, for the most part, the outward exercises; their faith they do not imitate.

After this semblance of wisdom and righteousness has deceived men, then infinite evils follow; the Gospel concerning the righteousness of faith in Christ is obscured, and vain confidence in such works succeeds. Then the commandments of God are obscured; these works arrogate to themselves the title of a perfect and spiritual life, and are far preferred to the works of God's commandments [the true, holy, good works], as, the works of one's own calling, the administration of the state, the management of a family, married life, the bringing up of children. Compared with those ceremonies, the latter are judged to be profane, so that they are exercised by many with some doubt of conscience. For it is known that many have abandoned the administration of the state and married life, in order to embrace these observances as better and holier [have gone into cloisters in order to become holy and spiritual].

Nor is this enough. When the persuasion has taken possession of minds that such observances are necessary to justification, consciences are in miserable anxiety because they cannot exactly fulfil all observances. For how many are there who could enumerate all these observances? There are immense books, yea whole libraries, containing not a syllable concerning Christ, concerning faith in Christ, concerning the good works of one's own calling, but which only collect the traditions and interpretations by which they are sometimes rendered quite rigorous and sometimes relaxed. [They write of such precepts as of fasting for forty days, the four canonical hours for prayer, etc.] How that most excellent man, Gerson, is tortured while he searches for the grades and extent of the precepts! Nevertheless, he is not able to fix *epieicheian* [mitigation] in a definite grade [and yet cannot find any sure grade where he could confidently promise the heart assurance and peace]. Meanwhile, he deeply deplores the dangers to godly consciences which this rigid interpretation of the traditions produces.

Against this semblance of wisdom and righteousness in human rites, which deceives men, let us therefore fortify ourselves by the Word of God, and let us know, first of all that these neither merit before God the remission of sins or justification, nor are necessary for justification. We have above cited some testimonies. And Paul is full of them. To the Colossians, 2, 16. 17, he clearly says: Let no man, therefore, judge you in meat or in drink, or in respect of an holy-day, or of the new moon, or of the Sabbath-days, which are a shadow of things to come; but the body is of Christ. Here now he embraces at the same time both the Law of Moses and human traditions in order that the adversaries may not elude these testimonies, according to their custom, upon the ground that Paul is speaking only of the Law of Moses. But he clearly testifies here that he is speaking of human traditions. However, the adversaries do not see what they are saying; if the Gospel says that the ceremonies of Moses, which were divinely instituted, do not justify, how much less do human traditions justify!

Neither have the bishops the power to institute services, as though they justified, or were necessary for justification. Yea, the apostles, Acts 15, 10, say: Why tempt ye God to put a yoke, etc., where Peter declares this purpose to burden the Church a great sin. And Paul forbids the Galatians, 5, 1, to be entangled again with the yoke of bondage. Therefore, it is the will of the apostles that this liberty remain in the Church, that no services of the Law or of traditions be judged as necessary (just as in the Law ceremonies were for a time necessary), lest the righteousness of faith be obscured, if men judge that these services merit justification, or are necessary for justification. Many seek in traditions various *epieicheian* [mitigations] in order to heal consciences, and yet they do not find any sure grades by which to free consciences from these chains. But just as Alexander once for all solved the Gordian knot by cutting it with his sword when he could not disentangle it, so the apostles once for all free consciences from traditions, especially if they are taught to merit justification. The apostles compel us to oppose this doctrine by teaching and examples. They compel us to teach that traditions do not justify; that they are not necessary for justification; that no one ought to frame or receive traditions with the opinion that they merit justification. Then, even though any one should observe them, let him observe them without superstition as civil customs, just as without superstition soldiers are clothed in one way and scholars in another [as I regard my wearing of a German costume among the Germans and a French costume among the French as an observance of the usage of the land, and not for the purpose of being saved thereby]. The apostles violate traditions and are excused by Christ for the example was to be shown the Pharisees that these services are unprofitable. And if our people neglect some traditions that are of little advantage, they are now sufficiently excused, when these are required as though they merit justification. For such an opinion with regard to traditions is impious [an error not to be endured].

But we cheerfully maintain the old traditions [as, the three high festivals, the observance of Sunday, and the like] made in the Church for the sake of usefulness and tranquillity, and we interpret them in a more moderate way, to the exclusion of the opinion which holds that they justify. And our enemies falsely accuse us of abolishing good ordinances and churchdiscipline. For we can truly declare that the public form of the churches is more becoming with us than with the adversaries [that the true worship of God is observed in our churches in a more Christian, honorable way]. And if any one will consider it aright, we conform to the canons more truly than do the adversaries. [For the adversaries, without shame, tread under foot the most honorable canons, just as they do Christ and the Gospel.] With the adversaries, unwilling celebrants, and those hired for pay, and very frequently only for pay, celebrate the Masses. They sing psalms, not that they may learn or pray [for the greater part do not understand a verse in the psalms], but for the sake of the service as though this work were a service, or at feast, for the sake of reward. [All this they cannot deny. Some who are upright among them are even ashamed of this baffle, and declare that the clergy is in need of reformation.] With us many use the Lord's Supper [willingly and without constraint] every Lord's Day, but after having been first instructed, examined [whether they know and understand anything of the Lord's Prayer, the Creed, and the Ten Commandments], and absolved.

The children sing psalms in order that they may learn [become familiar with passages of Scripture], the people also sing [Latin and German psalms], in order that they may either learn or pray. With the adversaries there is no catechization of the children whatever, concerning which even the canons give commands. With us the pastors and ministers of the churches are compelled publicly [and privately] to instruct and hear the youth; and this ceremony produces the best fruits. [And the Catechism is not a mere childish thing, as is the bearing of banners and tapers, but a very profitable instruction.] Among the adversaries, in many regions [as in Italy and Spain], during the entire year no sermons are delivered, except in Lent [Here they ought to cry out and justly make grievous complaint, for this means at one blow to overthrow completely all worship. For of all acts that is the greatest most holy, most necessary, and highest, which God has required as the highest in the First and the Second Commandment, namely, to preach the Word of God. For the ministry is the highest office in the Church. Now, if this worship is omitted, how can there be knowledge of God, the doctrine of Christ, or the Gospel,] But the chief service of God is to teach the Gospel. And when the adversaries do preach, they speak of human traditions, of the worship of saints [of consecrated water], and similar tripes, which the people justly loathe, therefore they are deserted immediately in the beginning, after the text of the Gospel has been recited. [This practise may have started because the people did not wish to hear the other lies.] A few better ones begin now to speak of good works, but of the righteousness of faith, of faith in Christ, of the consolation of consciences, they say nothing; yea, this most wholesome part of the Gospel they rail at with their reproaches. [This blessed doctrine, the precious holy Gospel, they call Lutheran.] On the contrary, in our churches all the sermons are occupied with such topics as these: of repentance, of the fear of God, of faith in Christ, of the righteousness of faith, of the consolation of consciences by faith, of the exercises of faith; of prayer, what its nature should be, and that we should be fully confident that it is efficacious, that it is heard of the cross; of the authority of magistrates and all civil ordinances [likewise, how each one in his station should live in a Christian manner, and, out of obedience to the command of the Lord God, should conduct himself in reference to every worldly ordinance and law]; of the distinction between the kingdom of Christ, or the spiritual kingdom and political affairs, of marriage; of the education and instruction of children, of chastity; of all the offices of love. From this condition of the churches it may be judged that we diligently maintain church-discipline and godly ceremonies and good churchcustoms.

And of the mortification of the flesh and discipline of the body we thus teach, just as the Confession states, that a true and not a feigned mortification occurs through the cross and afflictions by which God exercises us [when God breaks our will, inflicts the cross and trouble]. In these we must obey God's will, as Paul says, Rom. 12, 1: Present your bodies a living sacrifice. And these are the spiritual exercises of fear and faith. But in addition to this mortification which occurs through the cross [which does not depend upon our will] there is also a voluntary kind of exercise necessary, of which Christ says Luke 21, 34: Take heed to yourselves lest at any time your hearts be overcharged with surfeiting. And Paul, 1 Cor. 9, 27: I keep under my body, and bring it into subjection, etc. And these exercises are to be undertaken not because they are services that justify, but in order to curb the flesh, lest satiety may overpower us, and render us secure and indifferent, the result of which is that men indulge and obey the dispositions of the flesh. This diligence ought to be perpetual, because it has the perpetual command of God. And this prescribed form of certain meats and times does nothing [as experience shows] towards curbing the flesh. For it is more luxurious and sumptuous than other feasts [for they were at greater expense, and practised greater gluttony with fish and various Lenten meats than when the fasts were not observed], and not even the adversaries observe the form given in the canons.

This topic concerning traditions contains many and difficult questions of controversy and we have actually experienced that traditions are truly snares of consciences. When they are exacted as necessary, they torture in wonderful ways the conscience omitting any observance [as godly hearts, indeed, experience when in the canonical hours they have omitted a compline, or offended against them in a similar way]. Again their abrogation has its own evils and its own questions. [On the other hand, to teach absolute freedom has also its doubts and questions, because the common people need outward discipline and instruction.] But we have an easy and plain case, because the adversaries condemn us for teaching that human traditions do not merit the remission of sins. Likewise they require universal traditions, as they call them, as necessary for justification [and place them in Christ's stead].

Here we have Paul as a constant champion, who everywhere contends that these observances neither justify nor are necessary in addition to the righteousness of faith. And nevertheless we teach that in these matters the use of liberty is to be so controlled that the inexperienced may not be offended, and, on account of the abuse of liberty, may not become more hostile to the true doctrine of the Gospel, or that without a reasonable cause nothing in customary rites be changed, but that, in order to cherish harmony, such old customs be observed as can be observed without sin or without great inconvenience. And in this very assembly we have shown sufficiently that for love's sake we do not refuse to observe adiaphora with others, even though they should have some disadvantage; but we have judged that such public harmony as could indeed be produced without offense to consciences ought to be preferred to all other advantages [all other less important matters]. But concerning this entire subject we shall speak after a while, when we shall treat of vows and ecclesiastical power.

Part 21

Article XVI: *Of Political Order.*

The Sixteenth Article the adversaries receive without any exception, in which we have confessed that it is lawful for the Christian to bear civil office, sit in judgment, determine matters by the imperial laws, and other laws in present force, appoint just punishments engage in just wars, act as a soldier, make legal contracts, hold property, take an oath when magistrates require it, contract marriage; finally, that legitimate civil ordinances are good creatures of God and divine ordinances, which a Christian can use with safety. This entire topic concerning the distinction between the kingdom of Christ and a political kingdom has been explained to advantage [to the remarkably great consolation of many consciences] in the literature of our writers, [namely] that the kingdom of Christ is spiritual [inasmuch as Christ governs by the Word and by preaching], to wit, beginning in the heart the knowledge of God, the fear of God and faith, eternal righteousness, and eternal life; meanwhile it permits us outwardly to use legitimate political ordinances of every nation in which we live, just as it permits us to use medicine or the art of building, or food, drink, air. Neither does the Gospel bring new laws concerning the civil state, but commands that we obey present laws, whether they have been framed by heathen or by others, and that in this obedience we should exercise love. For Carlstadt was insane in imposing upon us the judicial laws of Moses. Concerning these subjects, our theologians have written more fully, because the monks diffused many pernicious opinions in the Church. They called a community of property the polity of the Gospel; they said that not to hold property, not to vindicate one's self at law [not to have wife and child], were evangelical counsels. These opinions greatly obscure the Gospel and the spiritual kingdom [so that it was not understood at all what the Christian or spiritual kingdom of Christ is; they concocted the secular kingdom with the spiritual whence much trouble and seditions, harmful teaching resulted], and are dangerous to the commonwealth. For the Gospel does not destroy the State or the family [buying, selling, and other civil regulations], but much rather approves them, and bids us obey them as a divine ordinance, not only on account of punishment, but also on account of conscience.

Julian the Apostate, Celsus, and very many others made the objection to Christians that the Gospel would rend asunder states, because it prohibited legal redress, and taught certain other things not at all suited to political association. And these questions wonderfully exercised Origen, Nazianzen, and others, although, indeed, they can be most readily explained, if we keep in mind the fact that the Gospel does not introduce laws concerning the civil state, but is the remission of sins and the beginning of a new life in the hearts of believers; besides, it not only approves outward governments, but subjects us to them, Rom. 13, 1, just as we have been necessarily placed under the laws of seasons, the changes of winter and summer, as divine ordinances. [This is no obstacle to the spiritual kingdom.] The Gospel forbids private redress [in order that no one should interfere with the office of the magistrate], and Christ inculcates this so frequently with the design that the apostles should not think that they ought to seize the governments from those who held otherwise, just as the Jews dreamed concerning the kingdom of the Messiah, but that they might know they ought to teach concerning the spiritual kingdom that it does not change the civil state. Therefore private redress is prohibited not by advice, but by a command, Matt. 5, 39; Rom. 12, 19. Public redress which is made through the office of the magistrate, is not advised against, but is commanded, and is a work of God, according to Paul, Rom. 13, 1 sqq. Now the different kinds of public redress are legal decisions, capital punishment, wars, military service. It is manifest how incorrectly many writers have judged concerning these matters [some teachers have taught such pernicious errors that nearly all princes, lords, knights, servants regarded their proper estate as secular, ungodly, and damnable, etc. Nor can it be fully expressed in words what an unspeakable peril and damage has resulted from this to souls and consciences], because they were in the error that the Gospel is an external, new and monastic form of government, and did not see that the Gospel brings eternal righteousness to hearts [teaches how a person is redeemed, before God and in his conscience, from sin, hell, and the devil], while it outwardly approves the civil state.

It is also a most vain delusion that it is Christian perfection not to hold property. For Christian perfection consists not in the contempt of civil ordinances, but in dispositions of the heart, in great fear of God, in great faith, just as Abraham, David, Daniel, even in great wealth and while exercising civil power, were no less perfect than any hermits. But the monks [especially the Barefoot monks] have spread this outward hypocrisy before the eyes of men, so that it could not be seen in what things true perfection exists. With what praises have they brought forward this communion of property, as though it were evangelical! But these praises have the greatest danger, especially since they differ much from the Scriptures. For Scripture does not command that property be common, but the Law of the Decalog, when it says, Ex. 20, 15: Thou shalt not steal, distinguishes rights of ownership, and commands each one to hold what is his own. Wyclif manifestly was raging when he said that priests were not allowed to hold property. There are infinite discussions concerning contracts, in reference to which good consciences can never be satisfied unless they know the rule that it is lawful for a Christian to make use of civil ordinances and laws. This rule protects consciences when it teaches that contracts are lawful before God just to the extent that the magistrates or laws approve them.

This entire topic concerning civil affairs has been so clearly set forth by our theologians that very many good men occupied in the state and in business have declared that they have been greatly benefited, who before, troubled by the opinion of the monks, were in doubt as to whether the Gospel allowed these civil offices and business. Accordingly, we have recounted these things in order that those without also may understand that by the kind of doctrine which we follow, the authority of magistrates and the dignity of all civil ordinances are not undermined, but are all the more strengthened [and that it is only this doctrine which gives true instruction as to how eminently glorious an office, full of good Christian works, the office of rulers is]. The importance of these matters was greatly obscured previously by those silly monastic opinions, which far preferred the hypocrisy of poverty and humility to the state and the family, although these have God's command, while this Platonic communion [monasticism] has not God's command.

Part 22

Article XVII: *Of Christ's Return to Judgment.*

The Seventeenth Article the adversaries receive without exception, in which we confess that at the consummation of the world Christ shall appear, and shall raise up all the dead, and shall give to the godly eternal life and eternal joys, but shall condemn the ungodly to be punished with the devil without end.

Part 23

Article XVIII: *Of Free Will.*

The Eighteenth Article, Of Free Will, the adversaries receive, although they add some testimonies not at all adapted to this case. They add also a declamation that neither, with the Pelagians, is too much to be granted to the free will, nor, with the Manicheans, is all freedom to be denied it. Very well; but what difference is there between the Pelagians and our adversaries, since both hold that without the Holy Ghost men can love God and perform God's commandments with respect to the substance of the acts, and can merit grace and justification by works which reason performs by itself, without the Holy Ghost? How many absurdities follow from these Pelagian opinions, which are taught with great authority in the schools! These Augustine, following Paul, refutes pith great emphasis, whose judgment we have recounted above in the article Of Justification. (See p. 119 and 153.) Nor, indeed, do we deny liberty to the human will. The human will has liberty in the choice of works and things which reason comprehends by itself. It can to a certain extent render civil righteousness or the righteousness of works; it can speak of God, offer to God a certain service by an outward work, obey magistrates, parents; in the choice of an outward work it can restrain the hands from murder, from adultery, from theft. Since there is left in human nature reason and judgement concerning objects subjected to the senses, choice between these things, and the liberty and power to render civil righteousness, are also left. For Scripture calls this the righteousness of the flesh which the carnal nature, i.e., reason renders by itself, without the Holy Ghost. Although the power of concupiscence is such that men more frequently obey evil dispositions than sound judgment.

And the devil, who is efficacious in the godless, as Paul says Eph. 2, 2, does not cease to incite this feeble nature to various offenses. These are the reasons why even civil righteousness is rare among men, as we see that not even the philosophers themselves, who seem to have aspired after this righteousness, attained it. But it is false to say that he who performs the works of the commandments without grace does not sin. And they add further that such works also merit *de congruo* the remission of sins and justification. For human hearts without the Holy Ghost are without the fear of God; without trust toward God, they do not believe that they are heard, forgiven, helped, and preserved by God. Therefore they are godless. For neither can a corrupt tree bring forth good fruit, Matt. 7, 18. And without faith it is impossible to please God, Heb. 11, 6.

Therefore, although we concede free will the liberty and power to perform the outward works of the Law, yet we do not ascribe to free will these spiritual matters, namely, truly to fear God, truly to believe God, truly to be confident and hold that God regards us, hears us, forgives us, etc. These are the true works of the First Table, which the heart cannot render without the Holy Ghost, as Paul says, 1 Cor. 2, 14: The natural man, i.e., man using only natural strength, receiveth not the things of the Spirit of God [That is a person who is not enlightened by the Spirit of God does not, by his natural reason, receive anything of God's will and divine matters.] And this can be decided if men consider what their hearts believe concerning God's will, whether they are truly confident that they are regarded and heard by God. Even for saints to retain this faith [and, as Peter says (1 Ep. 1, 8), to risk and commit himself entirely to God, whom he does not see, to love Christ, and esteem Him highly, whom he does not see] is difficult, so far is it from existing in the godless. But it is conceived, as we have said above, when terrified hearts hear the Gospel and receive consolation [when we are born anew of the Holy Ghost].

Therefore such a distribution is of advantage in which civil righteousness is ascribed to the free will and spiritual righteousness to the governing of the Holy Ghost in the regenerate. For thus the outward discipline is retained, because all men ought to know equally, both that God requires this civil righteousness [God will not tolerate indecent, wild, reckless conduct], and that, in a measure, we can afford it. And yet a distinction is shown between human and spiritual righteousness, between philosophical doctrine and the doctrine of the Holy Ghost and it can be understood for what there is need of the Holy Ghost. Nor has this distribution been invented by us, but Scripture most clearly teaches it. Augustine also treats of it, and recently it has been well treated of by William of Paris, but it has been wickedly suppressed by those who have dreamt that men can obey God's Law without the Holy Ghost, but that the Holy Ghost is given in order that, in addition, it may be considered meritorious.

Part 24

Article XIX: *Of the Cause of Sin.*

The Nineteenth Article the adversaries receive, in which we confess that, although God only and alone has framed all nature, and preserves all things which exist, yet [He is not the cause of sin, but] the cause of sin is the will in the devil and men turning itself away from God, according to the saying of Christ concerning the devil, John 8, 44: When he speaketh a lie, he speaketh of his own.

Part 25

Article XX: *Of Good Works.*

In the Twentieth Article they distinctly lay down these words, namely, that they reject and condemn our statement that men do not merit the remission of sins by good works. [Mark this well!] They clearly declare that they reject and condemn this article. What is to be said on a subject so manifest? Here the framers of the *Confutation* openly show by what spirit they are led. For what in the Church is more certain than that the remission of sins occurs freely for Christ's sake, that Christ, and not our works, is the propitiation for sins, as Peter says, Acts 10, 43: To Him give all the prophets witness that through His name, whosoever believeth on Him, shall receive remission of sins? [This strong testimony of all the holy prophets may duly be called a decree of the catholic Christian Church. For even a single prophet is very highly esteemed by God and a treasure worth the whole world.] To this Church of the prophets we would rather assent than to these abandoned writers of the Confutation, who so impudently blaspheme Christ. For although there were writers who held that after the remission of sins men are just before God, not by faith, but by works themselves, yet they did not hold this, namely, that the remission of sins itself occurs on account of our works, and not freely for Christ's sake.

Therefore the blasphemy of ascribing Christ's honor to our works is not to be endured. These theologians are now entirely without shame if they dare to bring such an opinion into the Church. Nor do we doubt that His Most Excellent Imperial Majesty and very many of the princes would not have allowed this passage to remain in the *Confutation* if they had been admonished of it. Here we could cite infinite testimonies from Scripture and from the Fathers [that this article is certainly divine and true, and this is the sacred and divine truth. For there is hardly a syllable, hardly a leaf in the Bible, in the principal books of the Holy Scriptures where this is not clearly stated.] But also above we have said enough on this subject. And there is no need of more testimonies for one who knows why Christ has been given to us, who knows that Christ is the propitiation for our sins. [God-fearing, pious hearts that know well why Christ has been given, who for all the possessions and kingdoms of the world would not be without Christ as our only Treasure, our only Mediator and Redeemer must here be shocked and terrified that God's holy Word and Truth should be so openly despised and condemned by poor men.] Isaiah says, 53, 6: The Lord hath laid on Him the iniquities of us all. The adversaries, on the other hand, [accuse Isaiah and the entire Bible of lying and teach that God lays our iniquities not on Christ, but on our [beggarly] works. Neither are we disposed to mention here the sort of works [rosaries, pilgrimages, and the like] which they teach. We see that a horrible decree has been prepared against us, which would terrify us still more if we were contending concerning doubtful or trifling subjects. Now, since our consciences understand that by the adversaries the manifest truth is condemned, whose defense is necessary for the Church and increases the glory of Christ, we easily despise the terrors of the world, and with a strong spirit will bear whatever is to be suffered for the glory of Christ and the advantage of the Church. Who would not rejoice to die in the confession of such articles as that we obtain the remission of sins by faith freely for Christ's sake, that we do not merit the remission of sins by our works? [Experience shows--and the monks themselves must admit it--that] The consciences of the pious will have no sufficiently sure consolation against the terrors of sin and of death, and against the devil soliciting to despair [and who in a moment blows away all our works like dust], if they do not know that they ought to be confident that they have the remission of sins freely for Christ's sake. This faith sustains and quickens hearts in that most violent conflict with despair [in the great agony of death, in the great anguish, when no creature can help, yea, when we must depart from this entire visible creation into another state and world, and must die].

Therefore the cause is one which is worthy that for its sake we should refuse no danger. Whosoever you are that has assented to our Confession, "do not yield to the wicked, but, on the contrary, go forward the more boldly," when the adversaries endeavor, by means of terrors and tortures and punishments, to drive away from you that consolation which has been tendered to the entire Church in this article of ours [but with all cheerfulness rely confidently and gladly on God and the Lord Jesus, and joyfully confess this manifest truth in opposition to the tyranny, wrath, threatening, and terrors of all the world, yea, in opposition to the daily murders and persecution of tyrants. For who would suffer to have taken from him this great, yea, everlasting consolation on which the entire salvation of the whole Christian Church depends? Any one who picks up the Bible and reads it earnestly will soon observe that this doctrine has its foundation everywhere in the Bible]. Testimonies of Scripture will not be wanting to one seeking them, which will establish his mind. For Paul at the top of his voice, as the saying is, cries out, Rom. 3, 24 f., and 4, 16, that sins are freely remitted for Christ's sake. It is of faith, he says, that it might be by grace, to the end the promise might be sure. That is, if the promise would depend upon our works, it would not be sure. If remission of sins would be given on account of our works, when would we know that we had obtained it, when would a terrified conscience find a work which it would consider sufficient to appease God's wrath? But we spoke of the entire matter above. Thence let the reader derive testimonies. For the unworthy treatment of the subject has forced from us the present, not discussion, but complaint that on this topic they have distinctly recorded themselves as disapproving of this article of ours, that we obtain remission of sins not on account of our works, but by faith and freely on account of Christ.

The adversaries also add testimonies to their own condemnation, and it is worth while to recite several of them. They quote from Peter, 2. Ep. 1, 10: Give diligence to make your calling sure, etc.. Now you see, reader, that our adversaries have not wasted labor in learning logic, but have the art of inferring from the Scriptures whatever pleases them [whether it is in harmony with the Scriptures or out of harmony; whether it is correctly or incorrectly concluded. For they conclude thus:] "Make your calling sure by good works." Therefore works merit the remission of sins. A very agreeable mode of reasoning, if one would argue thus concerning a person sentenced to capital punishment, whose punishment has been remitted: "The magistrate commands that hereafter you abstain from that which belongs to another. Therefore you have merited the remission of the penalty, because you are now abstaining from what belongs to another." Thus to argue is to make a cause out of that which is not a cause. For Peter speaks of works following the remission of sins, and teaches why they should be done, namely, that the calling may be sure, i.e., lest they may fall from their calling if they sin again. Do good works that you may persevere in your calling, that you [do not fall away again, grow cold and] may not lose the gifts of your calling, which were given you before, and not on account of works that follow, and which now are retained by faith, for faith does not remain in those who lose the Holy Ghost, who reject repentance, just as we have said above (p. 253) that faith exists in repentance.

They add other testimonies cohering no better. Lastly they say that this opinion was condemned a thousand years before, in the time of Augustine. This also is quite false. For the Church of Christ always held that the remission of sins is obtained freely. Yea, the Pelagians were condemned, who contended that grace is given on account of our works. Besides, we have above shown sufficiently that we hold that good works ought necessarily to follow faith. For we do not make void the Law, says Paul, Rom. 3, 31; yea, we establish the Law, because when by faith we have received the Holy Ghost, the fulfilling of the Law necessarily follows, by which love, patience, chastity, and other fruits of the Spirit gradually grow.

Part 26

The Twenty-first Article they absolutely condemn, because we do not require the invocation of saints. Nor on any topic do they speak more eloquently and with more prolixity. Nevertheless they do not effect anything else than that the saints should be honored; likewise, that the saints who live pray for others; as though, indeed, the invocation of dead saints were on that account necessary. They cite Cyprian, because he asked Cornelius while yet alive to pray for his brothers when departing. By this example they prove the invocation of the dead. They quote also Jerome against Vigilantius. "On this field" [in this matter], they say, "eleven hundred years ago, Jerome overcame Vigilantius." Thus the adversaries triumph, as though the war were already ended. Nor do those asses see that in Jerome, against Vigilantius, there is not a syllable concerning invocation. He speaks concerning honors for the saints, not concerning invocation. Neither have the rest of the ancient writers before Gregory made mention of invocation. Certainly this invocation, with these opinions which the adversaries now teach concerning the application of merits, has not the testimonies of the ancient writers.

Our Confession approves honors to the saints. For here a threefold honor is to be approved. The first is thanksgiving. For we ought to give thanks to God because He has shown examples of mercy, because He has shown that He wishes to save men; because He has given teachers or other gifts to the Church. And these gifts, as they are the greatest, should be amplified, and the saints themselves should be praised, who have faithfully used these gifts, just as Christ praises faithful businessmen, Matt. 25, 21. 23. The second service is the strengthening of our faith when we see the denial forgiven Peter we also are encouraged to believe the more that grace truly superabounds over sin, Rom. 5, 20. The third honor is the imitation, first, of faith, then of the other virtues which every one should imitate according to his calling. These true honors the adversaries do not require. They dispute only concerning invocation, which, even though it would have no danger, nevertheless is not necessary.

Besides, we also grant that the angels pray for us. For there is a testimony in Zech. 1, 12, where an angel prays: O Lord of hosts, how long wilt Thou not have mercy on Jerusalem? Although concerning the saints we concede that, just as, when alive, they pray for the Church universal in general, so in heaven they pray for the Church in general, albeit no testimony concerning the praying of the dead is extant in the Scriptures, except the dream taken from the Second Book of Maccabees, 15, 14.

Moreover, even supposing that the saints pray for the Church ever so much, yet it does not follow that they are to be invoked; although our Confession affirms only this, that Scripture does not teach the invocation of the saints, or that we are to ask the saints for aid. But since neither a command, nor a promise, nor an example can be produced from the Scriptures concerning the invocation of saints, it follows that conscience can have nothing concerning this invocation that is certain. And since prayer ought to be made from faith, how do we know that God approves this invocation? Whence do we know without the testimony of Scripture that the saints perceive the prayers of each one? Some plainly ascribe divinity to the saints namely, that they discern the silent thoughts of the minds in us. They dispute concerning morning and evening knowledge, perhaps because they doubt whether they hear us in the morning or the evening. They invent these things, not in order to treat the saints with honor, but to defend lucrative services. Nothing can be produced by the adversaries against this reasoning, that, since invocation does not have a testimony from God's Word, it cannot be affirmed that the saints understand our invocation, or, even if they understand it, that God approves it. Therefore the adversaries ought not to force us to an uncertain matter, because a prayer without faith is not prayer. For when they cite the example of the Church, it is evident that this is a new custom in the Church; for although the old prayers make mention of the saints, yet they do not invoke the saints. Although also this new invocation in the Church is dissimilar to the invocation of individuals.

Again, the adversaries not only require invocation in the worship of the saints, but also apply the merits of the saints to others, and make of the saints not only intercessors, but also propitiators. This is in no way to be endured. For here the honor belonging only to Christ is altogether transferred to the saints. For they make them mediators and propitiators, and although they make a distinction between mediators of intercession and mediators [the Mediator] of redemption, yet they plainly make of the saints mediators of redemption. But even that they are mediators of intercession they declare without testimony of Scripture, which, be it said ever so reverently, nevertheless obscures Christ's office, and transfers the confidence of mercy due Christ to the saints. For men imagine that Christ is more severe and the saints more easily appeased, and they trust rather to the mercy of the saints than to the mercy of Christ, and fleeing from Christ [as from a tyrant], they seek the saints. Thus they actually make of them mediators of redemption.

Therefore we shall show that they truly make of the saints, not only intercessors, but propitiators, i.e., mediators of redemption. Here we do not as yet recite the abuses of the common people [how manifest idolatry is practiced at pilgrimages]. We are still speaking of the opinions of the Doctors. As regards the rest, even the inexperienced [common people] can judge.

In a propitiator these two things concur. In the first place, there ought to be a word of God from which we may certainly know that God wishes to pity, and hearken to, those calling upon Him through this propitiator. There is such a promise concerning Christ, John 16 23: Whatsoever ye shall ask the Father in My name, He will give it you. Concerning the saints there is no such promise. Therefore consciences cannot be firmly confident that by the invocation of saints we are heard. This invocation, therefore, is not made from faith. Then we have also the command to call upon Christ, according to Matt. 11, 28: Come unto Me, all ye that labor, etc., which certainly is said also to us. And Isaiah says, 11,10: In that day there shall be a root of Jesse, which shall stand for an ensign to the people; to it shall the Gentiles seek. And Ps. 45, 12: Even the rich among the people shall entreat Thy favor. And Ps. 72, 11. 16: Yea, all kings shall fall down before Him. And shortly after: Prayer also shall be made for Him continually. And in John 6, 23 Christ says: That all men should honor the Son even as they honor the Father. And Paul, 2 Thess. 2, 16. 17, says, praying: Now our Lord Jesus Christ Himself, and God, even our Father,... comfort your hearts and stablish you. [All these passages refer to Christ.] But concerning the invocation of saints, what commandment, what example can the adversaries produce from the Scriptures? The second matter in a propitiator is, that his merits have been presented as those which make satisfaction for others, which are bestowed by divine imputation on others, in order that through these, just as by their own merits, they may be accounted righteous. As when any friend pays a debt for a friend, the debtor is freed by the merit of another, as though it were by his own. Thus the merits of Christ are bestowed upon us, in order that, when we believe in Him, we may be accounted righteous by our confidence in Christ's merits as though we had merits of our own.

And from both, namely, from the promise and the bestowment of merits, confidence in mercy arises [upon both parts must a Christian prayer be founded]. Such confidence in the divine promise, and likewise in the merits of Christ, ought to be brought forward when we pray. For we ought to be truly confident, both that for Christ's sake we are heard, and that by His merits we have a reconciled Father.

Here the adversaries first bid us invoke the saints, although they have neither God's promise, nor a command, nor an example from Scripture. And yet they cause greater confidence in the mercy of the saints to be conceived than in that of Christ, although Christ bade us come to Him and not to the saints. Secondly, they apply the merits of the saints, just as the merits of Christ, to others, they bid us trust in the merits of the saints as though we were accounted righteous on account of the merits of the saints, in like manner as we are accounted righteous by the merits of Christ. Here we fabricate nothing. In indulgences they say that they apply the merits of the saints [as satisfactions for our sins]. And Gabriel, the interpreter of the canon of the Mass, confidently declares: According to the order instituted by God we should betake ourselves to the aid of the saints, in order that we may be saved by their merits and vows. These are the words of Gabriel. And nevertheless in the books and sermons of the adversaries still more absurd things are read here and there. What is it to make propitiators if this is not? They are altogether made equal to Christ if we must trust that we are saved by their merits.

But where has this arrangement, to which he refers when he says that we ought to resort to the aid of the saints, been instituted by God? Let him produce an example or command from the Scriptures. Perhaps they derive this arrangement from the courts of kings, where friends must be employed as intercessors. But if a king has appointed a certain intercessor, he will not desire that eases be brought to him through others. Thus, since Christ has been appointed Intercessor and High Priest, why do we seek others? [What can the adversaries say in reply to this?]

Here and there this form of absolution is used: The passion of our lord Jesus Christ the merits of the most blessed Virgin Mary and of all the saints, be to thee for the remission of sins. Here the absolution is pronounced on the supposition that we are reconciled and accounted righteous not only by the merits of Christ, but also by the merits of the other saints. Some of us have seen a doctor of theology dying, for consoling whom a certain theologian, a monk, was employed. He pressed on the dying man nothing but this prayer: Mother of grace, protect us from the enemy; receive us in the hour of death.

Granting that the blessed Mary prays for the Church, does she receive souls in death, does she conquer death [the great power of Satan], does she quicken? What does Christ do if the blessed Mary does these things? Although she is most worthy of the most ample honors, nevertheless she does not wish to be made equal to Christ, but rather wishes us to consider and follow her example [the example of her faith and her humility]. But the subject itself declares that in public opinion the blessed Virgin has succeeded altogether to the place of Christ. Men have invoked her, have trusted in her mercy, through her have desired to appease Christ, as though He were not a Propitiator, but only a dreadful judge and avenger. We believe, however, that we must not trust that the merits of the saints are applied to us, that on account of these God is reconciled to us, or accounts us just, or saves us. For we obtain remission of sins only by the merits of Christ, when we believe in Him. Of the other saints it has been said, 1 Cor. 3, 8: Every man shall receive his own reward according to his own labor, i.e., they cannot mutually bestow their own merits, the one upon the other, as the monks sell the merits of their orders. Even Hilary says of the foolish virgins: And as the foolish virgins could not go forth with their lamps extinguished, they besought those who were prudent to lend them oil; to whom they replied that they could not give it because peradventure there might not be enough for all; i.e., no one can be aided by the works and merits of another, because it is necessary for every one to buy oil for his own lamp. [Here he points out that none of us can aid another by other people's works or merits.]

Since, therefore, the adversaries teach us to place confidence in the invocation of saints, although they have neither the Word of God nor the example of Scripture [of the Old or of the New Testament]; since they apply the merits of the saints on behalf of others, not otherwise than they apply the merits of Christ, and transfer the honor belonging only to Christ to the saints, we can receive neither their opinions concerning the worship of the saints, nor the practise of invocation. For we know that confidence is to be placed in the intercession of Christ, because this alone has God's promise. We know that the merits of Christ alone are a propitiation for us. On account of the merits of Christ we are accounted righteous when we believe in Him, as the text says, Rom. 9, 33 (cf. 1 Pet. 2, 6 and Is. 28, 16): Whosoever believeth on Him shall not be confounded. Neither are we to trust that we are accounted righteous by the merits of the blessed Virgin or of the other saints.

With the learned this error also prevails namely, that to each saint a particular administration has been committed, that Anna bestows riches [protects from poverty], Sebastian keeps off pestilence, Valentine heals epilepsy, George protects horsemen. These opinions have clearly sprung from heathen examples. For thus, among the Romans Juno was thought to enrich, Febris to keep off fever, Castor and Pollux to protect horsemen, etc. Even though we should imagine that the invocation of saints were taught with the greatest prudence, yet since the example is most dangerous, why is it necessary to defend it when it has no command or testimony from God's Word? Aye, it has not even the testimony of the ancient writers. First because, as I have said above, when other mediators are sought in addition to Christ, and confidence is put in others, the entire knowledge of Christ is suppressed. The subject shows this. In the beginning, mention of the saints seems to have been admitted with a design that is endurable, as in the ancient prayers. Afterwards invocation followed, and abuses that are prodigious and more than heathenish followed invocation. From invocation the next step was to images; these also were worshiped, and a virtue was supposed to exist in these, just as magicians imagine that a virtue exists in images of the heavenly bodies carved at a particular time. In a certain monastery we [some of us] have seen a statue of the blessed Virgin, which moved automatically by a trick [within by a string], so as to seem either to turn away from [those who did not make a large offering] or nod to those making request.

Still the fabulous stories concerning the saints, which are publicly taught with great authority, surpass the marvelous tales of the statues and pictures. Barbara, amidst her torments, asks for the reward that no one who would invoke her should die without the Eucharist. Another, standing on one foot, recited daily the whole psaltery. Some wise man painted [for children] Christophorus [which in German means Bearer of Christ], in order by the allegory to signify that there ought to be great strength of mind in those who would bear Christ, i.e., who would teach or confess the Gospel, because it is necessary to undergo the greatest dangers [for they must wade by night through the great sea, i.e., endure all kinds of temptations and dangers]. Then the foolish monks taught among the people that they ought to invoke Chistophorus, as though such a Polyphemus [such a giant who bore Christ through the sea] had once existed. And although the saints performed very great deeds, either useful to the state or affording private examples the remembrance of which would conduce much both toward strengthening faith and toward following their example in the administration of affairs, no one has searched for these from true narratives. [Although God Almighty through His saints, as a peculiar people, has wrought many great things in both realms, in the Church and in worldly trans-actions; although there are many great examples in the lives of the saints which would be very profitable to princes and lords, to true pastors and guardians of souls, for the government both of the world and of the Church, especially for strengthen-ing faith in God, yet they have passed these by, and preached the most insignificant matters concerning the saints, concerning their hard beds their hair shirts, etc., which, for the greater part, are falsehoods.] Yet indeed it is of advantage to hear how holy men administered governments [as in the Holy Scriptures it is narrated of the kings of Israel and Judah], what calamities, what dangers they underwent, how holy men were of aid to kings in great dangers, how they taught the Gospel, what encounters they had with heretics. Examples of mercy are also of service, as when we see the denial forgiven Peter, when we see Cyprian forgiven for having been a magician, when we see Augustine, having experienced the power of faith in sickness steadily affirming that God truly hears the prayers of believers. It was profitable that such examples as these, which contain admonitions for either faith or fear or the administration of the state, be recited. But certain triflers, endowed with no knowledge either of faith or for governing states, have invented stories in imitation of poems, in which there are nothing but superstitious examples concerning certain prayers, certain fastings, and certain additions of service for bringing in gain [where there are nothing but examples as to how the saints wore hair shirts, how they prayed at the seven canonical hours how they lived upon bread and water]. Such are the miracles that have been invented concerning rosaries and similar ceremonies. Nor is there need here to recite examples. For the legends, as they call them, and the mirrors of examples, and the rosaries, in which there are very many things not unlike the true narratives of Lucian, are extant.

The bishops, theologians, and monks applaud these monstrous and wicked stories [this abomination set up against Christ, this blasphemy, these scandalous, shameless lies, these lying preachers; and they have permitted them so long, to the great injury of consciences, that it is terrible to think of it] because they aid them to their daily bread. They do not tolerate us, who, in order that the honor and office of Christ may be more conspicuous, do not require the invocation of saints, and censure the abuses in the worship of saints. And although [even their own theologians], all good men everywhere [a long time before Dr. Luther began to write] in the correction of these abuses, greatly longed for either the authority of the bishops or the diligence of the preachers, nevertheless our adversaries in the *Confutation* altogether pass over vices that are even manifest, as though they wish, by the reception of the Confutation, to compel us to approve even the most notorious abuses.

Thus the *Confutation* has been deceitfully written, not only on this topic, but almost everywhere. [They pretend that they are as pure as gold, that they have never muddled the water.] There is no passage in which they make a distinction between the manifest abuses and their dogmas. And nevertheless, if there are any of sounder mind among them they confess that many false opinions inhere in the doctrine of the scholastics and canonists, and, besides, that in such ignorance and negligence of the pastors many abuses crept into the Church. For Luther was not [the only one nor] the first to complain of [innumerable] public abuses. Many learned and excellent men long before these times deplored the abuses of the Mass, confidence in monastic observances, services to the saints intended to yield a revenue, the confusion of the doctrine concerning repentance [concerning Christ], which ought to be as clear and plain in the Church as possible [without which there cannot be nor remain a Christian Church]. We ourselves have heard that excellent theologians desire moderation in the scholastic doctrine which contains much more for philosophical quarrels than for piety. And nevertheless, among these the older ones are generally nearer Scripture than are the more recent. Thus their theology degenerated more and more. Neither had many good men, who from the very first began to be friendly to Luther, any other reason than that they saw that he was freeing the minds of men from these labyrinths of most confused and infinite discussions which exist among the scholastic theologians and canonists, and was teaching things profitable for godliness.

The adversaries, therefore, have not acted candidly in passing over the abuses when they wished us to assent to the Confutation. And if they wished to care for the interests of the Church [and of Buffeted consciences, and not rather to maintain their pomp and avarice] especially on that topic, at this occasion they ought to exhort our most excellent Emperor to take measures for the correction of abuses [which furnish grounds for derision among the Turks, the Jews, and all unbelievers], as we observe plainly enough that he is most desirous of healing and well establishing the Church. But the adversaries do not act as to aid the most honorable and most holy will of the Emperor, but so as in every way to crush [the truth and] us. Many signs show that they have little anxiety concerning the state of the Church. [They lose little sleep from concern that Christian doctrine and the pure Gospel be preached.] They take no pains that there should be among the people a summary of the dogmas of the Church. [The office of the ministry they permit to be quite desolate.] They defend manifest abuses [they continue every day to shed innocent blood] by new and unusual cruelty. They allow no suitable teachers in the churches. Good men can easily judge whither these things tend. But in this way they have no regard to the interest either of their own authority or of the Church. For after the good teachers have been killed and sound doctrine suppressed, fanatical spirits will rise up, whom the adversaries will not be able to restrain, who both will disturb the Church with godless dogmas, and will overthrow the entire ecclesiastical government, which we are very greatly desirous of maintaining.

Therefore, most excellent Emperor Charles for the sake of the glory of Christ, which we have no doubt that you desire to praise and magnify, we beseech you not to assent to the violent counsels of our adversaries, but to seek other honorable ways of so establishing harmony that godly consciences are not burdened, that no cruelty is exercised against innocent men, as we have hitherto seen, and that sound doctrine is not suppressed in the Church. To God most of all you owe the duty [as far as this is possible to man] to maintain sound doctrine and hand it down to posterity, and to defend those who teach what is right. For God demands this when He honors kings with His own name and calls them gods, saying, Ps. 82, 6: I have said, Ye are gods, namely, that they should attend to the preservation and propagation of divine things, i.e., the Gospel of Christ, on the earth, and, as the vicars of God, should defend the life and safety of the innocent [true Christian teachers and preachers].

Part 27

Article XXII (X): *Of Both Kinds in the Lord's Supper.*

It cannot be doubted that it is godly and in accordance with the institution of Christ and the words of Paul to use both parts in the Lord's Supper. For Christ instituted both parts, and instituted them not for a part of the Church, but for the entire Church. For not only the presbyters, but the entire Church uses the Sacrament by the authority of Christ, and not by human authority, and this, we suppose, the adversaries acknowledge. Now, if Christ has instituted it for the entire Church, why is one kind denied to a part of the Church? Why is the use of the other kind prohibited? Why is the ordinance of Christ changed, especially when He Himself calls it His testament? But if it is not allowable to annul man's testament, much less will it be allowable to annul the testament of Christ. And Paul says, 1 Cor. 11, 23 ff., that he had received of the Lord that which he delivered. But he had delivered the use of both kinds, as the text, 1 Cor. 11, clearly shows. This do [in remembrance of Me], he says first concerning His body; afterwards he repeats the same words concerning the cup [the blood of Christ]. And then: Let a man examine himself, and so let him eat of that bread and drink of that cup. [Here he names both.] These are the words of Him who has instituted the Sacrament. And, indeed, he says before that those who will use the Lord's Supper should use both. It is evident, therefore, that the Sacrament was instituted for the entire Church. And the custom still remains in the Greek churches, and also once obtained in the Latin churches, as Cyprian and Jerome testify. For thus Jerome says on Zephaniah: The priests who administer the Eucharist, and distribute the Lord's blood to the people, etc. The Council of Toledo gives the same testimony. Nor would it be difficult to accumulate a great multitude of testimonies. Here we exaggerate nothing; we but leave the prudent reader to determine what should be held concerning the divine ordinance [whether it is proper to prohibit and change an ordinance and institution of Christ].

The adversaries in the **Confutation** do not endeavor to [comfort the consciences or] excuse the Church, to which one part of the Sacrament has been denied. This would have been becoming to good and religious men. For a strong reason for excusing the Church, and instructing consciences to whom only a part of the Sacrament could be granted, should have been sought. Now these very men maintain that it is right to prohibit the other part, and forbid that the use of both parts be allowed. First, they imagine that, in the beginning of the Church, it was the custom at some places that only one part was administered. Nevertheless they are not able to produce any ancient example of this matter. But they cite the passages in which mention is made of bread, as in Luke 24, 35 where it is written that the disciples recognized Christ in the breaking of bread. They quote also other passages, Acts 2, 42. 46; 20, 7, concerning the breaking of bread. But although we do not greatly oppose if some receive these passages as referring to the Sacrament, yet it does not follow that one part only was given, because, according to the ordinary usage of language, by the naming of one part the other is also signified. They refer also to Lay Communion which was not the use of only one kind, but of both; and whenever priests are commanded to use Lay Communion [for a punishment are not to consecrate themselves, but to receive Communion, however, of both kinds from another], it is meant that they have been removed from the ministry of consecration. Neither are the adversaries ignorant of this, but they abuse the ignorance of the unlearned, who, when they hear of Lay Communion, immediately dream of the custom of our time, by which only a part of the Sacrament is given to the laymen.

And consider their impudence. Gabriel recounts among other reasons why both parts are not given that a distinction should be made between laymen and presbyters. And it is credible that the chief reason why the prohibition of the one part is defended is this, namely, that the dignity of the order may be the more highly exalted by a religious rite. To say nothing more severe, this is a human design; and whither this tends can easily be judged. In the **Confutation** they also quote concerning the sons of Eli that after the loss of the high-priesthood, they were to seek the one part pertaining to the priests, 1 Sam. 2, 36 [the text reads: Every one that is left in thine house shall come and crouch him for a piece of silver and a morsel of bread, and shall say, Put me, I pray thee, into one of the priest's offices (German: *Lieber, lass mich zu einem Priesterteil*) that I may eat a piece of bread]. Here they say that the use of one kind was signified. And they add: "Thus, therefore, our laymen ought also to be content, with one part pertaining to the priests, with one kind." The adversaries [the masters of the *Confutation* are quite shameless, rude asses, and] are clearly trifling when they are transferring the history of the posterity of Eli to the Sacrament. The punishment of Eli is there described. Will they also say this, that as a punishment the laymen have been removed from the other party [They are quite foolish and mad.] The Sacrament was instituted to console and comfort terrified minds when they believe that the flesh of Christ given for the life of the world, is food, when they believe that, being joined to Christ [through this food], they are made alive. But the adversaries argue that laymen are removed from the other part as a punishment. "They ought," they say, "to be content." This is sufficient for a despot. [That, surely, sounds proud and defiant enough.] But [my lords, may we ask the reason] why ought they? "The reason must not be asked but let whatever the theologians say be law." [Is whatever you wish and whatever you say to be sheer truth? See now and be astonished how shameless and impudent the adversaries are: they dare to set up their own words as sheer commands of lords, they frankly say: The laymen must be content. But what if they must not?] This is a concoction of Eck. For we recognize those vainglorious words, which if we would wish to criticize, there would be no want of language. For you see how great the impudence is. He commands, as a tyrant in the tragedies: "Whether they wish or not, they must be content." Will the reasons which he cites excuse, in the judgment of God, those who prohibit a part of the Sacrament, and rage against men using an entire Sacrament? [Are they to take comfort in the fact that it is recorded concerning the sons of Eli: They will go begging? That will be a shuffling excuse at the judgment-seat of God.] If they make the prohibition in order that there should be a distinguishing mark of the order, this very reason ought to move us not to assent to the adversaries, even though we would be disposed in other respects to comply with their custom. There are other distinguishing marks of the order of priests and of the people, but it is not obscure what design they have for defending this distinction so earnestly. That we may not seem to detract from the true worth of the order, we will not say more concerning this shrewd design.

They also allege the danger of spilling and certain similar things, which do not have force sufficient to change the ordinance of Christ. [They allege more dreams like these for the sake of which it would be improper to change the ordinance of Christ.] And, indeed, if we assume that we are free to use either one part or both, how can the prohibition [to use both kinds] be defended? Although the Church does not assume to itself the liberty to convert the ordinances of Christ into matters of indifference. We indeed excuse the Church which has borne the injury [the poor consciences which have been deprived of one part by force], since it could not obtain both parts; but the authors who maintain that the use of the entire Sacrament is justly prohibited, and who now not only prohibit, but even excommunicate and violently persecute those using an entire Sacrament, we do not excuse. Let them see to it how they will give an account to God for their decisions. Neither is it to be judged immediately that the Church determines or approves whatever the pontiffs determine, especially since Scripture prophesies concerning the bishops and pastors to effect this as Ezekiel says, 7, 28: The Law shall perish from the priest [there will be priests or bishops who will know no command or law of God].

Part 28

Article XXIII (XI): *Of the Marriage of Priests.*

Despite the great infamy of their defiled celibacy, the adversaries have the presumption not only to defend the pontifical law by the wicked and false pretext of the divine name, but even to exhort the Emperor and princes, to the disgrace and infamy of the Roman Empire, not to tolerate the marriage of priests. For thus they speak. [Although the great, unheard-of lewdness, fornication, and adultery among priests, monks, etc., at the great abbeys, in other churches and cloisters, has become so notorious throughout the world that people sing and talk about it, still the adversaries who have presented the **Confutation** are so blind and without shame that they defend the law of the Pope by which marriage is prohibited, and that, with the specious claim that they are defending a spiritual state. Moreover, although it would be proper for them to be heartily ashamed of the exceedingly shameful, lewd, abandoned loose life of the wretches in their abbeys and cloisters, although on this account alone they should not have the courage to show their face in broad daylight, although their evil, restless heart and conscience ought to cause them to tremble, to stand aghast, and to be afraid to lift their eyes to our excellent Emperor, who loves uprightness, still they have the courage of the hangman, they act like the very devil and like all reckless, wanton people, proceeding in blind defiance and forgetful of all honor and decency. And these pure chaste gentlemen dare to admonish His Imperial Majesty, the Electors and Princes not to tolerate the marriage of priests *ad infamiam et ignominiam imperti*, that is, to ward off shame and disgrace from the Roman Empire. For these are their words, as if their shameful life were a great honor and glory to the

Church.]

What greater impudence has ever been read of in any history than this of the adversaries? [Such shameless advocates before a Roman Emperor will not easily be found. If all the world did not know them, if many godly, upright people among them, their own canonical brethren, had not complained long ago of their shameful, lewd, indecent conduct, if their vile, abominable, ungodly, lewd, heathenish, Epicurean life, and the dregs of all filthiness at Rome were not quite manifest, one might think that their great purity and their inviolate virgin chastity were the reason why they could not bear to hear the word woman or marriage pronounced, and why they baptize holy matrimony, which the Pope himself calls a sacrament, *infamiam imperil*.] For the arguments which they use we shall afterwards review. Now let the wise reader consider this, namely, what shame these good-for-nothing men have who say that marriages [which the Holy Scriptures praise most highly and command] produce infamy and disgrace to the government, as though, indeed, this public infamy of flagitious and unnatural lusts which glow among these very holy fathers, who feign that they are Curii and live like bacchanals, were a great ornament to the Church! And most things which these men do with the greatest license cannot even be named without a breach of modesty. And these their lusts they ask you to defend with your chaste right hand, Emperor Charles (whom even certain ancient predictions name as the king of modest face, for the saying appears concerning you: "One modest in face shall reign everywhere"). For they ask that, contrary to divine law, contrary to the law of nations, contrary to the canons of Councils you sunder marriages, in order to impose merely for the sake of marriage atrocious punishments upon innocent men, to put to death priests, whom even barbarians reverently spare, to drive into exile banished women and fatherless children. Such laws they bring to you, most excellent and most chaste Emperor, to which no barbarity, however monstrous and cruel, could lend its ear. But because the stain of no disgrace or cruelty falls upon your character, we hope that you will deal with us mildly in this matter, especially when you have learned that we have the weightiest reasons for our belief derived from the Word of God to which the adversaries oppose the most trifling and vain opinions.

And nevertheless they do not seriously defend celibacy. For they are not ignorant how few there are who practise chastity, but [they stick to that comforting saying which is found in their treatise, *Si non caste, tamen caue* (If not chastely, at least cautiously) and] they devise a sham of religion for their dominion, which they think that celibacy profits, in order that we may understand Peter to have been right in admonishing, 2 Ep. 2, 1, that there will be false teachers who will deceive men with feigned words. For the adversaries say, write, or do nothing truly [their words are merely an argument *ad hominem*], frankly, and candidly in this entire case, but they actually contend only concerning the dominion which they falsely think to be imperiled, and which they endeavor to fortify with a wicked pretense of godliness [they support their case with nothing but impious, hypocritical lies; accordingly, it will endure about as well as butter exposed to the sun].

We cannot approve this law concerning celibacy which the adversaries defend, because it conflicts with divine and natural law and is at variance with the very canons of the Councils. And that it is superstitious and dangerous is evident. For it produces infinite scandals, sins, and corruption of public morals [as is seen in the real towns of priests, or, as they are called, their residences]. Our other controversies need some discussion by the doctors; in this the subject is so manifest to both parties that it requires no discussion. It only requires as judge a man that is honest and fears God. And although the manifest truth is defended by us, yet the adversaries have devised certain reproaches for satirizing our arguments.

First. Gen. 1, 28 teaches that men were created to be fruitful, and that one sex in a proper way should desire the other. For we are speaking not of concupiscence, which is sin, but of that appetite which was to have been in nature in its integrity [which would have existed in nature even if it had remained uncorrupted], which they call physical love. And this love of one sex for the other is truly a divine ordinance. But since this ordinance of God cannot be removed without an extraordinary work of God, it follows that the right to contract marriage cannot be removed by statutes or vows.

The adversaries cavil at these arguments; they say that in the beginning the commandment was given to replenish the earth but that now since the earth has been replenished, marriage is not commanded. See how wisely they judge! The nature of men is so formed by the word of God that it is fruitful not only in the beginning of the creation, but as long as this nature of our bodies will exist just as the earth becomes fruitful by the word Gen. 1, 11: Let the earth bring forth grass, yielding seed. Because of this ordinance the earth not only commenced in the beginning to bring forth plants, but the fields are clothed every year as long as this natural order will exist. Therefore, just as by human laws the nature of the earth cannot be changed, so, without a special work of God the nature of a human being can be changed neither by vows nor by human law [that a woman should not desire a man, nor a man a woman].

Secondly. And because this creation or divine ordinance in man is a natural right, jurists have accordingly said wisely and correctly that the union of male and female belongs to natural right. But since natural right is immutable, the right to contract marriage must always remain. For where nature does not change, that ordinance also with which God has endowed nature does not change, and cannot be removed by human laws. Therefore it is ridiculous for the adversaries to prate that marriage was commanded in the beginning, but is not now. This is the same as if they would say: Formerly, when men were born, they brought with them sex; now they do not. Formerly, when they were born, they brought with them natural right, now they do not. No craftsman (Faber) could produce anything more crafty than these absurdities, which were devised to elude a right of nature. Therefore let this remain in the case which both Scripture teaches and the jurist says wisely, namely, that the union of male and female belongs to natural right. Moreover, a natural right is truly a divine right, because it is an ordinance divinely impressed upon nature. But inasmuch as this right cannot be changed without an extraordinary work of God, it is necessary that the right to contract marriage remains, because the natural desire of sex for sex is an ordinance of God in nature, and for this reason is a right; otherwise, why would both sexes have been created? And we are speaking, as it has been said above, not of concupiscence, which is sin, but of that desire which they call physical love [which would have existed between man and woman even though their nature had remained pure], which concupiscence has not removed from nature, but inflames, so that now it has greater need of a remedy, and marriage is necessary not only for the sake of procreation, but also as a remedy [to guard against sins]. These things are clear, and so well established that they can in no way be overthrown.

Thirdly. Paul says, 1 Cor. 7, 2: To avoid fornication, let every man have his own wife. This now is an express command pertaining to all who are not fit for celibacy. The adversaries ask that a commandment be shown them which commands priests to marry. As though priests are not men! We judge indeed that the things which we maintain concerning human nature in general pertain also to priests. Does not Paul here command those who have not the gift of continence to marry? For he interprets himself a little after when he says, v. 9: It is better to marry than to burn. And Christ has clearly said Matt. 19, 11: All men cannot receive this saying, save they to whom it is given. Because now, since sin [since the fall of Adam], these two things concur, namely, natural appetite and concupiscence, which inflames the natural appetite, so that now there is more need of marriage than in nature in its integrity, Paul accordingly speaks of marriage as a remedy, and on account of these flames commands to marry. Neither can any human authority, any law, any vows remove this declaration: It is better to marry than to burn, because they do not remove the nature or concupiscence. Therefore all who burn, retain the right to marry. By this commandment of Paul: To avoid fornication, let every man have his own wife, all are held bound who do not truly keep themselves continent; the decision concerning which pertains to the conscience of each one.

For as they here give the command to seek continence of God, and to weaken the body by labors and hunger, why do they not proclaim these magnificent commandments to themselves? But, as we have said above, the adversaries are only playing; they are doing nothing seriously. If continence were possible to all, it would not require a peculiar gift. But Christ shows that it has need of a peculiar gift; therefore it does not belong to all. God wishes the rest to use the common law of nature which He has instituted. For God does not wish His ordinances, His creations to be despised. He wishes men to be chaste in this way, that they use the remedy divinely presented, just as He wishes to nourish our life in this way, that we use food and drink. Gerson also testifies that there have been many good men who endeavored to subdue the body, and yet made little progress. Accordingly, Ambrose is right in saying: Virginity is only a thing that can be recommended, but not commanded; it is a matter of vow rather than of precept. If any one here would raise the objection that Christ praises those which have made themselves eunuchs for the kingdom of heaven's sake, Matt. 19, 12, let him also consider this, that He is praising such as have the gift of continence, for on this account He adds: He that is able to receive it, let him receive it. For an impure continence [such as there is in monasteries and cloisters] does not please Christ. We also praise true continence. But now we are disputing concerning the law and concerning those who do not have the gift of continence. The matter ought to be left free and snares ought not to be cast upon the weak through this law.

Fourthly. The pontifical law differs also from the canons of the Councils. For the ancient canons do not prohibit marriage, neither do they dissolve marriages that have been contracted, even if they remove from the administration of their office those who have contracted them in the ministry. At those times this dismissal was an act of kindness [rather than a punishment]. But the new canons, which have not been framed in the Synods, but have been made according to the private judgment of the Popes, both prohibit the contraction of marriages, and dissolve them when contracted; and this is to be done openly, contrary to the command of Christ, Matt. 19, 6: What God hath joined together, let not man put asunder. In the ***Confutation*** the adversaries exclaim that celibacy has been commanded by the Councils. We do not find fault with the decrees of the Councils; for under a certain condition these allow marriage, but we find fault with the laws which, since the ancient Synods, the Popes of Rome have framed contrary to the authority of the Synods. The Popes despise the authority of the Synods, just as much as they wish it to appear holy to others [under peril of God's wrath and eternal damnation]. Therefore this law concerning perpetual celibacy is peculiar to this new pontifical despotism. Nor is it without a reason. For Daniel, 11, 37, ascribes to the kingdom of Antichrist this mark, namely, the contempt of women.

Fifthly. Although the adversaries do not defend the law because of superstition, [not because of its sanctity, as from ignorance], since they see that it is not generally observed, nevertheless they diffuse superstitious opinions, while they give a pretext of religion. They proclaim that they require celibacy because it is purity. As though marriage were impurity and a sin, or as though celibacy merited justification more than does marriage! And to this end they cite the ceremonies of the Mosaic Law, because, since under the Law, the priests, at the time of ministering, were separated from their wives, the priest in the New Testament, inasmuch as he ought always to pray, ought always to practise continence. This silly comparison is presented as a proof which should compel priests to perpetual celibacy, although, indeed, in this very comparison marriage is allowed, only in the time of ministering its use is interdicted. And it is one thing to pray; another, to minister. The saints prayed even when they did not exercise the public ministry; nor did conjugal intercourse hinder them from praying.

But we shall reply in order to these figments. In the first place, it is necessary for the adversaries to acknowledge this, namely, that in believers marriage is pure because it has been sanctified by the Word of God, i.e., it is a matter that is permitted and approved by the Word of God, as Scripture abundantly testifies. For Christ calls marriage a divine union, when He says, Matt. 19, 6: What God hath joined together [let not man put asunder. Here Christ says that married people are joined together by God. Accordingly, it is a pure, holy, noble, praiseworthy work of God]. And Paul says of marriage, of meats and similar things, I Tim. 4, 6: It is sanctified by the Word of God and prayer, i.e., by the Word, by which consciences become certain that God approves; and by prayer, i.e., by faith, which uses it with thanksgiving as a gift of God. Likewise, 1 Cor. 7, 14: The unbelieving husband is sanctified by the wife, etc., i.e.. the use of marriage is permitted and holy on account of faith in Christ, just as it is permitted to use meat, etc. Likewise, 1 Tim. 2, 16: She shall, be saved in childbearing [if they continue in faith], etc. If the adversaries could produce such a passage concerning celibacy, then indeed they would celebrate a wonderful triumph. Paul says that woman is saved by child-bearing. What more honorable could be said against the hypocrisy of celibacy than that woman is saved by the conjugal works themselves, by conjugal intercourse, by bearing children and the other duties? But what does St. Paul mean? Let the reader observe that faith is added, and that domestic duties without faith are not praised. If they continue, he says, in faith. For he speaks of the whole class of mothers. Therefore he requires especially faith [that they should have God's Word and be believing], by which woman receives the remission of sins and justification. Then he adds a particular work of the calling, just as in every man a good work of a particular calling ought to follow faith. This work pleases God on account of faith. Thus the duties of the woman please God on account of faith, and the believing woman is saved who in such duties devoutly serves her calling.

These testimonies teach that marriage is a lawful [a holy and Christian] thing. If therefore purity signifies that which is allowed and approved before God, marriages are pure, because they have been approved by the Word of God. And Paul says of lawful things, Titus 1, 15: Unto the pure all things are pure, i.e., to those who believe in Christ and are righteous by faith. Therefore, as virginity is impure in the godless, so in the godly marriage is pure on account of the Word of God and faith.

Again, if purity is properly opposed to concupiscence, it signifies purity of heart, i.e., mortified concupiscence, because the Law does not prohibit marriage, but concupiscence, adultery, fornication. Therefore celibacy is not purity. For there may be greater purity of heart in a married man, as in Abraham or Jacob, than in most of those who are even truly continent [who even, according to bodily purity, really maintain their chastity].

Lastly, if they understand that celibacy is purity in the sense that it merits justification more than does marriage, we most emphatically contradict it. For we are justified neither on account of virginity nor on account of marriage, but freely for Christ's sake, when we believe that for His sake God is propitious to us. Here perhaps they will exclaim that, according to the manner of Jovinian, marriage is made equal to virginity. But, on account of such clamors we shall not reject the truth concerning the righteousness of faith, which we have explained above. Nevertheless we do not make virginity and marriage equal. For just as one gift surpasses another, as prophecy surpasses eloquence, the science of military affairs surpasses agriculture, and eloquence surpasses architecture, so virginity is a more excellent gift than marriage. And nevertheless, just as an orator is not more righteous before God because of his eloquence than an architect because of his skill in architecture, so a virgin does not merit justification by virginity more than a married person merits it by conjugal duties but each one ought faithfully to serve in his own gift, and to believe that for Christ's sake he receives the remission of sins and by faith is accounted righteous before God.

Neither does Christ or Paul praise virginity because it justifies, but because it is freer and less distracted with domestic occupations, in praying, teaching, [writing,] serving. For this reason Paul says, 1 Cor. 7, 32: He that is unmarried careth for the things which belong to the Lord. Virginity, therefore, is praised on account of meditation and study. Thus Christ does not simply praise those who make themselves eunuchs, but adds, for the kingdom of heaven's sake, i.e., that they may have leisure to learn or teach the Gospel; for He does not say that virginity merits the remission of sins or salvation.

To the examples of the Levitical priests we have replied that they do not establish the duty of imposing perpetual celibacy upon the priests. Furthermore, the Levitical impurities are not to be transferred to us. [The law of Moses, with the ceremonial statutes concerning what is clean or unclean, do not at all concern us Christians.] Then intercourse contrary to the Law was an impurity. Now it is not impurity, because Paul says, Titus 1, 15: Unto the pure all things are pure. For the Gospel frees us from these Levitical impurities [from all the ceremonies of Moses, and not alone from the laws concerning uncleanness]. And if any one defends the law of celibacy with the design to burden consciences by these Levitical observances, we must strive against this, just as the apostles in Acts 15, 10 sqq. strove against those who required circumcision and endeavored to impose the Law of Moses upon Christians.

Yet, in the mean while, good men will know how to control the use of marriage, especially when they are occupied with public offices, which often, indeed, give good men so much labor as to expel all domestic thoughts from their minds. [For to be burdened with great affairs and transactions, which concern commonwealths and nations, governments and churches, is a good remedy to keep the old Adam from lustfulness.] Good men know also this, that Paul, 1 Thess. 4, 4, commands that every one possess his vessel in sanctification [and honor, not in the lust of concupiscence]. They know likewise that they must sometimes retire, in order that there may be leisure for prayer, but Paul does not wish this to be perpetual, 1 Cor. 7, 5. Now such continence is easy to those who are good and occupied. But this great crowd of unemployed priests which is in the fraternities cannot afford, in this voluptuousness, even this Levitical continence, as the facts show. [On the other hand, what sort of chastity can there be among so many thousands of monks and priests who live without worry in all manner of delights, being idle and full, and, moreover, have not the Word of God, do not learn it, and have no regard for it. Such conditions bring on all manner of inchastity. Such people can observe neither Levitical nor perpetual chastity.] And the lines are well known: The boy accustomed to pursue a slothful life hates those who are busy.

Many heretics understanding the Law of Moses incorrectly have treated marriage with contempt, for whom, nevertheless, celibacy has gained extraordinary admiration. And Epiphanius complains that, by this commendation especially, the

Encratites captured the minds of the unwary. They abstained from wine even in the Lord's Supper; they abstained from the flesh of all animals, in which they surpassed the Dominican brethren who live upon fish. They abstained also from marriage; and just this gained the chief admiration. These works, these services, they thought, merited grace more than the use of wine and flesh, and than marriage, which seemed to be a profane and unclean matter, and which scarcely could please God, even though it were not altogether condemned.

Paul to the Colossians, 2, 18, greatly disapproves these angelic forms of worship. For when men believe that they are pure and righteous on account of such hypocrisy, they suppress the knowledge of Christ, and suppress also the knowledge of God's gifts and commandments. For God wishes us to use His gifts in a godly way. And we might mention examples where certain godly consciences were greatly disturbed on account of the lawful use of marriage. This evil was derived from the opinions of monks superstitiously praising celibacy [and proclaiming the married estate as a life that would be a great obstacle to salvation, and full of sins]. Nevertheless we do not find fault with temperance or continence, but we have said above that exercises and mortifications of the body are necessary. We indeed deny that confidence should be placed in certain observances, as though they made righteous. And Epiphanies has elegantly said that these observances ought to be praised dia tehn egkrateian kai dia tehn politeian, i.e., for restraining the body or on account of public morals; just as certain rites were instituted for instructing the ignorant, and not as services that justify.

But it is not through superstition that our adversaries require celibacy, for they know that chastity is not ordinarily rendered [that at Rome, also in all their monasteries, there is nothing but undisguised, unconcealed inchastity. Nor do they seriously intend to lead chaste lives, but knowingly practise hypocrisy before the people]. But they feign superstitious opinions, so as to delude the ignorant. They are therefore more worthy of hatred than the Encratites, who seem to have erred by show of religion; these Sardanapali [Epicureans] designedly misuse the pretext of religion.

Sixthly. Although we have so many reasons for disapproving the law of perpetual celibacy, yet, besides these, dangers to souls and public scandals also are added, which even, though the law were not unjust, ought to deter good men from approving such a burden as has destroyed innumerable souls.

For a long time all good men [their own bishops and canons] have complained of this burden, either on their own account, or on account of others whom they saw to be in danger. But no Popes give ear to these complaints. Neither is it doubtful how greatly injurious to public morals this law is, and what vices and shameful lusts it has produced. The Roman satires are extant. In these Rome still recognizes and reads its own morals.

Thus God avenges the contempt of His own gift and ordinance in those who prohibit marriage. But since the custom in regard to other laws was that they should be changed if manifest utility would advise it, why is the same not done with respect to this law, in which so many weighty reasons concur, especially in these last times, why a change ought to be made? Nature is growing old and is gradually becoming weaker, and vices are increasing; wherefore the remedies divinely given should have been employed. We see what vice it was which God denounced before the Flood, what He denounced before the burning of the five cities. Similar vices have preceded the destruction of many other cities, as of Sybaris and Rome. And in these there has been presented an image of the times which will be next to the end of things. Accordingly, at this time, marriage ought to have been especially defended by the most severe laws and warning examples, and men ought to have been invited to marriage. This duty pertains to the magistrates, who ought to maintain public discipline. [God has now so blinded the world that adultery and fornication are permitted almost without punishment, on the contrary, punishment is inflicted on account of marriage. Is not this terrible to hear?] Meanwhile the teachers of the Gospel should do both, they should exhort incontinent men to marriage, and should exhort others not to despise the gift of continence.

The Popes daily dispense and daily change other laws which are most excellent, yet, in regard to this one law of celibacy, they are as iron and inexorable, although, indeed, it is manifest that this is simply of human right. And they are now making this law more grievous in many ways. The canon bids them suspend priests, these rather unfriendly interpreters suspend them not from office, but from trees. They cruelly kill many men for nothing but marriage. [It is to be feared therefore, that the blood of Abel will cry to heaven so loudly as not to be endured, and that we shall have to tremble like Cain.] And these very parricides show that this law is a doctrine of demons. For since the devil is a murderer, he defends his law by these parricides.

We know that there is some offense in regard to schism, because we seem to have separated from those who are thought to be regular bishops. But our consciences are very secure, since we know that, though we most earnestly desire to establish harmony, we cannot please the adversaries unless we cast away manifest truth, and then agree with these very men in being willing to defend this unjust law, to dissolve marriages that have been contracted, to put to death priests if they do not obey, to drive poor women and fatherless children into exile. But since it is well established that these conditions are displeasing to God, we can in no way grieve that we have no alliance with the multitude of murderers among the adversaries.

We have explained the reasons why we cannot assent with a good conscience to the adversaries when they defend the pontifical law concerning perpetual celibacy, because it conflicts with divine and natural law and is at variance with the canons themselves, and is superstitious and full of danger, and, lastly, because the whole affair is insincere. For the law is enacted not for the sake of religion [not for holiness' sake, or because they do not know better; they know very well that everybody is well acquainted with the condition of the great cloisters, which we are able to name], but for the sake of dominion, and this is wickedly given the pretext of religion. Neither can anything be produced by sane men against these most firmly established reasons. The Gospel allows marriage to those to whom it is necessary. Nevertheless, it does not compel those to marry who can be continent, provided they be truly continent. We hold that this liberty should also be conceded to the priests, nor do we wish to compel any one by force to celibacy, nor to dissolve marriages that have been contracted.

We have also indicated incidentally, while we have recounted our arguments, how the adversaries cavil at several of these; and we have explained away these false accusations. Now we shall relate as briefly as possible with what important reasons they defend the law. First, they say that it has been revealed by God. You see the extreme impudence of these sorry fellows. They dare to affirm that the law of perpetual celibacy has been divinely revealed, although it is contrary to manifest testimonies of Scripture, which command that to avoid fornication each one should have his own wife, 1 Cor. 7, 2; which likewise forbid to dissolve marriages that have been contracted; cf. Matt. 6, 32; 19, 6; 1 Cor. 7, 27. [What can the knaves say in reply? And how dare they wantonly and shamelessly misapply the great, most holy name of the divine Majesty?] Paul reminds us what an author such a law was to have when he calls it a doctrine of demons, 1 Tim. 4, 1. And the fruits show their author, namely, so many monstrous lusts and so many murders which are now committed under the pretext of that law [as can be seen at Rome].

The second argument of the adversaries is that the priests ought to be pure, according to Is. 52, 11: Be ye clean that bear the vessels of the Lord. And they cite many things to this effect. This reason which they display we have above removed as especially specious. For we have said that virginity without faith is not purity before God, and marriage, on account of faith, is pure, according to Titus 1, 16: Unto the pure all things are pure. We have said also this, that outward purity and the ceremonies of the Law are not to be transferred hither, because the Gospel requires purity of heart, and does not require the ceremonies of the Law. And it may occur that the heart of a husband, as of Abraham or Jacob, who were polygamists, is purer and burns less with lusts than that of many virgins who are even truly continent. But what Isaiah says: Be ye clean that bear the vessels of the Lord, ought to be understood as referring to cleanness of heart and to the entire repentance. Besides, the saints will know in the exercise of marriage how far it is profitable to restrain its use, and as Paul says, 1 Thess. 4, 4, to possess his vessel in sanctification. Lastly, since marriage is pure, it is rightly said to those who are not continent in celibacy that they should marry wives in order to be pure. Thus the same law: Be ye clean that bear the vessels of the Lord, commands that impure celibates become pure husbands [impure unmarried priests become pure married priests].

The third argument is horrible, namely, that the marriage of priests is the heresy of Jovinian. Fine-sounding words! [Pity on our poor souls, dear sirs; proceed gently!] This is a new crime, that marriage [which God instituted in Paradise] is a heresy! [In that case all the world would be children of heretics.] In the time of Jovinian the world did not as yet know the law concerning perpetual celibacy. [This our adversaries know very well.] Therefore it is an impudent falsehood that the marriage of priests is the heresy of Jovinian, or that such marriage was then condemned by the Church. In such passages we can see what design the adversaries had in writing the ***Confutation***. They judged that the ignorant would be thus most easily excited, if they would frequently hear the reproach of heresy, if they pretend that our cause had been dispatched and condemned by many previous decisions of the Church. Thus they frequently cite falsely the judgment of the Church. Because they are not ignorant of this, they were unwilling to exhibit to us a copy of their Apology, lest this falsehood and these reproaches might be exposed. Our opinion, however, as regards the case of Jovinian, concerning the comparison of virginity and marriage, we have expressed above. For we do not make marriage and virginity equal, although neither virginity nor marriage merits justification.

By such false arguments they defend a law that is godless and destructive to good morals. By such reasons they set the minds of princes firmly against God's judgment [the princes and bishops who believe this teaching will see whether their reasons will endure the test when the hour of death arrives], in which God will call them to account as to why they have dissolved marriages, and why they have tortured [flogged and impaled] and killed priests [regardless of the cries, wails, and tears of so many widows and orphans]. For do not doubt but that, as the blood of dead Abel cried out, Gen. 4, 10, so the blood of many good men against whom they have unjustly raged, will also cry out. And God will avenge this cruelty; there you will discover how empty are these reasons of the adversaries, and you will perceive that in God's judgment no calumnies against God's Word remain standing, as Isaiah says, 40, 6: All flesh is grass, and all the goodliness thereof is as the flower of the field [that their arguments are straw and hay, and God a consuming fire, before whom nothing but God's Word can abide, 1 Pet. 1, 24].

Whatever may happen, our princes will be able to console themselves with the consciousness of right counsels, because even though the priests would have done wrong in contracting marriages, yet this disruption of marriages, these proscriptions, and this cruelty are manifestly contrary to the will and Word of God. Neither does novelty or dissent delight our princes, but especially in a matter that is not doubtful more regard had to be paid to the Word of God than to all other things.

Part 29

Article XXIV (XII): *Of the Mass.*

At the outset we must again make the preliminary statement that we do not abolish the Mass, but religiously maintain and defend it. For among us masses are celebrated every Lord's Day and on the other festivals, in which the Sacrament is offered to those who wish to use it, after they have been examined and absolved. And the usual public ceremonies are observed, the series of lessons of prayers, vestments, and other like things.

The adversaries have a long declamation concerning the use of the Latin language in the Mass, in which they absurdly trifle as to how it profits [what a great merit is achieved by] an unlearned hearer to hear in the faith of the Church a Mass which he does not understand. They evidently imagine that the mere work of hearing is a service, that it profits without being understood. We are unwilling to malignantly pursue these things, but we leave them to the judgment of the reader. We mention them only for the purpose of stating in passing, that also among us the Latin lessons and prayers are retained.

Since ceremonies, however, ought to be observed both to teach men Scripture, and that those admonished by the Word may conceive faith and fear [of God, and obtain comfort] and thus also may pray (for these are the designs of ceremonies), we retain the Latin language on account of those who are learning and understand Latin, and we mingle with it German hymns, in order that the people also may have something to learn, and by which faith and fear may be called forth. This custom has always existed in the churches. For although some more frequently, and others more rarely, introduced German hymns, nevertheless the people almost everywhere sang something in their own tongue. [Therefore, this is not such a new departure.] It has, however, nowhere been written or represented that the act of hearing lessons not understood profits men, or that ceremonies profit, not because they teach or admonish, but *ex opere operato*, because they are thus performed or are looked upon. Away with such pharisaic opinions! [Ye sophists ought to be heartily ashamed of such dreams!]

The fact that we hold only Public or Common Mass [at which the people also commune, not Private Mass] is no offense against the Church catholic. For in the Greek churches even to-day private Masses are not held, but there is only a public Mass, and that on the Lord's Day and festivals. In the monasteries daily Mass is held, but this is only public. These are the traces of former customs. For nowhere do the ancient writers before Gregory make mention of private Masses. We now omit noticing the nature of their origin. It is evident that after the mendicant monks began to prevail, from most false opinions and on account of gain they were so increased that all good men for a long time desired some limit to this thing. Although St. Francis wished to provide aright for this matter, as he decided that each fraternity should be content with a single common Mass daily, afterwards this was changed, either by superstition or for the sake of gain. Thus, where it is of advantage, they themselves change the institutions of the Fathers; and afterwards they cite against us the authority of the Fathers. Epiphanius writes that in Asia the Communion was celebrated three times a week, and that there were no daily Masses. And indeed he says that this custom was handed down from the apostles. For he speaks thus: Assemblies for Communion were appointed by the apostles to be held on the fourth day, on Sabbath eve, and the Lord's Day.

Moreover, although the adversaries collect many testimonies on this topic to prove that the Mass is a sacrifice, yet this great tumult of words will be quieted when the single reply is advanced that this line of authorities, reasons and testimonies, however long, does not prove that the Mass confers grace er opere operato, or that, when applied on behalf of others, it merits for them the remission of venial and mortal sins, of guilt and punishment. This one reply overthrows all objections of the adversaries, not only in this *Confutation*, but in all writings which they have published concerning the Mass.

And this is the issue [the principal question] of the case of which our readers are to be admonished, as Aeschines admonished the judges that just as boxers contend with one another for their position, so they should strive with their adversary concerning the controverted point, and not permit him to wander beyond the case. In the same manner our adversaries ought to be here compelled to speak on the subject presented. And when the controverted point has been thoroughly understood, a decision concerning the arguments on both sides will be very easy.

For in our Confession we have shown that we hold that the Lord's Supper does not confer *grace ex opere operato*, and that, when applied on behalf of others, alive or dead, it does not merit for them *ex opere operato* the remission of sins, of guilt or of punishment. And of this position a clear and firm proof exists in that it is impossible to obtain the remission of our sins on account of our own work *ex opere operato* [even when there is not a good thought in the heart], but the terrors of sin and death must be overcome by faith when we comfort our hearts with the knowledge of Christ, and believe that for Christ's sake we are forgiven, and that the merits and righteousness of Christ are granted us, Rom. 5, 1: Being justified by faith, we have peace. These things are so sure and so firm that they can stand against all the gates of hell.

If we are to say only as much as is necessary, the case has already been stated. For no sane man can approve that pharisaic and heathen opinion concerning the *opus operatum*. And nevertheless this opinion inheres in the people, and has increased infinitely the number of masses. For masses are purchased to appease God's wrath, and by this work they wish to obtain the remission of guilt and of punishment; they wish to procure whatever is necessary in every kind of life [health riches, prosperity, and success in business]. They wish even to liberate the dead. Monks and sophists have taught this pharisaic opinion in the Church.

But although our case has already been stated, yet, because the adversaries foolishly pervert many passages of Scripture to the defense of their errors, we shall add a few things on this topic. In the *Confutation* they have said many things concerning "sacrifice," although in our Confession we purposely avoided this term on account of its ambiguity. We have set forth what those persons whose abuses we condemn now understand as a sacrifice. Now, in order to explain the passages of Scripture that have been wickedly perverted, it is necessary in the beginning to set forth what a sacrifice is. Already for an entire period of ten years the adversaries have published almost infinite volumes concerning sacrifice, and yet not one of them thus far has given a definition of sacrifice. They only seize upon the name "sacrifices" either from the Scriptures or the Fathers [and where they find it in the Concordances of the Bible apply it here, whether it fits or not]. Afterward they append their own dreams, as though indeed a sacrifice signifies whatever pleases them.

Part 30

What a Sacrifice Is, and What Are the Species of Sacrifice.

[Now, lest we plunge blindly into this business, we must indicate, in the first place, a distinction as to what is, and what is not, a sacrifice. To know this is expedient and good for all Christians.] Socrates, in the Phaedrus of Plato, says that he is especially fond of divisions, because without these nothing can either be explained or understood in speaking, and if he discovers any one skilful in making divisions, he says that he attends and follows his footsteps as those of a god. And he instructs the one dividing to separate the members in their very joints, lest, like an unskilful cook, he break to pieces some member. But the adversaries wonderfully despise these precepts, and, according to Plato, are truly *kakoi mageiroi* (poor butchers), since they break the members of "sacrifice," as can be understood when we have enumerated the species of sacrifice. Theologians are rightly accustomed to distinguish between a Sacrament and a sacrifice. Therefore let the genus comprehending both of these be either a ceremony or a sacred work. A Sacrament is a ceremony or work in which God presents to us that which the promise annexed to the ceremony offers; as Baptism is a work, not which we offer to God but in which God baptizes us, i.e., a minister in the place of God; and God here offers and presents the remission of sins, etc., according to the promise, Mark 16, 16: He that believeth and is baptized shall be saved. A sacrifice, on the contrary, is a ceremony or work which we render God in order to afford Him honor.

Moreover, the proximate species of sacrifice are two, and there are no more. One is the propitiatory sacrifice, i.e., a work which makes satisfaction for guilt and punishment, i.e., one that reconciles God, or appeases God's wrath, or which merits the remission of sins for others. The other species is the eucharistic sacrifice, which does not merit the remission of sins or reconciliation, but is rendered by those who have been reconciled, in order that we may give thanks or return gratitude for the remission of sins that has been received, or for other benefits received.

These two species of sacrifice we ought especially to have in view and placed before the eyes in this controversy, as well as in many other discussions; and especial care must be taken lest they be confounded. But if the limits of this book would suffer it, we would add the reasons for this division. For it has many testimonies in the Epistle to the Hebrews and elsewhere. And all Levitical sacrifices can be referred to these members as to their own homes [genera]. For in the Law certain sacrifices were named propitiatory on account of their signification or similitude; not because they merited the remission of sins before God, but because they merited the remission of sins according to the righteousness of the Law, in order that those for whom they were made might not be excluded from that commonwealth [from the people of Israel]. Therefore they were called sin-offerings and burnt offerings for a trespass. Whereas the eucharistic sacrifices were the oblation, the drink-offering, thank-offerings, first-fruits, tithes.

[Thus there have been in the Law emblems of the true sacrifice.] But in fact there has been only one propitiatory sacrifice in the world, namely, the death of Christ, as the Epistle to the Hebrews teaches, which says, 10, 4: It is not possible that the blood of bulls and of goats should take away sins. And a little after, of the [obedience and] will of Christ, v. 10: By the which will we are sanctified by the offering of the body of Jesus Christ once for all. And Isaiah interprets the Law, in order that we may know that the death of Christ is truly a satisfaction for our sins, or expiation, and that the ceremonies of the Law are not, wherefore he says, 53, 10: When Thou shalt make His soul an offering for sin, He will see His seed, etc. For the word employed here, *'shm*, signifies a victim for transgression; which signified in the Law that a certain Victim was to come to make satisfaction for our sins and reconcile God in order that men might know that God wishes to be reconciled to us, not on account of our own righteousnesses, but on account of the merits of another, namely, of Christ. Paul interprets the same word *'shm* as sin, Rom. 8, 3: For sin (God) condemned sin, i.e., He punished sin for sin, i.e., by a Victim for sin. The significance of the word can be the more easily understood from the customs of the heathen, which, we see, have been received from the misunderstood expressions of the Fathers. The Latins called a victim that which in great calamities, where God seemed to be especially enraged, was offered to appease God's wrath, a *piaculum*; and they sometimes sacrificed human victims, perhaps because they had heard that a human victim would appease God for the entire human race. The Greeks sometimes called them *katharmata* and sometimes *peripsehmata*. Isaiah and Paul, therefore, mean that Christ became a victim i.e., an expiation, that by His merits, and not by our own, God might be reconciled. Therefore let this remain established in the case namely, that the death of Christ alone is truly a propitiatory sacrifice. For the Levitical propitiatory sacrifices were so called only to signify a future expiation. On account of a certain resemblance, therefore, they were satisfactions redeeming the righteousness of the Law, lest those persons who sinned should be excluded from the commonwealth. But after the revelation of the Gospel [and after the true sacrifice has been accomplished] they had to cease, and because they had to cease in the revelation of the Gospel, they were not truly propitiations, since the Gospel was promised for this very reason, namely, to set forth a propitiation.

Now the rest are eucharistic sacrifices which are called sacrifices of praise, Lev. 3, 1 f.; 7, 11 f.; Ps. 56, 12 f., namely, the preaching of the Gospel, faith, prayer, thanksgiving, confession, the afflictions of saints yea, all good works of saints. These sacrifices are not satisfactions for those making them, or applicable on behalf of others, so as to merit for these, ex opere operato, the remission of sins or reconciliation. For they are made by those who have been reconciled. And such are the sacrifices of the New Testament, as Peter teaches, 1. Ep. 2, 5: An holy priesthood, to offer up spiritual sacrifices. Spiritual sacrifices, however, are contrasted not only with those of cattle, but even with human works offered *ex opere operato*, because spiritual refers to the movements of the Holy Ghost in us. Paul teaches the same thing Rom. 12, 1: Present your bodies a living sacrifice, holy, acceptable, which is your reasonable service. Reasonable service signifies, however, a service in which God is known and apprehended by the mind, as happens in the movements of fear and trust towards God. Therefore it is opposed not only to the Levitical service, in which cattle are slain, but also to a service in which a work is imagined to be offered *ex opere operato*. The Epistle to the Hebrews, 13, 15, teaches the same thing: By Him, therefore, let us offer the sacrifice of praise to God continually; and he adds the interpretation, that is, the fruit of our lips, giving thanks to His name. He bids us offer praises, i.e., prayer, thanksgiving, confession, and the like. These avail not *ex opere operato*, but on account of faith. This is taught by the clause: By Him let us offer, i.e., by faith in Christ.

In short, the worship of the New Testament is spiritual, i.e., it is the righteousness of faith in the heart and the fruits of faith. It accordingly abolishes the Levitical services. [In the New Testament no offering avails *ex opere operato, sine bono motu utentis*, i.e. on account of the work, without a good thought in the heart.] And Christ says, John 4, 23. 24: True worshipers shall worship the Father in spirit and in truth, for the Father seeketh such to worship Him. God is a Spirit; and they that worship Him must worship Him in spirit and in truth [that is from the heart, with heartfelt fear and cordial faith]. This passage clearly condemns [as absolutely devilish, pharisaical, and antichristian] opinions concerning sacrifices which they imagine, avail *ex opere operato*, and teaches that men ought to worship in spirit i.e., with the dispositions of the heart and by faith. [The Jews also did not understand their ceremonies aright, and imagined that they were righteous before God when they had wrought works *ex opere operato*. Against this the prophets contend with the greatest earnestness.] Accordingly, the prophets also in the Old Testament condemn the opinion of the people concerning the opus operatum and teach the righteousness and sacrifices of the Spirit. Jer. 7, 22. 23: For I spake not unto your fathers, nor commanded them, in the day that I brought them out of the land of Egypt, concerning burnt offerings or sacrifices; but this thing commanded I them, saying, Obey My voice, and I will be your God, etc. How do we suppose that the Jews received this arraignment, which seems to conflict openly with Moses? For it was evident that God had given the fathers commands concerning burnt offerings and victims. But Jeremiah condemns the opinion concerning sacrifices which God had not delivered namely, that these services should please Him *ex opere operato*. But he adds concerning faith that God had commanded this: Hear Me, i.e., believe Me that I am your God; that I wish to become thus known when I pity and aid; neither have I need of your victims; believe that I wish to be God the Justifier and Savior, not on account of works, but on account of My word and promise, truly and from the heart seek and expect aid from Me.

Ps. 50, 13. 15, which rejects the victims and requires prayer, also condemns the opinion concerning the opus operatum: Will I eat the flesh of bulls? etc. (Call upon Me in the day of trouble; I will deliver thee, and thou shalt glorify Me. The Psalmist testifies that this is true service, that this is true honor, if we call upon Him from the heart.

Likewise Ps. 40, 6: Sacrifice and offering Thou didst not desire; mine ears hast Thou opened, i.e., Thou hast offered to me Thy Word that I might hear it, and Thou dost require that I believe Thy Word and The promises, that Thou truly desirest to pity, to bring aid, etc. Likewise Ps. 51, 16. 17: Thou delightest not in burnt offering. The sacrifices of God are a broken spirit; a broken and a contrite heart, O God, Thou wilt not despise. Likewise Ps. 4, 5: Offer the sacrifices of righteousness, and put your trust [hope, V.] in the Lord. He bids us hope, and says that this is a righteous sacrifice, signifying that other sacrifices are not true and righteous sacrifices. And Ps. 116, 17: I will offer to Thee the sacrifices of thanksgiving, and will call upon the name of the Lord They call invocation a sacrifice of thanksgiving.

But Scripture is full of such testimonies as teach that sacrifices *ex opere operato* do not reconcile God. Accordingly the New Testament, since Levitical services have been abrogated, teaches that new and pure sacrifices will be made, namely, faith, prayer, thanksgiving, confession, and the preaching of the Gospel, afflictions on account of the Gospel, and the like.

And of these sacrifices Malachi speaks, 1, 11: From the rising of the sun even unto the going down of the same My name shall be great among the Gentiles; and in every place incense shall be offered unto My name and a pure offering. The adversaries perversely apply this passage to the Mass, and quote the authority of the Fathers. A reply, however, is easy, for even if it spoke most particularly of the Mass, it would not follow that the Mass justifies *ex opere operato*, or that when applied to others, it merits the remission of sins, etc. The prophet says nothing of those things which the monks and sophists impudently fabricate. Besides, the very words of the prophet express his meaning. For they first say this, namely, that the name of the Lord will be great. This is accomplished by the preaching of the Gospel. For through this the name of Christ is made known, and the mercy of the Father, promised in Christ is recognized. The preaching of the Gospel produces faith in those who receive the Gospel. They call upon God, they give thanks to God, they bear afflictions for their confession, they produce good works for the glory of Christ. Thus the name of the Lord becomes great among the Gentiles. Therefore incense and a pure offering signify not a ceremony *ex opere operato* [not the ceremony of the Mass alone], but all those sacrifices through which the name of the Lord becomes great, namely, faith, invocation, the preaching of the Gospel, confession, etc. And if any one would have this term embrace the ceremony [of the Mass], we readily concede it, provided he neither understands the ceremony alone, nor teaches that the ceremony profits *ex opere operato*. For just as among the sacrifices of praise, i.e., among the praises of God, we include the preaching of the Word so the reception itself of the Lord's Supper can be praise or thanksgiving, but it does not justify *ex opere operato*; neither is it to be applied to others so as to merit for them the remission of sins. But after a while we shall explain how even a ceremony is a sacrifice. Yet, as Malachi speaks of all the services of the New Testament, and not only of the Lord's Supper; likewise, as he does not favor the pharisaic opinion of the *opus operatum*, he is not against us, but rather aids us. For he requires services of the heart, through which the name of the Lord becomes truly great.

Another passage also is cited from Malachi 3, 3: And He shall purify the sons of Levi, and purge them as gold and silver, that they may offer unto the Lord an offering of righteousness. This passage clearly requires the sacrifices of the righteous, and hence does not favor the opinion concerning the *opus operatum*. But the sacrifices of the sons of Levi i.e., of those teaching in the New Testament, are the preaching of the Gospel, and the good fruits of preaching, as Paul says, Rom. 15, 16: Ministering the Gospel of God, that the offering up of the Gentiles might be acceptable, being sanctified by the Holy Ghost, i.e., that the Gentiles might be offerings acceptable to God by faith, etc. For in the Law the slaying of victims signified both the death of Christ and the preaching of the Gospel, by which this oldness of flesh should be mortified, and the new and eternal life be begun in us.

But the adversaries everywhere perversely apply the name sacrifice to the ceremony alone. They omit the preaching of the Gospel, faith, prayer, and similar things, although the ceremony has been established on account of these, and the New Testament ought to have sacrifices of the heart, and not ceremonials for sin that are to be performed after the manner of the Levitical priesthood.

They cite also the daily sacrifice (cf. Ex. 29, 38 f.; Dan. 8, ll f., 12, 11), that, just as in the Law there was a daily sacrifice, so the Mass ought to be a daily sacrifice of the New Testament. The adversaries have managed well if we permit ourselves to be overcome by allegories. It is evident, however, that allegories do not produce firm proofs [that in matters so highly important before God we must have a sure and clear word of God, and not introduce by force obscure and foreign passages, such uncertain explanations do not stand the test of God's judgment]. Although we indeed readily suffer the Mass to be understood as a daily sacrifice, provided that the entire Mass be understood, i.e., the ceremony with the preaching of the Gospel, faith, invocation, and thanksgiving. For these joined together are a daily sacrifice of the New Testament, because the ceremony [of the Mass, or the Lord's Supper] was instituted on account of these things, neither is it to be separated from these. Paul says accordingly, 1 Cor. 11, 26: As often as ye eat this bread and drink this cup, ye do show the Lord's death till He come. But it in no way follows from this Levitical type that a ceremony justifying *ex opere operato* is necessary, or ought to be applied on behalf of others, that it may merit for them the remission of sins.

And the type aptly represents not only the ceremony, but also the preaching of the Gospel. In Num. 28, 4 f. three parts of that daily sacrifice are represented, the burning of the lamb, the libation, and the oblation of wheat flour. The Law had pictures or shadows of future things. Accordingly, in this spectacle Christ and the entire worship of the New Testament are portrayed. The burning of the lamb signifies the death of Christ. The libation signifies that everywhere in the entire world, by the preaching of the Gospel, believers are sprinkled with the blood of that Lamb, i.e., sanctified, as Peter says, 1. Ep. 1, 2: Through sanctification of the Spirit, unto obedience and sprinkling of the blood of Jesus Christ. The oblation of wheat flour signifies faith, prayer, and thanksgiving in hearts. As, therefore, in the Old Testament, the shadow is perceived, so in the New the thing signified should be sought, and not another type, as sufficient for a sacrifice.

Therefore, although a ceremony is a memorial of Christ's death, nevertheless it alone is not the daily sacrifice; but the memory itself is the daily sacrifice, i.e., preaching and faith, which truly believes that, by the death of Christ, God has been reconciled. A libation is required, i.e., the effect of preaching, in order that, being sprinkled by the Gospel with the blood of Christ, we may be sanctified, as those put to death and made alive. Oblations also are required, i.e., thanksgiving, confessions, and afflictions.

Thus the pharisaic opinion of the *opus operatum* being cast aside, let us understand that spiritual worship and a daily sacrifice of the heart are signified, because in the New Testament the substance of good things should be sought for [as Paul says: In the Old Testament is the shadow of things to come but the body and the truth is in Christ], i.e., the Holy Ghost, mortification, and quickening. From these things it is sufficiently apparent that the type of the daily sacrifice testifies nothing against us, but rather for us, because we seek for all the parts signified by the daily sacrifice. [We have clearly shown all the parts that belonged to the daily sacrifice in the law of Moses, that it must mean a true cordial offering, not an ***opus operatum***.] The adversaries falsely imagine that the ceremony alone is signified, and not also the preaching of the Gospel, mortification, and quickening of heart, etc. [which is the best part of the Mass, whether they call it a sacrifice or anything else].

Now, therefore, good men will be able to judge readily that the complaint against us that we abolish the daily sacrifice is most false. Experience shows what sort of Antiochi they are who hold power in the Church; who under the pretext of religion assume to themselves the kingdom of the world, and who rule without concern for religion and the teaching of the Gospel; who wage war like kings of the world, and have instituted new services in the Church. For in the Mass the adversaries retain only the ceremony, and publicly apply this to sacrilegious gain. Afterward they feign that this work, as applied on behalf of others, merits for them grace and all good things. In their sermons they do not teach the Gospel, they do not console consciences they do not show that sins are freely remitted for Christ's sake, but they set forth the worship of saints, human satisfactions, human traditions, and by these they affirm that men are justified before God. And although some of these traditions are manifestly godless, nevertheless they defend them by violence. If any preachers wish to be regarded more learned, they treat of philosophical questions, which neither the people nor even those who propose them understand. Lastly, those who are more tolerable teach the Law, and say nothing concerning the righteousness of faith.

The adversaries in the ***Confutation*** make a great ado concerning the desolation of churches, namely, that the altars stand unadorned, without candles and without images. These trifles they regard as ornaments to churches. [Although it is not true that we abolish all such outward ornaments; yet, even if it were so, Daniel is not speaking of such things as are altogether external and do not belong to the Christian Church.] It is a far different desolation which Daniel means, 11, 31; 12, 11, namely, ignorance of the Gospel. For the people, overwhelmed by the multitude and variety of traditions and opinions, were in no way able to embrace the sum of Christian doctrine. [For the adversaries preach mostly of human ordinances, whereby consciences are led from Christ to confidence in their own works.] For who of the people ever understood the doctrine of repentance of which the adversaries treat? And yet this is the chief topic of Christian doctrine.

Consciences were tormented by the enumeration of offenses and by satisfactions. Of faith by which we freely receive the remission of sins, no mention whatever was made by the adversaries. Concerning the exercises of faith struggling with despair, and the free remission of sins for Christ's sake, all the books and all the sermons of the adversaries were silent [worse than worthless, and, moreover, caused untold damage]. To these, the horrible profanation of the masses and many other godless services in the churches were added. This is the desolation which Daniel describes.

On the contrary, by the favor of God, the priests among us attend to the ministry of the Word, teach the Gospel concerning the blessings of Christ, and show that the remission of sins occurs freely for Christ's sake. This doctrine brings sure consolation to consciences. The doctrine of [the Ten Commandments and] good works which God commands is also added. The worth and use of the Sacraments are declared.

But if the use of the Sacrament would be the daily sacrifice, nevertheless we would retain it rather than the adversaries, because with them priests hired for pay use the Sacrament. With us there is a more frequent and more conscientious use. For the people use it, but after having first been instructed and examined. For men are taught concerning the true use of the Sacrament that it was instituted for the purpose of being a seal and testimony of the free remission of sins, and that, accordingly, it ought to admonish alarmed consciences to be truly confident and believe that their sins are freely remitted. Since, therefore, we retain both the preaching of the Gospel and the lawful use of the Sacrament, the daily sacrifice remains with us.

And if we must speak of the outward appearance, attendance upon church is better among us than among the adversaries. For the audiences are held by useful and clear sermons. But neither the people nor the teachers have ever understood the doctrine of the adversaries. [There is nothing that so attaches people to the church as good preaching. But our adversaries preach their people out of the churches; for they teach nothing of the necessary parts of Christian doctrine; they narrate the legends of saints and other fables.] And the true adornment of the churches is godly, useful, and clear doctrine, the devout use of the Sacraments, ardent prayer, and the like. Candles, golden vessels [tapers, altar-cloths, images], and similar adornments are becoming, but they are not the adornment that properly belongs to the Church. But if the adversaries make worship consist in such matters, and not in the preaching of the Gospel, in faith, and the conflicts of faith they are to be numbered among those whom Daniel describes as worshiping their God with gold and silver, Dan. 11, 38.

They quote also from the Epistle to the Hebrews, 5, 1: Every high priest taken from among men is ordained for men in things pertaining to God that he may offer both gifts and sacrifices for sins. Hence they conclude that, since in the New Testament there are high priests and priests, it follows that there is also a sacrifice for sins. This passage particularly makes an impression on the unlearned, especially when the pomp of the priesthood [the garments of Aaron, since in the Old Testament there were many ornaments of gold, silver, and purple] and the sacrifices of the Old Testament are spread before the eyes. This resemblance deceives the ignorant, so that they judge that, according to the same manner, a ceremonial sacrifice ought to exist among us, which should be applied on behalf of the sins of others, just as in the Old Testament. Neither is the service of the masses and the rest of the polity of the Pope anything else than false zeal in behalf of the misunderstood Levitical polity. [They have not understood that the New Testament is occupied with other matters, and that, if such ceremonies are used for the training of the young, a limit must be fixed for them.]

And although our belief has its chief testimonies in the Epistle to the Hebrews, nevertheless the adversaries distort against us mutilated passages from this Epistle, as in this very passage, where it is said that every high priest is ordained to offer sacrifices for sins. Scripture itself immediately adds that Christ is High Priest, Heb. 5, 5. 6. 10. The preceding words speak of the Levitical priesthood, and signify that the Levitical priesthood was an image of the priesthood of Christ. For the Levitical sacrifices for sins did not merit the remission of sins before God; they were only an image of the sacrifice of Christ, which was to be the one propitiatory sacrifice, as we have said above. Therefore the Epistle is occupied to a great extent with the topic that the ancient priesthood and the ancient sacrifices were instituted not for the purpose of meriting the remission of sins before God or reconciliation, but only to signify the future sacrifice of Christ alone. For in the Old Testament it was necessary for saints to be justified by faith derived from the promise of the remission of sins that was to be granted for Christ's sake, just as saints are also justified in the New Testament. From the beginning of the world it was necessary for all saints to believe that Christ would be the promised offering and satisfaction for sins, as Isaiah teaches, 53, 10: When Thou shalt make His soul an offering for sin.

Since, therefore, in the Old Testament, sacrifices did not merit reconciliation, unless by a figure (for they merited civil reconciliation), but signified the coming sacrifice, it follows that Christ is the only sacrifice applied on behalf of the sins of others. Therefore, in the New Testament no sacrifice is left to be applied for the sins of others, except the one sacrifice of Christ upon the cross.

They altogether err who imagine that Levitical sacrifices merited the remission of sins before God, and, by this example in addition to the death of Christ, require in the New Testament sacrifices that are to be applied on behalf of others. This imagination absolutely destroys the merit of Christ's passion and the righteousness of faith, and corrupts the doctrine of the Old and New Testaments, and instead of Christ makes for us other mediators and propitiators out of the priests and sacrificers, who daily sell their work in the churches.

Therefore, if any one would thus infer that in the New Testament a priest is needed to make offering for sins, this must be conceded only of Christ. And the entire Epistle to the Hebrews confirms this explanation. And if, in addition to the death of Christ, we were to seek for any other satisfaction to be applied for the sins of others and to reconcile God, this would be nothing more than to make other mediators in addition to Christ. Again, as the priesthood of the New Testament is the ministry of the Spirit, as Paul teaches 2 Cor. 3, 6, it, accordingly, has but the one sacrifice of Christ, which is satisfactory and applied for the sins of others. Besides it has no sacrifices like the Levitical, which could be applied *ex opere operato* on behalf of others, but it tenders to others the Gospel and the Sacraments, that by means of these they may conceive faith and the Holy Ghost and be mortified and quickened, because the ministry of the Spirit conflicts with the application of an *opus operatum*. [For, unless there is personal faith and a life wrought by the Holy Spirit, the *opus operatum* of another cannot render me godly nor save me.] For the ministry of the Spirit is that through which the Holy Ghost is efficacious in hearts; and therefore this ministry is profitable to others, when it is efficacious in them, and regenerates and quickens them. This does not occur by the application *ex opere operato* of the work of another on behalf of others.

We have shown the reason why the Mass does not justify *ex opere operato*, and why, when applied on behalf of others, it does not merit remission, because both conflict with the righteousness of faith. For it is impossible that remission of sins should occur, and the terrors of death and sin be overcome by any work or anything, except by faith in Christ, according to Rom. 5, 1: Being justified by faith, we have peace.

In addition, we have shown that the Scriptures, which are cited against us, in no way favor the godless opinion of the adversaries concerning the opus operatum. All good men among all nations can judge this. Therefore the error of Thomas is to be rejected, who wrote: That the body of the Lord, once offered on the cross for original debt, is continually offered for daily offenses on the altar in order that, in this, the Church might have a service whereby to reconcile God to herself. The other common errors are also to be rejected, as, that the Mass *ex opere operato* confers grace upon one employing it; likewise that when applied for others, even for wicked persons, provided they do not interpose an obstacle, it merits for them the remission of sins, of guilt and punishment. All these things are false and godless, and lately invented by unlearned monks, and obscure the glory of Christ's passion and the righteousness of faith.

And from these errors infinite others sprang, as, that the masses avail when applied for many, just as much as when applied individually. The sophists have particular degrees of merit, just as money-changers have grades of weight for gold or silver. Besides they sell the Mass, as a price for obtaining what each one seeks: to merchants, that business may be prosperous; to hunters, that hunting may be successful, and infinite other things. Lastly, they apply it also to the dead; by the application of the Sacrament they liberate souls from the pains of purgatory; although without faith the Mass is of service not even to the living. Neither are the adversaries able to produce even one syllable from the Scriptures in defense of these fables which they teach with great authority in the Church, neither do they have the testimonies of the ancient Church nor of the Fathers. [Therefore they are impious and blind people who knowingly despise and trample under foot the plain truth of God.]

Part 31

What the Fathers Thought concerning Sacrifice.

And since we have explained the passages of Scripture which are cited against us, we must reply also concerning the Fathers. We are not ignorant that the Mass is called by the Fathers a sacrifice; but they do not mean that the Mass confers grace ***ex opere operato***, and that, when applied on behalf of others, it merits for them the remission of sins, of guilt and punishment. Where are such monstrous stories to be found in the Fathers? But they openly testify that they are speaking of thanksgiving. Accordingly they call it a eucharist. We have said above, however, that a eucharistic sacrifice does not merit reconciliation, but is made by those who have been reconciled, just as afflictions do not merit reconciliation, but are eucharistic sacrifices when those who have been reconciled endure them.

And this reply, in general, to the sayings of the Fathers defends us sufficiently against the adversaries. For it is certain that these figments concerning the merit of the opus operatum are found nowhere in the Fathers. But in order that the whole case may be the better understood, we also shall state those things concerning the use of the Sacrament which actually harmonize with the Fathers and Scripture.

Part 32

Some clever men imagine that the Lord's Supper was instituted for two reasons. First, that it might be a mark and testimony of profession, just as a particular shape of hood is the sign of a particular profession. Then they think that such a mark was especially pleasing to Christ, namely, a feast to signify mutual union and friendship among Christians, because banquets are signs of covenant and friendship. But this is a secular view; neither does it show the chief use of the things delivered by God; it speaks only of the exercise of love, which men, however profane and worldly, understand, it does not speak of faith, the nature of which few understand.

The Sacraments are signs of God's will toward us, and not merely signs of men among each other, and they are right in defining that Sacraments in the New Testament are signs of grace. And because in a sacrament there are two things, a sign and the Word, the Word, in the New Testament, is the promise of grace added. The promise of the New Testament is the promise of the remission of sins, as the text, Luke 22, 19, says: This is My body, which is given for you. This cup is the New Testament in My blood which is shed for many for the remission of sins. Therefore the Word offers the remission of sins. And a ceremony is, as it were, a picture or seal, as Paul, Rom. 4, 11, calls it, of the Word, making known the promise. Therefore, just as the promise is useless unless it is received by faith, so a ceremony is useless unless such faith is added as is truly confident that the remission of sins is here offered. And this faith encourages contrite minds. And just as the Word has been given in order to excite this faith, so the Sacrament has been instituted in order that the outward appearance meeting the eyes might move the heart to believe [and strengthen faith]. For through these, namely, through Word and Sacrament, the Holy Ghost works.

And such use of the Sacrament, in which faith quickens terrified hearts, is a service of the New Testament, because the New Testament requires spiritual dispositions, mortification and quickening. [For according to the New Testament the highest service of God is rendered inwardly in the heart.] And for this use Christ instituted it, since He commanded them thus to do in remembrance of Him. For to remember Christ is not the idle celebration of a show [not something that is accomplished only by some gestures and actions], or one instituted for the sake of example, as the memory of Hercules or Ulysses is celebrated in tragedies, but it is to remember the benefits of Christ and receive them by faith so as to be quickened by them. Psalm 111, 4. 5 accordingly says: He hath made His wonderful works to be remembered: the Lord is gracious and full of compassion. He hath given meat unto them that fear Him. For it signifies that the will and mercy of God should be discerned in the ceremony. But that faith which apprehends mercy quickens. And this is the principal use of the Sacrament, in which it is apparent who are fit for the Sacrament, namely, terrified consciences and how they ought to use it.

The sacrifice [thank-offering or thanksgiving] also is added. For there are several ends for one object. After conscience encouraged by faith has perceived from what terrors it is freed, then indeed it fervently gives thanks for the benefit and passion of Christ, and uses the ceremony itself to the praise of God, in order by this obedience to show its gratitude; and testifies that it holds in high esteem the gifts of God. Thus the ceremony becomes a sacrifice of praise.

And the Fathers, indeed, speak of a twofold effect, of the comfort of consciences, and of thanksgiving, or praise. The former of these effects pertains to the nature [the right use] of the Sacrament; the latter pertains to the sacrifice. Of consolation Ambrose says: Go to Him and be absolved, because He is the remission of sins. Do you ask who He is? Hear Him when He says, John 6, 35: I am the Bread of life; he that cometh to Me shall never hunger; and he that believeth on Me shall never thirst. This passage testifies that in the Sacrament the remission of sins is offered; it also testifies that this ought to be received by faith. Infinite testimonies to this effect are found in the Fathers, all of which the adversaries pervert to the ***opus operatum***, and to a work to be applied on behalf of others; although the Fathers clearly require faith, and speak of the consolation belonging to every one, and not of the application.

Besides these, expressions are also found concerning thanksgiving, such as that most beautifully said by Cyprian concerning those communing in a godly way. Piety, says he, in thanksgiving the Bestower of such abundant blessing, makes a distinction between what has been given and what has been forgiven, i.e., piety regards both what has been given and what has been forgiven, i.e., it compares the greatness of God's blessings and the greatness of our evils, sin and death, with each other, and gives thanks, etc. And hence the term eucharist arose in the Church. Nor indeed is the ceremony itself, the giving of thanks ex opere operato, to be applied on behalf of others, in order to merit for them the remission of sins, etc., in order to liberate the souls of the dead. These things conflict with the righteousness of faith, as though, without faith, a ceremony can profit either the one performing it or others.

Part 33

Of the Term Mass.

T he adversaries also refer us to philology. From the names of the Mass they derive arguments which do not require a long discussion. For even though the Mass be called a sacrifice, it does not follow that it must confer grace *ex opere operato*, or, when applied on behalf of others, merit for them the remission of sins, etc. *Leitourgia*, they say, signifies a sacrifice, and the Greeks call the Mass liturgy. Why do they here omit the old appellation synaxris, which shows that the Mass was formerly the communion of many? But let us speak of the word liturgy. This word done not properly signify a sacrifice, but rather the public ministry, and agrees aptly with our belief, namely, that one minister who consecrates tenders the body and blood of the lord to the rest of the people, just as one minister who preaches tenders the Gospel to the people, as Paul says, 1 Cor. 4, 1: Let a man so account of us as of the ministers of Christ and stewards of the mysteries of God, i.e., of the Gospel and the Sacraments. And 2 Cor. 5, 20: We are ambassadors for Christ as though God did beseech you by us; we pray you in Christ's stead, Be ye reconciled to God. Thus the term *Leitourgia* agrees aptly with the ministry. For it is an old word, ordinarily employed in public civil administrations, and signified to the Greeks public burdens, as tribute, the expense of equipping a fleet, or similar things, as the oration of Demosthenes, *FOR LEPTINES*, testifies, all of which is occupied with the discussion of public duties and immunities: *Phehsei de anaxious tinas anthrohpous euromenous ateleian ekdedukenai tas leitourgias*, i.e.: He will say that some unworthy men, having found an immunity, have withdrawn from public burdens. And thus they spoke in the time of the Romana, as the rescript of Pertinax, *De Iure Immunitatis*, l. Semper, shows: ***Ei kai meh pasohn leitour-giohn tous pateras ho tohn teknohn arithmos aneitai***, Even though the number of children does not liberate parents from all public burdens. And the Commentary upon Demosthenes states that *leitourgia* is a kind of tribute, the expense of the games, the expense of equipping vessels, of attending to the gymnasia and similar public offices. And Paul in 2 Cor. 9, 12 employs it for a collection. The taking of the collection not only supplies those things which are wanting to the saints, but also causes them to give more thanks abundantly to God, etc. And in Phil. 2, 25 he calls Epaphroditus a *leitourgos*, one who ministered to my wants, where assuredly a sacrificer cannot be understood. But there is no need of more testimonies, since examples are everywhere obvious to those reading the Greek writers, in whom *lei-tourgia* is employed for public civil burdens or ministries. And on account of the diphthong, grammarians do not derive it from *liteh*, which signifies prayers, but from public goods, which they call *leita*, so that *leitourgeoh* means, I attend to, I administer public goods.

Ridiculous is their inference that, since mention is made in the Holy Scriptures of an altar, therefore the Mass must be a sacrifice; for the figure of an altar is referred to by Paul only by way of comparison. And they fabricate that the Mass has been so called from *mzbh*, an altar. What need is there of an etymology so far fetched, unless it be to show their knowledge of the Hebrew language? What need is there to seek the etymology from a distance, when the term Mass is found in Deut. 16, 10, where it signifies the collections or gifts of the people, not the offering of the priest? For individuals coming to the celebration of the Passover were obliged to bring some gift as a contribution. In the beginning the Christians also retained this custom. Coming together they brought bread, wine, and other things, as the Canons of the Apostles testify. Thence a part was taken to be consecrated; the rest was distributed to the poor. With this custom they also retained Mass as the name of the contributions. And on account of such contributions it appears also that the Mass was elsewhere called *agapeh*, unless one would prefer that it was so called on account of the common feast. But let us omit these trifles. For it is ridiculous that the adversaries should produce such trifling conjectures concerning a matter of such great importance. For although the Mass is called an offering, in what does the term favor the dreams concerning the **opus operatum**, and the application which, they imagine, merits for others the remission of sins? And it can be called an offering for the reason that prayers, thanksgivings, and the entire worship are there offered, as it is also called a eucharist. But neither ceremonies nor prayers profit **ex opere operato**, without faith. Although we are disputing here not concerning prayers, but particularly concerning the Lord's Supper.

[Here you can see what rude asses our adversaries are. They say that the term **missa** is derived from the term **misbeach**, which signifies an altar; hence we are to conclude that the Mass is a sacrifice; for sacrifices are offered on an altar. Again, the word **liturgia**, by which the Greeks call the Mass, is also to denote a sacrifice. This claim we shall briefly answer. All the world sees that from such reasons this heathenish and antichristian error does not follow necessarilv, that the Mass benefits **ex opere operato sine bono motu utentis**. Therefore they are asses, because in such a highly important matter they bring forward such silly things. Nor do the asses know any grammar. For missa and liturgia do not mean sacrifice. **Missa**, in Hebrew, denotes a joint contribution. For this may have been a custom among Christians, that they brought meat and drink for the benefit of the poor to their assemblies. This custom was derived from the Jews, who had to bring such contributions on their festivals, these they called **missa**. Likewise, **liturgia**, in Greek, really denotes an office in which a person ministers to the congregation. This is well applied to our teaching, because with us the priest, as a common servant of those who wish to commune, ministers to them the holy Sacrament.

Some think that **missa** is not derived from the Hebrew, but signifies as much as **remissio** the forgiveness of sin. For, the communion being ended, the announcement used to be made: **Ite, missa est**: Depart, you have forgiveness of sins. They cite, as proof that this is so, the fact that the Greeks used to say: Lais Aphesis (laois aphsesis), *which also means that they had been pardoned. If this were so, it would be an excellent meaning, for in connection with this ceremony forgiveness of sins must always be preached and proclaimed. But the case before us is little aided, no matter what the meaning of the word* missa is.]

The Greek canon says also many things concerning the offering, but it shows plainly that it is not speaking properly of the body and blood of the Lord, but of the whole service of prayers and thanksgivings. For it says thus: ***Kai poiehson hemas axious genesthai tou prospserein soi deehseis kai hikesias kai thusias anaimaktous huper pantos laou.*** When this is rightly understood, it gives no offense. For it prays that we be made worthy to offer prayers and supplications and bloodless sacrifices for the people. For he calls even prayers bloodless sacrifices. Just as also a little afterward: ***Eti prospheromen soi tehn logikehn tautehn kai anaimakton latreian***, We offer, he says this reasonable and bloodless service. For they explain this inaptly who would rather interpret this of a reasonable sacrifice, and transfer it to the very body of Christ, although the canon speaks of the entire worship, and in opposition to the ***opus operatum*** Paul has spoken of ***logikeh latreia*** [reasonable service], namely, of the worship of the mind, of fear, of faith, of prayer, of thanksgiving, etc.

Part 34

Of the Mass for the Dead.

Our adversaries have no testimonies and no command from Scripture for defending the application of the ceremony for liberating the souls of the dead, although from this they derive infinite revenue. Nor, indeed, is it a light sin to establish such services in the Church without the command of God and without the example of Scripture, and to apply to the dead the Lord's Supper, which was instituted for commemoration and preaching among the living [for the purpose of strengthening the faith of those who use the ceremony]. This is to violate the Second Commandment, by abusing God's name.

For, in the first place, it is a dishonor to the Gospel to hold that a ceremony ***ex opere operato***, without faith, is a sacrifice reconciling God, and making satisfaction for sins. It is a horrible saying to ascribe as much to the work of a priest as to the death of Christ. Again, sin and death cannot be overcome unless by faith in Christ, as Paul teaches, Rom. 5, 1: Being justified by faith, we have peace with God, and therefore the punishment of purgatory cannot be overcome by the application of the work of another.

Now we shall omit the sort of testimonies concerning purgatory that the adversaries have: what kinds of punishments they think there are in purgatory, what grounds the doctrine of satisfactions has, which we have shown above to be most vain. We shall only present this in opposition: It is certain that the Lord's Supper was instituted on account of the remission of guilt. For it offers the remission of sins, where it is necessary that guilt be truly understood. [For what consolation would we have if forgiveness of sin were here offered us, and yet there would be no remission of guilt?] And nevertheless it does not make satisfaction for guilt, otherwise the Mass would be equal to the death of Christ. Neither can the remission of guilt be received in any other way than by faith. Therefore the Mass is not a satisfaction, but a promise and Sacrament that require faith.

And, indeed, it is necessary that all godly persons be seized with the most bitter grief [shed tears of blood, from anguish and sorrow] if they consider that the Mass has been in great part transferred to the dead and to satisfactions for punishments. This is to banish the daily sacrifice from the Church; this is the kingdom of Antiochus, who transferred the most salutary promises concerning the remission of guilt and concerning faith to the most vain opinions concerning satisfactions; this is to defile the Gospel, to corrupt the use of the Sacraments. These are the persons [the real blasphemers] whom Paul has said, 1 Cor. 11, 27, to be guilty of the body and blood of the Lord, who have suppressed the doctrine concerning faith and the remission of sins, and, under the pretext of satisfactions, have devoted the body and blood of the Lord to sacrilegious gain. And they will at some time pay the penalty for this sacrilege. [God will one day vindicate the Second Commandment, and pour out a great, horrible wrath upon them.] Therefore we and all godly consciences should be on our guard against approving the abuses of the adversaries.

But let us return to the case. Since the Mass is not a satisfaction, either for punishment or for guilt, ***ex opere operato***, without faith, it follows that the application on behalf of the dead is useless. Nor is there need here of a longer discussion. For it is evident that these applications on behalf of the dead have no testimonies from the Scriptures. Neither is it safe, without the authority of Scripture, to institute forms of worship in the Church. And if it will at any time be necessary, we shall speak at greater length concerning this entire subject. For why should we now contend with adversaries who understand neither what a sacrifice, nor what a sacrament, nor what remission of sins, nor what faith is?

Neither does the Greek canon apply the offering as a satisfaction for the dead, because it applies it equally for all the blessed patriarchs, prophets, apostles. It appears therefore that the Greeks make an offering as thanksgiving, and do not apply it as satisfaction for punishments. [For, of course, it is not their intention to deliver the prophets and apostles from purgatory, but only to offer up thanks along and together with them for the exalted eternal blessings that have been given to them and us.] Although they speak, moreover, not of the offering alone of the body and blood of the Lord, but of the other parts of the Mass, namely, prayers and thanksgiving. For after the consecration they pray that it may profit those who partake of it, they do not speak of others. Then they add: ***Eti prospheromen soi tehn logikehn tautehn latreian huper tohn en pistei anapausamenohn propatorohn, paterohn, patriarchohn, prophertohn, apostolohn***, etc. ["Yet we offer to you this reasonable service for those having departed in faith, forefathers, fathers, patriarchs prophets, apostles," etc.] Reasonable service, however, does not signify the offering itself, but prayers and all things which are there transacted. Now, as regards the adversaries' citing the Fathers concerning the offering for the dead, we know that the ancients speak of prayer for the dead, which we do not prohibit, but we disapprove of the application ***ex opere operato*** of the Lord's Supper on behalf of the dead. Neither do the ancients favor the adversaries concerning the ***opus operatum***. And even though they have the testimonies especially of Gregory or the moderns, we oppose to them the most clear and certain Scriptures. And there is a great diversity among the Fathers. They were men, and could err and be deceived. Although if they would now become alive again, and would see their sayings assigned as pretexts for the notorious falsehoods which the adversaries teach concerning the opus operatum, they would interpret themselves far differently.

The adversaries also falsely cite against us the condemnation of Aerius, who, they say was condemned for the reason that he denied that in the Mass an offering is made for the living and the dead. They frequently use this dexterous turn, cite the ancient heresies and falsely compare our cause with these in order by this comparison to crush us. [The asses are not ashamed of any lies. Nor do they know who Aerius was and what he taught.] Epiphanius testifies that Aerius held that prayers for the dead are useless. With this he finds fault. Neither do we favor Aerius, but we on our part are contending with you who are defending a heresy manifestly conflicting with the prophets, apostles and holy Fathers, namely, that the Mass justifies ***ex opere operato***, that it merits the remission of guilt and punishment even for the unjust, to whom it is applied, if they do not present an obstacle. Of these pernicious errors, which detract from the glory of Christ's passion, and entirely overthrow the doctrine concerning the righteousness of faith, we disapprove. There was a similar persuasion of the godless in the Law, namely, that they merited the remission of sins, not freely by faith, but through sacrifices ***ex opere operato***.

Therefore they increased these services and sacrifices, instituted the worship of Baal in Israel, and even sacrificed in the groves in Judah. Therefore the prophets condemn this opinion, and wage war not only with the worshipers of Baal, but also with other priests who, with this godless opinion, made sacrifices ordained by God. But this opinion inheres in the world, and always will inhere namely, that services and sacrifices are propitiations. Carnal men cannot endure that alone to the sacrifice of Christ the honor is ascribed that it is a propitiation, because they do not understand the righteousness of faith, but ascribe equal honor to the rest of the services and sacrifices. Just as, therefore, in Judah among the godless priests a false opinion concerning sacrifices inhered, just as in Israel, Baalitic services continued, and, nevertheless, a Church of God was there which disapproved of godless services, so Baalitic worship inheres in the domain of the Pope, namely, the abuse of the Mass, which they apply, that by it they may merit for the unrighteous the remission of guilt and punishment. [And yet, as God still kept His Church, i.e., some saints, in Israel and Judah, so God still preserved His Church, i.e., some saints, under the Papacy, so that the Christian Church has not entirely perished.] And it seems that this Baalitic worship will endure as long as the reign of the Pope, until Christ will come to judge, and by the glory of His advent destroy the reign of Antichrist. Meanwhile all who truly believe the Gospel [that they may truly honor God and have a constant comfort against sins; for God has graciously caused His Gospel to shine, that we might be warned and saved] ought to condemn these wicked services, devised, contrary to God's command, in order to obscure the glory of Christ and the righteousness of faith.

We have briefly said these things of the Mass in order that all good men in all parts of the world may be able to understand that with the greatest zeal we maintain the dignity of the Mass and show its true use, and that we have the most just reasons for dissenting from the adversaries. And we would have all good men admonished not to aid the adversaries in the profanation of the Mass lest they burden themselves with other men's sin. It is a great cause and a great subject not inferior to the transaction of the prophet Elijah, who condemned the worship of Baal. We have presented a case of such importance with the greatest moderation, and now reply without casting any reproach. But if the adversaries will compel us to collect all kinds of abuses of the Mass, the case will not be treated with such forbearance.

Part 35

Article XXVII (XIII): *Of Monastic Vows.*

In the town of Eisenach, in Thuringia, there was, to our knowledge, a monk, John Hilten, who, thirty years ago, was cast by his fraternity into prison because he had protested against certain most notorious abuses. For we have seen his writings, from which it can be well understood what the nature of his doctrine was [that he was a Christian, and preached according to the Scriptures]. And those who knew him testify that he was a mild old man, and serious indeed, but without moroseness. He predicted many things, some of which have thus far transpired, and others still seem to impend which we do not wish to recite, lest it may be inferred that they are narrated either from hatred toward one or from partiality to another. But finally, when, either on account of his age or the foulness of the prison, he fell into disease, he sent for the guardian in order to tell him of his sickness; and when the guardian, inflamed with pharisaic hatred, had begun to reprove the man harshly on account of his kind of doctrine, which seemed to be injurious to the kitchen, then, omitting all mention of his sickness, he said with a sigh that he was bearing these injuries patiently for Christ's sake, since he had indeed neither written nor taught anything which could overthrow the position of the monks, but had only protested against some well-known abuses. But another one he said, will come in A.D. 1516, who will destroy you, neither will you be able to resist him. This very opinion concerning the downward career of the power of the monks, and this number of years, his friends afterwards found also written by him in his commentaries, which he had left, concerning certain passages of Daniel. But although the outcome will teach how much weight should be given to this declaration, yet there are other signs which threaten a change in the power of the monks, that are no less certain than oracles. For it is evident how much hypocrisy, ambition, avarice there is in the monasteries, how much ignorance and cruelty among all the unlearned, what vanity in their sermons and in devising continually new means of gaining money. [The more stupid asses the monks are, the more stubborn, furious bitter, the more venomous asps they are in persecuting the truth and the Word of God.] And there are other faults, which we do not care to mention. While they once were [not jails or everlasting prisons, but] schools for Christian instruction, now they have degenerated, as though from a golden to an iron age, or as the Platonic cube degenerates into bad harmonies, which, Plato says brings destruction. [Now this precious gold is turned to dross, and the wine to water.] All the most wealthy monasteries support only an idle crowd, which gluttonizes upon the public alms of the Church. Christ, however, teaches concerning the salt that has lost its savor that it should be cast out and be trodden under foot, Matt. 5, 13. Therefore the monks by such morals are singing their own fate [requiem, and it will soon be over with them]. And now another sign is added, because they are in many places, the instigators of the death of good men. [This blood of Abel cries against them and] These murders God undoubtedly will shortly avenge. Nor indeed do we find fault with all, for we are of the opinion that there are here and there some good men in the monasteries who judge moderately concerning human and factitious services, as some writers call them, and who do not approve of the cruelty which the hypocrites among them exercise.

But we are now discussing the kind of doctrine which the composers of the *Confutation* are now defending and not the question whether vows should be observed. For we hold that lawful vows ought to be observed; but whether these services merit the remission of sins and justification; whether they are satisfactions for sins, whether they are equal to Baptism, whether they are the observance of precepts and counsels; whether they are evangelical perfection; whether they have the merits of supererogation; whether these merits, when applied on behalf of others save them, whether vows made with these opinions are lawful; whether vows are lawful that are undertaken under the pretext of religion, merely for the sake of the belly and idleness, whether those are truly vows that have been extorted either from the unwilling or from those who on account of age were not able to judge concerning the kind of life, whom parents or friends thrust into the monasteries that they might be supported at the public expense, without the loss of private patrimony, whether vows are lawful that openly tend to an evil issue, either because on account of weakness they are not observed, or because those who are in these fraternities are compelled to approve and aid the abuses of the Mass, the godless worship of saints, and the counsels to rage against good men: concerning these questions we are treating. And although we have said very many things in the Confession concerning such vows as even the canons of the Popes condemn, nevertheless the adversaries command that all things which we have produced be rejected. For they have used these words.

And it is worth while to hear how they pervert our reasons, and what they adduce to fortify their own cause. Accordingly, we will briefly run over a few of our arguments, and in passing, explain away the sophistry of the adversaries in reference to them. Since, however, this entire cause has been carefully and fully treated by Luther in the book to which he gave the title *De Votis Monasticis*, we wish here to consider that book as reiterated.

First, it is very certain that a vow is not lawful by which he who vows thinks that he merits the remission of sins before God, or makes satisfaction before God for sins. For this opinion is a manifest insult to the Gospel, which teaches that the remission of sins is freely granted us for Christ's sake, as has been said above at some length. Therefore we have correctly quoted the declaration of Paul to the Galatians, Gal. 5, 4: Christ is become of no effect unto you, whosoever of you are justified by the Law; ye are fallen from grace. Those who seek the remission of sins not by faith in Christ, but by monastic works detract from the honor of Christ, and crucify Christ afresh. But hear, hear how the composers of the *Confutation* escape in this place! They explain this passage of Paul only concerning the Law of Moses, and they add that the monks observe all things for Christ's sake, and endeavor to live the nearer the Gospel in order to merit eternal life. And they add a horrible peroration in these words: Wherefore those things are wicked that are here alleged against monasticism. O Christ, how long wilt Thou bear these reproaches with which our enemies treat Thy Gospel? We have said in the Confession that the remission of sins is received freely for Christ's sake, through faith. If this is not the very voice of the Gospel, if it is not the judgment of the eternal Father, which Thou who art in the bosom of the Father hast revealed to the world, we are justly blamed. But Thy death is a witness, Thy resurrection is a witness, the Holy Ghost is a witness, Thy entire Church is a witness, that it is truly the judgment of the Gospel that we obtain remission of sins, not on account of our merits, but on account of Thee, through faith.

When Paul denies that by the Law of Moses men merit the remission of sins, he withdraws this praise much more from human traditions, and this he clearly testifies Col. 2, 16. If the Law of Moses, which was divinely revealed, did not merit the remission of sins, how much less do these silly observances [monasticism rosaries, etc.], averse to the civil custom of life, merit the remission of sins!

The adversaries feign that Paul abolishes the Law of Moses, and that Christ succeeds in such a way that He does not freely grant the remission of sins, but on account of the works of other laws, if any are now devised. By this godless and fanatical imagination they bury the benefit of Christ. Then they feign that among those who observe this Law of Christ, the monks observe it more closely than others, on account of their hypocritical poverty, obedience, and chastity, since indeed all these things are full of sham. In the greatest abundance of all things they boast of poverty. Although no class of men has greater license than the monks [who have masterfully decreed that they are exempt from obedience to bishops and princes], they boast of obedience. Of celibacy we do not like to speak, how pure this is in most of those who desire to be continent, Gerson indicates. And how many of them desire to be continent [not to mention the thoughts of their hearts]?

Of course, in this sham life the monks live more closely in accordance with the Gospel! Christ does not succeed Moses in such a way as to remit sins on account of our works, but so as to set His own merits and His own propitiation on our behalf against God's wrath that we may be freely forgiven. Now, he who apart from Christ's propitiation, opposes his own merits to God's wrath, and on account of his own merits endeavors to obtain the remission of sins, whether he present the works of the Mosaic Law, or of the Decalog, or of the rule of Benedict, or of the rule of Augustine, or of other rules, annuls the promise of Christ, has cast away Christ, and has fallen from grace. This is the verdict of Paul.

But, behold, most clement Emperor Charles behold, ye princes, behold, all ye ranks, how great is the impudence of the adversaries! Although we have cited the declaration of Paul to this effect, they have written: Wicked are those things that are here cited against monasticism. But what is more certain than that men obtain the remission of sins by faith for Christ's sake? And these wretches dare to call this a wicked opinion! We do not at all doubt that if you had been advised of this passage, you would have taken [will take] care that such blasphemy be removed from the *Confutation.*

But since it has been fully shown above that the opinion is wicked, that we obtain the remission of sins on account of our works, we shall be briefer at this place. For the prudent reader will easily be able to reason thence that we do not merit the remission of sins by monastic works. Therefore this blasphemy also is in no way to be endured which is read in

Thomas, that the monastic profession is equal to Baptism. It is madness to make human tradition, which has neither God's command nor promise, equal to the ordinance of Christ which has both the command and promise of God, which contains the covenant of grace and of eternal life.

Secondly. Obedience, poverty, and celibacy, provided the latter is not impure, are, as exercises, adiaphora [in which we are not to look for either sin or righteousness]. And for this reason the saints can use these without impiety, just as Bernard, Franciscus, and other holy men used them. And they used them on account of bodily advantage, that they might have more leisure to teach and to perform other godly offices, and not that the works themselves are, by themselves, works that justify or merit eternal life. Finally they belong to the class of which Paul says, 1 Tim. 4, 8: Bodily exercise profiteth little. And it is credible that in some places there are also at present good men, engaged in the ministry of the Word, who use these observances without wicked opinions [without hypocrisy and with the understanding that they do not regard their monasticism as holiness]. But to hold that these observances are services on account of which they are accounted just before God, and through which they merit eternal life, conflicts with the Gospel concerning the righteousness of faith, which teaches that for Christ's sake righteousness and eternal life are granted us. It conflicts also with the saying of Christ, Matt. 15, 9: In vain do they worship Me, teaching for doctrines the commandments of men. It conflicts also with this statement, Rom. 14, 23: Whatsoever is not of faith is sin. But how can they affirm that they are services which God approves as righteousness before Him when they have no testimony of God's Word?

But look at the impudence of the adversaries! They not only teach that these observances are justifying services, but they add that these services are more perfect, i.e. meriting more the remission of sins and justification, than do other kinds of life [that they are states of perfection, i.e., holier and higher states than the rest, such as marriage, rulership]. And here many false and pernicious opinions concur. They imagine that they [are the most holy people who] observe [not only] precepts and [but also] counsels [that is, the superior counsels, which Scripture issues concerning exalted gifts, not by way of command but of advice]. Afterwards these liberal men, since they dream that they have the merits of supererogation, sell these to others. All these things are full of pharisaic vanity. For it is the height of impiety to hold that they satisfy the Decalog in such a way that merits remain, while such precepts as these are accusing all the saints: Thou shalt love the Lord, thy God, with all shine heart, Deut. 6, 5. Likewise: Thou shalt not covet, Rom. 7, 7. [For

as the First Commandment of God (Thou shalt love the Lord, thy God, with all thy heart and with all thy soul and with all thy mind) is higher than a man upon earth can comprehend as it is the highest theology, from which all the prophets and all the apostles have drawn as from a spring their best and highest doctrines, yea, as it is such an exalted commandment, according to which alone all divine service, all honor to God, every offering, all thanksgiving in heaven and upon earth, must be regulated and judged, so that all divine service high and precious and holy though it appear if it be not in accordance with this commandment, is nothing but husks and shells without a kernel, yea, nothing but filth and abomination before God; which exalted commandment no saint whatever has perfectly fulfilled, so that even Noah and Abraham, David, Peter and Paul acknowledged themselves imperfect and sinners: it is an unheard-of, pharisaic, yea, an actually diabolical pride for a sordid Barefooted monk or any similar godless hypocrite to say, yea, preach and teach, that he has observed and fulfilled the holy high commandment so perfectly, and according to the demands and will of God has done so many good works, that merit even superabounds to him. Yea, dear hypocrites, if the holy Ten Commandments and the exalted First Commandment of God were fulfilled as easily as the bread and remnants are put into the sack! They are shameless hypocrites with whom the world is plagued in this last time.] The prophet says, Ps. 116, 11: All men are liars, i.e., not thinking aright concerning God, not fearing God sufficiently, not believing Him sufficiently. Therefore the monks falsely boast that in the observance of a monastic life the commandments are fulfilled, and more is done than what is commanded [that their good works and several hundredweights of superfluous, superabundant holiness remain in store for them].

Again, this also is false, namely, that monastic observances are works of the counsels of the Gospel. For the Gospel does not advise concerning distinctions of clothing and meats and the renunciation of property. These are human traditions, concerning all of which it has been said, 1 Cor. 8, 8: Meat commendeth us not to God. Therefore they are neither justifying services nor perfection; yea, when they are presented covered with these titles, they are mere doctrines of demons.

Virginity is recommended, but to those who have the gift, as has been said above. It is, however, a most pernicious error to hold that evangelical perfection lies in human traditions. For thus the monks even of the Mohammedans would be able to boast that they have evangelical perfection. Neither does it lie in the observance of other things which are called adiaphora, but because the kingdom of God is righteousness and life

in hearts, Rom. 14, 17, perfection is growth in the fear of God, and in confidence in the mercy promised in Christ, and in devotion to one's calling just as Paul also describes perfection 2 Cor. 3, 18: We are changed from glory to glory, even as by the Spirit of the Lord. He does not say: We are continually receiving another hood, or other sandals, or other girdles. It is deplorable that in the Church such pharisaic, yea, Mohammedan expressions should be read and heard as, that the perfection of the Gospel of the kingdom of Christ, which is eternal life, should be placed in these foolish observances of vestments and of similar trifles.

Now hear our Areopagites [excellent teachers] as to what an unworthy declaration they have recorded in the Confutation. Thus they say: It has been expressly declared in the Holy Scriptures that the monastic life merits eternal life if maintained by a due observance, which by the grace of God any monk can maintain; and, indeed, Christ has promised this as much more abundant to those who have left home or brothers, etc., Matt. 19, 29. These are the words of the adversaries in which it is first said most impudently that it is expressed in the Holy Scriptures that a monastic life merits eternal life. For where do the Holy Scriptures speak of a monastic life! Thus the adversaries plead their case thus men of no account quote the Scriptures. Although no one is ignorant that the monastic life has recently been devised, nevertheless they cite the authority of Scripture, and say, too, that this their decree has been expressly declared in the Scriptures.

Besides, they dishonor Christ when they say that by monasticism men merit eternal life. God has ascribed not even to His Law the honor that it should merit eternal life, as He clearly says in Ezek. 20, 25: I gave them also statutes that were not good, and judgments whereby they should not live. In the first place, it is certain that a monastic life does not merit the remission of sins, but we obtain this by faith freely, as has been said above. Secondly, for Christ's sake, through mercy, eternal life is granted to those who by faith receive remission, and do not set their own merits against God's judgment, as Bernard also says with very great force: It is necessary first of all to believe that you cannot have the remission of sine unless by God's indulgence. Secondly, that you can have no good work whatever, unless He has given also this. Lastly, that you can merit eternal life by no works, unless this also is given freely. The rest that follows to the same effect we have above recited. Moreover, Bernard adds at the end: Let no one deceive himself, because if he will reflect well, he will undoubtedly find that with ten thousand he cannot meet Him [namely, God] who cometh against him with twenty thousand. Since however, we do not

merit the remission of sins or eternal life by the works of the divine Law, but it is necessary to seek the mercy promised in Christ, much less is this honor of meriting the remission of sins or eternal life to be ascribed to monastic observances since they are mere human traditions.

Thus those who teach that the monastic life merits the remission of sins or eternal life, and transfer the confidence due Christ to these foolish observances, altogether suppress the Gospel concerning the free remission of sins and the promised mercy in Christ that is to be apprehended. Instead of Christ they worship their own hoods and their own filth. But since even they need mercy, they act wickedly in fabricating works of supererogation, and selling them [their superfluous claim upon heaven] to others.

We speak the more briefly concerning these subjects, because from those things which we have said above concerning justification, concerning repentance, concerning human traditions, it is sufficiently evident that monastic vows are not a price on account of which the remission of sins and life eternal are granted. And since Christ calls traditions useless services, they are in no way evangelical perfection.

But the adversaries cunningly wish to appear as if they modify the common opinion concerning perfection. They say that a monastic life is not perfection, but that it is a state in which to acquire perfection. It is prettily phrased! We remember that this correction is found in Gerson. For it is apparent that prudent men, offended by these immoderate praises of monastic life, since they did not venture to remove entirely from it the praise of perfection, have added the correction that it is a state in which to acquire perfection. If we follow this, monasticism will be no more a state of perfection than the life of a farmer or mechanic. For these are also states in which to acquire perfection. For all men, in every vocation, ought to seek perfection, that is, to grow in the fear of God in faith, in love towards one's neighbor, and similar spiritual virtues.

In the histories of the hermits there are examples of Anthony and of others which make the various spheres of life equal. It is written that when Anthony asked God to show him what progress he was making in this kind of life, a certain shoemaker in the city of Alexandria was indicated to him in a dream to whom he should be compared. The next day Anthony came into the city, and went to the shoemaker in order to ascertain his exercises and gifts, and, having conversed with the man, heard nothing except that early in the morning he prayed in a few words for the entire state, and then attended to his trade. Here Anthony learned that justification is not to be ascribed to the kind of life which he had entered [what God had meant by the revelation; for we are justified before God not through this or that life, but alone through faith in Christ].

But although the adversaries now moderate their praises concerning perfection, yet they actually think otherwise. For they sell merits, and apply them on behalf of others under the pretext that they are observing precepts and counsels, hence they actually hold that they have superfluous merits. But what is it to arrogate to one's self perfection, if this is not? Again, it has been laid down in the ***Confutation*** that the monks endeavor to live more nearly in accordance with the Gospel. Therefore it ascribes perfection to human traditions if they are living more nearly in accordance with the Gospel by not having property, being unmarried, and obeying the rule in clothing, meats, and like trifles.

Again, the ***Confutation*** says that the monks merit eternal life the more abundantly, and quotes Scripture, Matt. 19, 29: Every one that hath forsaken houses, etc. Accordingly, here, too, it claims perfection also for factitious religious rites. But this passage of Scripture in no way favors monastic life. For Christ does not mean that to forsake parents, wife, brethren, is a work that must be done because it merits the remission of sins and eternal life. Yea, such a forsaking is cursed. For if any one forsakes parents or wife in order by this very work to merit the remission of sins or eternal life, this is done with dishonor to Christ.

There is, moreover, a twofold forsaking. One occurs without a call, without God's command; this Christ does not approve, Matt. 15, 9. For the works chosen by us are useless services. But that Christ does not approve this flight appears the more clearly from the fact that He speaks of forsaking wife and children. We know, however, that God's commandment forbids the forsaking of wife and children. The forsaking which occurs by God's command is of a different kind, namely, when power or tyranny compels us either to depart or to deny the Gospel. Here we have the command that we should rather bear injury, that we should rather suffer not only wealth, wife, and children, but even life, to be taken from us. This forsaking Christ approves, and accordingly He adds: For the Gospel's sake, Mark 10, 29, in order to signify that He is speaking not of those who do injury to wife and children, but who bear injury on account of the confession of the Gospel. For the Gospel's sake we ought even to forsake our body. Here it would be ridiculous to hold that it would be a service to God to kill one's self, and without God's command to leave the body. So, too, it is ridiculous to hold that it is a service to God without God's command to forsake possessions, friends, wife, children.

Therefore it is evident that they wickedly distort Christ's word to a monastic life. Unless perhaps the declaration that they "receive a hundredfold in this life" be in place here. For very many become monks not on account of the Gospel but on account of sumptuous living and idleness, who find the most ample riches instead of slender patrimonies. But as the entire subject of monasticism is full of shams, so, by a false pretext they quote testimonies of Scripture, and as a consequence they sin doubly, i.e., they deceive men, and that, too, under the pretext of the divine name.

Another passage is also cited concerning perfection Matt. 19, 21: If thou wilt be perfect, go and sell that thou hast, and give to the poor, and come and follow Me. This passage has exercised many, who have imagined that it is perfection to cast away possessions and the control of property. Let us allow the philosophers to extol Aristippus, who cast a great weight of gold into the sea. [Cynics like Diogenes, who would have no house, but lay in a tub, may commend such heathenish holiness.] Such examples pertain in no way to Christian perfection. [Christian holiness consists in much higher matters than such hypocrisy.] The division, control and possession of property are civil ordinances, approved by God's Word in the commandment, Ex. 20, 15: Thou shalt not steal. The abandonment of property has no command or advice in the Scriptures. For evangelical poverty does not consist in the abandonment of property, but in not being avaricious, in not trusting in wealth, just as David was poor in a most wealthy kingdom.

Therefore, since the abandonment of property is merely a human tradition, it is a useless service. Excessive also are the praises in the Extravagant, which says that the abdication of the ownership of all things for God's sake is meritorious and holy, and a way of perfection. And it is very dangerous to extol with such excessive praises a matter conflicting with political order. [When inexperienced people hear such commendations, they conclude that it is unchristian to hold property whence many errors and seditions follow, through such commendations Muentzer was deceived, and thereby many Anabaptists were led astray.] But [they say] Christ here speaks of perfection. Yea, they do violence to the text who quote it mutilated. Perfection is in that which Christ adds: Follow Me. An example of obedience in one's calling is here presented. And as callings are unlike [one is called to rulership, a second to be father of a family, a third to be a preacher], so this calling does not belong to all, but pertains properly to

that person with whom Christ there speaks, just as the call of David to the kingdom, and of Abraham to slay his son, are not to be imitated by us. Callings are personal, just as matters of business themselves vary with times and persons; but the example of obedience is general. Perfection would have belonged to that young man if he had believed and obeyed this vocation. Thus perfection with us is that every one with true faith should obey his own calling. [Not that I should undertake a strange calling for which I have not the commission or command of God.]

Thirdly. In monastic vows chastity is promised. We have said above, however, concerning the marriage of priests, that the law of nature [or of God] in men cannot be removed by vows or enactments. And as all do not have the gift of continence, many because of weakness are unsuccessfully continent. Neither, indeed, can any vows or any enactments abolish the command of the Holy Ghost 1 Cor. 7, 2: To avoid fornication, let every man have his own wife. Therefore this vow is not lawful in those who do not have the gift of continence, but who are polluted on account of weakness. Concerning this entire topic enough has been said above, in regard to which indeed it is strange, since the dangers and scandals are occurring before men's eyes that the adversaries still defend their traditions contrary to the manifest command of God. Neither does the voice of Christ move them, who chides the Pharisees, Matt. 23, 13 f., who had made traditions contrary to God's command.

Fourthly. Those who live in monasteries are released from their vows by such godless ceremonies as of the Mass applied on behalf of the dead for the sake of gain, the worship of saints, in which the fault is twofold, both that the saints are put in Christ's place, and that they are wickedly worshiped, just as the Dominicasters invented the rosary of the Blessed Virgin, which is mere babbling not less foolish than it is wicked, and nourishes the most vain presumption. Then, too, these very impieties are applied only for the sake of gain. Likewise, they neither hear nor teach the Gospel concerning the free remission of sins for Christ's sake, concerning the righteousness of faith, concerning true repentance, concerning works which have God's command. But they are occupied either in philosophic discussions or in the handing down of ceremonies that obscure Christ.

We will not here speak of the entire service of ceremonies, of the lessons, singing, and similar things, which could be tolerated if they [were regulated as regards number, and if they] would be regarded as exercises, after the manner of lessons in the schools [and preaching], whose design is to teach the hearers, and, while teaching, to move some to fear or faith.

But now they feign that these ceremonies are services of God, which merit the remission of sins for themselves and for others. For on this account they increase these ceremonies. But if they would undertake them in order to teach and exhort the hearers, brief and pointed lessons would be of more profit than these infinite babblings. Thus the entire monastic life is full of hypocrisy and false opinions [against the First and Second Commandments, against Christ]. To all these this danger also is added, that those who are in these fraternities are compelled to assent to those persecuting the truth. There are, therefore, many important and forcible reasons which free good men from the obligation to this kind of life.

Lastly, the canons themselves release many who either without judgment [before they have attained a proper age] have made vows when enticed by the tricks of the monks, or have made vows under compulsion by friends. Such vows not even the canons declare to be vows. From all these considerations it is apparent that there are very many reasons which teach that monastic vows such as have hitherto been made are not vows; and for this reason a sphere of life full of hypocrisy and false opinions can be safely abandoned.

Here they present an objection derived from the Law concerning the Nazarites, Num. 6, 2f. But the Nazarites did not take upon themselves their vows with the opinions which, we have hitherto said we censure in the vows of the monks. The rite of the Nazarites was an exercise [a bodily exercise with fasting and certain kinds of food] or declaration of faith before men, and did not merit the remission of sins before God, did not justify before God. [For they sought this elsewhere, namely, in the promise of the blessed Seed.] Again, just as circumcision or the slaying of victims would not be a service of God now, so the rite of the Nazarites ought not to be presented now as a service, but it ought to be judged simply as an adiaphoron. It is not right to compare monasticism, devised without God's Word, as a service which should merit the remission of sins and justification, with the rite of the Nazarites, which had God's Word, and was not taught for the purpose of meriting the remission of sins, but to be an outward exercise, just as other ceremonies of the Law. The same can be said concerning other ceremonies prescribed in the Law.

The Rechabites also are cited, who did not have any possessions, and did not drink wine, as Jeremiah writes, chap. 35, 6f. Yea, truly, the example of the Rechabites accords beautifully with our monks, whose monasteries excel the palaces of kings, and who live most sumptuously! And the Rechabites, in their poverty of all things, were nevertheless married. Our monks, although abounding in all voluptuousness, profess celibacy.

Besides, examples ought to be interpreted according to the rule, i.e., according to certain and clear passages of Scripture, not contrary to the rule, that is, contrary to the Scriptures. It is very certain, however, that our observances do not merit the remission of sins or justification. Therefore, when the Rechabites are praised, it is necessary [it is certain] that these have observed their custom, not because they believed that by this they merited remission of sins, or that the work was itself a justifying service, or one on account of which they obtained eternal life, instead of, by God's mercy, for the sake of the promised Seed. But because they had the command of their parents, their obedience is praised, concerning which there is the commandment of God: Honor thy father and mother.

Then, too, the custom had a particular purpose: Because they were foreigners, not Israelites, it is apparent that their father wished to distinguish them by certain marks from their countrymen, so that they might not relapse into the impiety of their countrymen. He wished by these marks to admonish them of the [fear of God, the] doctrine of faith and immortality. Such an end is lawful. But for monasticism far different ends are taught. They feign that the works of monasticism are a service, they feign that they merit the remission of sins and justification. The example of the Rechabites is therefore unlike monasticism; to omit here other evils which inhere in monasticism at present.

They cite also from 1 Tim. 5, 11ff. concerning widows, who, as they served the Church, were supported at the public expense, where it is said: They will marry, having damnation, because they have cast off their first faith. First, let us suppose that the Apostle is here speaking of vows [which, however, he is not doing]; still this passage will not favor monastic vows, which are made concerning godless services, and in this opinion that they merit the remission of sins and justification. For Paul with ringing voice condemns all services, all laws, all works, if they are observed in order to merit the remission of sins, or that, on account of them instead of through mercy on account of Christ we obtain remission of sins. On this account the vows of widows, if there were any, must have been unlike monastic vows.

Besides, if the adversaries do not cease to misapply the passage to vows, the prohibition that no widow be selected who is less than sixty years, 1 Tim. 5, 9, must be misapplied in the same way. Thus vows made before this age will be of no account. But the Church did not yet know these vows. Therefore Paul condemns widows, not because they marry, for he commands the younger to marry; but because, when supported at the public expense, they became wanton, and thus cast off faith. He calls this first faith, clearly not in a monastic vow, but in Christianity [of their Baptism, their Christian duty, their Christianity]. And in this sense he understands faith in the same chapter, v. 8: If any one provide not for his own, and specially for those of his own house, he hath denied the faith. For he speaks otherwise of faith than the sophists. He does not ascribe faith to those who have mortal sin. He, accordingly, says that those cast off faith who do not care for their relatives. And in the same way he says that wanton women cast off faith.

We have recounted some of our reasons and, in passing, have explained away the objections urged by the adversaries. And we have collected these matters, not only on account of the adversaries, but much more on account of godly minds, that they may have in view the reasons why they ought to disapprove of hypocrisy and fictitious monastic services, all of which indeed this one saying of Christ annuls, which reads, Matt. 15, 9: In vain they do worship Me, teaching for doctrines the commandments of men. Therefore the vows themselves and the observances of meats, lessons, chants, vestments, sandals, girdles are useless services in God's sight. And all godly minds should certainly know that the opinion is simply pharisaic and condemned that these observances merit the remission of sins; that on account of them we are accounted righteous, that on account of them, and not through mercy on account of Christ, we obtain eternal life. And the holy men who have lived in these kinds of life must necessarily have learned, confidence in such observance having been rejected, that they had the remission of sins freely, that for Christ's sake through mercy they would obtain eternal life, and not for the sake of these services [therefore godly persons who were saved and continued to live in monastic life had finally come to this, namely, that they despaired of their monastic life, despised all their works as dung, condemned all their hypocritical service of God, and held fast to the promise of grace in Christ, as in the example of St. Bernard, saying, ***Perdite vixi***, I have lived in a sinful way], because God only approves services instituted by His Word, which services avail when used in faith.

Part 36

Article XXVIII (XIV): *Of Ecclesiastical Power.*

Here the adversaries cry out violently concerning the privileges and immunities of the ecclesiastical estate, and they add the peroration: All things are vain which are presented in the present article against the immunity of the churches and priests. This is mere calumny; for in this article we have disputed concerning other things. Besides, we have frequently testified that we do not find fault with political ordinances, and the gifts and privileges granted by princes.

But would that the adversaries would hear, on the other hand, the complaints of the churches and of godly minds! The adversaries courageously guard their own dignities and wealth; meanwhile, they neglect the condition of the churches; they do not care that the churches are rightly taught, and that the Sacraments are duly administered. To the priesthood they admit all kinds of persons indiscriminately. [They ordain rude asses; thus the Christian doctrine perished, because the Church was not supplied with efficient preachers.] Afterwards they impose intolerable burdens, as though they were delighted with the destruction of their fellowmen, they demand that their traditions be observed far more accurately than the Gospel. Now, in the most important and difficult controversies, concerning which the people urgently desire to be taught, in order that they may have something certain which they may follow, they do not release the minds which are most severely tortured with doubt, they only call to arms. Besides, in manifest matters [against manifest truth] they present decrees written in blood, which threaten horrible punishments to men unless they act clearly contrary to God's command. Here, on the other hand, you ought to see the tears of the poor, and hear the pitiable complaints of many good men, which God undoubtedly considers and regards, to whom one day you will render an account of your stewardship.

But although in the Confession we have in this article embraced various topics, the adversaries make no reply [act in true popish fashion], except that the bishops have the power of rule and coercive correction, in order to direct their subjects to the goal of eternal blessedness; and that the power of ruling requires the power to judge, to define, to distinguish and fix those things which are serviceable or conduce to the aforementioned end. These are the words of the **Confutation**, in which the adversaries teach us [but do not prove] that the bishops have the authority to frame laws [without the authority of the Gospel] useful for obtaining eternal life. The controversy is concerning this article.

[Regarding this matter we submit the following:] But we must retain in the Church this doctrine, namely, that we receive the remission of sins freely for Christ's sake, by faith. We must also retain this doctrine, namely, that human traditions are useless services, and therefore neither sin nor righteousness should be placed in meat drink, clothing and like things, the use of which Christ wished to be left free, since He says, Matt. 15, 11: Not that which goeth into the mouth defileth the man; and Paul, Rom. 14, 17: The kingdom of God is not meat and drink. Therefore the bishops have no right to frame traditions in addition to the Gospel, that they may merit the remission of sins, that they may be services which God is to approve as righteousness and which burden consciences, as though it were a sin to omit them. All this is taught by that one passage in Acts, 15, 9ff., where the apostles say [Peter says] that hearts are purified by faith. And then they prohibit the imposing of a yoke, and show how great a danger this is, and enlarge upon the sin of those who burden the Church. Why tempt ye God they say. By this thunderbolt our adversaries are in no way terrified, who defend by violence traditions and godless opinions.

For above they have also condemned Article XV, in which we have stated that traditions do not merit the remission of sins, and they here say that traditions conduce to eternal life. Do they merit the remission of sins? Are they services which God approves as righteousness? Do they quicken hearts! Paul to the Colossians, 2, 20ff., says that traditions do not profit with respect to eternal righteousness and eternal life; for the reason that food, drink, clothing and the like are things that perish with the using. But eternal life [which begins in this life inwardly by faith] is wrought in the heart by eternal things, i.e., by the Word of God and the Holy Ghost. Therefore let the adversaries explain how traditions conduce to eternal life.

Since, however, the Gospel clearly testifies that traditions ought not to be imposed upon the Church in order to merit the remission of sins; in order to be services which God shall approve as righteousness; in order to burden consciences, so that to omit them is to be accounted a sin, the adversaries will never be able to show that the bishops have the power to institute such services.

Besides, we have declared in the Confession what power the Gospel ascribes to bishops. Those who are now bishops do not perform the duties of bishops according to the Gospel although, indeed, they may be bishops according to canonical polity, which we do not censure. But we are speaking of a bishop according to the Gospel. And we are pleased with the ancient division of power into power of the order and power of jurisdiction [that is the administration of the Sacraments and the exercise of spiritual jurisdiction]. Therefore the bishop has the power of the order, i.e., the ministry of the Word and Sacraments; he has also the power of jurisdiction, i.e., the authority to excommunicate those guilty of open crimes, and again to absolve them if they are converted and seek absolution. But their power is not to be tyrannical, i.e., without a fixed law; nor regal, i.e., above law; but they have a fixed command and a fixed Word of God, according to which they ought to teach and according to which they ought to exercise their jurisdiction. Therefore, even though they should have some jurisdiction, it does not follow that they are able to institute new services. For services pertain in no way to jurisdiction. And they have the Word, they have the command, how far they ought to exercise jurisdiction, namely, if any one would do anything contrary to that Word which they have received from Christ. [For the Gospel does not set up a rule independently of the Gospel; that is quite clear and certain.]

Although in the Confession we also have added how far it is lawful for them to frame traditions, namely, not as necessary services, but so that there may be order in the Church, for the sake of tranquillity. And these traditions ought not to cast snares upon consciences, as though to enjoin necessary services; as Paul teaches when he says, Gal. 5, 1: Stand fast, therefore, in the liberty wherewith Christ hath made us free, and be not entangled again with the yoke of bondage. The use of such ordinances ought therefore to be left free, provided that offenses be avoided, and that they be not judged to be necessary services; just as the apostles themselves ordained [for the sake of good discipline] very many things which have been changed with time. Neither did they hand them down in such a way that it would not be permitted to change them. For they did not dissent from their own writings, in which they greatly labor lest the Church be burdened with the opinion that human rites are necessary services.

This is the simple mode of interpreting traditions, namely, that we understand them not as necessary services, and nevertheless, for the sake of avoiding offenses, we should observe them in the proper place. And thus many learned and great men in the Church have held. Nor do we see what can be said against this. For it is certain that the expression Luke 10, 16: He that heareth you heareth Me, does not speak of traditions, but is chiefly directed against traditions. For it is not a *mandatum cum libera* (a bestowal of unlimited authority), as they call it, but it is a *cautio de rato* (a caution concerning something prescribed), namely, concerning the special command [not a free, unlimited order and power, but a limited order, namely, not to preach their own word, but God's Word and the Gospel], i.e., the testimony given to the apostles that we believe them with respect to the word of another, not their own. For Christ wishes to assure us, as was necessary, that we should know that the Word delivered by men is efficacious, and that no other word from heaven ought to be sought. He that heareth you heareth Me, cannot be understood of traditions. For Christ requires that they teach in such a way that [by their mouth] He Himself be heard, because He says: He heareth Me. Therefore He wishes His own voice, His own Word, to be heard, not human traditions. Thus a saying which is most especially in our favor, and contains the most important consolation and doctrine, these stupid men pervert to the most trifling matters, the distinctions of food, vestments, and the like.

They quote also Heb. 13, 17: Obey them that have the rule over you. This passage requires obedience to the Gospel. For it does not establish a dominion for the bishops apart from the Gospel. Neither should the bishops frame traditions contrary to the Gospel, or interpret their traditions contrary to the Gospel. And when they do this, obedience is prohibited, according to Gal. 1, 9: If any man preach any other gospel, let him be accursed.

We make the same reply to Matt. 23, 3: Whatsoever they bid you observe, that observe, because evidently a universal command is not given that we should receive all things [even contrary to God's command and Word], since Scripture elsewhere, Acts 5, 29, bids us obey God rather than men. When, therefore they teach wicked things, they are not to be heard. But these are wicked things, namely, that human traditions are services of God that they are necessary services, that they merit the remission of sins and eternal life.

They present, as an objection, the public offenses and commotions which have arisen under pretext of our doctrine. To these we briefly reply. If all the scandals be brought together, still the one article concerning the remission of sins, that for Christ's sake through faith we freely obtain the remission of sins, brings so much good as to hide all evils. And this, in the beginning, gained for Luther not only our favor, but also, that of many who are now contending against us. "For former favor ceases, and mortals are forgetful," says Pindar. Nevertheless, we neither desire to desert truth that is necessary to the Church, nor can we assent to the adversaries in condemning it. For we ought to obey God rather than men. Those who in the beginning condemned manifest truth, and are now persecuting it with the greatest cruelty, will give an account for the schism that has been occasioned. Then, too, are there no scandals among the adversaries? How much evil is there in the sacrilegious profanation of the Mass applied to gain! How great disgrace in celibacy! But let us omit a comparison. This is what we hare replied to the ***Confutation*** for the time being. Now we leave it to the judgment of all the godly whether the adversaries are right in boasting that they have actually refuted our Concession from the Scriptures.

Part 37

THE END.

[As regards the slander and complaint of the adversaries at the end of the *Confutation*, namely, that this doctrine is causing disobedience and other scandals, this is unjustly imputed to our doctrine. For it is evident that by this doctrine the authority of magistrates is most highly praised. Moreover, it is well known that in those localities where this doctrine is preached, the magistrates have hitherto by the grace of God, been treated with all respect by the subjects.

But as to the want of unity and dissension in the Church, it is well known how these matters first happened, and who have caused the division, namely, the sellers of indulgences, who shamelessly preached intolerable lies, and afterwards condemned Luther for not approving of those lies, and besides, they again and again excited more controversies, so that Luther was induced to attack many other errors. But since our opponents would not tolerate the truth, and dared to promote manifest errors by force, it is easy to judge who is guilty of the schism. Surely, all the world, all wisdom, all power ought to yield to Christ and His holy Word. But the devil is the enemy of God, and therefore rouses all his might against Christ, to extinguish and suppress the Word of God. Therefore the devil with his members, setting himself against the Word of God, is the cause of the schism and want of unity. For we have most zealously sought peace, and still most eagerly desire it, provided only we are not forced to blaspheme and deny Christ. For God, the discerner of all men's hearts, is our witness that we do not delight and have no joy in this awful disunion. On the other hand, our adversaries have so far not been willing to conclude peace without stipulating that we must abandon the saving doctrine of the forgiveness of sin by Christ without our merit; though Christ would be most foully blasphemed thereby.

And although, as is the custom of the world it cannot be but that offenses have occurred in this schism through malice and by imprudent people; for the devil causes such offenses, to disgrace the Gospel, yet all this is of no account in view of the great comfort which this teaching has brought men, that for Christ's sake, without our merit, we have forgiveness of sins and a gracious God. Again, that men have been instructed that forsaking secular estates and magistracies is not a divine worship, but that such estates and magistracies are pleasing to God and to be engaged in them is a real holy work and divine service.

If we also were to narrate the offenses of the adversaries, which, indeed, we have no desire to do, it would be a terrible list: what an abominable, blasphemous fair the adversaries have made of the Mass; what unchaste living has been instituted by their celibacy; how the Popes have for more than 400 years been engaged in wars against the emperors, have forgotten the Gospel, and only sought to be emperors themselves, and to bring all Italy into their power how they have juggled the possessions of the Church; how through their neglect many false teachings and forms of worship have been set up by the monks. Is not their worship of the saints manifest pagan idolatry? All their writers do not say one word concerning faith in Christ, by which forgiveness of sin is obtained; the highest degree of holiness they ascribe to human traditions, it is chiefly of these that they write and preach. Moreover this, too, ought to be numbered with their offenses, that they clearly reveal what sort of a spirit is in them, because they are now putting to death so many innocent, pious people on account of Christian doctrine. But we do not now wish to say more concerning this; for these matters should be decided in accordance with God's Word, regardless of the offenses on either aide.

We hope that all God-fearing men will sufficiently see from this writing of ours that ours is the Christian doctrine and comforting and salutary to all godly men. Accordingly, we pray God to extend His grace to the end that His holy Gospel may be known and honored by all, for His glory, and for the peace, unity, and salvation of all of us. Regarding all these articles we offer to make further statements if required.]

www.bookjungle.com *email: sales@bookjungle.com fax: 630-214-0564 mail: Book Jungle PO Box 2226 Champaign, IL 61825*

The Codes Of Hammurabi And Moses
W. W. Davies

QTY

The discovery of the Hammurabi Code is one of the greatest achievements of archaeology, and is of paramount interest, not only to the student of the Bible, but also to all those interested in ancient history...

Religion   **ISBN:** *1-59462-338-4*   **Pages:132**
MSRP $12.95

The Theory of Moral Sentiments
Adam Smith

QTY

This work from 1749. contains original theories of conscience amd moral judgment and it is the foundation for systemof morals.

Philosophy **ISBN:** *1-59462-777-0*   **Pages:536**
MSRP $19.95

Jessica's First Prayer
Hesba Stretton

QTY

In a screened and secluded corner of one of the many railway-bridges which span the streets of London there could be seen a few years ago, from five o'clock every morning until half past eight, a tidily set-out coffee-stall, consisting of a trestle and board, upon which stood two large tin cans, with a small fire of charcoal burning under each so as to keep the coffee boiling during the early hours of the morning when the work-people were thronging into the city on their way to their daily toil...

Pages:84

Childrens   **ISBN:** *1-59462-373-2*   *MSRP $9.95*

My Life and Work
Henry Ford

QTY

Henry Ford revolutionized the world with his implementation of mass production for the Model T automobile. Gain valuable business insight into his life and work with his own auto-biography... "We have only started on our development of our country we have not as yet, with all our talk of wonderful progress, done more than scratch the surface. The progress has been wonderful enough but..."

Pages:300

Biographies/ **ISBN:** *1-59462-198-5*   *MSRP $21.95*

The Art of Cross-Examination
Francis Wellman

QTY

I presume it is the experience of every author, after his first book is published upon an important subject, to be almost overwhelmed with a wealth of ideas and illustrations which could readily have been included in his book, and which to his own mind, at least, seem to make a second edition inevitable. Such certainly was the case with me; and when the first edition had reached its sixth impression in five months, I rejoiced to learn that it seemed to my publishers that the book had met with a sufficiently favorable reception to justify a second and considerably enlarged edition. ..

Pages:412

Reference   **ISBN:** *1-59462-647-2*   *MSRP $19.95*

On the Duty of Civil Disobedience
Henry David Thoreau

QTY

Thoreau wrote his famous essay, On the Duty of Civil Disobedience, as a protest against an unjust but popular war and the immoral but popular institution of slave-owning. He did more than write—he declined to pay his taxes, and was hauled off to gaol in consequence. Who can say how much this refusal of his hastened the end of the war and of slavery ?

Law   **ISBN:** *1-59462-747-9*   **Pages:48**
MSRP $7.45

Dream Psychology
Psychoanalysis for Beginners

Sigmund Freud

Dream Psychology Psychoanalysis for Beginners
Sigmund Freud

QTY

Sigmund Freud, born Sigismund Schlomo Freud (May 6, 1856 - September 23, 1939), was a Jewish-Austrian neurologist and psychiatrist who co-founded the psychoanalytic school of psychology. Freud is best known for his theories of the unconscious mind, especially involving the mechanism of repression; his redefinition of sexual desire as mobile and directed towards a wide variety of objects; and his therapeutic techniques, especially his understanding of transference in the therapeutic relationship and the presumed value of dreams as sources of insight into unconscious desires.

Pages:196

Psychology   **ISBN:** *1-59462-905-6*   *MSRP $15.45*

The Miracle of Right Thought
Orison Swett Marden

QTY

Believe with all of your heart that you will do what you were made to do. When the mind has once formed the habit of holding cheerful, happy, prosperous pictures, it will not be easy to form the opposite habit. It does not matter how improbable or how far away this realization may see, or how dark the prospects may be, if we visualize them as best we can, as vividly as possible, hold tenaciously to them and vigorously struggle to attain them, they will gradually become actualized, realized in the life. But a desire, a longing without endeavor, a yearning abandoned or held indifferently will vanish without realization.

Pages:360

Self Help   **ISBN:** *1-59462-644-8*   *MSRP $25.45*

www.bookjungle.com *email: sales@bookjungle.com fax: 630-214-0564 mail: Book Jungle PO Box 2226 Champaign, IL 61825*

QTY

The Rosicrucian Cosmo-Conception Mystic Christianity *by Max Heindel*   ISBN: *1-59462-188-8*   **$38.95**
The Rosicrucian Cosmo-conception is not dogmatic, neither does it appeal to any other authority than the reason of the student. It is: not controversial, but is: sent forth in the, hope that it may help to clear...   *New Age/Religion Pages 646*

Abandonment To Divine Providence *by Jean-Pierre de Caussade*   ISBN: *1-59462-228-0*   **$25.95**
"The Rev. Jean Pierre de Caussade was one of the most remarkable spiritual writers of the Society of Jesus in France in the 18th Century. His death took place at Toulouse in 1751. His works have gone through many editions and have been republished...   *Inspirational/Religion Pages 400*

Mental Chemistry *by Charles Haanel*   ISBN: *1-59462-192-6*   **$23.95**
Mental Chemistry allows the change of material conditions by combining and appropriately utilizing the power of the mind. Much like applied chemistry creates something new and unique out of careful combinations of chemicals the mastery of mental chemistry...   *New Age Pages 354*

The Letters of Robert Browning and Elizabeth Barret Barrett 1845-1846 vol II   ISBN: *1-59462-193-4*   **$35.95**
by Robert Browning and Elizabeth Barrett   *Biographies Pages 596*

Gleanings In Genesis (volume I) *by Arthur W. Pink*   ISBN: *1-59462-130-6*   **$27.45**
Appropriately has Genesis been termed "the seed plot of the Bible" for in it we have, in germ form, almost all of the great doctrines which are afterwards fully developed in the books of Scripture which follow...   *Religion/Inspirational Pages 420*

The Master Key *by L. W. de Laurence*   ISBN: *1-59462-001-6*   **$30.95**
In no branch of human knowledge has there been a more lively increase of the spirit of research during the past few years than in the study of Psychology, Concentration and Mental Discipline. The requests for authentic lessons in Thought Control, Mental Discipline and...   *New Age/Business Pages 422*

The Lesser Key Of Solomon Goetia *by L. W. de Laurence*   ISBN: *1-59462-092-X*   **$9.95**
This translation of the first book of the "Lernegton" which is now for the first time made accessible to students of Talismanic Magic was done, after careful collation and edition, from numerous Ancient Manuscripts in Hebrew, Latin, and French...   *New Age/Occult Pages 92*

Rubaiyat Of Omar Khayyam *by Edward Fitzgerald*   ISBN:*1-59462-332-5*   **$13.95**
Edward Fitzgerald, whom the world has already learned, in spite of his own efforts to remain within the shadow of anonymity, to look upon as one of the rarest poets of the century, was born at Bredfield, in Suffolk, on the 31st of March, 1809. He was the third son of John Purcell...   *Music Pages 172*

Ancient Law *by Henry Maine*   ISBN: *1-59462-128-4*   **$29.95**
The chief object of the following pages is to indicate some of the earliest ideas of mankind, as they are reflected in Ancient Law, and to point out the relation of those ideas to modern thought.   *Religion/History Pages 452*

Far-Away Stories *by William J. Locke*   ISBN: *1-59462-129-2*   **$19.45**
"Good wine needs no bush, but a collection of mixed vintages does. And this book is just such a collection. Some of the stories I do not want to remain buried for ever in the museum files of dead magazine-numbers an author's not unpardonable vanity..."   *Fiction Pages 272*

Life of David Crockett *by David Crockett*   ISBN: *1-59462-250-7*   **$27.45**
"Colonel David Crockett was one of the most remarkable men of the times in which he lived. Born in humble life, but gifted with a strong will, an indomitable courage, and unremitting perseverance...   *Biographies/New Age Pages 424*

Lip-Reading *by Edward Nitchie*   ISBN: *1-59462-206-X*   **$25.95**
Edward B. Nitchie, founder of the New York School for the Hard of Hearing, now the Nitchie School of Lip-Reading, Inc, wrote "LIP-READING Principles and Practice". The development and perfecting of this meritorious work on lip-reading was an undertaking...   *How-to Pages 400*

A Handbook of Suggestive Therapeutics, Applied Hypnotism, Psychic Science   ISBN: *1-59462-214-0*   **$24.95**
by Henry Munro   *Health/New Age/Health/Self-help Pages 376*

A Doll's House: and Two Other Plays *by Henrik Ibsen*   ISBN: *1-59462-112-8*   **$19.95**
Henrik Ibsen created this classic when in revolutionary 1848 Rome. Introducing some striking concepts in playwriting for the realist genre, this play has been studied the world over.   *Fiction/Classics/Plays 308*

The Light of Asia *by sir Edwin Arnold*   ISBN: *1-59462-204-3*   **$13.95**
In this poetic masterpiece, Edwin Arnold describes the life and teachings of Buddha. The man who was to become known as Buddha to the world was born as Prince Gautama of India but he rejected the worldly riches and abandoned the reigns of power when...   *Religion/History/Biographies Pages 170*

The Complete Works of Guy de Maupassant *by Guy de Maupassant*   ISBN: *1-59462-157-8*   **$16.95**
"For days and days, nights and nights, I had dreamed of that first kiss which was to consecrate our engagement, and I knew not on what spot I should put my lips..."   *Fiction/Classics Pages 240*

The Art of Cross-Examination *by Francis L. Wellman*   ISBN: *1-59462-309-0*   **$26.95**
Written by a renowned trial lawyer, Wellman imparts his experience and uses case studies to explain how to use psychology to extract desired information through questioning.   *How-to/Science/Reference Pages 408*

Answered or Unanswered? *by Louisa Vaughan*   ISBN: *1-59462-248-5*   **$10.95**
Miracles of Faith in China   *Religion Pages 112*

The Edinburgh Lectures on Mental Science (1909) *by Thomas*   ISBN: *1-59462-008-3*   **$11.95**
This book contains the substance of a course of lectures recently given by the writer in the Queen Street Hall, Edinburgh. Its purpose is to indicate the Natural Principles governing the relation between Mental Action and Material Conditions...   *New Age/Psychology Pages 148*

Ayesha *by H. Rider Haggard*   ISBN: *1-59462-301-5*   **$24.95**
Verily and indeed it is the unexpected that happens! Probably if there was one person upon the earth from whom the Editor of this, and of a certain previous history, did not expect to hear again...   *Classics Pages 380*

Ayala's Angel *by Anthony Trollope*   ISBN: *1-59462-352-X*   **$29.95**
The two girls were both pretty, but Lucy who was twenty-one who supposed to be simple and comparatively unattractive, whereas Ayala was credited, as her Bombwhat romantic name might show, with poetic charm and a taste for romance. Ayala when her father died was nineteen...   *Fiction Pages 484*

The American Commonwealth *by James Bryce*   ISBN: *1-59462-286-8*   **$34.45**
An interpretation of American democratic political theory. It examines political mechanics and society from the perspective of Scotsman James Bryce   *Politics Pages 572*

Stories of the Pilgrims *by Margaret P. Pumphrey*   ISBN: *1-59462-116-0*   **$17.95**
This book explores pilgrims religious oppression in England as well as their escape to Holland and eventual crossing to America on the Mayflower, and their early days in New England...   *History Pages 268*

QTY

The Fasting Cure *by Sinclair Upton*   ISBN: *1-59462-222-1*   **$13.95**
In the Cosmopolitan Magazine for May, 1910, and in the Contemporary Review (London) for April, 1910, I published an article dealing with my experi-
ences in fasting. I have written a great many magazine articles, but never one which attracted so much attention... New Age/Self Help/Health Pages 164

Hebrew Astrology *by Sepharial*   ISBN: *1-59462-308-2*   **$13.45**
In these days of advanced thinking it is a matter of common observation that we have left many of the old landmarks behind and that we are now pressing
forward to greater heights and to a wider horizon than that which represented the mind-content of our progenitors... Astrology Pages 144

Thought Vibration or The Law of Attraction in the Thought World   ISBN: *1-59462-127-6*   **$12.95**
by William Walker Atkinson   Psychology/Religion Pages 144

Optimism *by Helen Keller*   ISBN: *1-59462-108-X*   **$15.95**
Helen Keller was blind, deaf, and mute since 19 months old, yet famously learned how to overcome these handicaps, communicate with the world, and
spread her lectures promoting optimism. An inspiring read for everyone... Biographies/Inspirational Pages 84

Sara Crewe *by Frances Burnett*   ISBN: *1-59462-360-0*   **$9.45**
In the first place, Miss Minchin lived in London. Her home was a large, dull, tall one, in a large, dull square, where all the houses were alike, and all the
sparrows were alike, and where all the door-knockers made the same heavy sound... Childrens/Classic Pages 88

The Autobiography of Benjamin Franklin *by Benjamin Franklin*   ISBN: *1-59462-135-7*   **$24.95**
The Autobiography of Benjamin Franklin has probably been more extensively read than any other American historical work, and no other book of its kind
has had such ups and downs of fortune. Franklin lived for many years in England, where he was agent... Biographies/History Pages 332

Name	
Email	
Telephone	
Address	
City, State ZIP	

☐ **Credit Card**   ☐ **Check / Money Order**

Credit Card Number	
Expiration Date	
Signature	

Please Mail to: Book Jungle
PO Box 2226
Champaign, IL 61825
or Fax to: 630-214-0564

ORDERING INFORMATION

web*: www.bookjungle.com*
email*: sales@bookjungle.com*
fax*: 630-214-0564*
mail*: Book Jungle PO Box 2226 Champaign, IL 61825*
or PayPal *to sales@bookjungle.com*

Please contact us for bulk discounts

DIRECT-ORDER TERMS

**20% Discount if You Order
Two or More Books**
Free Domestic Shipping!
Accepted: Master Card, Visa,
Discover, American Express

www.ingramcontent.com/pod-product-compliance
Lightning Source LLC
Chambersburg PA
CBHW080954020726

47505CB00009B/2195